BEYOND A DARKENED SHORE

BEYOND A DARKENED SHORE

JESSICA LEAKE

An Imprint of HarperCollinsPublishers

HarperTeen is an imprint of HarperCollins Publishers.

Library of Congress Control Number: 2017949557
ISBN 978-0-06-266626-0 (trade bdg.)

Typography by Michelle Taormina
18 19 20 21 22   PC/LSCH   10 9 8 7 6 5 4 3 2 1

First Edition

For Karina, who wouldn't let this book go
gently onto that good shelf.

BEYOND

A

DARKENED

SHORE

I

Kingdom of Mide, Ireland, AD 1035

I learned to hate the sea. Not because it was unbearably cold, and not because I loathed swimming in its salty depths. I hated it because, in spite of its raw beauty, it brought death to our doorstep.

Today, though, I was on the shore below my father's castle because of my two little sisters. After being practically locked inside the keep for days, they'd begged me for the chance to breathe fresh air. I couldn't blame my mother for hiding them away in the keep—the place where my family and our most trusted servants lived, as it was the most fortified structure within the castle walls. Indeed, she was so obsessed with their safety that she and my sisters attended Mass at a different time from everyone else. Though I couldn't blame her for that—not after what had happened the last time we were all in church together.

But unlike our mother, I had trouble telling my sisters no. Nothing made them happier: the sounds of the sea crashing against the rock that made me clench my teeth, the salty breeze that tangled my hair, the gritty sand that swallowed my boots—they loved it all. With so much darkness plaguing our family, the girls needed these moments of happiness.

So when they'd awoken just after dawn, I hadn't hesitated to follow them down to the stables to retrieve their fat ponies. I knew as well as they that early morning, when our mother was at Lauds, was also the only chance for a proper riding lesson. Our mother had ordered that my sisters' ponies be kept on leads while they rode, but I was determined to make them independent riders: an essential skill to have should we ever have to flee the castle. And the best way to become more comfortable was to ride without saddles—something I would do only with the sand and water to cushion their falls, and with my mother not around to hassle us.

"Keep your heels down, Bran," I reminded my younger sister as she trotted her pony toward me. Her blond braid bounced on her back in time to the pony's hoofbeats, and her eyes narrowed in concentration. For a moment, she looked so much like her older sister Alana that my breath hitched in my throat. I pushed the memories away. Alana was never far from my thoughts, but thinking of her was like the dull throb of pain from a wound not yet healed.

"I thought I was," Branna said, her tone a little impatient. I didn't take offense—it was how my sister always sounded, at least since the moment she'd reached her thirteenth birthday. She was only four years younger than I was, though in some ways, it might as well have been ten.

But then, she hadn't seen the things I had. Nor been the cause of them.

Branna decided to listen to me in spite of herself, and pushed her heels down, which straightened her spine and strengthened her balance.

"That's much better," I said, and she smiled. My attention shifted to my youngest sister, trailing not far behind Branna. "You're doing well, Deirdre." She glanced down at her pony's mane—shy as always in the face of a compliment.

The breeze brought the noxious smell of salt and fish to my nose, distracting me from my sisters. Out of habit, I checked the horizon for any sign of square sails. My father and many of my clansmen had answered the call of the nearby monastery two days ago, after the barbaric Northmen were spotted off their coast, too close to the monastery under my father's protection to ignore. As my father's heir and the most skilled warrior left behind, I was in charge of protecting his kingdom in his absence. And that meant protecting my sisters as well. The worry weighed heavily on me as I scanned the horizon again. It had been seven years since the Northmen had landed on our shores, but there were frequent raids along the coast. The Northmen never stopped trying to invade the shores of our land.

Thankfully the only movement on the water today was the seagulls—crying stridently to one another and darting just below the water's crest. In the distance, bells from our small church rang out, signaling the end of Lauds. Our mother would be among the faithful, and there were many prayers being offered today for the deliverance of both the monastery and our men who'd gone to defend it. Had I been welcome in the small chapel, I would have no doubt offended God by my fervent prayers that each and every Northman be shown no mercy and preferably be killed in as painful a way as possible. Devils.

"Do we have to return already?" Bran asked, her eyes on the looming castle. She knew as well as I that the end of Lauds meant the return of our mother.

I considered the weak morning sun. Our mother usually remained in the church for at least another half hour after Lauds to help Father Briain.

"We have a few more minutes. Deirdre, give a little tug on the reins—don't let him get his head down," I said as her pony's nose kept inching closer to the sand. He was a placid beast, but he loved to roll, and I'd rather he didn't do it with my sister on his back.

A flutter of feathers drew my attention to a rocky outcropping not far from where my sisters rode. I expected to see the white and gray of a gull, but a little jolt of surprise ran through me when I saw the fathomless black of a crow. I tried to relax my tense shoulders. It could be just a normal crow, after all—just an everyday crow out searching for food like any other bird. It could be, but the hair risen on the back of my neck told me it wasn't.

It cocked its head at me once before letting loose a harsh *caw-caw-caw*. The sound sprang memories free in my mind: a murder of crows so large it was like a blot against the gray of the sky. My clansmen dying, and my own sister . . . no, I wouldn't allow my mind to stray to such a place. Again, I looked toward the sea, but the line of water stretching toward the horizon was unbroken.

"Ciara!" Deirdre called, her tone sharp. I jerked my head up in time to see her pony sink to its front knees in preparation for a roll.

I rushed to her side and grabbed the pony's reins. Ignoring me, the pony grunted as he continued to lower his considerable bulk to the sand. I held my hand out to Deirdre, an exasperated smile playing on my lips. "You'll have to jump down. He won't be dissuaded."

She slid the short distance to the ground, and I pulled her out of the way. Free of his rider, the pony rolled nearly all the way onto his back, kicking his hooves into the air and snorting.

"Stubborn thing." I shook my head. Beside me, Deirdre giggled.

"Oh no," Branna groaned from somewhere nearby.

I turned to see our mother hurrying down the winding path

to the shore, the velvet of her skirts swishing angrily in her wake.

"Ciara!" Máthair called as soon as she was within hearing range, her voice as sharp as a blade. Her entire focus was on me.

Her sleeves trailed nearly to the sands of the beach as she stopped before me, her long blond hair in waves down her back. She reached out and pulled Deirdre to her. "Did you fall, child?" she asked, her hands cupping Deirdre's cheeks.

"No, Máthair," Deirdre said.

"Ciara was only giving us a riding lesson," Branna said from the back of her pony.

"Come down from there, Branna," our mother said, letting go of Deirdre. She gestured vehemently toward Bran as though she was astride a great menacing wolf rather than a docile pony.

Frustration evident in the set of her shoulders, Branna slid down.

Máthair's attention shifted to me, her mouth tight. "How could you have endangered them like this, Ciara?" She swept her arm out to indicate the shore. "*Here*, of all places?"

Her words triggered a heavy guilt, but I forced my back to straighten. She wasn't truly upset over the fact that my sisters were riding. Ever since Alana, she feared anything that could potentially endanger them—even if it was a necessary skill like riding. "I wanted them to learn to ride without having someone lead them. The soft sands of the beach are safer than the rocky meadow. They wouldn't have been harmed if they fell."

"But the Northmen have been spotted not far from here.

Why did you not at least bring a guard?"

Because none would want to accompany me willingly. I met her narrowed gaze. "Because I can keep my sisters safe."

The bluster seemed to leave her all at once, and she let out her breath. She couldn't argue with the truth. "Ask for my permission next time," she said. "Come, girls. We missed you at Lauds, but it's not too late to go before the altar and pray for your father's safe return." With her arms around my sisters, she started back toward the keep, toward the chapel where my presence was so unwelcome that the faithful members of our clan believed I tainted its sacred ground. I schooled my features to hide the twinge of sadness I always felt at being so painfully excluded—it would only upset my sisters.

"I should help Ciara with the ponies," Branna said, but I waved her off.

"I can get them," I said, taking hold of the ponies' reins.

As I followed behind, winding slowly upward on the rocky path that led to our father's castle, a flickering shadow drew my gaze to the cloudless sky. The same crow circled high above, its inky feathers slicing through the weak morning sun.

It watched me with an interest no ordinary crow would have. And then I knew for sure.

They're coming, a voice whispered in my mind, and a cold shiver snaked down my back. It wasn't the first time I'd heard the crow's voice, and I knew it warned of only one thing: death. There could be no doubt: the Northmen were coming to our shores.

Then the crow let out a *caw-caw-caw* so startling even my mother and sisters paused.

Branna's eyes were on the crow. "What does it mean?" she asked, her voice hushed. She had learned long ago that no omen should be ignored.

I met Máthair's worried glance—a shared fear we couldn't voice. *Northmen.*

"We should get back to the castle." I gave the ponies another gentle tug to keep pace with me.

As we entered the castle bailey, where the stables, the kitchens, and the armory were located, I scanned the wide expanse, wondering if anyone else had noticed anything amiss. The morning buzzed with activity; two men guiding pigs and sheep through the bailey bowed their heads briefly when they noticed me watching. Kitchen servants beat the dust and ash from two matching red-and-gold rugs, chatting, oblivious to the tension that thrummed through the air and made the hair on the back of my neck rise.

Then a sound came that made my heart pound: a horn's bellow echoed across the crowded courtyard, grinding everything to a stop. The color in our mother's face drained away, and she tightened her grip on my sisters.

A shout from one of my clansmen rang out. Everything that was frozen leaped into frantic motion. Children were herded alongside livestock as too few of the men hurried to gather weapons.

I took a steadying breath, forcing down the panic that

threatened to engulf me. Memories overtook my mind—

The horn's bellow calling our clansmen to war.

The clang of axes meeting swords.

The smell of coppery blood in the air.

The pale form of my sister broken and bleeding on the hard ground, her hair spread out behind her.

And me, powerless to help.

But I wasn't powerless now. I'd spent years training and honing my skills through battle, ensuring I'd never be powerless again.

Máthair pulled my sisters toward the safety of the keep, practically dragging them in her wake. Before they could reach the steps, Branna freed herself from her grasp and ran to me.

"Branna!" our mother cried.

"Come with us," Branna said, her eyes pleading with me.

"Go to Máthair. Stay hidden." I pressed a hurried kiss to the top of her head.

She grabbed my arm before I could run for my own horse, her grip almost painful. "Please don't go. The Northmen—"

"I must," I said, my tone firm. "Now hurry." I gave her a little push toward the keep, and hopefully, to safety.

Before I turned away, I met Máthair's gaze. "God keep you safe," she said, and fled into the castle.

2

As I ran to the stables—ponies in tow—my mind already shifted to the battle ahead. Without my father here, I would lead my clansmen, and I clenched my teeth at the thought of giving them orders. I might have been heir to the throne, but my strange abilities ensured that I didn't have the trust of my clansmen. They would listen to me, but they wouldn't like it.

Killing Northmen was far easier.

All around me, women and children ran to take cover. They relied on the steep, rocky cliff to protect them from the Northmen raiders. But I knew better. It hadn't kept them out seven years ago.

More worrisome was the fact that the Northmen were here instead of at the monastery with its rich treasures. Had they defeated my father? Or had my father defended the monks only to have the raiders turn their eyes toward our home as vengeance?

The stables greeted me with a torrent of sounds: men shouted to one another, warhorses trumpeted, and swords clanged as they were pulled from the rack. My sisters' ponies eagerly returned to their own stalls as soon as I pulled their bridles free. When the men caught sight of me, a whisper of unease ran through them.

I straightened my spine and pulled my own broadsword free before I turned to address the men in the now uncomfortable silence. "With the king and half our army gone, we are few in number, but we are the only thing standing between the Northmen and our families." Most of them just stared at me, but a few nodded tersely. They couldn't argue with the need to protect our own. We knew how much was at stake. "They will hope to ambush us, to catch us unawares, but we will meet them at the top of the cliff." My grip tightened on my sword. "We will slaughter them one by one."

The men shouted their approval, brandishing their own weapons high in the air as horses neighed and stamped their feet.

Fergus, one of the few clansmen who I considered a friend, grinned. His teeth looked whiter than usual against the dark blue paint slathered on his face. "We have nothing to fear, lads. Not with Princess Ciara leading us."

He meant it ironically, of course—*I* was the one they feared.

It was one of the reasons my father had banned me from the church—my people welcomed my power on the battlefield, but they believed it tainted any sacred space.

I smiled in return, but didn't stop on my way to my horse's stall. Riordan, a man whose arms and chest bulged with muscle, shied away from me like a horse from a snake. *Demon*, he had said about me once, and I could practically hear him thinking it now. I forced myself to stand unflinchingly in the face of such rejection even as pain and loneliness clawed at me.

There was little I wouldn't do, and little I wouldn't endure, to keep my sisters safe.

I continued toward my horse and another of my clansmen caught my eye—Séamus. For one painful moment, I thought he might grin at me like he used to while we worked with the young warhorses together, the smile softening his sharp features. But instead he turned away, his face paling beneath his war paint. My mouth drew into a grim line, and pinpricks of shame sneaked across my skin. It had been two winters since he'd been forced to train with me, but it might as well have been yesterday.

I remembered how he looked standing before me: wary but strong.

Even he hadn't been able to withstand my power.

My hand reached for the carved wooden horse hidden on its fraying piece of leather beneath my armor. *It's the only thing I know how to carve,* he had said with a nervous smile, *but I wanted to give you something to show you how much you mean to me.* That was years ago, before he knew who I really was. I could still see him in the stable where we'd first met, surrounded by the soft sounds of horses.

He'd sworn he didn't fear my abilities, but that was before he was subjected to them. My mind assaulted me with another memory: Séamus on his knees.

Stay away from me, he'd shouted, his hands curled protectively around his head.

I blinked rapidly and let the necklace fall back in place against my chest.

I didn't want to speak to him, but I knew I must. With so many of the other clansmen gone, his skill with a sword and as a horseman would be more useful than ever. Squaring my shoulders, I walked over to where he was saddling his horse.

"Séamus," I said, and his whole body tensed. "I will need your skills at the top of the cliff—you'll be able to cut the Northmen down faster than anyone."

"Yes, milady," he said, keeping his eyes on his saddle—on anything but me.

A flash of pain cut through me at his formal address. There was a time when I was only Ciara, his friend, not "milady" . . . not the heir to the throne . . . or worse, someone to be feared. Just me.

I watched him for a moment more, his long fingers making quick work of the saddle's cinch, but he never looked up.

"May God keep you safe," I whispered, and hurried toward my own horse.

I threw open the stall door to my horse, Sleipnir, a stallion as black as pitch. I named him after the Norse god's eight-legged horse, mostly as an insult to Northmen I defeated, but also because if any horse had the personality of a god's horse, it was Sleipnir. He charged out of his stall, impatient as always for war. Despite his massive size, he pulled himself to a dead halt in front of me. With a fistful of his long black mane in one hand, I leaped astride.

After my short, painful conversation with Séamus, I wanted nothing more than to touch my heels to Sleipnir's sides and gallop until every thought in my mind disappeared. Instead, I held Sleipnir in check until the men rode out ahead of me, their chests bare and their faces painted. The smell of sweat, metal, and paint from the battle-hungry men, and the sweeter smell of horses, filled my nostrils. It was better than the coppery tang of blood, which would be all I could smell soon.

I took up my position in the rear after everyone had passed by, and Sleipnir tossed his head in annoyance at being behind the other horses. It couldn't be helped, though—my power was more useful after the enemy had already been engaged.

I kept my eyes on the sea as Sleipnir descended the steep, rocky slope. Small stones dislodged beneath his heavy hooves as we wound our way down. There were two cliffs near my father's castle: one that was closest to shore with an easier climb and a second with a much more treacherous path. It was on this second cliff, one that jutted out into the sea itself, that the castle was located. Between the two cliffs was a small valley, and it was at this descent that we found ourselves. Our horses were used to the cliff that was our home and protection, but any other army would find it difficult not to break a leg.

When we climbed to the top of the outcropping, which allowed us to view the length of the shore, I pulled Sleipnir to a stop and surveyed the twenty men before me. Compared to the Northmen, our armor was practically nonexistent: light leather leggings, soft leather boots, and no helmets. Unwilling to join my fellow clansmen in simply covering my chest with paint, I wore a leather chest piece over my linen tunic. Most of the men had broadswords, though a few fought with axes. The Northmen would come with their chain mail and their shields, but we would be faster, and more agile.

The waves viciously beat against the worn rock, sending sprays of white water into the air. It should have been deterrent enough, but the Northmen were relentless. Their longship had already landed. Men poured from its side like a wave of death. As I took in the square sail—white with a skeletal crimson dragon—my heart beat a furious rhythm in my chest. I'd fought countless Northmen in battles throughout our kingdom, but the sight of that sail still made every muscle in my body clench in warring fear and anger—and memory.

My clansmen's blood staining the earth red—

—my sister's hand in mine as we tried to escape—

—her eyes wide as the blood trailed down her throat, and *me*, screaming, screaming—

I shook my head, banishing the memories before they could

weaken my mind further. Sleipnir snorted and pawed the ground in response. Like other horses, he could sense my emotions. But unlike other horses, my apprehension only made him bolder.

Fergus wheeled his horse over to me and spat on the ground. "Let us pray the blood of the raiders will flow this day."

I glanced at the men assembled beside me and frowned. A Northman longship of the size of the one on our shore could hold at least sixty men, far more than our own crew. "The battle can go no farther than this cliff—not this time."

"I will cover you as best I can," Fergus said. "You search for their leader."

I tightened my grip on the hilt of my sword. My arm muscles tensed, and my heart pounded. Anticipation of the battle was always the hardest: the prickling adrenaline, the torrent of memories, the cold dread. I endured it all because my sisters and mother were huddled in fear in their room. We were the only things preventing them from being killed.

I snapped my attention back to the battle. The Northmen had begun the treacherous climb to our stronghold. With any luck, we would pick them off as they emerged at the top of the cliff. The Northman raiding strategy was always to ambush. Instead of recognizing such actions as dishonorable, they seemed happy to live to fight again. They wouldn't expect us to be waiting for them, and if we could defeat their leader quickly enough, they might retreat. There was no dishonor in retreat in their eyes either, not when their strategy to ambush meant they were usually slinking into a castle and catching its warriors unawares.

Holding the high ground was our advantage. We had to make it count.

With a shout, the first man made it to the top. He showed a momentary flash of surprise that we were lying in wait for him, but he recovered quickly. Battle-axe raised and shield in front of his chest, he charged. More of the enemy followed, their armor and long beards making them indistinguishable from one another. My clansmen made rivers of their blood.

Still, more made it over the rise, until there were two of them to every one of us. I swept my gaze over the battling men for their leader—usually the one with a shield guard. It was my job to kill him, but that would come later. After he had outlived his usefulness to me.

The chaos of the battle overwhelmed my senses as men swarmed us. Sleipnir reared when one of the Northmen came dangerously close. His flinty hooves smashed the pitiful shield the light-haired man used to protect his face. I met his axe with my sword. The clash sent painful echoes all the way to my bones, and my muscles strained.

Our eyes met—my dark with his muddy green. And in that moment, he was caught, as helpless as a fly in a spider's web.

Pain flared behind my eyes, intense but brief—nothing like the first time. I reached out—an invisible extension of my mind, but as natural to me now as extending my arm. His axe fell away as I took possession of his mind. A torrent of emotions washed over me like a sudden driving rain: bright surprise, hot anger, but most of all, sickening fear.

He was mine to control.

It was a monstrous ability to take possession of someone else—to control them as though they were merely an extension of my own body. Still, it was a strength I wasn't afraid to use on the battlefield because while I knew I wasn't the stongest fighter, nor the fastest, what power I did have made the difference between life and death for my clansmen. For my family.

I forced my new bodyguard forward. His will rebelled against mine, straining for independence. My will was stronger.

You aren't the leader, but you'll do for now, I told him in his mind, and felt a surge of answering fear and impotent rage. I ignored it. *Protect me from your comrades until you fall.*

Two enemies charged me, their faces grimly determined. My Northman bodyguard met them with his axe. As their weapons clashed, confusion slowed their movements. They halted in their attack, their disbelief paralyzing them. Despite the angry hum of protest within my bodyguard's mind, he raised his axe again and brought it down upon his comrade's head. The other I killed with my own sword.

It had taken years, many battles, and many training sessions to be able to divide my attention so totally as to be able to control someone while still maintaining my sense of self. It wasn't unlike being able to sword fight while still holding a fully engaged conversation. Difficult, but not impossible.

As I fought, I searched for the leader, but there were so many men locked in combat I couldn't pick him out.

Another Northman attacked from behind. Sleipnir aided me

once again, biting and kicking. I swung his big body around so his haunches slammed into the man. My guard was engaged in a battle of his own. This was one of the weaknesses of my ability: I could take possession of only one man at a time.

I was vulnerable to attack.

The man's hand grabbed my thigh, and I kicked in reflex. He must have been as tall as Sleipnir and almost as broad. He tugged again. I tried to bring my blade down on his head, but he met it with his axe. He smiled, his teeth the color of old leather.

Instead of fighting the Northman, I leaned into his hand. Surprised by the sudden loss of tension, he loosened his grip. I kicked again, and he lost his hold entirely.

All the while I could feel my guard at the other end of my mental tether—he had taken one of his own men by surprise and was currently fending off a second.

When the leather-toothed man came at me again, I smashed the hilt of my sword into his nose. He bellowed and swung his axe wildly. I deflected as it came dangerously close to cutting into Sleipnir's side. Anger blazed within me at the thought of my horse being injured, and my control slipped. Sensing my distraction, my guard struggled against my mental hold. His desperate fear and frustration hit me with such force that my eyes closed against my will. I had to focus. I brought to mind the lessons my father had drilled into me: when in a desperate situation, take the enemy by surprise.

I wrenched my eyes open again just in time to see the

leather-toothed Northman striding toward me, his nose spurting blood.

This time, his eyes were on my horse. I surged into a standing position on Sleipnir's broad back. The man's eyes widened. I launched myself at him, bringing my sword down at the same time. He brought his shield up, but the blade smashed through it, into the soft flesh of his neck.

The big man fell to his knees before falling face-first into the rocks. Blood haloed around him, but I wouldn't stop to think. I wouldn't let myself absorb the carnage around me—both of my fallen clansmen and of Northmen. I needed to find their leader.

My gaze landed on the corpse of a man cleaved in two. It was Cormac, one of the few who would greet me with a kind word. He had a new babe at home, a bright-eyed boy who would now be raised with no father. The pain of his loss stole my breath away.

And then I felt it: the severing of a connection, like the tautness of string suddenly gone slack. My guard was dead.

Arms grabbed me from behind. I forced my elbow into my assailant's gut. The grunt I heard in response sounded too youthful to have come from one of the burly Northmen. I spun around and came face-to-face with a boy who couldn't have been older than thirteen years.

For a moment, all I saw was my sister Alana. Why had these monsters brought a child to battle? I was many things, but I wasn't a murderer of children—even a Northman child. The rage within died down to a pulse.

He raised his sword, and I couldn't help but laugh. "Run along, boy," I said, sure that if he couldn't understand my words, he would understand my meaning. "The battlefield is no place for a child."

His eyes narrowed. "No place for a lady either," he said in heavily accented Gaelic.

I laughed again because he had a point. My smile faded when he charged.

He was quick, I had to give him that. He met every blow of my admittedly half-hearted attacks. But when he knocked my legs out from under me, my amusement disappeared entirely.

He leaped on top of me, kept me pinned to the ground. He slashed my face with his sword, and I tasted blood. Still, I couldn't bring myself to kill him.

I scanned the bloodied cliff. Where was their leader? I shouldn't be wasting my time with a boy. If I could take possession of the leader, force him to turn on his own, I'd learned from experience that his men would be so taken by surprise that they were easier to kill. Sometimes it so disturbed them that they turned on the leader himself.

An approaching Northman distracted me from my search. I was running out of time. The man shouted and the boy stiffened, but he didn't stop trying to cut my throat.

With my left hand, I felt around for one of the stones that littered the cliff. I wouldn't kill the boy, but I had to stop him. As my arm swung the stone into his skull, my eyes met the Northman who had appeared behind us.

His expression almost stopped me. His features were twisted with panic.

The boy slumped, knocked unconscious. Lucky for him, to my clansmen, he'd appear dead. I might be willing to spare his life, but the others wouldn't.

I pushed him off me and scrambled to my feet to greet the Northman who now towered over me, his shield bearing the insignia of the skeletal red dragon—the same as the one on the sail. Instead of an axe, he carried a massive claymore. He wasn't surrounded by his own personal shield guard like most I'd battled, but still, I was sure. The leader had found me.

I held my sword at the ready, and as I tried to reach his mind, I studied him. This Northman was different from the others. Surprise trickled through me as I realized how young he was—perhaps only a year older than I was. He was tall, but it was his lightly muscled form that suggested youth. Beneath the splatters of blood, his face was a handsome one with a straight nose, unmarred by multiple breakings like the other men's. A strong jaw, full lips.

His ice-blue eyes cut to the boy at my feet. When we both watched the boy's chest rise, the leader's attention returned to me. Our eyes locked, and once again, I bore the intense pain as I tried to take his mind.

But my power slammed into a wall, as real as the stones surrounding my father's castle. I took a step back in surprise. Gritting my teeth, I *pushed* with my mind. Nothing. He didn't even blink.

But he did swing his sword.

I brought my own blade up at the last moment. The impact was so jarring I felt it in my bones, the metals of the swords coming together in an earsplitting clatter.

Before I could formulate a plan of attack, he was on me again. His blows were powerful, and yet there was something about the way he wielded his sword—almost a hesitation every time he brought it down upon mine. It was as though he was holding himself back. But why would he do such a thing? Because I was a girl? Or because he'd seen me refuse to kill the boy?

When next he attacked, I dodged and swung my sword, hoping to catch him off balance. He deflected it easily with his own blade. I was by no means a novice swordsman, but it was clear his skill far outshone mine.

I circled him, all the while seeking some way of gaining control of his mind. My every effort was met with an impenetrable wall. His repeated attacks made it impossible to concentrate. Was he toying with me?

Who will stand between these barbarians and my sisters if I fall? I thought. All around me, my clansmen continued to fight. But our limited numbers meant if I didn't end this soon, we would all die. They'd take the castle and then my sisters. And I'd have let them down—again.

The sudden sharp *caw* of a crow rang out above us, and the Northman paused, his brows drawing low over his eyes. I took his distraction to my advantage. He was powerful, but was he fast? I feinted left and swung around behind him. My blade slammed down on the chain mail covering his broad back.

It didn't bring him to his knees, but it did stun him.

I swung my sword, taking advantage of his slow reaction. He parried at the last second. My blade slipped off his sword and nicked his neck. Blood snaked down his throat, and I quickly scanned the ground beneath him. Stones even larger than the one I'd used to knock out the boy were scattered all around us. I threw my sword down and dived for one.

As he bent down to grab me, I snatched a rock and smashed it against his head. He fell heavily with a dull thud upon stone. I retrieved my sword and held it high over my head, poised to keep the Northman down permanently.

But before I could deliver the final blow, something stayed my hand. A silvery voice filled my mind, whispering, *Not him*. It was the crow's voice again. It had never been wrong, but still I resisted. Why would it want me to spare my enemy? Did this Northman know what had happened to my father? Was he the reason my clansmen and father had gone to the monastery's defense? I watched the man's chest rise and fall, my gaze moving upward to study his face. His cheeks were smooth, and his golden lashes gave him a deceptively innocent appearance. The possibility that my father had been defeated, possibly even killed, made me want to shake the Northman until he woke.

My lip curled. Never mind the crow. I hated this man who'd brought these demons to my doorstep. The world would be better off with one less Northman. My arms trembled, suddenly weak under the weight of my sword as I warred with myself. In sleep, he was no threat, and I was no murderer.

I sheathed my sword as I panted for breath.

Another Northman warrior stumbled close to me. He saw his leader at my feet. I latched hold of him with my mind as fast as a hawk snatches an unsuspecting mouse from a field. This one was tired and bloody; he barely had the strength to resist. I made him open his mouth and shout in his own language, *"Hrokkva!"* Fall back. The fighting continued for several heart-beats, and I forced the Northman warrior to repeat his call. One by one, the Northmen caught sight of their fallen leader and obeyed the order to retreat.

The surviving Northmen—twenty or so by my count—turned and ran as my remaining clansmen chased them to the edge of the cliff.

The man I controlled remained behind, still swaying under my influence. I moved him toward the younger unconscious boy. I could sense the pain of his injuries as I forced him to scoop up the boy: the cut on his thigh bleeding freely that burned as he bent down, the searing pain of bruised or broken ribs with his every breath, the sting of the blood and sweat in his eyes. Still, he was strong enough to retreat with the boy, and that's all I cared about.

Take the boy and never return, but your leader is mine, I told him. Let him remember me for the monster I was.

I glanced back down at the fallen Northman leader as my twelve remaining clansmen gathered around me.

"Cut his head from his shoulders and end this," said Conall, one of my cousins.

"No," I said, my eyes holding his. He immediately dropped his gaze. "I want him kept alive."

"Your father—"

"My father isn't here," I snapped, "and this Northman may know about—may even be responsible for—the attack on the monastery. I need to know if my father survived." I moved to stand over the Northman's fallen body like a wolf guarding her pup. The crow's voice had told me to spare him, so I would . . . for now. But more than anything, I wanted to know how this Northman was able to resist me. I let out a sharp whistle for Sleipnir. He trotted over, gracefully avoiding trampling the fallen. All my clansmen save Fergus and Conall backed away, eyeing me warily. I stared at the two of them for several heart-beats—just long enough to remind them I could force them if I wanted to—before they finally hefted the Northman onto my horse.

I leaped onto Sleipnir's back behind my prisoner.

Apprehension at what I'd done filled me. If my father returned—no, *when*, I corrected myself angrily—I'd have to explain why I hadn't immediately killed the Northman when I had the chance.

But first, I'd have to explain my logic to myself.

There was only one place I trusted to keep a prisoner both secure and secret—at least for a while. A tiny cave carved into the high cliffs by the sea, easily the most miserable place in our kingdom.

The sea roared beneath us as we hugged the side of the cliff. Conall and Fergus grunted under the weight of their unconscious charge, and I led the way over the rocky path to the cave. It was only the three of us who were able to drag our captive to his new prison; the rest stayed behind to guard the way until the enemy fully retreated. We followed a steep goat trail to a small cave carved out of the rock. Jagged rocks awaited us if we fell, but this was a path we knew well. Once I slipped inside, I helped pull the Northman into the cool darkness.

Manacles dangled from chains attached to the wall, and I fastened them around the Northman's wrists. I gritted my teeth as I touched him in such a familiar way. His arms were surprisingly heavy, the lean bands of muscles pulling the chains taut as soon as they were fastened. He slumped forward, his head on his chest, arms outstretched. His long hair escaped the leather thong that kept it bound, some of the blond strands preventing me from seeing his face.

I leaned back on my heels. I didn't understand why the voice had made me spare this man's life. Many times it had warned of battles to come, but it had never intervened in any other way—especially never to *spare* an enemy's life. Sometimes the crow appeared with the voice, but not always, proving this was more than simply an enchanted crow. I'd asked it many times what—or who—it was, but I'd never been given an answer. A spirit, a god, a demon . . . it made no difference. All that mattered was that it enabled me to prepare for battle. And now, it had spared my enemy's life.

I tilted my head as I studied the warrior before me. He looked like any other Northman—so why had the voice commanded he live? But if I was being truly honest with myself, I knew there was another reason I'd spared him.

I wanted to know how he'd been able to resist my mind control. After all, who was this warrior whose mind was nothing but a stone wall? Who could resist even my power?

"Is everything all right, milady?" Conall's voice snapped me back to the cave. In the dim light, it was hard to see my clansmen, but I knew both had minor injuries from the battle. Conall's forearm was sticky with clotted blood, and Fergus had added yet another scar to the collection on his craggy face. For all I knew, the Northman I had spared had put those marks on men I'd grown up with. Men who were perhaps the only two who treated me as an equal rather than someone to be feared. I closed my eyes tightly as if the simple act would erase the greasy guilt swirling inside me. Maybe the Northman would awake in a fury and I would be forced to do what I should have done on the battlefield.

"Go home and tend to your wounds," I said to Conall and Fergus. "There's no reason for all three of us to keep watch."

Conall, who loved to argue for the pleasure of it, crossed his arms over his chest. "It would be wrong for us to leave you with this barbarian, milady." He held his arm up to the light. "This is a mere scratch."

"Even scratches can fester," I said. "Go and tell my sisters I'll be home before nightfall."

"Come, Conall," Fergus said with a grin. "The princess can handle herself, and I'm tired of the blood dripping in my eye."

Conall's face was a mask of disapproval. "That may be, but we shouldn't leave her here for long. There's always the possibility the other raiders saw where we took their leader." His jaw flexed. "Are you sure you wouldn't rather just kill him and be done with it? The king will not approve of him being kept prisoner. If he finds out—"

"And what if this Northman knows what happened at the

monastery? What if my father is dead?"

Fergus and Conall glanced at each other, sharing a look of dismay. Losing my father would be unthinkable for many reasons, the least of which being that it was no secret King Sigtrygg in Dubhlinn wanted our kingdom for himself. Or rather, its riches. And if my father was dead, the king of Dubhlinn wouldn't waste time waging war to get it.

"He's not dead," Conall said, but anyone could see he said it to comfort himself.

"The princess has a point," Fergus said. "If these Northmen raided the monastery, it's unlikely they left anyone alive to send us word."

I glanced at the Northman prisoner again. "And I'd rather know now."

"If he'll even answer you," Conall said.

I glanced back at the Northman. "He'll answer me."

Fergus unsheathed his sword, still tinged red from the battle. "I have no doubt of that, milady. Conall, we should scout around before returning to the castle."

Conall watched the prisoner for a moment as if hoping he'd suddenly wake. His lip curled when the Northman remained slumped over. "We'll be back soon, cousin," he said, and stalked out of the cave, Fergus on his heels.

I stood at the mouth of the cave until their footsteps had long since become undetectable. I hadn't lied about wanting to find out if these Northmen were responsible for the raid, but I was also glad to be alone with my strange prisoner. I'd taken over the minds of men bigger and wiser and older than this boy, and yet he'd been able to resist. What was so special about him? It made me feel an unfamiliar sense of vulnerability.

And then the thought appeared in my mind: *What if he's like me—someone with power?*

It wasn't a wild thought. I knew I wasn't entirely alone in having abilities beyond those of most people. There were those who had true visions, who could prophesy. Traders told of people who could do incredible things, like calm a storm at sea. And then there was what my own clansmen whispered about me: that I was a changeling. A faerie child switched at birth with her real human counterpart. Though changelings were rare, they weren't unheard of, and none had ever turned out to be friendly toward humans—even to the ones who'd raised them. Everyone knew magic was alive and well in Éirinn, despite the majority of its citizens being Christians. Christianity kept some of the monsters at bay . . . but not all.

My father forbade such talk about me; even rumors of it caused his face to go ruddy with rage. But it did not keep the talk from the castle, whispered behind our backs. As painful as it was to see the apprehension in the servants' eyes, I couldn't blame them. Truly, my power was terrifying.

Was this man powerful in ways I hadn't encountered before? I picked a spot far out of reach of his chains and sat against the wall. I pulled my legs close to my body and wished I had my green-and-gold-trimmed cloak to ward off the chill. It was cold outside and still colder inside the cave, but at least I was sheltered from the wind. When my mind inevitably wandered to thoughts of the battle, I forced myself to think of other things. The story I would tell my sisters that night when they inevitably demanded one before bed, the sound of the waves crashing on the rock just outside, the chill dampness beneath my legs—anything but the blood and death and violence of battle.

After a time, the rattle of chains broke the silence. I turned to find the Northman staring at me with eyes that appeared dark in the low light. "I find it strange I am not dining in the halls of Valhalla this night," he said in Norse-accented Gaelic.

It took me a moment to puzzle out his meaning. Valhalla was the "hall of the slain"—the Norse equivalent of heaven. Even in death, the Northmen continued their raiding and drinking.

I stood, and he watched my every move, his gaze tracing the lines of my body. I tried to remember I was a warrior in this instance and not a maiden. Still, heat crept up my neck. "I kept you for questioning," I said. "There are things I need to know."

"What makes you think I will answer?" he asked, his voice lightly taunting.

"Either that or I leave you here to die."

A ghost smile appeared briefly. "Fair enough, *meyja*."

I knew only a handful of words in Norse, so I didn't know what he'd called me, but his expression said it was meant to be mocking. "How do you speak Gaelic so well?" I asked, an edge creeping into my voice. "I thought you Northmen too barbaric to bother learning other languages."

"Is this why you kept me from Valhalla? To hold a useless

conversation on my knowledge of languages?"

I glared. The fact that I couldn't understand anything but the simplest words in Norse, but he could converse with me fluently in my own language, made me uncomfortable. "I spared your life to determine whether you raided the monastery north of here."

Silent, he only stared back at me. Inwardly I forced my rising frustration down; I knew better than to say anything else. Letting silence grow until it settled on one's shoulders like a sodden wool cape was enough to force someone to talk. Usually, the mere threat of my mental abilities was enough to loosen stubborn tongues. But this particular prisoner had been immune.

Well, there were always blades.

But before I could reach for my sword, he spoke. "My life is in the hands of the gods." I enjoyed a small thrill at him having capitulated first. "I owe you nothing."

"Your Norse gods hold no power here. By all rights, I should have killed you on the battlefield, but I didn't. I could kill you now. And still you will not answer?"

He stared mutely, as though he no longer understood Gaelic.

I considered the chains that bound him for a moment, and it occurred to me that if I wasn't able to take possession of his mind on the battlefield, perhaps now that he was in a weakened state, I'd be successful at forcing the answers from his mind. I stared him down as though trying to intimidate him. All the while, I opened myself to my power, pushing through the blinding pain behind my eyes. I concentrated, my entire being focused on the prisoner in front of me.

And again I hit a wall, an impregnable nothingness. Most people's minds had no defenses; their every thought and feeling pelted me like rain the moment I reached out. But with the Northman, there was only silence. I pushed harder. A hint of confusion flitted across his face for a moment—he felt something, at least. When I pushed again, the nothingness repelled my mental attack.

The pain in my head intensified, and the many small wounds on my body from the battle throbbed. With fatigue came the severing of my patience.

"I hope your gods will keep you warm in this cave tonight. When the tide rises and the wind beats at the door, perhaps you will consider my request for answers."

His face revealed no emotion, no evidence that he had even heard or understood my threat.

I turned on my heel and stalked out of the cave. Already the night had turned bitterly cold, the type of cold that made one desperate for a fire. The kind of cold that should loosen a prisoner's tongue to guarantee he's never abandoned in such an environment again.

The goat trail was as inhospitable as always, causing me to choose my footholds carefully. Heavy footsteps announced Fergus's approach, and once I had reached the bottom of the trail, I held my hand aloft in greeting.

Fergus's eyebrows rose the moment he took in my frustrated expression. "The prisoner refused to answer you?" he asked.

"But how—with your . . . abilities . . ." He trailed off, and I was surprised he'd said as much as he had. My mental powers weren't a subject many enjoyed talking about.

I shook my head. "I wish I had an answer for you." I glanced up at the darkened cave. "The wind and tide will do the job well enough, I'm sure. If not . . ."

"I could break his silence for you, milady." He smiled then, for both Conall and Fergus loved nothing more than the chance to use their swords.

"You may get the chance," I said. My muscles tensed as I remembered the prisoner's mute stare, but even so, torture wasn't one of my strengths. "You needn't make the trek to the cave. It was hard going just now, and if you've nominated yourself as guard, then you'd be much warmer here."

He shrugged, and the flame from the torch he held danced merrily. "I would be glad to escort ye back, milady. The Northman scum will keep in his prison tonight—the manacles will see to that. And even if he should escape, he will surely fall to his death."

I glanced back at the dizzying height of the cliff, and the rocks and sea waiting hungrily at the bottom. Escape would indeed be risky, even for an uninjured warrior.

"I can see well enough in this light. I have no need for an escort. But what of my mother and sisters? Are they well?"

"Aye, milady. Only eager to see ye."

A relieved breath escaped me. Thanks be to God. "I will go to them, then. Thank you, Fergus." As I walked away, I called back over my shoulder, "I'll be sure to relieve you of your post in the morning."

Fergus chuckled, settling himself down among the rocks. "I have no doubt you'll be back. It's not many who would stand up to ye."

My muscles were drawn as tight as a bow as I hurried back to the castle keep. Fergus was wrong. I wasn't angry because the Northman had defied me—that was to be expected. No, it was the fact that he continued to resist me that fueled my anger. With him so physically weak, it should have been easy to break through his mental defenses and access the information I needed. It was too great a risk to send anyone to the monastery now, not after we had lost so many in battle; we needed his information. But what if we stalled too long and the Northmen should come back for their leader? Truly, the man was a liability. It would be better to chop off his head and throw him into the sea.

You need him, the dangerous voice whispered.

Warily, I scanned the environment around me. I didn't see the crow, just darkness around me.

Who are you? I asked.

No answer, and in this, at least, I found comfort. The voice never responded. Perhaps I was foolish to listen, possibly even reckless. For all I knew, it was a demon whispering warnings to me.

It wouldn't have been the first time such a thing had happened here. The coast could be a dangerous place, not just because of the hungry sea, heights that could maim as easily as kill, or rocks lying in wait to break one's bones, but because of the creatures that made it their home.

As a child, I was told a tale of a sluagh who tormented an old woman who lived in a fisherman's hut not far from here. The restless spirit took the form of a vulture, and followed her night and day, perching on her roof, its talons scraping across the thatching until it drove her mad. It whispered things to her, evil things, and after a time, she succumbed to it. She plucked out her husband's eyes in the night and threw herself into the sea.

But this was a familiar voice, even though the intercession was unusual. Needed him for what? What could a Northman pagan possibly help me with?

Suddenly, I was angry at myself. I shouldn't have spared the Northman's life. I was feared and disliked enough within my own clan. Why bring more trouble upon myself? But even as I thought that, I knew I couldn't execute him.

Not without reason.

4

When I returned to the castle, my sisters were huddled under a bear's pelt in front of the fire in my room, their deft fingers weaving needles in and out of embroidery, their golden hair shimmering in the light. Branna threw her needlework down as soon as she saw me. She wrapped her slim, freckled arms around me for a tight embrace. Deirdre, ever the more reserved of the two, hung back by the fireplace.

I held out my arm to her, and she joined in. "I'm so thankful you are both unharmed," I said.

"We were never in any danger," Branna said. "Thanks to you."

Deirdre nodded solemnly and tucked a lock of hair behind her ear. "Why must you fight with the men, Ciara? It's so frightening, and I couldn't bear it if anything should happen to you."

"I never wanted to leave you, but I have a duty to you and to this clan. As long as I have the power to keep those who would harm us away, I must use it."

"Branna is right in saying we were all afraid for you," my mother said from the doorway of the room. Her long blond hair was plaited, and she wore her warmest fur-trimmed robe. With the same sky-blue eyes as my sisters, she was often mistaken for their older sibling. With my hair as dark as crows' feathers, pale skin, and dark eyes, it was no wonder I was rumored to be a changeling. Not for the first time, the similarities in the three of them caused a dark feeling of foreboding to make its home in my chest.

"Máthair, it is for you and my sisters that I fight. It would be sinful of me to remain here when I can make a difference on the battlefield."

"You didn't allow me to finish," my mother scolded. "Branna, Deirdre, we must be strong for Ciara. She risks much for us, and it only burdens her heart to have us beg her not to leave."

Deirdre hung her head. "Yes, Máthair."

But Branna regarded me with a determined expression that reminded me of the Northman boy of the battlefield. "Since the battle is over, will you accompany us to the market tomorrow?"

God willing, I would be extracting answers from a prisoner tomorrow. "Bran, I—"

"Your sister cannot leave the castle," our mother said, her voice quietly firm. "Especially with so many of our men away."

"Ciara never comes with us," Branna persisted. She was right. Máthair rarely, if ever, asked me to accompany them away from the castle.

"She is of more use here. We must all play our part—for the good of all." She held her arm out, the sleeves of her robe hanging down to her waist. "Come now, girls. Ciara needs her rest."

"Please, Máthair," Deirdre said. "Can't we sleep here with Ciara?"

Máthair met my eyes, wariness evident in the thin press of her lips. There had been a time when the three of us slept in the same bed every night. But that was before I had become of age, before my abilities had manifested and my own mother treated me as though I were more wolf than daughter—one to be respected and feared.

Indeed, the first time I'd used my abilities was when I'd accidentally used them on my own mother.

I remembered being furious with her. She'd forbidden me from riding for the rest of the week because I hadn't gotten up in time to go to Mass.

"You've shamed us, acting like a pagan," she'd said, her face red with anger.

"No one wants me there anyway!" I'd thrown back at her. Even before my true abilities had manifested, many were uneasy in my company. It was as if they sensed from the very beginning that I was different.

I was more hurt that she never defended me. She knew what the others said about me, but she never attempted to silence them. It was as if she silently agreed. And when she took away riding, the one thing that made me feel free and useful and accomplished, something inside me broke.

It was as if my fury took on the form of an invisible hand, reaching from my mind to hers. It grabbed hold of her and pushed hard enough that she stumbled backward into the wall. Her anger and disappointment in me quickly changed to an icy, paralyzing fear.

She's just like her, my mother had thought, her words tumbling over themselves, echoing in her mind. *Too powerful. Too dangerous.*

Just like who? I'd thought back, but I was already letting go of her mind. Shaking with the horror of what I'd done to her, with the fact that she was *afraid* of me, I watched her flee my room.

That was five years ago.

Ever since then, my mother had been cautious in my company, like one would be cautious with any wild thing. My father, when he'd heard what I'd done, had locked me in my room for two days. On the third, he'd asked me to join him on the training field with a single rule: I was never to use my abilities on members of our family. And once others found out what I could do, I was no longer welcome in church.

"I would take great comfort from it if they stayed," I said to Máthair now.

She hesitated, and I felt my heart twist in response. What had my sisters to fear from me? "Very well," Máthair said. "Just for tonight." She rubbed her hand gently over Branna's head, and bent down to kiss Deirdre's cheek.

She left as quietly as she'd come, and I pointed to the fastenings of my armor. "I will have to remove all this before bed. Will you help me, Bran?"

"Of course," she said, her nimble fingers making quick work of the stubborn buckles.

I'd washed the blood and gore from my armor before entering the keep, but it still took the effort of the three of us to remove it. The leather leggings were the worst of all, practically molded to my skin.

Branna sat back on her haunches with an exasperated groan after several unsuccessful attempts to free me from them. "I think I will have to cut you free," she announced.

"Do whatever you must," I said.

She retrieved a dagger from my wall and cut them off in strips. I breathed a sigh of relief when they fell in a clump at my feet, and I was left in my linen tunic.

"Here's your robe," Deirdre said, holding the heavy velvet aloft. "Now will you tell us a story?"

I glanced at my wooden tub longingly but knew it would have to wait. I smiled. "I would love to."

Deirdre threw herself into my bed and buried herself beneath the thick pelts. Branna and I joined her, laughing. "What kind of story?" I asked.

"A scary one," Branna said. She gave Deirdre a nudge with her shoulder, and Deirdre nodded.

"Now what kind of older sister would I be to scare you both witless before bed? Haven't you had enough fear for the day?"

Branna shook her head while Deirdre watched me solemnly. "Better to think of a story and be afraid than to think of the Northmen," Branna said. "We won't be scared because we'll all be together. It's only when we're separated that we're afraid."

Guilt spiraled inside me. Depending on what I learned from the Northman prisoner about my father, I might have to leave them again soon. "Very well, then. I shall tell you a story about one of the scariest water creatures."

Branna's face lit up. "Is this about a each-uisce? Shauna swears her grandfather tamed one once."

"Shauna is wrong," I said, holding her gaze so she knew I was to be taken seriously. "Each-uisce can never be tamed. They may appear as sleek black horses, eerily beautiful, or even ponies, deceptively small. Always their manes and tails are dripping wet, and their eyes glow like a wolf's."

Deirdre shuddered and pressed closer to Branna.

"That doesn't sound so bad," Branna said, but I could see the gooseflesh on her arms.

"Their appearances are meant to draw you in," I said. "You see, there was a girl, long ago, who was the lone survivor of an each-uisce encounter—though her friends were not so fortunate. On one of the darkest nights the world had ever seen, with thunder roaring so loud in the sky it seemed as though the rocks beneath their feet would crumble away, a young girl and her friends were on their way home."

"Why were they out wandering in the dark? I've never heard of anything more foolish."

"*Shh*," Deirdre said to her sister. "It's just a story."

"It's a warning," I corrected. "They had strayed too far from home and had lost their way in the storm. Another lesson you'd do well to learn. The craggy hills and coast can all look the same; that's why Brother Mac Máel spends so much time on lessons of the land with you."

"He hardly teaches us anything else," Branna said, and Deirdre shushed her again.

"There were four of them altogether, the youngest Deirdre's age. They held hands and kept close to one another, but they were afraid they'd never find home again. Lightning lit up the sky, and a magnificent black stallion appeared before them. His mane dripped, water flowing in rivers down his sleek body, but the girls thought nothing of it. He was in the midst of a thunderstorm, after all. He knelt down before them, inviting them onto his back. The girl's friends said, 'He wants us to ride him, and he's big enough for all of us. We'll be sure to make it home now.' But the girl was afraid. She remembered the tale of the each-uisce her older sister had told her," I said with a pointed look at my own sisters. "The horse's nightmarish eyes sent chills racing up her spine. 'I'm afraid this horse is a demon in disguise,' the girl said, but she was too late. Her friends leaped astride, and the each-uisce galloped away so far and so fast not even a hawk could keep up from the sky."

Both Branna and Deirdre listened with wide eyes, so quiet I could hardly hear their breaths. "Why did they not throw themselves from its back?" Branna asked.

"Its skin becomes like the stickiest sap. There is no escape."

"What happened to them?" Deirdre asked, her voice barely more than a whisper.

"The each-uisce took them back to his pond and dived to the very bottom. He trapped them under until they drowned, and then he ate everything but their hearts and livers. He came back for the girl, for an each-uisce has never had his fill, but she hid from him in a cave. She watched him change into the most beautiful man, with a voice like an angel, but still she did not leave the safety of the rock at her back. Morning came, and the each-uisce disappeared, along with the thunderstorm. In the light of day, the girl realized her keep was within sight and walked back home without her friends, but alive just the same."

A hush fell over us, the crackling fire the only sound in the room. "That was a sad story," Deirdre said finally.

"It is, so you must promise me you will remember it. It's no secret there are monsters that roam all over the coast." I leaned closer to them and whispered, "Especially at night," and they both jumped and then laughed. "Truly, though, you should only ride the horses and ponies we have here."

"Then you must also promise to keep teaching us in secret," Branna said. "We're tired of Brother Mac Máel keeping our ponies on leads."

I smiled. "That all depends on Máthair. She's the one who fears you will hurt yourselves." Our mother had an unusual fear of horses, preferring to walk unless absolutely forced to ride. I had always wondered if perhaps she had encountered an each-uisce in her younger years, but as with many things, she would never say.

"Will you tell us another story?" Deirdre asked. She yawned so wide I could see every tooth.

I laughed quietly and gave her a hug. "You're too tired to hear another, and I need a proper bath. I'm sure I've smelled better."

To my surprise, no further argument was given. They burrowed under the furs, and after a few minutes of tossing and turning, they were quiet, and asleep.

After kissing each of their cheeks good night, I turned to my wide wooden tub in front of the fire.

Many viewed bathing as a luxury necessary only every cycle of the moon, but I had a different opinion on the matter, especially after a battle—I might no longer have been covered in blood and sweat, but I still felt unclean.

My handmaiden had painstakingly prepared a bath for me earlier in the evening—when I should have arrived home. I didn't dare rouse her from her warm bed now to bring the bath back to a comfortable temperature. The scent of lavender and mint still perfumed the air invitingly, despite the cold.

The water in my tub was too cold to soak in, so I bathed quickly, scrubbing my skin until it was pink from abuse.

Finished, I stood, and as my hands grasped both sides of the tub, I suddenly went blind. My heart pounded in my chest like the thundering hooves of a herd of horses. The water dripped from my body; I could hear it falling back into the tub with a *drip, drip, drip*. A cry for help clawed its way up my throat, but my lips would not part to release it. I could not move.

I sensed rather than saw the mist rise up around me, colder even than my bath had been. It snaked up my legs and blanketed my body until gooseflesh covered my skin. My breaths came in a panicked pant, and I willed my legs, my arms, to move, but not even my strength could force them to. As suddenly as it had disappeared, my vision returned, but I was still paralyzed. Then came a flash of blinding light, and in the midst of it, a crow appeared. Its eyes held mine, worlds of knowledge contained within.

Ciara, it said, and the blood in my veins seemed to turn to ice. It was the same voice I had always heard. Now that I heard it clearly, it was a hoarse, dangerous sort of voice. *Do you know who I am?*

Still in the hold of the same paralysis, I could only stare.

I am one of the Tuatha Dé Danann, the first men of Éirinn who were once worshipped as gods. The Morrigan, Phantom Queen, and goddess of war and death. It tilted its head, and the feathers shifted, oily and black. In rapid succession, images poured into my mind, until I was sure I was in the grip of madness: a misty wood, the fog slowly taking shape until I could almost make out the figure of a woman; but then she turned, and her face was that of a crow's, her hair made of feathers. *But then, you have always known me.*

The crow's harsh *caw-caw-caw* blasted through the room. It flew so close to my face I feared it would tear out my eyes with its talons, but it only buffeted my cheeks with its greasy black feathers. In its eye, I saw my memories, all the times I had seen the crow before: the day I received my first blood as a woman; the day I had taken control of one of my fellow clansmen during training; on the battlefield at Fir Tulach, when Northman raiders had sailed all the way down the river to lay siege to the village there; and then earlier today, before the Northman prisoner had landed on our shore.

The crow's eye seemed to shimmer and grow, until it soon blotted out everything else. I was trapped; the Morrigan's voice was all I could hear.

For hundreds of years, the Tuatha Dé Danann have allowed the raiders from the north to rape and pillage our lands.

In my vision I saw Northman longships, with prows of gaping dragon heads, make landfall on the coast of Éirinn. Cold nausea gripped me as I watched them slaughter every monk they encountered at the monasteries along the coast, their axes making quick work of men who had virtually no defenses. From there they moved on to the villages. Houses with thatched roofs went up in infernos, children ran screaming, men were cut down as women were taken as slaves. The raiders took everything of value, packing captured slaves and treasures until their longships hung low in the water from the sheer weight of it all.

And then: the night they attacked my father's castle for the first time. I tried to block out the vision, one I had long since kept at bay, but I was helpless to stop it.

No, I said when I found myself back in the front pew of the church.

No, I said again when Father Teagan, now long dead, lifted his hands in prayer.

The horn rang out across the bailey, loud and urgent.

Run, you fools! I tried to shout to all the people in the church, who glanced at one another in confusion.

My father stood and hauled my mother to her feet. "Take the hidden passageway," he said, and pushed her along as my sisters and I clutched at her skirts. "Go!" he said when she hesitated.

Finally, she obeyed. Máthair carried Deirdre, then a mere baby, in her arms, while she kept a firm hold on six-year-old Bran's hand. Both were crying, their eyes wide with terror.

"Keep hold of your sister," Máthair said to me urgently, and I did. I held Alana's hand until the moment she was dragged from me.

Why show me this? I tried to shout at the Morrigan, but it was like shouting into the wind. I shook with the effort to keep the images at bay, for I knew what came next.

Máthair raced across the bailey, keeping Bran's face pressed against her skirts as best she could. But I saw everything: men taller than my father, axes cutting into my clansmen, women screaming, while still others were caught and bound. Blood everywhere. It tinted my world red as though my own eyes were bleeding.

Alana was so quiet, her face twisted in terror and disbelief, but she didn't utter a sound. The steps to the keep were only a yard away. But then she tugged me to a stop. "Moira!" she screamed. She was looking at her friend who lay dead, blood pooling around her while her mother clutched her broken body to her breast. I remember thinking: *But she's a child. Children don't die in battle.*

Our mother reached the steps of the keep. She whirled around when she realized we were no longer behind her.

"Alana," I said with another tug, but my sister was frozen in horror.

When I turned back toward our mother, a Northman loomed above us, cutting off our escape. He was as big as a bull, his straw-colored hair long and braided. The axe in his hand was stained red, and a fresh wound—a deep cut from his eyebrow down to his cheek—dripped blood. His blue eyes shifted to my mother. Somewhere across the bailey, I heard my father shout.

Áthair is coming, I told myself. *He'll save us.*

Alana finally turned away from the sight of her fallen friend, only to scream as she saw the massive man before us.

He grabbed her, yanking her from my grasp. "These must be your children," he said, his voice loud enough to carry across the bailey. He spoke our language—he wanted my father to hear him. "This one will make a fine slave."

"No!" my father shouted, running toward us, but he was cut off by another Northman.

"No?" the enemy before us repeated. He glanced down at

my struggling sister. "You'd rather she be dead, then? You cut down my nephew who was barely older than a child himself." His upper lip curled, his expression turning feral. His gaze was fixed on the body of an adolescent boy, one of the fallen Northmen. "Blood for blood," he said, and slit my sister's throat.

My father barreled into him then, knocking him to the ground as my mother screamed and ran to Alana. I couldn't look away from the blood bubbling from her throat.

More men came to the Northman's aid, but not before my father ducked beneath the man's axe and drove the blade of his sword into the enemy's leg. The remaining ranks of our clansmen joined the battle, and eventually, the Northmen retreated—taking my sister's murderer with them.

I could only hope he had later died of his injuries.

A cold sweat broke out over my skin, and I shook as though I were feverish. I begged for the images to end, to be released from the vision, but they continued mercilessly.

Another vision of Éirinn, this time of green hills, the sky above steel gray. Northmen ran across the hills, armed for battle. The men seemed different, somehow; their features were twisted, and some had deformities that made them appear less than human. They called to one another in a strange tongue, like Norse, only more guttural. More and more appeared until there was an entire army. They moved as one, swarming over the meadows, killing even sheep in their path.

As they ran, they grew taller and wider, until they were as big as mountains. The earth shook with their steady footsteps, and soon, all of Éirinn was covered by the massive men. With their axes and their legs as wide as oak trees, they destroyed everything, burning what they did not reduce to rubble. The scene changed, the land becoming more familiar: the coast where Branna and Deirdre gathered seashells, the meadow where they rode their ponies, my father's castle upon the cliff. My clansmen lay torn apart, blood spilling upon the ground, turning the earth red. High-pitched screams came from the keep: my sisters begging for mercy. I tried to shake my head, to close my eyes against the terrible vision, but the Morrigan was relentless.

Then I saw my sisters in my room, huddled together on my bed as though they had come looking for me to save them. Over them loomed a creature whose head brushed the stone ceiling, whose muscled body was nearly as wide as my bed. He was a man and yet not . . . too tall, too craggy and mountainous to be considered human. He reached for Deirdre first, and I fought anew against the vision—I wanted to take control of his mind and destroy him before he could even touch her—yet I could do nothing but watch as he yanked her up as though she were only a doll. She was screaming and fighting; Branna leaped off the bed in an attempt to stop him, and to my horror, he grabbed her, too. Lifting both of his massive arms, he dangled my sisters from his hands and squeezed. Their faces turned red, then purple; they clawed at his hands.

And then they were dead, hanging limp from his fists. He threw them to the floor and stomped over their bodies. I shook, tears streaking down my cheeks—it was so real, so vivid. I suddenly understood how the old woman with the sluagh had thrown herself into the sea. At that moment, I would have done *anything* to make the vision stop.

Screams continued from the keep as the vision shifted from my sisters' lifeless bodies to more scenes of death, to the destruction of everything I'd ever known. And everywhere, fire . . . fire burning through the meadow and roaring into the bailey. Soon, the whole of the Emerald Isle was nothing but ash.

Why torture me with such visions? I demanded, no longer able to watch the destruction of my clansmen, my family, my world.

The gods of the old world have stood aside, obeyed the ancient laws giving free will to men, the Morrigan said, her voice echoing in my mind, *and now, when our realm and yours hang in the balance, we are still bound by our covenants. The laws are clear: we can act only through man. And in all the world, there are only two strong enough to defeat them. One born for it, the other through great sacrifice.*

The vision shifted yet again in my mind, to show a pool of mist that concealed the figures of two people. They stepped into the light, and to my horror, I saw who the Morrigan spoke of: myself . . . and the Northman I currently held prisoner.

What has he to do with it? I thought, even as I remembered the voice telling me, *You need him.*

It was I who brought the two of you together, for only your alliance can save us all.

No, I thought. *No, I cannot join forces with my enemy.*

You must. The monsters will not be satisfied with the destruction of Éirinn. They will slaughter everyone you love, and they will not rest until the world is destroyed. A war is coming. Will you fight it, Ciara of Mide?

In a rush, the crow, the Morrigan, and everything I had seen, evaporated like water in the sun. Released from the paralysis, I stumbled out of the tub and fell to the floor, wet and shaking. I curled in on myself and took great gulping breaths.

"That cannot be true," I whispered. "Please, let it not be true."

It's no lie, the voice answered. *Make ready*.

5

Dawn's weak light barely illuminated the goat trail up to the cave, and the rocks were slick from the recent high tide. I picked my way carefully, my mind on the revelations of the night before. The residual terror of what I'd seen still held me in its grasp, and I couldn't free myself from watching my sisters' brutal deaths. Once the visions had passed the night before and I could finally walk again—shivering and sick—I had gone to where Branna and Deirdre slept peacefully and held them so tightly they'd both made sounds of protest. Instead of sleeping, I'd stood guard over them all night, terrified that the moment I closed my eyes would be the moment the vision would come true.

Now as I walked toward my prisoner, my head felt heavy and

throbbed mercilessly as though I'd caught a chill, and my limbs trembled. I'd been in many people's heads, seen their darkest thoughts, been in battles that were gruesome and violent, but nothing was as soul-crushingly terrible as the Morrigan's vision. Not only had I been forced to relive what happened to my sister Alana—something I hadn't allowed myself to fully remember for years now—but also I was forced to witness the threat to my surviving sisters in such vivid detail that my stomach churned with horror just thinking about it. Worse still was the threat that such a fate could befall not only my family and kingdom, but all of Éirinn.

The Morrigan. It had been her voice, her crows that had warned me of impending death. I'd always wondered, though of course any belief in her would only brand me a heretic. She was part of the Tuatha Dé Danann. Though the people of Éirinn were now Christian, it didn't erase the magic from our land, nor the creatures who had always made it their home. The Tuatha Dé Danann were powerful immortals, and the Morrigan was perhaps the most frightening. Some called her the Phantom Queen because she was a specter on the battlefield, often flying above it as a crow, warning of bloody and gruesome death. She was even known for determining the outcome of battle, choosing who would be the victor.

In this, at least, she had always seemed to favor me.

Again, I thought of her words on the battlefield. *Not him*, she had said, and I'd been compelled to spare his life. Did she really mean for me to join forces with my Northman prisoner?

I shook my head. What if he had raided the monastery and killed my father? Was I to join forces with my father's murderer? I would gladly fight the monsters from the Morrigan's vision myself, but I could not join forces with my enemy. It was far too much to ask of me.

One born for it, the other through great sacrifice.

The words filled me with unease. I didn't understand what she meant, but neither did I want to. I'd spent many years wondering where my powers came from and why I was the only one in my family with such abilities, but did this mean I was the one who was born to it? Or was I the one who'd make a great sacrifice? Thinking such things only elicited more questions. There must be another goal in mind.

And somehow, the Northman fit into those goals.

The prisoner watched me with his ice-blue eyes as I crossed the threshold of the cave. He had stood tall in the Morrigan's vision, his hair braided and face not smattered with blood and dirt, not battered and beaten as he was now.

I held aloft the hunk of bread and flagon of wine I'd brought him. "I will loosen your irons and allow you to eat and drink, if you will swear to answer my questions."

He said nothing, only shifted with a soft rattle of chains.

"You must be uncomfortable after a night spent in such a position," I said.

The smallest of smiles crossed his lips so fast I wasn't sure I had seen it at all. "You are persistent, *meyja*. I will give you that."

I took a step toward the end of his chains. "Does this mean you agree to my terms?"

"That small bit of bread and puny flagon will only stir my appetite," he said, a taunting smile curving his mouth. "If you will bring me a real meal, fit for a warrior after a battle, then I will answer you."

I strode forward and ripped the irons free from their stays; the sudden slack caused him to pitch forward, and he barely caught himself at the last moment. "You will answer me now. If I am satisfied with your response, then I will bring you more food and drink."

The muscles in his arms bulged as he pushed himself upright. His eyes flicked to the ends of the chains, still attached to a ring on either side of him. I had merely removed the pins that kept the length of links so short. "You play a dangerous game," he said, holding one of the chains aloft.

If he lunged, he could pin me. I became suddenly aware of the familiar weight of the dagger hidden beneath my cloak, but I didn't want to use it. Not yet. "Do you still sneer at my offering?"

We stared at each other, tension a thrum of power between us. After a moment, he held out his hand. I stepped within reach of his chains, my head held high, and gave him the bread and wine. A low chuckle escaped him as I returned to a relatively safe distance unscathed.

He tore into the bread and gulped the wine in two swallows. He wiped his mouth with the back of his hand and reclined, one arm resting on his knee. "Come, then. Ask your questions."

I opened my mouth to ask about the northern monastery, or to ask if he knew anything about monstrous invaders who threatened my family, but I realized all at once that he would never answer me. It was clear he didn't fear me, and I couldn't force his mind as I did others'—something that still nagged at my thoughts—but I could do what anyone must do who wanted answers: gain his trust. I remembered the boy I'd spared on the battlefield and how this Northman had seemed to fear for him. "That boy on the battlefield. Who is he to you?"

His face darkened like a sudden storm cloud. "Where is he?" The length of chain rattled ominously.

"Safe. Or as much as he can be, I suppose, with your men."

The threatening aura he had been emitting just moments before receded. "You spared him."

"He's a child."

"Celts have killed our children before."

And Northmen have killed our *children before*, I wanted to say. With force, I pushed down the flare of anger that burned within me. He was not my sister's murderer. "I haven't." I risked a glance at him. "Why would you force a child to fight?"

To my surprise, he avoided my gaze. "I didn't realize he was on the ship until we landed on your shores."

"A stowaway." It was something Branna would have done. A flash of the look on his face when he saw me battling the boy appeared in my mind then: the gut-wrenching fear. "You were afraid I would kill him."

"He is my brother. The only sibling I have left." He shook his head as though his admission surprised him. "After watching what you did to my men, I was afraid you'd make quick work of him." He was silent for several heartbeats. "You have my thanks," he added, his voice gruffer than before.

"And the monastery I asked about?" I held my breath.

"We did not raid a monastery."

My shoulders slumped. I couldn't hide my relief. "Thanks be to God." All too soon, a cold feeling settled in my stomach. "But your longship came from the north."

"What of it?"

"Why pass up the opportunity for a monastery? Why disembark on our shores?"

He hesitated, as though debating whether or not to answer. Finally, he said, "A bird. A *kráka*."

My eyes snapped to his. "What did you say?" I had to be sure—with his accent, it was hard to tell.

He made an impatient sort of noise before letting out a harsh *caw-caw-caw*. I felt the color drain from my face. The Morrigan.

"Did it lead you?" I asked, my voice hushed.

"It landed on the prow of my ship, and I saw myself within its eyes. It wanted me to land here, so I did. I didn't expect to be greeted by a warrior maiden and her band of Celts."

"And I'm supposed to believe you never intended to raid my home?"

"Of course we were there to raid. Your castle was a challenge, and one that I ultimately failed. My first failure, thanks to you."

"My apologies, Northman," I said with a curl to my upper lip Conall would be proud of. But inwardly, the Morrigan's visions haunted me. If the Morrigan had led him here, if she was bringing us both together, then the horrific scenes she'd shown me . . .

No, it couldn't be true.

But even as I denied it, I heard my sisters screaming before the life was squeezed from their bodies.

"What now, maiden?" the Northman said, pulling me from my morbid thoughts. "I have told you everything you asked of me and more. Will you keep me chained here until my flesh falls from my bones?"

But how could I ask him what he knew about the Morrigan? What if he hadn't seen what I'd seen? He'd think I was mad. "What would you have me do? Set you free?" I scoffed. "So that you might continue your raiding all the way to Dubhlinn?"

His gaze shifted to the entrance of the cave. "I have seen many things, but a maiden as a prison guard is one of the strangest. Are the Celts so weak they allow their women to interrogate prisoners? Where are the men?"

"I am no maiden," I said. I crossed my arms over my chest.

He laughed. "A warrior maiden, perhaps, but a maiden just the same. Do you think me blind? You are far too beautiful to be a mere servant."

"Honeyed words do nothing but anger me. All you need know about me is that I am your captor."

His expression turned skeptical. "The Celts allow their

women to hold prisoners captive? To shed blood on the battle-field?"

"If the woman has proven abilities, then yes. Isn't it true you Northmen have your own female warriors—shieldmaidens, I believe?"

He didn't answer me, but instead leaned back, raising his chin just slightly, as though challenging me. "And what would a maiden want with a warrior chained in a cave?" His eyebrows rose, the suggestion clear.

I stared at him, aghast. My heart belied my calm tone, beat-ing a furious pace in my chest. It was clear I was losing control of this conversation.

He only laughed, obviously enjoying my embarrassment.

"If your plan is to insult me, then I will only leave you here to starve." I turned to go.

"By all means, milady. Go, bring me a meal fit for a warrior, and I will tell you what it is the *kráka* said to me."

I paused. "It spoke to you?" This could be what I needed to know: if the Northman knew of the Morrigan's vision.

"It did, but I will tell you nothing more until I have eaten my fill."

I looked away for a moment, a muscle in my jaw twitching. His tone was flippant, but I could also hear the truth in his words. "I suppose I could find you some bread and cheese."

He smirked. "Come, do not toy with me. I will accept noth-ing less than meat, brown bread, dark beer, and cheese."

I scoffed. "I would also like some meat. But we are a stone's throw from the sea. You will have fish like the rest of us."

"A stew, I hope," he called as I left the cave. I shook my head at his audacity.

A short raid in the kitchen was a small price to pay to discover what the Northman knew, but the prospect of giving in to his demands was as noxious to me as swimming in a each-uisce's pond.

The bailey was a bustle of activity as I made my way through to the kitchens. Brother Mac Máel and Father Briain hurried to the chapel for Lauds; the smith's hammer beat out a steady rhythm, replacing blades broken the day before; and many of the servants were enjoying the rare sunshine, repairing torn cloaks, dresses, or even the leggings Branna had cut from me the night before—though they'd be repurposed into something else now.

As I passed the smithy, a low, welcoming horn sounded. I froze and jerked my head toward the stockade bridge. Just as it had the day before, everything ground to a halt, only this time, everyone wore looks of anticipation.

I ran to the center of the bailey, in full view of the bridge. The warriors who had left with my father were returning, their faces weary, yet triumphant. Their horses perked up noticeably as they trotted over the bridge, no doubt anticipating a rest in the stables. My clansmen broke out into grins as they caught sight of loved ones, their green-and-gold cloaks billowing out behind them. The clan crest, a fierce griffin embroidered in gold and surrounded by a Celtic knot, was emblazoned on the long cloak of each man. Behind them came a wagon heavily laden with wooden chests—from the monastery? I held my breath as I watched each man pass, counting as they went. Thirty men. Everyone was accounted for. Everyone but my father.

The horn blew low again, and everyone bowed.

My breath let out in a sigh as I caught sight of the next rider. My father rode in on his dapple-gray charger, his cloak of green and gold flowing behind him like a sail. A small circlet of gold sat atop his light hair, nearly the same color save for the gray streaks that had recently taken over the blond. His face bore the determined expression it always did, with no sign of wear.

Relief weakened my knees. He was alive.

I ran to my father's side, and he smiled from atop his tall horse. "Ciara, we came as soon as we received word. I'm glad to hear you did your duty and protected your mother and sisters."

"Yes, Áthair. The raid took us by surprise, but we were able to defeat the leader." Though, of course, I had broken every rule by taking the leader prisoner, but I wasn't about to volunteer such information. "Had the monastery been raided? Are the monks safe?"

"It was nearly raided, but not by Northmen—this was King Sigtrygg's doing," Áthair said with a look of disgust he reserved for the king of Dubhlinn. "We fought them off and brought the monastery's gold and silver and relics back here for safekeeping."

It wasn't unusual for Sigtrygg to go on raids; with the whole of Éirinn divided into five different overkingdoms—including

Mide—and countless smaller clan territories and kingdoms, there were frequent raids from within the country by other kingdoms seeking to gain more resources. Sigtrygg, though, had recently aligned himself with the High King by marrying his daughter, but this addition to his power clearly hadn't stopped him raiding other kingdoms for more land, more gold, more power. As a half Northman, however, Sigtrygg was one of the most hated kings, and he had never raided so close to our castle before. I didn't need the Morrigan's crow to sense that a battle was brewing between our kingdoms. "I'm glad you were able to stop them."

He nodded. "Now where are your mother and sisters? I missed them terribly while I was away."

I kept a smile on my face though his words pained me. My father never concerned himself with me, seeing me more as a fellow clansman than as his daughter. "They must have already left for the market." I could almost see Branna and Deirdre's crestfallen faces when they realized they'd missed Áthair's homecoming. They loved watching the clansmen parade through the bailey, Áthair striking such a proud figure on his big dapple gray.

"How disappointing." His horse stamped its hoof as though impatient to move on. "Well, come speak to me in the throne room. I would hear a full report on all that transpired."

I hesitated for a moment, struggling to think of an excuse, but there was nothing so important that would allow me to ignore my father's command. I dipped my head in acquiescence, and he rode away, giving orders to the clansmen to rest.

Before I could follow, I watched Conall move to meet my father as he dismounted from his horse. Áthair bent his head toward Conall, and the two of them continued walking toward the castle keep.

It was Conall's duty as much as it was mine to tell the king what had passed in the battle, but would Conall tell him of the Northman prisoner?

A sense of urgency nipped at my heels as I followed. If—no, when—my father discovered I kept the Northman prisoner in the cave, he would order him beheaded without question. In my mind, I saw the young prisoner and his younger brother, and a sort of desperation built within me. I winced as images of my sisters' murders assaulted my mind. Forcefully, I pushed the terrorizing thoughts away. If the Northman knew some-thing—*anything*—that could help me stop the crow's vision, then I could not let him be killed.

Even if it meant facing Áthair's wrath.

I strode into the keep's great hall, my soft leather boots barely making a sound upon the stone floor. The cavernous room was quiet, the rows upon rows of wooden benches empty. Ahead of me, my father made his way toward his wide wooden throne, elevated on a stone dais. He would expect me to stand before him and make my report on the battle like any other clansman. For a moment, I imagined what it would be like to have him express concern for me, to inquire about the battle with his face twisted in anxiety instead of calculation. Even as I thought these things, I shook my head. My parents had always kept me at a distance; imagining anything different would only cause me pain.

The first time I'd stood before his disappointed gaze in this very room, I'd been thirteen. It was after our first battle against Northman raiders, and my leg had been cut so badly I could barely walk. As I limped the length of the room, my father watched my slow progress dispassionately.

"You have the blood of a warrior, Ciara," my father had said, his eyes intense on mine. "It's been a year since you first discovered your extraordinary powers, and still you have not mastered them." He glanced down at my leg. "That injury you bear will be the least of what you—and others—may suffer if you cannot gain control of them. But we cannot rely on chance battles and raids to train you." He waved forward one of our clansmen, a superior fighter as strong as an ox. "You will have to learn to take over the minds of our allies so that you may be able to do so against our enemies in battle."

I wish I could say I hadn't wanted to. That I'd refused my father and learned to hone my skills some other way. But the truth was, while my abilities disgusted and even shamed me, in the midst of using them, I reveled in them. I felt invincible, all-powerful, and most of all, I felt useful. So while part of me shriveled in horror at what I did to men and boys I'd grown up with, the other rejoiced at the power I displayed.

But such things came at a price.

My steps slowed, echoing in the great hall, as I tried unsuccessfully to fight off a yawning feeling of loneliness. As a child, I could never have been described as affable, but I did have a handful of friends. Now, it was only my sisters who sought my company—and Fergus, on occasion. As a princess, my clansmen couldn't shun me outright, but they avoided me, until some days I felt like I'd go mad from the isolation. A writhing remorse deep in my abdomen surfaced—for men, much older than I, who watched me with suspicion and flinched when I entered the room. Of Séamus, who had once been my closest friend, a boy I'd thought I loved, but who now despised me.

Demon, they called me in their minds. *Changeling. Cursed.* And every time I took hold of someone's mind, I wondered if perhaps they were right.

Reaching his throne before me, Áthair sat down heavily. When I stood before the dais, he glanced down at me and nodded. His elegant clothing looked dull—a fine layer of dust had settled upon his fur-trimmed cloak, his boots were scuffed, and his tunic was rumpled beneath his leather breastplate. For a moment, he looked so weary that I almost asked if he'd rather I came back later, but I knew drawing attention to any weakness of his made him bearish. As though sensing my thoughts, he straightened.

"You are to be commended for driving the pagans off," Áthair began, but I waited bracingly, knowing his compliments were almost always followed by a criticism. "However, I was informed that there were survivors."

My heart beat faster in my chest. So Conall must have told him. I kept my gaze very carefully on his eyes, afraid I'd betray myself by looking anxiously at the door. "They retreated when their leader was defeated."

He leaned forward. "And you let them?"

I could see now that what I had originally taken for weariness was actually disappointment . . . in me. "Should I have hunted them all down as animals, then?"

"What you did was far worse. Tell me, what *exactly* were you planning to do with a prisoner?"

Suddenly, the room was much too warm. I needed the Northman alive, but if my father already knew, then had he sent one of the others to kill him? A niggling feeling crept up my neck. I knew what needed to be done—this was my father, yes, but also the king. And the king should be informed of a vision of monstrous beings who would not only bring about the destruction of Éirinn but the deaths of my own sisters. But would he believe me?

"I held him for questioning when I suspected he had attacked the northern monastery."

Some of the anger in my father's face lessened.. "You feared for me?"

"I did, Áthair."

"Why interrogate him when you could simply take over his mind?"

I raised my eyebrows in surprise. Áthair rarely discussed my abilities. Forced me to endlessly practice them on the training grounds, yes. But rarely spoke of them. "He was able to resist me," I admitted.

Áthair looked taken aback for a moment, but quickly recovered. "A rare talent. Unfortunately for him, it's not enough to preserve his life." He let out a sigh and leaned back. "You're a good daughter, Ciara. But it's time you cleaned up your own mess. Go to the prisoner, kill him, and burn the body. Return to me when you are done."

I froze, my heartbeat throbbing in my ears. It was now or never. Áthair needed to know why I couldn't kill the Northman, why we might even need him to face the new enemies that would soon be at our door.

"Áthair," I said, proud that my voice managed to not waver, "the prisoner must be kept alive." His eyes narrowed, but I forged ahead. "After the battle with the Northmen raiders, I endured a vision of not only our kingdom falling under attack, but the whole of Éirinn."

"You've never had visions before. Where did this come from, and why should you believe it?"

I took a deep breath. My pious father would not like to hear it had been given to me not by God, but by a pagan goddess. "The Morrigan appeared to me."

His face paled, and he started to come out of his throne before sitting back down again. "The Morrigan?"

"Yes, Áthair," I said. "The Phantom—"

"I know who she is," he roared, his voice echoing throughout the throne room. "Why would you listen to one of the Old

Ones? You know they're dangerous. Many have been led to their death by the Old Ones, and many more have lost their souls."

"I listened to her because it's her voice I've been hearing all along—the one that has warned me of battles and death." His face paled again, but at least he'd stopped shouting long enough to listen to me. "I listened because she showed our castle being attacked, and my sisters . . ." I swallowed hard as I remembered helplessly watching as the giant killed them both. "My sisters were killed by enemies I've never encountered before. They were like the Northmen we have battled, only giant, taller than an oak tree and stronger than any man I've ever seen. The Morrigan warned they wouldn't rest with Éirinn; they meant to take over the world."

"We have battled Northmen before and won," Áthair said. "A pagan creature shows you differently, and you believe her. You are being led astray."

I took a step toward the throne, desperation rising within me. "You don't understand. I have heard her voice before, and she has never been wrong. You don't understand what's at stake." I thought again of my sisters, of the whole isle turning to ash, and I painstakingly described every horrific image the Morrigan had shown me, but still, he shook his head angrily.

"Enough of this, Ciara," he said, his voice rising again. "Listening to the Old Ones is heresy, and I will not tolerate it in my kingdom. Go to the Northman prisoner. Kill him. Be done with this—it matters not what the Morrigan told you. Their race is full of lies and deceit."

"I cannot."

Silence descended as Áthair stared at me. "You dare to tell me no?" His tone was dangerously calm.

Like a flame touched to dry wood, it ignited my own anger. "The Morrigan said the Northman is the only one aside from myself with the power to stop the inhuman invaders. If there's even the slightest chance this is true, if it means keeping my sisters safe, then I will keep him alive."

Áthair flew out of his throne, red-faced with rage. "If you defy me in this, Ciara, then I swear by all the saints that I will send you away to the other side of Éirinn and kill the Northman myself."

His eyes were narrowed, his hands fists at his sides. I knew he wouldn't listen to me, and I knew he'd stand by his words. He never listened to me, at least not like a father should listen to his daughter. The anger built and built within me, until every muscle tightened to the point it was painful. I thought of Alana, dead at the Northmen's hands, of Branna and Deirdre writhing and clawing for breaths as they were murdered in my own room, and something within me snapped. If he wouldn't listen to me, then I would *make* him understand. Without stopping to think of the consequences, I lashed out with my mind.

I grabbed hold of my father's mind, and his shock and outrage spewed forth a torrent of memories that washed over me: the Morrigan on a battlefield, standing naked before Áthair, a murder of crows flying above them.

There will come a day, the Morrigan said in her terrible voice, *when your own blood will join forces with your enemy.*

He struggled against my hold on his mind, but I delved deeper until the thought he'd been trying to hide from me surfaced: the image of myself standing before him on the throne, telling him of the Morrigan's vision, and Áthair, hearing the echo of the Morrigan's warning all those years ago.

I shoved him back into his throne. "You knew the Morrigan's vision was true." The horror of that shook me enough that my mental grip on him weakened.

Áthair fought anew until he was able to wrench free of my hold. He gripped his head in his hands, and I knew he was in agony—taking control of someone by force could have that effect. I took a step forward as though I could help him, desperate to undo what I'd just done. "Áthair, I—"

"You dare turn on me like a mad dog?" His voice was gruff with pain but also anger. The fury rolled off him like black smoke.

"I just wanted you to understand. You have to listen to me—"

"Your mother always said I was wrong to train you after what you did to her."

I flinched like I'd been struck. We never spoke of that day. It made me feel sick to be reminded of it after doing the same to Áthair. He stood, and again I reached out as if to steady him, but his words stopped me.

"She was right. You are an abomination, a monster who threatens her own family." His eyes leveled on me, remorseless. "You leave me with no choice, despite the terrible loss of you as a warrior. But I can no longer fear who you will turn on next."

His words hung heavily in the air, and I took a step back in horror when I realized who he was implying: my sisters.

"I want you to leave. There are convents far from here—the kingdoms of Connacht or Munster on the other side of Éirinn. They will take you in. Go there, and may God have mercy on your soul."

I held on to my swelling rage; I knew once I took a moment to absorb my father's words that I would face endless despair. Exile! I thought again of Branna and Deirdre, of my clansmen, and the kingdom of Mide. The Morrigan had said I had the ability to save them. I couldn't let anything stand in my way. Not even my own father.

I did the only thing I could do: I turned and ran.

No one tried to stop me as I flew out of the castle, angrily brushing away the tears that fell unchecked from my eyes. I had broken the one rule I'd vowed to always uphold: to never use my abilities on a member of our family. Certainly not him. Never him.

"I *am* a monster," I whispered to myself.

I had always been a monster in his eyes. But I would gladly be a monster if it meant saving my sisters.

Banishment. Exile. I never thought I'd hear those words directed toward me, and as the initial anger slowly abated, I had the strongest urge to run back to the castle and beg his forgiveness. The mere thought of having to leave the kingdom and not see my sisters again was so devastating I let out a cry of pain. It didn't matter that I was the princess. Áthair was known for his quick temper, and many clansmen who had committed far lesser crimes had been exiled before. My particular crime subjected me to both Brehon Law, the law all kingdoms obeyed, and the Church. I wouldn't be brought before a tribunal of judges, though—no, my father had already issued my punishment. As soon as he had recovered from my attack on him, he'd send his guards after me to escort me out of the kingdom.

There was only one place I could go . . . to the Northman.

And then what? I demanded of myself. Even if he knew of the invaders to our land, what would I do? Ask him to join me in exile?

I let out a noise that was disgust and frustration in one.

If I wanted the prisoner to answer me, it was in my best interest to bring him the food he demanded. There wouldn't be time to force the information from him, no matter how desperate I was.

It was easy enough to retrieve bread and cheese from the larder, as well as a flagon of water, but I ground my teeth when I found a massive cauldron of fish stew bubbling over a fire. How I would hate the look of triumph on the Northman's face when I brought him exactly what he had asked for.

I was as nervous as a hare that scented the fox as I hurried back through the bailey with my parcels of food. I couldn't be detained. Lying was not my strength, and I was short on daylight.

A shock of red hair drew my attention as I made my way to the stockade. The Lord had mercy on me. It was Fergus and not Conall, for obviously it was he who had told my father about the prisoner. I should have anticipated it, really. Conall's loyalties above all were to his king. I shouldn't have expected him to keep silent on something like a captured Northman prisoner.

Fergus hailed me, one hand raised. "I was just coming to find you, milady. I checked on the prisoner not long ago, and he seemed to be asleep. Pity, that."

I tried not to dance in place. I was desperate to continue on my way, but running off now would only make him suspicious. "Thank you, Fergus. I'm sorry to have left you at the foot of the trail for so long. Áthair summoned me the moment he returned."

"And I apologize for having to leave my post, but the king will want to see me."

My hands tightened on the food I carried. "Of course."

Thoughts of how Fergus would react when he learned I'd attacked my own father and had been exiled for it tried to fill my mind, but I pushed them aside. They were too painful. His gaze drifted to the food I carried, and both bushy eyebrows lifted questioningly.

"It's better not to ask," I said.

He frowned. "You are feeding him now?"

I kept walking. "It's none of your concern, Fergus."

"It is, milady. I'm to keep watch over ye." He touched his

hand to my arm. "Does your father know?"

In this, at least, I need not lie. "He does. This is to be the prisoner's last meal."

That silenced him for a moment. "Should I come with you?"

"No," I said—a little too sharply. "I must speak to him privately first."

I tried to hurry away from Fergus, but his words stopped me. "What more do you need to know? The king has returned to us safely. The Northman has nothing to offer you now."

I stopped and turned toward my clansman. I held his watery gaze with mine, praying that I could convey the direness of the situation. "Fergus, do you believe the talk about me? That I'm a changeling?"

He floundered, all round eyes and gaping mouth. "I—" He seemed to gather his thoughts. "I wouldn't consider myself an authority on such a matter. I only know you have the ability to . . ." And there he trailed off. ". . . control others in battle," he said. "You are able to interpret omens."

"Then know this. I have seen things, Fergus. Terrible things, destruction to our world I pray never comes to pass. I believe this Northman may have answers, and I will do anything to get them."

"Even bringing him food like a servant?"

"Even that."

Fergus nodded. "Very well, milady. But once you have your answers, if you find you cannot bring yourself to do what must be done, only call on me, and I will help you."

He was offering to take the burden of executing the Northman for me. Not that I intended to go through with the act—not when the Northman could be the only remaining ally I had. "Thank you, Fergus, but you can be most helpful in making sure my interrogation stays private."

He nodded once before watching me go, his brows a dark furrow of concern. My heart twisted to see his expression. Fergus had always been a friend to me. And now, because of my monstrous abilities, I'd lose him, too. With the bowl of stew still balanced precariously in my hand, I walked as fast as I could to the cave.

On the path, the wind threatened to tear the food from my hands, but I held on tenaciously. *He will likely complain the stew has gone cold*, I thought, squishing the bread in my clenched fist.

Silence greeted me when I entered the cave, and it took a moment for my eyes to adjust to the darkness. When they did, the bowl of stew shattered at my feet. The Northman was gone, the chains torn from their rings on the wall.

I flew back down the trail as fast as I dared, cursing the Northman as I went. Obviously he'd escaped the moment Fergus had left his post. I nearly stumbled once; the goat trail was treacherous, but not nearly as dangerous in the light of day. I'd seen for myself in battle how agile the Northman was—and clearly much stronger than I'd anticipated. No doubt he'd had enough time to put distance between us. Sleipnir was my only chance of catching him now.

But as soon as I reached the bottom, I slid to a stop. Chasing after the Northman alone was madness, but what did I have left to lose?

Exiled, I told myself again, just to test the amount of pain the word would cause me—much like someone might test a wound. It nearly doubled me over. Physical pain, I could take, but the torturous thought of having to leave my home . . . my family . . .

My mind filled with the previous night's vision: Éirinn reduced to ashes, my sisters broken and lifeless, and I knew exile meant nothing to me if they could be saved. I would follow him to the depths of hell if it meant preventing that from becoming reality.

I was on my own.

"Milady!" Fergus called as I raced past. I didn't stop, only continued to the stables. I couldn't risk telling Fergus where I was going—if my father discovered Fergus let an exile get away, no matter if that exile was me, he would most certainly be punished. Better if he never knew at all.

My feet pounded against the hard-packed dirt of the stables, and Sleipnir flung his head up. His nostrils flared, and he snorted, as though sensing my anxiety. I stopped only to grab my sword and a bridle. The heavy wooden bar to Sleipnir's stall clattered to the ground as I released him. He emerged and eagerly accepted the bit. Grasping a lock of long mane, I hauled myself astride, and the massive horse sprang forward.

Before we could make our escape, red hair at the entrance to the stables made my heart seize in my chest. But as the figure stepped into the light, I saw that it was Séamus instead of Fergus. His gaze fell on me, and on Sleipnir dancing in place, my hand on his neck the only thing restraining Sleipnir from galloping over him.

Séamus's expression was as cold as ever, but I could still hear the sound of his laugh, unbridled and impossible to resist.

I opened my mouth—I wanted to say *something*—but before I could, he turned and left. For a heartbeat, I thought I'd call out to him, but there was nothing I could say. I had seen the depths of his mind, and I knew his true feelings toward me.

You don't deserve to live, he had shouted at me over and over as I laid waste to his mental defenses. *May the next battle be your last.*

I flinched from the ghost of his words, turning my mind to what I'd do when I found the Northman. At least the Northman was unarmed; I could easily confront him once I found him.

I looked back at the castle . . . at my sisters' windows. They weren't even here to tell me good-bye. What would they say when they discovered I'd been exiled? When they'd learned what I'd done?

"Forgive me," I whispered, and touched my heels to Sleipnir's sides once again.

Sleipnir galloped over the stockade bridge amid frightened shouts, but still I did not slow. We wound down the hillside, and at the crossroads, I sat back on my tailbone and brought Sleipnir to a sliding halt. Which way would he have gone?

South, toward Dubhlinn, I thought, and turned Sleipnir in that direction.

His heavy hooves sent rocks flying in our wake, and the sea crashed against the shore to our left, seemingly urging us on. A *caw-caw-caw* cried out from above, and I glanced up to see a crow soaring above us. A prickly feeling of unease descended upon me, but with it a feeling of tentative hope that I was choosing the right course. The bird's black wings beat the air, speeding ahead of us.

"Fly, Sleipnir," I said, and the stallion surged ahead.

My heart hammered in perfect rhythm with the pounding of Sleipnir's hooves. I stretched low against his body, and his coarse mane billowed back in my face. We covered much ground, the scenery a blur on either side. We would catch the Northman; we had to.

The crow's call split the air again, and up ahead, I saw my quarry. He was sprinting at a fast clip on the relatively flat terrain where the rocky ground gave way to green grass. He was faster than any man I'd seen, and my mind whispered with the impossibility of it all—he had been weakened in the cave, injured, and had spent the night in a position guaranteed to stiffen his muscles. Yet he raced ahead as if the wind itself gave him speed.

Still, he was no match for Sleipnir.

I urged Sleipnir on until we galloped parallel to the Northman. Another couple of strides and Sleipnir pulled far ahead. I threw my weight entirely on my tailbone, digging my heel into the stallion's left side. He skidded to a stop and reared, his flinty hooves a hairsbreadth from the Northman's face.

With a hoarse shout, the Northman threw himself to the ground and rolled, just missing Sleipnir's powerful hooves.

Our eyes met and held. In one fluid motion, the Northman

vaulted upright. Before I could urge Sleipnir to move, the Northman had launched himself at me.

He pulled me from my horse, and I fell to the ground. Sleipnir trumpeted a warning, his ears flat against his skull, but the Northman kept me pinned against the rock with his heavy body.

"Did others follow?" he demanded, his accent almost too thick to understand.

My sword dug into my spine as I struggled against him, but it was like grappling against a mountain. He pushed me down until I could scarce draw breath, but still he didn't try to kill me.

"Were you followed?" he asked again.

I didn't want to tell him—the risk was far too great—and yet, without my ability to control his mind, he had the advantage. "I cannot be sure," I said in a growl. "I think not." He needn't know the truth: no one would come for me, not once they all learned what I had done to my father. Once they learned I was exiled.

The pressure on my arms lessened. "You came alone?" he asked incredulously.

"As you see."

He rolled off me with a chuckle. "That was foolish. Just what did you plan to do when you caught up with me? Besides having that useless mare knock me on my arse."

I pushed myself up until I was standing once again, my jaw clenched in anger. In stiff movements, I removed the satchel of the bread and cheese I had tied to my belt. I threw it at his feet.

"I brought you the meal you asked for. Payment for what you promised me."

He scooped it up and examined the contents. "What use is this? This stingy bit of bread and cheese?"

"There was a lovely fish stew to accompany it," I said in saccharine tones, "only you were not there when I carried it all the way to the top of the cave."

The sudden call of a crow distracted us both, drawing our attention to the sky. The Northman frowned. "The *kráka* again." His gaze shifted to me, his expression turning pensive. "Well, do you still wish to know what it said?"

Warily, I nodded.

"It said it would lead me to a warrior who would help me on my quest. But it lied. It led me to a *meyja* instead." My brow furrowed. "A little girl," he supplied.

White-hot fury shot through me, and I drew my sword. His eyes widened, but he held his ground. He was unarmed, with nothing but a satchel of bread and cheese to defend himself with.

"This *kráka* you speak of is more than just a crow. It is the Morrigan, the Phantom Queen, the goddess of war and death." Adrenaline fueled by my anger raced through my blood, pouring strength into my muscles, until my grip on my sword turned my knuckles white. "She revealed a vision to me, one where murderous Northman giants destroy Éirinn. Tell me what you know of this, or I swear I will end you."

For a moment, it appeared he wouldn't answer me. His eyes

flashed a warning, his jaw tightened, but then he said, "You insult me gravely to call such filth by the name of Northman. If you were truly given a vision, then you would know they are not men."

Cold fingers touched the back of my neck. No, they were not men. "It's true, then? There are such . . . monstrosities? Men like giants?"

"There have always been tales of giants among my people— the jötnar of Jötunheimr. Man-eaters, gluttons who are bigger than mountains. We always believed they were confined to their realm. We were wrong."

"Jötnar?" I repeated, the unfamiliar word sticking to my tongue. "This is the name of the creatures that will descend upon Éirinn?"

He shook his head as though frustrated with my lack of understanding. "You needn't concern yourself, maiden. Run along home and leave such a quest to men with skill."

Fury flushed across my cheeks. Skill? Wasn't I the warrior the Morrigan had led the Northman to? And yet he insulted me. "Are you forgetting that I am the one holding the sword?"

He took a step forward, until the point of the sword was inches from his throat. "If you think a little girl with a sword will keep me from my quest, then you have made a grave error."

There was something about the look in his eyes, like a cornered lion, that gave me pause. "Your quest . . . do you mean you have been searching for the giants? Is that what brought you to our land?"

"Yes."

I took a step back so my sword was no longer at his throat. "Why you? What can you do to stop them?"

He met my gaze. "There is no one stronger. I paid the ultimate price to ensure this was true."

"You'd go to such lengths to protect this land?"

"I care nothing for your land." A muscle in his jaw flexed. "I came for revenge."

Vengeance. This was something I could understand.

Above us, the crow circled. "Well, the crow was right. I want to stop them, same as you."

His look was wary and calculating both—before it turned into a defensive sneer. "And what can you do about it? I've fought many Celts and heard much talk of their infighting among clans. Your band of Celts would not stir themselves to join our fight—not until it is much too late."

I thought of the way my father had dismissed the Morrigan's vision. If he didn't believe me, no one would.

I couldn't go home, and even if I could, I knew my clansmen would never join with me on a quest like this. The Northman was right.

My hand shook on my sword as the weight of that realization sank in. I couldn't go home. I couldn't see my sisters again.

The only way I could redeem myself was to save them.

I swallowed my pride, my disgust, at joining such a hated enemy. "My clansmen may not join you, but I will."

His gaze traveled the length of me, as though taking my

measure. "A brave offer, to be sure, but you could not even keep a single man captive, much less battle enemies who can level entire villages."

Frustration and anger at his insult—no matter how true it was—erupted within me. I brought my sword up in a sweeping arc, nicking his throat in the same place as I had on the battlefield. To his credit, he did not flinch, only brought his fingers to the small trail of blood.

"I was also the one who brought you to your knees, Northman."

His scowl melted away, and he threw back his head in a laugh. On edge still, the bark of laughter nearly caused me to attack him again. "You may have imprisoned me, warrior maiden, but I can't help but like you."

"My name is Ciara of Mide," I corrected, my tone waspish.

"Ciara, then," he said, mirth still visible in his eyes. "I am Leif Olafsson. You would prove an interesting distraction, it is true. But what use can you be against giants?"

I could see he was wavering. I would have to explain to him—and pray he believed me. "I can take possession of someone's mind and force them to do whatever I command."

His eyebrows rose. "Impressive. Though, if you have such an ability, why haven't you used it on me?"

"How do you know I haven't?"

He grinned. "Because you wouldn't have had to waste time begging me for answers."

I shifted briefly from foot to foot. "You are the first person

I haven't been able to take control of," I admitted grudgingly.

"I would call you a liar or mad, but I have to admit I saw what you did on the battlefield. I didn't understand it at the time—I only knew someone had cast some dark spell on one of my men to make him turn on his own. You did that. You made my men turn on each other."

"It's not a spell," I said, though to me, the truth was much worse.

"It doesn't matter how you do it—only that you can—and there's no doubt it would be useful." He nodded as though he had finally found me acceptable, and I felt sweat bead on my forehead with the effort to not bash him over the head again.

"More useful than brute strength," I said heatedly.

"You sound jealous," he said, and then laughed as my grip tightened on my sword. "I can see you want to attempt to use that on me again, so I will relent." He glanced at the crow still flying above us. "You wanted answers from me—what is it you wish to know?"

"What is your plan? How do you intend to stop the giants?"

"My men wait for me in Dyflin, and so I must reunite with them and speak with the king." I crossed my arms over my chest at the mention of the Northman word for the city of Dubhlinn. They had changed the name when they had conquered the city, and it still rankled me to hear it called thus. Worse still was the fact that he was referring to King Sigtrygg, my kingdom's enemy.

"Sigtrygg won't help you. He doesn't care about anything

but raids and amassing riches. I'd be more inclined to agree with you if you said your plan was to attack him and take over Dubhlinn."

Leif grinned. "And you called my people bloodthirsty. Sigtrygg will help us because he is bound to; my father lent him ships and men for his raids, long before he was king. Now he owes us the same—ships and men. I need his help if I am to defeat Fenris, the leader of the jötnar."

"I still don't understand why it has to be Sigtrygg of all people, but I will admit that having ships and men could be useful. Will you tell me about Fenris? How do you plan to defeat him?"

"Fenris was the leader in the jötnar's own realm. Fenris entered into our realm and now that he is here, he has gathered more of my people to his cause, naming himself Jarl of Skien—one of our most important ports. The jötnar Fenris brought with him from Jötunheimr have set up camp in Skien, along with many men. But man or jötunn, I will fight them. I must gather as many warriors as I can and return to kill Fenris and whoever tries to get in my way."

A direct attack and a show of force of the magnitude Leif was suggesting would certainly intimidate any mortal Northman raiders—it was simply not their preferred method of war. Did that hold true for monsters? "When will you set sail?"

"As soon as I am able. Though from what I heard, it might not be that easy." When I stared at him blankly, he said, "I have heard talk of men like giants here in Éirinn."

A cold wave of fear hit me. "You mean the . . . jötnar are here already?"

His eyes met mine, his grim expression answer enough.

I shook my head. "They cannot be allowed to wreak their destruction here."

"You will join me, then? Leave the comfortable trappings of your castle, your family, your clan, and follow your enemy?"

He didn't know that I'd already left all that behind—that I couldn't return if I wanted to. I couldn't even bear to utter the truth aloud. The crow had perched on a boulder, watching us, eyes bloodred in the light. My mind was quiet, both of the Morrigan's voice and of visions.

By now Áthair would have already announced my exile. How much worse would my punishment be when he discovered the Northman was alive? But knowing what I did about the jötnar, how could I possibly stand aside when I had the power to stop them? I would join forces with a murderous raider, a man who had killed many of my own people. Would stopping the greater evil of the giants negate the sin of aiding my enemy?

I didn't know how successful Leif had been in his quest so far, but I did know he was right about one thing: my clan would never lend their aid until it was too late. It was I who had been given this vision, and it was I who must make a stand.

I returned my sword to its sheath. With my right hand in a fist, I placed it over my heart. "I will join you in destroying the jötnar here in this land."

"I cannot say you have made the right decision, but I won't turn away from your offer." He strode toward Sleipnir. "Now come. All this talk has wasted too much time."

He grabbed hold of my warhorse as though it was his and hauled himself astride. It took Sleipnir only an instant to realize it wasn't me on his back. His ears flattened, and he bucked and twisted, his powerful muscles taut as a bow.

Leif's jaw was tense with concentration, but he managed to stay astride. Grudgingly impressed, I let it go on for another moment or two before finally saying, "Sleipnir."

My horse's ears remained flat, but he stopped trying to unseat the Northman.

"You should know better than to mount another's warhorse," I said with a smirk. "Or perhaps he took offense to being called a mare."

"He's stronger than he looks," Leif answered with a grin that suddenly made him appear much younger.

When he continued to smile at me, I shifted uncomfortably and said, "You'll have to make room for me."

Leif slid back along Sleipnir's spine a few inches—carefully. After giving Sleipnir a pat on the neck, I grabbed a handful of mane and pulled myself astride. It was an awkward affair, since I didn't have the room to swing my leg over with Leif in the way. But I managed it without the Northman's assistance, which was all I really cared about.

I went rigid as stone when Leif moved closer to me, and I was painfully aware my backside was now flush against his front. "Is it all right to take the reins?" Leif asked. "Or will he unseat us both this time?"

"Take them," I said through gritted teeth. I was positioned too close to Sleipnir's neck for me to hold them comfortably.

A low rumble of a chuckle vibrated through my back. "You cannot remain so stiff. Relax, or this will be a painful ride all the way to Dyflin."

He pressed his heels to Sleipnir's sides, and the stallion surged forward, throwing me against the Northman's chest.

"How can I relax when you are pressed so intimately against me?" I said, my tone sharp with embarrassment.

"There is a broadsword between us." Amusement was clear in his voice. "If you would like, you could hand it to me for safekeeping. Then we will both be more comfortable."

I snorted. "I will not part with it. You'll have to find your own weapon."

"I am weapon enough."

He guided Sleipnir away from the coast and into the green hills beyond. Fog rolled in from the sea and blanketed the land, until it became difficult to see much farther than a horse length in front of us. Still, he kept Sleipnir at a grueling pace.

"You needn't run him until he is blown," I snapped eventually. The lack of control was torturous.

"We've lost enough time already."

The fog thickened, lowering the temperature until I shivered. The sun had been shining not long ago, and even in this land with its capricious weather, it was almost unnatural to have such thick fog. I wanted to turn and look back at the kingdom I was rapidly leaving, but I resisted the urge. I would only get an eyeful of Northman chest for my effort anyway.

Besides, I had made my decision.

There would be no going back now.

Leif was silent, save for his quiet breathing, as Sleipnir cantered over hills of green. After a time, I allowed my body to relax, though I still kept as far from the Northman as I could. I was pressed uncomfortably against Sleipnir's withers, each stride bruising my inner thighs.

The sound of fresh water, a creek cutting through the hills, drew our attention. Leif slowed Sleipnir to a trot and guided him toward it.

The silvery-blue water gurgled over the rocks, invitingly fresh. I scanned the shores for any signs of river spirits guarding the river. Leif dismounted and strode toward the water brazenly, without a hint of caution. I shook my head in disgust.

He knelt down and washed both arms in the water before drinking his fill. When nothing attacked him, I dismounted and walked over to the water, alert for any signs of mischief.

Sleipnir's ears turned this way and that, but even he dipped his head to the water for a drink. I cupped my hands and scooped handfuls of the water, enjoying the coolness on my tongue. I drank until I could drink no more. When I stood again, I found Leif watching me.

He strode toward me and I backed away, sinking into a

defensive pose. A smile touched his lips. "Why would I choose now to harm you?" he asked. "I only wish to help you back onto your horse."

I didn't know what he intended, but I knew I didn't trust him. "I can manage it well enough myself."

I watched him until he shrugged and moved away. I had turned toward Sleipnir to mount when I felt the broadsword being pulled free from its sheath on my back. With an angry hiss, I whirled on Leif. In one smooth motion, I drew the dagger beneath my cloak.

He held up his hand and *my* sword in a gesture of peace. "You were bruising yourself against the horse's bones to keep from touching me. This sword kept me from moving closer so that we might both be comfortable. It's best that I carry it."

His casual disregard for my judgment filled me with such anger that my hands shook. "Is this how you would treat your men? Divesting them of their weapons, ordering them about like dogs?"

He smiled. "But you are not a man."

I glared. "I am the warrior who agreed to aid you in your quest. The one whose abilities you need, and yet you treat me like . . ." I struggled to remember the insult he had used earlier. "A *meyja*."

"If this is your only means of defense"—he gestured toward my sword at his back—"then you aren't the warrior I believed you to be."

I stared at the hilt, just visible over his shoulder. I'd honed my skills with a sword, but my true means of defense was my ability to control the mind of another. I gritted my teeth at the realization that he'd pinpointed the truth: though I had an otherworldly ability, I was still limited by my fighting ability. I had taken advantage of the terrain when I fought Leif, but there was no doubt he was more skilled.

I raised my chin until I was staring into his glacier-blue eyes. "Ask, then," I said. "Ask if you may carry my sword for me."

"I do not ask," he said. "I take."

"You take from your enemies; you ask of your allies. I am your ally. Treat me as such, or it'll be you who will walk all the way to Dubhlinn."

"Dyflin," he corrected, and my eyes narrowed to slits.

He drew himself up to his full height, which made him tower over me, but I caught a hint of respect in his eyes. "Please allow me to carry your sword for you, milady," he said, in a voice as gruff as stone.

I smiled and dipped my head. "As you wish."

After returning my dagger to its hiding place, I pulled myself astride Sleipnir. Leif settled in behind me, and without the solid presence of the sword between us, I could feel his every breath against my back.

While Sleipnir walked on, Leif drew in his breath as though he would say something, but then let it out again. Finally, he said, "I could help you hone your skills with a blade—if you'd be willing."

It occurred to me that I should feel insulted by his insinuation, but it was his hesitancy to suggest it that kept my indignation at bay. "You found my swordplay so terrible, then?" I asked with a self-deprecating laugh.

"Not terrible by any means, but I can tell it isn't your weapon of choice." I could hear the grin in his voice when he added, "Though of course I had no idea your mind was your weapon."

I thought of our brief clash of swords. "You were holding yourself back when you fought me," I said, almost to myself. It only confirmed what I had suspected during the battle.

He grunted in answer.

"Why?"

He was silent for so long I finally risked a glance at him. "You spared my brother's life. I saw that you were young and beautiful, and I couldn't bring myself to end your life." His eyes burned into mine, and I couldn't look away. I felt the spread of a flush born of surprise and something else . . . something that stirred within and filled me with warmth. "And then you bashed me over the head with a stone."

His rumbling laughter vibrated through me as I broke his gaze and urged Sleipnir into a smooth canter.

I willed myself to stop blushing like a maiden.

7

The sun had dipped low on the horizon by the time Leif slowed Sleipnir to a walk. Though it disturbed me to admit it, there were many times when I'd been lulled by Sleipnir's smooth gait, and had relaxed against Leif's chest . . . only to awake each time with a start, forcing my spine as straight as a sword. Leif never commented on it, despite the obvious chance to mock me.

With his endurance at its limit, Sleipnir's chest was heavily lathered with sweat. I leaned forward and patted his neck, whispering to him that we would soon stop. As though God-sent, a river snaked through the rock, beckoning us with its cool waters.

"We will make camp here, near the river," Leif said.

I gazed out over the vast landscape, interspersed with boulders and thick copses of trees. Anything could be hiding just out of our sight, and the water was a prime location for dangerous creatures. Stopping briefly to refresh ourselves was one thing; making camp was another. We'd been lucky before. We might not be lucky again.

"We risk the notice of things better left alone if we sleep near the river," I said, still warily scanning the area. "We should sleep with the rocks to our backs, so we'll know what is lurking nearby."

Leif scoffed and dismounted. He held out his arms to me to help me down, but I ignored him and dismounted on my own. Free of his burdens at last, Sleipnir shook himself and walked down to the water's edge.

"Éirinn has many dangers," I said. "We'll live longer if we're cautious."

His light eyebrows rose. "You think the northern lands are free from creatures who wish us harm?"

"It doesn't matter. What matters are the creatures of *this* land."

I was on the verge of throwing up my hands and telling him he could make camp wherever he damn well pleased, but instead of continuing to argue, he strode away from the shore, back toward several boulders at the foot of a hill. He started on a fire, his broad hands making quick work of the difficult task. I joined Sleipnir at the water's edge to hide my satisfaction that he had listened to me for once.

The river water was once again cold and refreshing, and as I cleaned myself of the dust from our travels, it occurred to me that I would soon be required to bed down for the night. With a Northman.

Well, it wouldn't be the first time I'd slept with my hand wrapped around my dagger.

"I'll hunt us hare to eat tonight," Leif said, coming up behind me with surprisingly light footsteps. He unstrapped my sword from his back and handed it to me. "So you won't be unarmed," he said in response to my questioning look.

"How will you catch anything without a weapon?" Not that a broadsword was particularly helpful in catching a hare, but it was better than bare hands.

He grinned, a flash of teeth really. "I have other means."

Too tired to contemplate how he thought he would chase down and kill a hare with his bare hands, I nodded and made myself comfortable by the fire. We still had bread and cheese, so we wouldn't starve tonight. I watched him as he followed the river farther south, struck by how agile he was despite his large size, like a lion instead of a man.

Sleipnir grazed on the long green grass by the river's edge, and I relaxed against the cool stone. Alone with my thoughts, a sort of melancholy homesickness descended upon me. My mother and sisters were surely home by now, and a knife's twist of pain began in my stomach. My absence would undoubtedly worry them, and though my regret over such a thing was pal-pable, I had to remind myself I had no other choice. Had they spoken to Áthair? What would Máthair say when she learned what I'd done? I winced as I imagined her reaction—disgust? Fear? Worse was how my sisters might react. Would they tell them the truth? That I'd attacked our father and been exiled?

I forced such thoughts from my head. I knew I would do everything exactly the same if given another chance. My flesh still crawled with what the Morrigan had shown me. There could be no doubt it would come to pass, and if forming an alliance with my enemy was the only way to stop it, then I would make my bed beside him.

But my father . . . Áthair's anger and disappointment would be as terrible as dragon's fire when he discovered that I had joined forces with our enemy. Even if I was successful in driving giants out of Éirinn, I wasn't sure that would change the way my father saw me: as a monster instead of a daughter. In my mind, I saw my family side by side, their blond hair, light eyes, and heart-shaped faces seeming to say that the possibility I was a changeling was not so difficult to believe after all.

"I leave for only a few minutes," Leif said, returning with a brace of rabbits, "and you look as though you may cry. Did you think I had abandoned you?"

"If only," I said, my eyes narrowed at his smirk. Unperturbed by my acidic tone, he sat down across from me and pulled out a small blade to skin the rabbits. "Where did you get the knife?"

He continued skinning the rabbit, but he spared me a moment's glance. "I've had it all along," he said. "Your men didn't search me well enough. Useless as those chains." A flash of teeth. "You didn't really think they'd hold me, did you?"

I had, actually, but of course I'd never admit that. My hand tightened on the grip of my sword when I thought about how easily he had escaped. His profile was to me, his nose as straight as a blade, his entire face as though it was chiseled from the rock itself, though his lips were surprisingly full. He was beautiful, a dangerous beauty, and again I thought of my earlier comparison to a lion. "If the chains were so ineffective, then why didn't you leave sooner?"

He quickly and efficiently finished skinning one rabbit and moved on to the next. "I wanted to hear what you had to say. And," he added with a grin, "if you'll recall, I had recently suffered a blow to my head."

He could have left at any time. A flush of embarrassment sneaked up my neck. "I could have killed you instead," I snapped, "though I suppose you would have liked that better, since you Northmen are all so eager to die."

"Not just die," Leif corrected. "Die in *battle*."

I scoffed. "Either way, you'd be dead."

He slid the rabbits onto two sticks and held them over the fire. "Would you have me explain to you about our afterworld, then? About Valhalla's golden halls overflowing with ale and mead—where we can fight all day and feast all night."

"How is that any different from what you do on earth?"

Amusement touched the edges of his mouth. "Because in Valhalla, we will never tire or grow old."

I shifted my gaze from the fire to his face. "And just how old are you? You can't be much older than I am."

He turned the rabbits expertly over the flames. "Old enough to have earned the right to sail my own longship, to lead my own men." I shook my head over his cryptic answer, but then he added, "I have seen eighteen years."

As I'd thought, only a year older than I was. But as I had learned long ago: power aged you. "Will you tell me more of the enemy we face?"

"That depends. How much do you know of our gods?"

"Nothing." Though that wasn't entirely true. I knew a little; it was hard not to, when the Northmen had infiltrated so many of our cities, intermarrying with my own people, bringing their strange gods with them. I knew that Odin was the father of the gods, and the god of war. His most famous son was Thor, the thunder god. "You said the giants wanted to overthrow the gods. Why do they want to do that?"

"The gods and jötnar may be descended from the same being, but they've been in a struggle against each other over control of the realms since the beginning of time. The jötnar are gluttons of all: gold, women, power, flesh. More than anything, they desire control over mankind—to be worshipped as the gods have been. Because of this, the gods banished them to their own realm: Jötunheimr. The jötnar have forever tried to break free of their realm, but we've always trusted the gods to keep them in check. Until the most powerful of them, led by Fenris, escaped."

My father would have immediately dismissed everything

Leif had said as heretical pagan nonsense, and part of me wanted to do the same, but there was a powerful ring of truth in his words. They raised the hair on the back of my neck.

"Why would men join with such monsters?"

"Because the men are drawn to the same thing as the jötnar. Promises of riches and power. In exchange for men helping them conquer the lands of both the Celtic gods and the Norse, they will defeat the gods, who have already become weak since the Christian God has spread throughout our lands. Not having to answer to our gods is a tempting proposition for many who are tired of bloody sacrifices that have gone unanswered by the gods."

Weak. The Morrigan certainly hadn't seemed weak when she was holding me captive in my own tub. But then, she was also working through me . . . and possibly through Leif. Was it because she didn't have the power to stop the jötnar on her own? It made me think of what the Morrigan had said before—that the old gods of Éirinn had grown weak and unable to interfere in the mortal realm. It was hard to believe, but the Morrigan was also a war goddess. She would have destroyed the giants already had she the power to do so.

"Have you seen these giants?"

His gaze shifted to mine briefly. "I have seen evidence of them, and talk of them has spread throughout the north."

"Must be strong evidence for you to take on such a quest."

"As strong as a crow's vision," he said with a smirk.

I looked away—I didn't want to be reminded of that horrible

vision. "What I saw was terrible enough to make me join with you, it's true." I glanced back at him. "What evidence did you find?"

A muscle in his jaw flexed—perhaps at the memory of them. "Not long ago I encountered a Norse village that had been reduced to splinters. There were no bodies to burn; only pools of blood were left. Like a herd of swine had been slaughtered— in some places, the blood dripped from the roof. My men and I found footprints, ten times the size of a normal man's, covering the village. It was clear to us what had happened—that the jöt- nar had escaped Jötunheimr. When we consulted with the seer, the warnings of our gods were passed along to us: that Fenris planned to overthrow them and take over Midgard."

A vein in my forehead pounded along with my heart. I had seen the destruction the jötnar were capable of in the Morri- gan's vision, but it was still hard to accept. There were those in my own clan who whispered of the old gods, but my clan had long since converted to Christianity. To believe in them branded me a heretic, and yet I could not argue against the Morrigan's existence.

"Why kill all those people?"

"In truth, I believed they were killing mortals for the same reason we kill livestock: to eat. But the seer thinks otherwise."

He paused to hand me one of the rabbits, and I only picked at it though I was famished. "The seer believes it's not so simple as that?"

"She has said that the jötnar have grown tired of their exiled existence," Leif said, tearing into his own rabbit with no shortage of appetite.

I looked at Leif. "The seer is a woman?"

"Most with such power are women. Are you surprised?" he added with a raised eyebrow. "The jötnar want us to believe they want to overthrow the gods and free mankind, but the seer believes the opposite is true. They want control of Asgard and the mortal realm of Midgard—to rule the world with all humans as their subjects. Odin's own mother is jötnar; they believe they have a claim."

Horror dwelled in the pit of my stomach. "And they plan to do this by slaughtering us?"

"Fear is a powerful motivator. They've spared the ones who have joined forces with them—they will need someone alive to worship them, after all."

In my mind, I saw Éirinn turn to ashes.

I felt colder than I ever had, as if I stood in the midst of a furious blizzard. Goose bumps erupted over my skin, and I could see this world he spoke of. Ruled by men who unleashed evil on us all.

We fell into a mutually disturbed silence.

"We shouldn't keep watch tonight," Leif said after some time, his voice as low as the crackling fire. "It is better if we both sleep. We'll need our strength tomorrow."

I shook out my cloak and covered myself with it, neck to toe, until only my head was visible. I curled up on my side, my back to the Northman. If I wasn't too tired to care, I would undoubtedly lie awake all night, self-conscious about my close proximity to a man not of my own blood. And an enemy besides.

"You are so sure my clansmen won't follow?" I asked.

"I never sleep deeply. You have nothing to fear."

Why would I fear my own clansmen? I thought, but soon, sleep was upon me, washing me into a sea of darkness.

I awoke slowly, with the sensation I was being watched. It was still dark, the moon covered by clouds and the sky an endless black. The fire had died down to a small flame, and I was chilled with only my cloak to cover me. My eyes adjusted to the darker edges surrounding the dying fire, until I could make out shapes: plants near the shore, larger river rocks, and the river itself.

Movement near the water's edge captured my attention, and I stiffened. It was a horse, as deep black in color as the night sky, its eyes reflecting the low light back to me with an eerie yellow glow.

"God save us," I whispered, and crossed myself.

"It's been watching us for some time now," Leif whispered. He lay motionless, but I could see the tautness of his muscles, as though he was ready to spring to his feet.

Sleipnir pawed the ground to my left, ears pricked toward the each-uisce near the river.

"Do not stare too long into its eyes," I warned. A chill of unease spread over me. I shifted into a crouched position as stealthily as possible.

"Does it guard the river?" Leif asked. "What brought it here?"

I shook my head as I thought of the story I had told my sisters. "I don't know. It isn't unheard of to see an each-uisce, but it's rare. It'll try to drown us to feast on our flesh. We mustn't touch any part of it, or we'll be ensnared upon its hide." I glanced at Leif.

He nodded once. "How do we defeat it?"

"We can't. We must wait for the dawn. If we try to escape now, it will only give chase."

He snorted. "Everything can be killed. What is its weakness?"

The each-uisce took a few steps toward us, but its gaze seemed focused on our fire. It tossed its head as though frustrated. Droplets of water flew from its dripping-wet mane. It paced, more as a wild cat or wolf would do than a horse, seeking our weak point. But we had solid rock to our backs, an outcropping from a steep hillside behind us, and a fire, though dying, before us. After a moment, it released a bloodcurdling neigh, high-pitched as a scream, its frustration evident.

Then it seemed to undulate before us, its skin shivering in the night. It transformed from a slick water horse into a man of such dark beauty, even I felt his siren call. His hair was long and black, his body leanly muscular.

"Come, my beauty," he said. "I have been waiting for you."

A fog seemed to descend upon my mind, and I was caught in that twilight between dreams and reality.

I came to my feet, and the beautiful man held out his hand, beckoning.

The rational part of my mind commanded my legs not to

move, but they did not listen. I had always considered my mind to be powerful, but as I strained and fought against the each-uisce, I quickly realized my defenses were as weak as a child's.

I took a step forward.

Beside me, Leif surged to his feet and pulled me to his side. "What has come over you? You see a pretty man and suddenly you abandon all sense?"

Help me, I thought. *I have lost control of myself.*

"What is your name, maiden?" the each-uisce asked.

"Do not answer him," Leif said in a growl even as my lips parted and spoke my name.

"Ciara," the each-uisce repeated, his voice more beautiful than a symphony of angels.

With my true name spoken from the demon's mouth, my mind seemed to shatter.

Who am I? I thought dreamily.

The man before me was so beautiful, and he watched me with such a captivating look in his eyes. I glanced down at the hand restraining me, and I snarled in frustration.

Who is this boy who restrains me? I must go to the other—the one who is so beautiful—he needs me.

The boy tightened his hold on my arm, and I struggled wildly against him, like a feral cat caught in a net.

"Be still!" the boy shouted, but I only struggled all the harder.

The beautiful man beckoned me again, and the hateful one shoved me behind him, his big body blocking my view. He backed us into the rock until the stone was pressed against my spine, trapping me.

"Ciara, my dark-haired beauty," the beautiful man said, and I struggled ever harder, the stone painful against my back. I pushed against the hateful one with everything I had, but still, he would not move.

The beautiful man reached out to me, and all at once, the fog in my mind deepened. Everything else disappeared—the rock at my back, the hateful one, the horse as black as pitch. All but the beautiful man and the river before me.

Why do you hide behind your enemy, Ciara? His hypnotic voice reverberated through my mind. *He is a plague, just like the giants from his land who will soon turn our world to ash, yet you follow him willingly. You have betrayed your family.*

Disgust sat in my stomach, dark and oily. I thought of the many Northmen I had battled; men who had killed my clansmen and sister. Men who had pillaged and burned monasteries. And I had turned away from my clan and joined them.

In my mind, my sisters appeared before me, pale and shaken. *Why did you leave us, Ciara?* Bran asked. Tears tracked down Deirdre's face. Behind them, my mother appeared. *I always knew you would betray us in the end*, she said.

Deirdre reached out her hand, and I tried to take it.

"No!" a deep voice shouted, penetrating the fog.

For a moment, I could almost think clearly, and then the beautiful man spoke again. *The Northman lies, Ciara. He has led you astray. He is in league with the giants. You must destroy him and escape. Only I can help you now.*

A black anger boiled up from within me, filling my body with an inhuman strength. I exploded past Leif and grabbed my sword.

Before me, Leif's face seemed to flicker and change, his features becoming more dragon-like. Distantly, I wondered if my mind had finally broken.

Kill him, the melodic voice said. *See how he is revealing his true form? The Northmen are nothing more than dragons who pillage and burn.*

I raised my sword. My arm shook as I fought against the force holding my mind captive. There was a reason I shouldn't attack this particular Northman . . . what was it?

The Northman would like nothing more than to murder your sisters, the voice said, more insistent this time.

A wave of burning anger crashed down upon me, but still I fought it. There was something about those words . . . something that rang false. It wasn't the Northman who would kill my sisters. . . .

My sisters . . . their faces flickered into my mind. Branna, her jaw set and determined. Deirdre, her eyes soft and sweet. Alana . . .

The power that gripped my mind tried to strengthen its hold, and in that moment, I regained enough control of myself to know one thing:

I had to fight back.

Intense pain shot through my head as though a sword had

smashed my skull, but still I pushed against the outside mind. It was the opposite of what I did to control another's mind: I thrust the each-uisce's power away instead of reaching toward it. He held on tenaciously, like a wild cat scrabbling for purchase on its prey, but I proved stronger. With one more powerful push with my mind, the each-uisce stumbled back and fell, as though I had physically pushed him.

The fogginess that had permeated my mind dissipated as though a strong wind had blown it away. The each-uisce tried to stand again. Before he could, Leif brought my sword down in a sweeping arc. It cleaved the each-uisce from shoulder to hip, dividing his body. Both sides crumpled to the ground, dark blood pouring out in the weak dawn light.

I met Leif's gaze, and we both panted for breath. Gone was any indication that he was anything less than human. The each-uisce had preyed upon my deepest fears—even the nightmares that Northmen were dragons wearing human skin.

Leif shook his head. "I thought I had lost you."

Breathing hard, I stared at the dead each-uisce at our feet. One less demon to threaten the children of Éirinn. How shameful that I fell victim to its spell, when even the child in the story I told my sisters had not. I couldn't help but shudder, though, as I realized that everything I'd felt in the grip of the each-uisce's mind control must be exactly what my victims experienced. Victims who included many of my clansmen.

"Thank you for helping me," I said to Leif.

"You saved yourself." He handed my sword back to me.

With the sun rising behind us, he rubbed the back of his neck before saying abruptly, "I will hunt us something to break our fast, and then we should continue to Dyflin."

He strode away without waiting for my response, and I let the sword slip from my hand. I was glad for Leif's absence, for I was shaking violently. Being trapped in the each-uisce's mind control had made me realize just how terrifying my abilities were.

The each-uisce was malevolent and powerful, but still, I understood it.

Worse still was the realization that while the battle with the each-uisce had been a struggle, it was nothing compared to what we would face with the jötnar.

With an afternoon sun intermittently hidden by clouds, we rode through a field of wheat, headed south toward Dubh-linn. The wind made the field seem like a golden sea as it blew the grasses like waves. I held out my hand as we passed, allow-ing the grain to brush against my palm. The wind was strong today; it tugged at my hair like a child before throwing it back in my face. Sleipnir's mane, too, billowed back onto my arms.

The farther we traveled through Mide, and the farther we traveled from my home, the more depressed my mood became. My father would have made the proclamation of my exile offi-cial by now. He would have forbidden anyone from seeking me out, though only Fergus would think of doing so. It wouldn't be the first time Áthair had forbidden others from following me, only this time, he didn't need to.

I had been younger than Branna then, and it was my second battle. My power was so new to me that I was barely able to understand it, much less able to successfully control it. When my father received word that Northmen were raiding along our northern coast, he took a small contingent of twenty men, including me, to stop them. When we finally reached the village, we were greeted by the dying screams of the people there. Most of them had gathered in the church for safety, but the Northmen had set it on fire to burn them out. They wanted the treasures contained within: the golden tabernacle, the chalice of silver and gemstones, pieces of silver and gold to honor God.

Two women were dragged out in chains, and seeing them plead with two merciless Northmen, their faces twisted with terror, unleashed something within me. Remnants of my own painful grief over my sister's death and rage over what was happening to the women before me broke over me like a wave upon the shore. I reached out and took control of the Northman who held the women's chains. I forced him to turn his weapon on himself, slitting his own throat with the edge of his axe. As soon as his blood flowed, I released his mind, delighting in the sheer panic I saw on his face.

Slack-jawed, the other man had watched his comrade kill himself. I reached out and took control of him, too, but instead of having him immediately take his own life, I forced him to slaughter the majority of his unsuspecting friends. Each man reacted in the same way: complete shock and disbelief that one of their own should turn on them.

They were as easy to kill as lambs.

The villagers had reacted to me not as their savior, but rather as a monster to be feared. They ran screaming from me just as they had run from the Northmen. As I stood amid the destruction, the rage that had brought it about disappeared as quickly as it had come. But it was when I saw the fear in my own clansmen's eyes that I leaped astride Sleipnir and ran.

Tears had blinded me, and Sleipnir galloped without direction. Before long, I was hopelessly lost in my own kingdom. When night fell, we took shelter in a cave, and as I stayed close to my horse for warmth, I told myself my father would come for me.

When dawn broke over the cave, it was Fergus who found me.

"Did my father send you?" I had asked.

He shook his head, the pity filling his eyes. "No, milady."

It was then I had realized that not only would I have to wrest control of the power within me, I could no longer rely on anyone but myself.

In the distance, white sheep bleated, drawing my attention away from my melancholy thoughts. Smoke from a small, stone farmhouse drifted toward the sky. The wind carried the smell of it to me: wood burning and freshly baked bread. A path cut through the earth toward the little farmhouse, worn down by wagons and horses, but Leif kept Sleipnir firmly pointed south.

"How do you know the way to Dubhlinn?" I asked. I was

surprised he was guiding us so easily without well-worn paths or the coast for reference.

"My father has maps of this land, and he had me study them long before I ever sailed on my first longship."

My jaw tensed. "So you could find the prime areas for raids?"

"Yes," he said without contrition, "but also because it's dangerous to sail to a completely unknown land."

I couldn't fault the wisdom in that, and it rankled. "Is your father still alive?"

"He is."

I thought of the many battles I'd fought with my own father. Strange that Leif's father wasn't with him. "Does he sail his own longship, then? Laying siege to other innocent monasteries?"

"Not anymore," he said. The amusement in his voice made my teeth clench. "I sail his longships for him now." He was quiet for a moment before adding, "One day when he is tired of this world, he'll join us on raids until he falls in battle."

I could hear the despondency in his voice, but also pride. "Valhalla again?"

He let out a breath in a quiet laugh. "Yes, Valhalla."

I knew enough of the Northmen to know that it was impressive that Leif led the raids at only eighteen. We fell silent again, as Sleipnir continued steadily on.

But when next we stopped for water, Leif stopped me before I could climb astride. "I asked you once before, and I think now would be as good a time as any. Will you spar with me?"

I shrugged, even as I itched for the chance to prove myself capable with a blade. "How will we practice with only one sword?"

He pulled out his dagger. "I'll attack with this, and you'll deflect with your sword."

I glanced at his distinctly smaller weapon with no small amount of skepticism, but in the end, I found I didn't care if he sustained a few nicks. I took hold of my broadsword with both hands and readied myself.

He attacked, so fast his body was a blur. It was nothing like fighting him the first time, and I realized with a cold trickle of horror down my spine that my instincts had been correct that day: he had been holding back. Instinctively, I raised my sword to protect my face, using the sharp side to deflect his blows.

"No," Leif said, halting abruptly. "Never use the edge of your sword to displace an attack. It will dull and weaken the metal." He stepped forward and took hold of my hands. "Use the flat of the blade." He gently rotated my wrists until the flat of the sword pointed outward.

I nodded slowly, already surprised to learn I'd been deflecting incorrectly for years. "Again."

It was unfathomable—he was attacking me with a dagger, and yet all I could do was try to block him. I danced and wove, trying to ward off the blows. Very soon, my arms and legs began to fatigue.

Leif relented. "You are tired?"

I panted in answer, and he smiled. He was enjoying this.

"That's because you're using ridiculous wide, sweeping motions." He gestured for me to hand over the sword, and I did so with narrowed eyes. Ridiculous indeed. He demonstrated what he meant, swinging the sword in a wide arc in front of us. The taut muscles in his arms bulged. "Instead, make your motions small, deliberate." He made a small twist of his wrist, as though deflecting an attack. "You want to set aside your opponent's blow so his thrust is broken but yours connects."

"Or I could take control of him mentally and have him fall upon my sword," I said with a mean smile.

"You could. But how many can you control at once?"

I shifted uncomfortably. "One."

"Then you're still vulnerable. I'll try to shield you in battle as best I can, but—"

"Make no mistake, Northman," I interrupted, my hands clenched in fists at my sides, "I need no protection from you."

He raised his eyebrows in mock surprise, but wisely kept silent. I took the broadsword back from him, and we continued our practice until my arms refused to wield the heavy weapon. By the end, though, I was able to successfully apply all the techniques he taught me—not perfectly but with some proficiency. I'd always been a quick study in swordplay.

As we remounted, I swore myself to silence—in all our conversations, when had I forgotten that we might be temporary allies, but he was still an enemy?—but it was as though my mouth couldn't obey. "The skill you have for battle," I said, my eyes focused on Sleipnir's mane, "it goes beyond a natural affinity for it, doesn't it?"

I risked a glance at him and saw amusement touch the edges of his mouth. "Yes."

"And you won't tell me how you came to be such a superior fighter?"

"I'll tell you when you tell me how you can use your mind to control others."

"I can't tell you because I don't know." He was quiet, and it was his silence that prompted me to offer more. "My clansmen always whispered that I was a changeling, but no one ever elaborated because my father forbade them from talking about it."

I could feel his eyes on me. "Yours isn't a gift of the Fae. They would never give up a child with your abilities to mere mortals."

A strange sense of relief combined with a yawning chasm of despair overcame me. A changeling would mean that the true princess, the babe with fair hair and light eyes like the rest of my family, lived a life of uncertain future surrounded by the Fae. For so long, it had tortured me to think I had taken the place of the human child. Yet I still didn't know where my power came from.

"Then I have no explanation for my power. It's something I've lived with for many years, but I've never known its source."

"A gift of the gods, then," he said.

"There is only one God." I said it automatically, the words as familiar to me as my own name.

"Your Christian God would never gift you with the power to kill so many men."

"He has seen it fit to grace others before me; Father Briain has told us many tales of such men."

He fixed me with a penetrating look. "And the *kráka*?"

I averted my eyes. The Morrigan had once been worshipped as a god, and may have been still. It wasn't unusual for my people to cling to superstitions that clearly contradicted the dogma of our Christian faith, but I still couldn't say exactly how the Morrigan fit into the belief system I'd always known.

"How you came by your power matters little," Leif continued. "What matters is how you use it."

I inwardly shook my head. "Why do you sound as sage as an old crone? You're barely older than I am." But I knew he made an excellent point. My abilities allowed me to protect the sisters I had left, which was all I truly cared about.

Again, the wind pulled and snatched at my hair, and I shoved it behind me in irritation.

"Take the reins," Leif said, dropping them into my lap.

I nearly jumped out of my skin when I first felt his hands upon my hair. With gentle yet efficient movements, he combed my hair back from my face. His fingers were warm and strong as they brushed against my neck, and I could feel an answering warmth stir inside me. No one but my handmaiden had ever touched my hair, and having a man touch it seemed intensely intimate. A few moments of a tugging sensation, and then my hair was neatly plaited behind me.

"Thank you," I said quietly. I reached back and felt the smooth braid. How strange that this Northman warrior should know how to do something so domestic. "How did you learn to do this?"

He retrieved the reins from my lap. "I had a sister once. She had long, unruly hair, and after our mother died, I was often called upon to help her subdue it."

His words were matter-of-fact, but I heard the sorrowful undercurrent to his tone. I turned toward him, and our gazes caught and held. An old wound was visible in his eyes, and I felt something move inside me in answer. He had two siblings— one who had later died. The similarities between us couldn't be ignored. An uncomfortable sensation of self-reproach roiled inside me at my earlier thoughts that he was a barbarian, beneath my notice. He was someone who had, in many ways, suffered just as much as I had.

But even as I felt my thoughts soften toward him, I heard the screams of my clansmen, saw Alana's blood pour down her neck.

I cleared my throat softly. "How did she die?"

"She was murdered," he said. The pain and wrath in his voice was so apparent that I flinched.

I couldn't stop my reply, not when I knew exactly what he was feeling. "I, too, lost a sister."

The same emotions seemed to flit across Leif's face, and so when he asked the inevitable question, I almost didn't want to answer him for fear of breaking the fragile friendship we'd created.

"How?" he asked.

"She was murdered," I answered, stealing his words. I turned around to look at him again.

He searched my face for a moment and found the answer there in the set of my jaw, in the shifting of my gaze. Thankfully he didn't force me to say it: that it was his own people who had killed her.

Thunder rumbled directly overhead, and I glanced up sharply.

Distracted by our conversation, I hadn't noticed the state of the weather around us. The wind had blown in a massive dark cloud, which loomed ominously above us. Unpredictable and rapidly changing weather wasn't unusual for Éirinn, but it seemed to happen the most when shelter wasn't available.

A torrent of rain released itself upon us, penetrating our cloaks and garments almost instantly, so they lay wet and flush against us.

Leif urged Sleipnir into a gallop toward a thick forest of towering oak and ash trees. A cave would be more welcome, but at least the leaves would filter some of the rain. The cold water ran in rivers down my face, chilling me until my teeth chattered.

As we galloped to the shelter of the wood, the muddy ground revealed a set of tracks left by animals with paws as big as Sleipnir's hooves. Much bigger than wolves. The hair on the back of my neck stood up.

My heart pounded in my chest. *Turn back*, my instincts screamed at me.

I shouted at Leif to stop, that we must turn back, but he could not hear me over the roar of the storm.

We made it to the forest, the trees filtering some of the rain, at least to the point that I could hear again. From deep within the forest came a small sound. Leif brought Sleipnir to a halt, and I strained to hear. The baying of hounds, followed by the low tones of a hunting horn.

My eyes widened in terror. "Move. We must leave now." The words tumbled out in a panicked rush.

"What ghoulish Gaelic creature is after us now?" Leif asked. There was more amusement to his tone than the dire situation warranted.

"Those sounds are the Wild Hunt, and if we're discovered, if we're even scented, we'll be hunted down and slaughtered like sheep."

Every nerve, every instinct within me was on fire with the need to escape.

Leif snorted and tightened his hold on me, urging Sleipnir once again into a gallop. "You also said the each-uisce couldn't be killed," he shouted above Sleipnir's hoofbeats. "Who is hunting us?"

The hair-raising sound of the baying grew still closer, until even Sleipnir snorted with terror. The path between the trees grew narrower and narrower. Twigs and branches grabbed at our sodden clothes. The fear within me grew to such colossal proportions that it developed a taste. It tasted like blood.

"Another of the Tuatha Dé Danann, Flidais," I said grimly.

"She is a protector of wild animals and hunts humans for sport, but it's strange to encounter her during the day."

I remembered the tales of the Wild Hunt—mostly stories to frighten children from wandering the forests alone, but they had clung to the recesses of my mind. The victims were herded into another realm, one from which there was no escape. The forest of the hunt was never-ending, the trees themselves aiding the hunter in trapping the prey. The hounds varied, from wolves to dog-boar hybrids, but always they tore the prey into pieces so small there was nothing left for even carrion birds.

With riotous barking to announce their presence, the hellhounds burst from the trees. They were enormous, almost as big as Sleipnir. I risked a glance as we raced on, only to see nothing but hideous creatures with yellow eyes, their coats the color of rotten leaves. One launched itself at us, sharp teeth snapping. Leif wrenched the reins to the right and used Sleipnir's powerful shoulder to slam the hound into a wide oak. Sleipnir tossed his head, the whites of his eyes nearly all I could see.

Leif wheeled Sleipnir around to where we'd entered the forest, and one of the hounds almost caught its strong jaw around Sleipnir's leg, but Sleipnir flew over it as though he had wings.

His hooves thundered across the muddy terrain, sending torrents of water up in his wake, and still the hounds closed in. They howled and snapped at Sleipnir's haunches, staying on him even as he zigzagged to avoid them.

We burst free of the forest only to find ourselves herded toward another copse of trees. Only this time, as we galloped closer, I realized this wasn't an ordinary forest. The tops of the trees had bowed over and entwined with each other on either side of a wide path, until they formed a tunnel made up of gnarled branches and leaves.

A deafening silence fell upon us as soon as Sleipnir entered the tunnel, as though the rain had cleared in an instant. The sounds of the hounds disappeared, but I sensed that we were far from safety. When I looked behind us, the torrent still fell, everywhere but over the forest entrance. I shuddered.

Sleipnir flicked his ears back and began to back up, but he was soon met with resistance.

I leaned forward and rubbed his neck in an effort to soothe him, though I was as terrified as he. "There is no use going back now. We have entered the Faerie Tunnel, and we will only be able to leave if and when it suits them."

"If we cannot go back, then we must continue on," Leif said, nudging a reluctant Sleipnir forward.

The eerie silence of the forest, completely absent of chirping birds, small animals moving through the underbrush, or even insects buzzing, filled me with as much dread as the howling of wolves. The fall of Sleipnir's hooves seemed like the loud banging of drums in comparison, and I scanned the trees for any sign of life as we passed.

I couldn't help but fear we'd been herded directly into a trap.

As we raced deeper into the forest with no way of knowing our direction, or if we would ever find our way out, the fear in me grew until it was as though fear itself was another monster that raced alongside us. I gripped Sleipnir's mane with whitened hands, and my heart thundered along to the sound of his hooves. When I glanced back at Leif, it made me even more afraid to see his face pale. He wrapped one arm around me, and the muscles were so tight it felt like stone.

The trees blurred by, but as I concentrated, I caught flashes of faces in the trees. They seemed to be part of the tree trunks, as though the trees themselves were alive: a white ash with the face of an old crone, an enormous oak tree with a slim face like a nymph, a haggard tree with gnarled, twisting branches forming a frightening face. And lights, blue lights in the trees. They danced merrily, enticingly. Will-o'-the-wisps, I was sure, to lead us astray, or even back toward the hunt.

For indeed, the baying had grown closer again, and Sleipnir snorted in fear. That same fear reached into my chest and grabbed hold, leaving ice in its place.

Where before us there were trees, now suddenly a rock wall rose out of the forest, blocking our path. Leif pulled Sleipnir to a sliding halt and threw himself from his back. I followed, taking up the same wide-legged defensive stance as Leif. We both stood together, pale and already panting for breath. Leif managed to shove away his fear first; he unsheathed the broadsword, and I pulled my dagger from beneath my cloak as soon as I'd steadied my breath. Holding the sword before him with both hands, Leif took a step in front of me.

With a growl of frustration, I moved away from him. "If you're so concerned for my safety, then give me my sword, you fool," I snapped.

He spared me the briefest of glances. "I can kill these creatures much faster with it—and keep us both alive."

The hounds burst out of the cover of the trees, stalking closer to us with bristly hackles raised. Out of the corner of my eye, I saw Leif raise the broadsword. Just as the lead hounds gathered themselves to leap at our throats, the ones at the rear yipped and barked excitedly. Like well-trained soldiers, they parted down the middle and stood at attention, allowing their leader to pass through.

A white stag, its antlers as sharp as daggers, leveled its gaze at us. Despite its male appearance, it was a female voice that resonated from it—and from all around us. It echoed from the trees and reverberated into our minds.

"I'm afraid you've found yourselves as prey for the Wild Hunt." The voice was softly menacing, beautiful and terrible all at once. "My hounds have herded you like sheep into my realm, and there is no escape."

I sensed the minds of all the creatures before us—feral and desperate for the kill. Beyond those minds, though, was a mind of a being so staggeringly powerful, I couldn't hope to breach it. The stag's mind made Leif's mental wall seem like a thin sheet of parchment. It was a fortress, a mountain—untouchable. There was something about the sheer awesome power of it that reminded me of the Morrigan. I probed harder, and the moment my mind touched hers, the voice let out an angry hiss.

A howling wind came from nowhere, and the forest darkened. The stag narrowed its eyes at Leif. "You have the same look about you as those abominations—those giants from the north who stomp all over this land, killing as they go, while you mortals do nothing. All the ancient creatures of Éirinn have been stirred free of their places of rest—each-uisces from their rivers, sluaghs from their forests and shores, even the Faerie Tunnel you find yourself trapped in—responding to their tainted presence."

Her words turned my blood to ice. She had seen the jötnar? My surprise broke my silence. "The giants—have you fought them? Where did you see them?" Pray not Mide. Surely we hadn't been gone long enough.

The stag lowered its head, its sharp antlers pointed toward us threateningly. "You dare question me? As though I am merely a mortal peasant for you to command?" Her words triggered the hounds to growl again, until the woods were filled with the sound of snarling. "I may not be able to hunt the abominations from the north in the mortal realm, but you are in *my* realm now." The stag reared, and the hounds' eyes glittered as they stalked toward us.

My hand tightened on my dagger. Fear again settled upon me like a great bird of prey, but I pushed past it and centered myself. I couldn't take control of the owner of the voice, but I might be able to grab hold of one of the hounds. I grasped for the mind of the creature closest to me, and once I connected, I nearly pulled myself free immediately, as the hound was picturing in vivid detail what it would feel like to rend my flesh, and to drink my blood while it was freshly flowing. Despite the horror of its black thoughts, I held on. The hound stopped in its advance, shaking its head wildly as though it might throw me from its mind. I pushed harder, bending its will to my own.

It broke under the force of my onslaught, capitulating to my desire to have it fight for *me* instead of the voice of the stag. Before one of other hounds could make the first leap for my throat, my chosen champion turned on it, sinking its teeth into the unsuspecting neck of the hound beside it.

Though I'd been spared for now, a massive hound launched

itself at Leif, who immediately cut it down with the sword. Two more replaced the first, but I could no longer track Leif's battle. Another hound, eyes glittering with malice, attacked me from the side. Its jaw snapped mere inches from my throat. I slashed with my dagger while simultaneously summoning my hound with enough force to make it lunge for my attacker, sending it slamming into the rocks behind us.

Another hound replaced the first with a vicious snarl. Before I could even take a breath, it launched itself at me. I deflected it as best I could with my dagger—catching it in its neck. It struggled wildly, leaving long scratches from my ribs to my hip. I cried out in pain but still held on until it collapsed. Panting, I turned to the next threat. Two stalked toward me, their muscles bunching. The hound I controlled cut them off before they could attack, and then they were growling and snapping and tearing at one another, the sound as loud and terrible as war.

Leif moved closer to me with every kill, the pile of dead hounds in his wake growing exponentially. His every movement was a fatal blow—no wasted effort. He was fast and he was strong, slicing the sword through multiple hounds as though they were as insubstantial as blades of grass. His fighting ability went beyond merely skilled and entered into the realm of inhuman.

And then, the worst possible outcome. The hound I controlled fell, its mind plunging into darkness as though a candle had been blown out.

The hounds that had killed it came at me.

I sank into a defensive position, balancing my weight on the balls of my feet. One feinted left as the other sprang, its heavy paws hitting me square in the chest. I was knocked to my back, and my head slammed onto one of the rocks. Darkness followed, and I blinked rapidly as the hound's fetid breath felt hot upon my face. My vision returned, but the world spun around me.

I shook myself free of my daze and grabbed the hound's throat, pushing against it from my prostrate position. Yellow teeth snapped inches from me. Its claws struggled for purchase against my leather chest piece. I couldn't get my hand free to stab it with my dagger. Desperately, I reached for its mind.

Leif shouted my name through the heavy sounds of the hounds he was defeating. Still, I knew he wouldn't reach me in time—I pushed past my own terror and flagging strength and grabbed hold of the hound's mind. The hound's teeth snapped closer; the muscles in my arms screamed with the effort of keeping it from tearing into my throat.

I forced the creature to stop in its efforts to kill me just as a flurry of beating wings rang out over the quiet wood.

Six ravens, as big as eagles, flew low over the heads of the hounds. They landed on the branches above us, watching with dark, intelligent eyes. The hounds glanced back at the stag, as though suddenly unsure.

Taking advantage of the hounds' momentary distraction, Leif raced to my side and cleaved the menacing hound in two. Spraying me with blood, the two halves sank wetly to either side of me. Leif kicked the hound away from me and spat on the ground. He hauled me to my feet. Deep scratches covered his arms, but he appeared whole.

A crow's *caw* drew our attention to the sky, where it circled far above us. It tucked its wings and dived. Just before it crashed into the ground, it transformed—but only partially. It was the body of a woman clad all in black except for her head, which was still that of a crow with its inky-black feathers and sharp beak: the Morrigan

It turned its gaze toward me, its eyes red. Beside me, even Leif looked suddenly unsure, his grip on the sword so tight his knuckles were pale.

The stag lowered its antlers and pawed the earth, but when it raised its head again, its dark eyes were anxious.

The Morrigan shot forward, as fast as a viper, and sank each hand into the chest of a hound. With a sickeningly wet sound, she pulled out their hearts. It happened so fast the beasts fell over dead without a sound.

I trembled as the blood dripped down her arms, so red against her pale white skin. Holding the hearts before her, she tore into each organ with her crow's beak, spraying blood until I was sure I would be sick. The stag seemed frozen in place— whether from fear or shock, I didn't know.

"I will feast on all their hearts," the Morrigan said. The voice was harsh and distorted and struck such fear in me I could not move.

The stag let out a breathy, distressed sound. If the two beings were conversing, it was a conversation we weren't privy to. I risked a glance at Leif. His every muscle was tense, his face pale.

Suddenly, the stag turned toward Leif and lowered its antlers. Leif raised the broadsword.

My whole body stiffened. *Not him*, I thought, surprising myself at my own vehemence.

Forgotten and silent until now, the ravens shifted in their branches, talons scraping across the wood ominously. All at once, the temperature in the forest dropped. Our breaths made plumes before us.

The Morrigan glanced up at the ravens before leveling her gaze on the stag. The meaning was clear: whoever the ravens were, they were on our side.

The hounds retreated to the stag's side. The ghostly white animal bowed its head just once before bounding away, hideous hounds following.

The Morrigan turned back to us. Her bloodred eyes met mine before black feathers erupted over the entirety of her body. A caw broke the air as she transformed back into a crow and took flight. With a heavy rustling of wings, the ravens followed, until only Sleipnir, Leif, and I remained.

With an explosive exhalation of breath, my knees buckled, and I sank to the ground.

A warm hand touched my shoulder, so steady that I realized I was shaking violently. "They're gone," Leif said, his voice more gentle than I had ever heard it. "Come, let me help you."

I held out my tremulous hands to him, and he pulled me to my feet. "Did you hear what she said before? About the giants? The jötnar are already here. That must have been why we encountered the each-uisce." We started to walk toward Sleipnir, but when I stumbled, Leif glanced down at me in alarm.

"How badly are you hurt?" Leif asked, true concern there instead of his usual sarcasm.

"I'll live," I said, gingerly touching the back of my head. When my fingertips came away with bright red blood, I felt the color drain from my face.

Leif gently examined it. "Head wounds always bleed horribly. How do you feel? If it feels like you're about to lose the contents of your stomach and everything around you is tilting like a ship in storm-tossed waters, then we shouldn't waste any time getting you to a healer."

I glanced around me, suddenly noticing the darkness. "Am I losing my vision, or has night fallen?"

Leif's fingers dropped away from my head as he looked at the bright moon above us. "No, it's not your vision. It appears to be the middle of the night, even though it was early afternoon when we entered that forest."

I shook my head and then winced. "It's the Faerie Tunnel. I've never been caught in one, but I know what they say: it's a realm between realms. Time is measured differently there. It may not even be the same day as it was when we entered."

Leif took a step back in alarm. "So we have lost days instead of hours?"

"It's possible," I mumbled, feeling suddenly like I needed to sit down.

"We should continue to Dyflin if you feel able—it's the only way we'll find a healer," Leif said.

The next moment, I was astride Sleipnir, lifted into the air by Leif. If I hadn't been so dazed, I would have remembered to be indignant for being treated like a helpless maiden. But even with such gentle treatment, my head pounded. The trees around me tilted, and I gripped Sleipnir's mane. Leif settled in behind me, only one hand on the reins, the other wrapped securely around my abdomen. I did nothing to discourage him; in fact, I leaned back against him, unable to help myself.

"You can trust me to keep you on this horse," he said softly. "Don't waste your strength trying to hold yourself upright."

Sleipnir shot forward eagerly, desperate to leave the macabre forest. A wide path appeared, guiding our way. In only a few strides, the trees disappeared, and rocky, green meadows lay before us. Each beat of Sleipnir's hooves brought terrible pain, which quickly spread throughout my body until I was shaking. As my vision blurred, I lost the fragile hold I had on my consciousness.

But even as the blackness swallowed me, I saw things in a dreamlike state. The world around me was hazy. Though I still made out Sleipnir and the rocky meadow beyond, it was through a mist that I viewed them. All color had been leached from the scene around me, and a terrible wind buffeted my ears such that no other sounds could penetrate.

With a terrible jolt of surprise, I realized that while my body remained astride Sleipnir, I could see my still form leaning against Leif. Without color, Leif and I were in shades of black and white, even in the bright light of the moon. Was this a vision, then? Or some hallucination brought on by the shock my body had endured?

Was I dead?

But no, I watched as my chest rose and fell. The moment I focused on my body, I saw a bright red spot amid all the black and white—a pulsing thing that glowed with vitality. It was where my heart was, and as I shifted my gaze to Leif, I realized he had the same.

I watched as Leif pulled Sleipnir to a halt and gently shook my shoulders. I could feel the pull on whatever form I'd taken now—an insistent tugging that seemed to come from my very core. I closed my eyes against the increasingly uncomfortable sensation . . . and opened them to the world full of color again.

Leif let out an explosive breath. I blinked slowly at him, still dazed. He had me draped across his lap so that I was looking directly into his eyes. His face was twisted into some expression I couldn't yet name, but once my mind cleared, I realized what it was. He was concerned for me.

"I thought I'd lost you," he said.

Something inside me softened at his kind words and his worried eyes, and this frightened me so terribly that I summoned my flagging strength and righted myself. My head ached, and my side where the hound had scratched it burned, but I found I could bear it. It certainly wasn't a serious enough injury to cause me to lose consciousness. The more I tried to puzzle out the strange occurrence, the more muddled my thoughts became.

Leif halted Sleipnir and helped me down, his hand lingering on my shoulder. "Will you be all right alone?" he asked. "I want to get you water, but . . ." He looked so unsure, so far from his usual arrogant bravado, that my breath hitched.

"Water would help," I said, just so he would leave and stop looking at me like that. *Fool*, I thought. *Someone—an enemy—shows you the least bit of kindness and your heart softens like—*

Like it did toward Séamus. Thinking of him made me reach toward the necklace he'd given me, but when I touched my collarbone, there was nothing but skin. With a painful stab of regret, I realized the hellhound must have ripped the necklace free during the battle. It was lost in the Faerie Tunnel now, and my throat swelled. The last connection to my life before my powers manifested had been torn away. As I spent many moments lost in that disturbing line of thought, I didn't notice right away that Leif had returned until he handed me the flask of water.

"Better?" he asked after I had guzzled most of the flask down.

"Yes."

He took the flask from me and sat down. "What happened?"

"I just fainted for a moment." *And somehow floated outside my body.* "I must have hit my head harder than I thought."

"We should make camp here. I don't think you will make it to Dyflin tonight."

He got to work on a fire, and I watched him, willing my head to stop spinning. I'd never lost control of my mind so much that I left my own body, and I feared it would happen again. If Leif hadn't been with me, I would have fallen. "Thank you for staying with me," I said quietly, without looking at him.

He turned. "Did you just thank me?" He laughed as my expression quickly turned to a scowl. "I wouldn't leave an injured ally. You fought well against those hounds."

Though I didn't want to be reminded of anything we'd just seen in the Faerie Tunnel, it made me think of our strange rescuers. "The ravens there," I said. "Who are they really?"

The smile fell from his face. "The Valkyrie—the Choosers of the Slain. They decide who lives and dies in battle, and the dead they carry to Valhalla."

Awareness trickled through the haze. As a pagan war goddess, the Morrigan was also said to be responsible for who lived and died on the battlefield.

A gift of the gods, then, Leif had said to me when we'd discussed my power, as though he had experience on the subject.

I thought of his otherworldly abilities in battle, and a slim connection formed in my mind. "What have the Valkyrie to do with your power?"

He was quiet for a moment. "I have a pact with the Valkyrie; they endowed me with the power to defeat Fenris and his kind."

"And the terms of this pact?"

"They are not something you need concern yourself over."

"Such a thing does not often end well for the mortal," I said quietly.

He chuckled humorlessly. "I care not."

"You told me you wanted vengeance on the giants. Is that why you sought out the Valkyrie?"

"You put things together quickly." He sounded grudgingly impressed. "Yes, vengeance was what motivated me."

We sat and listened to the fire hungrily consume the wooden branches, and I thought Leif would say nothing more, but then his voice joined the sounds of the fire. "That village I told you about—it wasn't just bloody footprints we found. We also found my sister . . . what was left of her."

I glanced at him, but his face could have been carved from rock. Every muscle in his body was tense. I was surprised by my desire to reach out to him—to place my hand on his arm to tell him without words how much I understood—but I knew it would stop him from continuing his tale, and I knew it needed to be told.

"Finna was visiting our aunt and uncle in our mother's home village—she spent every summer there for as long as I can remember. I think she needed that—to have someone be a mother to her. I could only do so much for her," he said, and nodded toward my braid with a ghost of a smile. "Summer is the best time for trade, so my father and I were often gone for many months anyway. But this time, we came home early. Father sent me to get her, and I remember as I rode there . . ." He trailed off, his mouth twisted in pain. "I remember thinking how excited she'd be to see the silks we'd brought back.

"When I got there, I kept telling myself that I'd taken a wrong turn somehow. I couldn't be at my mother's village. There was nothing left. Everything was blackened, and ashes floated in the air. I walked to where my uncle's house was, and that's where I found Finna on the ground just outside where the door used to be. She was mangled almost beyond recognition," he said, his voice gruff and angry. I couldn't look at him. I knew this pain: seeing your sister, once full of life, dead. "Her hair was soaked with blood, her chest was torn open from neck to navel, with her organs spilling out around her."

Nausea burned in my throat as I imagined not only his sister's body, but Alana's. This time, I couldn't stop myself. I reached over and touched his arm—just once, and only for a moment. "I know what it is to endure the loss of a sister, and I understand that need to have revenge on her murderers."

His eyes met mine. "Then you know there is nothing I wouldn't give to stop the jötnar."

"So you made a pact with the Valkyrie?" I thought of the way the Morrigan had always followed me as a crow, and how she'd finally revealed herself to me. I shivered and moved closer to the fire. "How did you find them?"

"When I brought my sister's body back to our village, I went immediately to the seer. I begged her to tell me what I could do to destroy the creatures that had done this to Finna. The seer told me I would have to cross a glacier and scale a mountain, and even then, I would have more to pay before I'd receive the power I needed to avenge my sister." His hand curled into a fist. "I started for the cave that same day. The Valkyrie only appear during midsummer solstice, in a cave where seers receive their first visions, high on the mountain. It left me a mere three days to get there.

"I was nearly frozen and exhausted from lack of food and sleep when I finally clawed my way to the cave. A red light glowed from within, as though Hel's fires burned in its depths, and I had to crawl inside like an animal. They weren't ravens in the cave—they were women dressed in identical golden armor, huge black wings soaring out from their shoulder blades. There were six of them, and they stood in front of the red fire, with their faces half in shadow."

I thought again of the Morrigan, appearing as half bird, half woman. "How terrifying it must have been to seek such creatures out."

Leif shook his head. "It wasn't bravery at that point. I was desperate and almost delirious from the cold and lack of food. Fear was the furthest thing from my mind." He scoffed. "Though now I think I should have been afraid."

"I think we've seen firsthand just how frightening these immortals can be," I said as my side and head throbbed in sympathy.

He passed me the water flask. "Do you think you can eat?"

"I'd rather hear the end of your story."

He flashed his teeth at me in a grim smile. "There's not much more to tell. They made predictions, one of which has already come true: that I'd be forced to ally myself with my enemy."

"Hm. We share the same prophecy, I see."

"Did I not save you from those hounds? It seems the prophecy worked in your favor."

"We saved ourselves," I said, but my heart wasn't in correcting his arrogant assumptions. "There must be more to the tale—what did the Valkyrie promise you?"

"They told me they would give me the power to defeat the jötnar—strength, fighting ability"—he glanced down at his arm, where scratches from the hounds were already fading—"fast healing. Strength of mind so I never lose focus during battle."

My gaze darted to his. "Is that how you resisted me? Your mind is as fortified by your goddesses' strength as your body?"

He nodded once.

Just what had he traded the Valkyrie for such power? I tilted my head. "And I'm sure they offered to do that freely—at no cost to you."

"There is nothing I wouldn't do to stop the jötnar," Leif said, echoing the words I'd sworn to myself. "The price is high, but higher still if I fail. If the jötnar overthrow the gods, they will enslave those who took up arms with them and slaughter the rest. The Valkyrie have also promised that if I fail, I will be denied a warrior's death in Valhalla and be taken straight to Hel's realm of torture."

"And should you succeed?"

His jaw tightened, discouraging any further questions. "It was necessary, and I would do it again no matter the cost." As I watched, a mist of foreboding seemed to creep across his features. "I've kept you awake for far too long. I'll hunt something to eat, and then you should sleep."

"Should I? I'm glad I have you to tell me when I should eat and sleep."

He snorted as he walked away, and then I was alone with my thoughts and the fire. The day's events had taken their toll—the Wild Hunt, the disturbing moment when I was outside my own body, and Leif's tale of the Valkyrie—and I barely wrapped my cloak around me before I toppled over on my side to sleep. As exhausted as I was, Leif's words haunted me. The brutal murder of his sister made his vendetta against the giants almost noble, and I hated that we had so much in common. Everything I'd ever known about the Northmen made it difficult to believe that he would go to such lengths over someone he loved. I had come to think of the Northmen as barbaric monsters who could no more love than a snake could.

There was no doubt, though: Leif loved his sister. Maybe as much I loved Alana. Enough that he would risk his own soul to avenge her.

I would do it again no matter the cost, he'd said.

Even as my eyelids drooped closed and I slipped away into sleep, one thing stuck out in my mind: the price of such power must be more terrible than I could imagine.

Dubhlinn, at last. The morning had revealed that we'd made camp close enough to see the river Liffey snaking through the land in the distance. It ran through the heart of Dubhlinn, so we'd known we weren't far from the city. Even still, Leif kept Sleipnir at a much slower pace, though I'd told him repeatedly my head injury was much more bearable this morning. But now, I couldn't help but feel a little dizzy and cover my nose with the edge of my cloak. The combined smell of animals, thick wood smoke, human waste, and refuse was so pungent—even through my cloak—that my eyes watered. The streets were narrow, pressing us close to the thatched houses made of mud, where I could hear the rise and fall of voices as we passed by. There was no privacy; I could view the entirety of their one-room houses from Sleipnir's back. I watched a pair of young boys carrying bread back to their mother, feet clad only in woolen socks. Their poverty caused my heart to twist in my chest; their lot was such that even if I gave them every coin I had with me, they would never escape their fate of living and dying in one of those one-roomed houses.

The farther we rode into the city, the more I began to dread the moment when we'd arrive at Sigtrygg's castle at the northern end of Dubhlinn.

As we entered the trade part of the city, the noise quickly vied with the pungent smell for most overwhelming stimulus. The pound of the blacksmith's hammer, the throngs of people, the bleats and calls of the animals, and the rise and fall of voices in Gaelic, English, and Norse created such a cacophony that I gritted my teeth so hard my jaw throbbed.

Rising above everything was a magnificent cathedral, with turrets that nearly blotted out the sun. It was constructed of dove-gray stone, so out of place in the dirty, crowded city that the cathedral rendered all the little thatched houses beneath it inferior. The cathedral's construction was one of the few things the Dubhlinn king had ever done that did not enrage me.

Leif guided Sleipnir through the narrow streets in the direction of the cathedral. Beyond the church was a castle, equally grand, with a stone wall encompassing its bailey. This, then, was the seat of King Sigtrygg.

The closer we got to the king's castle, the more trepidation filled me. I glanced down at my cloak in my clan's colors of green and gold. This was the king who was at odds with my father, who had raided a monastery under our kingdom's protection. How would he react to me? But there was another part of me—a much larger part—that welcomed such a confrontation. I was confident in my ability to protect myself, and I wanted to meet this half-pagan king, the one who would dare desecrate holy ground and raid like a Northman.

"I hope you remember that King Sigtrygg is no ally of mine," I told Leif. "I suspect he won't welcome me with open arms. Or, at least, if he does . . . it's most likely a trap."

"He will treat you the same way he treats any other highborn maiden," Leif said with a wry smile. "He will offer to take you to bed. Whether you accept or not is up to you, but I would advise against it."

I bristled at his teasing tone. "You don't understand. I am more than a mere maiden—"

"How well I know."

"I am a princess. Princess Ciara Leannán of Mide."

He fell into a surprised silence for a moment but recovered quickly. "Much more than a warrior maiden, then. We are allies, you and I." Leif's tone turned dangerous. "If he should do something so foolish as to attack you in my presence, then I will remove his head."

I wrapped my incriminatingly green-and-gold cloak closer about me. We were walking into the lion's den, but I had chosen this quest of my own free will, and I would see it to its conclusion. I didn't trust Leif—not yet—but I did have faith in my own abilities.

We crossed a sickly brownish-green moat, Sleipnir's hooves echoing hollowly on the wooden bridge. Two men hailed us before we entered the bailey, outfitted in chain mail. Their hair was closely cropped save for long braids in the back.

One of them squinted up at us, an ugly scar puckering the flesh of his forehead. "Your name, sir, or you will go no farther."

"Leif Olafsson," he said, with an edge to his tone.

"This is the one they told us to expect," the other said. His cheeks were as smooth as a boy's, and his hair was the color of wheat. He turned to Leif. "You are welcome here. The king was called away to another part of the kingdom, but he will give you audience as soon as he returns."

Leif tightened his hold on Sleipnir's reins until the horse fidgeted. "I care little for what the king is presently occupying himself with. My men." He enunciated slowly. "I will await them here. The lady will also need a healer."

The two must have sensed Leif's rising tension because one of the guards hurried off without another word, presumably to do as Leif demanded.

As we waited, Leif dismounted and helped me down gently, despite his obvious irritation. To my relief, I was able to stand. "You needn't speak to them as though they were dirt," I said with a glare. His jaw flexed repeatedly, tension evident in every muscle.

"I'll treat them as such until I see with my own eyes that Arinbjorn is well."

My brows furrowed until I realized he must mean his brother. In a gentler tone I said, "You said before, the king has always welcomed you. Do you doubt Arinbjorn's safety?"

His eyes flicked to mine briefly. "I won't know what to think until I see him. Arinbjorn is loyal to a fault—he may have decided to sneak out and come find me on his own—especially if the king has been unwelcoming to my people."

The two guards returned, followed by a small army of Northman warriors. As I always did when faced with numerous Northmen, I searched for the one who had murdered my sister and was relieved to find none that bore his resemblance. Leif strode toward them and clasped forearms with a Northman with graying hair who was as big as an ox. The others took turns pounding Leif roughly on the back.

As they all grinned widely at one another, I stepped closer to Sleipnir, my hand on his neck. A twinge of anger shot through me at the sight of them: the men who had killed many of my clansmen. The men who would have killed or enslaved our people and pillaged our castle if we had not fought to stop them. But now these were the allies of my ally. An image arose unbidden in my mind: of Leif's heated gaze, and my body's shameful reaction.

How could I have dishonored my family so abominably?

"What took you so long, Leif?" one of the warriors asked, drawing my attention away from my own thoughts. "We've all aged ten years waiting on you. We've waited a fortnight at least. We would have left, only the seer told us to stay."

The others laughed, but Leif and I shared a look. To us, it had been only three days. Anything could have happened in such a length of time. I glanced back at the entrance to the bailey. My sisters . . .

Leif, too, seemed taken aback. He leaned toward me as though to say something, but then a commotion drew our attention to the castle keep. Someone was coming toward us.

The Northman warriors parted, and a slip of a boy walked through, his head hung low. Leif watched his progress, his arms crossed, his face betraying no emotion.

Arinbjorn stopped in front of Leif, eyes cast to the ground, as though he expected censure from his brother. And I remembered: Leif had said when we first met that his brother had been a stowaway. "I'm sorry, brother. You won't tell our father, will you?"

Leif surprised us all by laughing. "I'm sure he already knows, Arin." He took a step forward and embraced his brother, and I let out the breath I hadn't even realized I was holding. Arin wrapped his slim arms as best he could around Leif's broad back.

Leif patted his brother's head of hair, as tawny as his own, and Arinbjorn smiled up at him. After a moment, Leif turned to me and called my name. Arinbjorn's smile quickly faded as I approached.

He rubbed the back of his head. "This is the maiden warrior who tried to bash in my head."

In my mind, I saw Leif as he was when first he appeared on the battlefield, like an avenging angel, swooping in to protect his younger brother. It was becoming clear that he cared for his siblings as much as I did mine.

Leif smiled. "If she had intended to brain you, Arin, she would have." He turned back to his warriors. "This is Princess Ciara of Mide."

The gray-haired ox of a Northman roared with laughter. "Only Leif War Hammer could so easily deceive his captor into joining his cause." He appraised me with small, dark eyes that lingered much too long on my chest, my hips, my legs. "I hope ye have convinced her to join you in your bed as well." The others laughed riotously as red-hot anger flared within me.

"You dare—" I started, but Leif stepped forward until he was only an inch away from the other Northman's face.

Leif's face was as darkly ominous as a thundercloud. "Gunnarr," he addressed the man, "this is no serving wench at a low tavern—this is a princess, and more importantly, my ally. Speak to her in such a way again, and I will personally make sure your next breath will be your last."

I attempted to hide the surprise from my face, but my eyes remained wide. I hadn't expected Leif to defend me so ferociously against his fellow men.

The smug smiles on the faces of all the Northmen disappeared as one. "You have my apologies, milady," Gunnarr said. "I hadn't realized how much—" He paused and seemed to choose his words more carefully. "I hadn't realized you were an ally."

I dipped my head but said nothing, neither accepting his apology nor refusing it. Many of the others were appraising me openly, their eyes scanning the length of me.

"Milady?" Just then a soft-spoken maidservant appeared at my side, giving the small army of Northmen a wide berth. "I am Aideen. I will serve as handmaiden to you during your stay. A room has been prepared for you, as well as new garments." Her gaze flicked over the blood matted in my hair. "The men also said you'd been injured, but our healer accompanied the king," she said apologetically. "I have some healing skills, though, and I'll prepare a bath and a poultice for you at once."

The many small wounds upon my body ached, as though calling attention to them only caused further injury. "That would be most welcome," I said.

"Follow me, milady," she said. She stopped short when I followed with Sleipnir in tow. "No groom has come for the horse yet? I will run and fetch one."

A shadow fell as she hurried away, and I looked up to find Leif towering over me. My heart raced in answer, and I scowled as though I could will away my feelings with a frown. The rest of Leif's men were moving back toward the castle, their heavy footsteps and loud voices creating so much clamor it was hard to hear anything else.

Even still Leif leaned close to my ear and said in a low voice, "You'll not listen to me, but I'll waste my breath anyway. Stay in your room tonight. Do not come down to the main hall."

"And why would I hide in my room like a frightened child?" I asked.

He let out an impatient breath. "Because you have sustained injury to your head, for one. And more so, these men are my best fighters, but they lose all sense after they have consumed their fill of mead. If they catch sight of you, they will want you, and they will not care about our alliance. Do you understand?"

If the maidservant's frightened demeanor was any indication, they had already exhibited such behavior. I thought of Gunnarr's vulgar words, and even though he'd seemed contrite enough when Leif had explained our alliance, I had little doubt what Leif said was true about their appetites. But these were men I would not soon be rid of. I'd have to earn their respect and guarantee my own safety—without Leif keeping me barred behind solid doors.

"Your maidservant returns," he said, watching the girl's progress across the bailey. "You must swear you'll stay in your room for the remainder of the evening."

"I will swear to nothing."

Leif took hold of my upper arms, his face determined. "You're strong, Ciara, stronger than most warriors I've seen, but I can see the pain and exhaustion in your face. You should rest."

I pulled away from his hold. "Don't make the mistake of treating me as a subordinate. It won't go well for you."

"Don't be so stubborn," he said in almost a growl. "You will not heed my warning?"

I narrowed my eyes at him, unwilling to answer. Anger rose within me like a great wave, washing away the sympathy I'd felt. I might have been injured, but I didn't require coddling.

Aideen returned to lead me to my room, and I was saved from making assurances I would not keep. Nothing would keep me confined to my room against my will, not even an arrogant Northman.

11

Aideen turned out to be more than an apprentice healer. After a brief examination of my head, she declared it only a mild injury, and then prepared me a bath scented with sweet herbs. With gentle fingers, she applied a salve to my head and the scratches on my side. When she finished, my light-headedness disappeared, my wound stopped throbbing, and my tight muscles finally relaxed. I lay upon the soft bed with the intention of resting for only a moment. But as soon as my eyes closed, I was swept away.

My dreams were full of violence. The Morrigan, tearing into the hound's heart; Alana with her throat cut before my eyes; and even Leif's sister, Finna, though I'd never seen her before, visited my dreams, her body gruesomely mangled.

In my dream, I watched as Leif wept over her broken body, and my own heart bled for him. I went to him as I couldn't do in life, running my hand over his golden head. He turned and took me into his arms, and I closed my eyes, listening to the strong beat of his heart. I pulled back to look at him, and just as his mouth was descending upon mine, I saw the red glow in his chest—the same I'd seen when I had floated above my body.

Before I could react to the fact that I was dreaming about Leif kissing me, he disappeared. Dark mist poured into the room in his place, and the Morrigan stepped forward. She wore a headdress of black crows' feathers, but the rest of her figure was obscured by fog.

Find the Northman's seer. There is a power you must master before you can complete your journey. The enemy is closer than you think. Every moment you waste brings them closer to their goal.

What power? I tried to ask, but in the way of dreams, the Morrigan had disappeared as quickly as she'd come.

The resounding boom of thunder awoke me, accompanied by the shouts of men. I sat up in the wide bed, my eyes adjusting to the low light of a fire burning cheerily in the massive stone fireplace. The Morrigan's words echoed in my mind, and I knew it was more than just a dream. Was she referencing my newfound ability to float outside my body? I failed to see how that was a power—it seemed more like a liability, especially in battle. If she meant that I needed to learn to control it so it didn't happen when I wasn't ready, then I agreed. It could mean my death if I lost control of myself at the wrong moment.

I shivered thinking of the rest of the Morrigan's message. *The enemy is closer than you think.* Leif's men had said before that their company included a seer, and though I hadn't met her when we first arrived, I had to believe she was in the castle somewhere.

Still dressed in the beautiful emerald-green gown Aideen had given me, I came to my feet slowly, and though the room seemed to tilt for a moment, everything righted itself after a few deep breaths. Again the thunderous boom came. Fully conscious now, I recognized it wasn't thunder at all, but the sound of tankards banging on wooden tables. The roar of drunken men rang out beneath my room. Would the seer be among them?

Only one way to find out.

I touched the sheathed dagger I'd strapped to my forearm before going to sleep. Leif's warning whispered through my mind, and for a moment I shamed myself by hesitating. Fear wouldn't keep me prisoner here, and neither would Leif.

The guest quarters in which I found myself were located in one of the turrets over the great room. A winding stone staircase led me down, and I yanked the heavy velvet skirt of my gown higher as I went. This was one of the many reasons I only ever wore my soft leather leggings. Gowns, though beautiful, were much too cumbersome.

The moon hung low in the sky; it was late, much too late for such revelry. I followed the low sounds of male voices until I walked through two enormous wooden doors. The cavernous hall was in such disarray, I was immediately thankful the king wasn't here, for he would surely throw us from his castle. Scraps of food littered every available surface; spilled goblets, empty plates, and the carcass of a pig were scattered as though hounds had been set free. But even that wasn't as chaotic a sight as the men, who lay across the tables in a state of total unconsciousness, guzzled great tankards of ale or mead, or played a game upon a carved wooden board.

In the chaos, it was difficult to find anyone, but it quickly became clear from the room full of burly men that the seer wasn't here. I'd have to find Leif instead and see if he knew where to find her. But among so many men of enormous stature and blond hair, I had to search the room several times before I found Leif. He sat at the head of the table where the game was played. Enthralled as they all were with their various activities, no one took note of me.

With a determined set to my chin, I strode toward Leif. Before I could reach his table, though, a great bear of a man stood in my way. He licked his lips as he boldly stared at me, mead dripping from his beard.

"Ah, the wench is lonely," he said with a lascivious sneer. "Come down from her tower for a tumble."

My first instinct was to backhand him, but I stayed my hand. There was more than lust in his eyes, something more akin to bloodlust, and I would do well to be on my guard. "If you lay hands on me, I will ensure you never do so again." I shifted to the balls of my feet, ready to move should he lunge for me.

As though I'd shouted, my comparatively high female voice

drew the attention of every Northman in the room—save those who had already fallen into a drunken stupor. At the head of his table, Leif stirred, but I could spare him only the briefest glance. My full attention was on the Northman before me.

The man's grin widened. "It is widely known that a spirited female is worth the effort." He leaned forward until I nearly choked on the smell of his filthy, braided beard. "Much more fun when she's finally broken."

With surprising speed for one so large, his hand darted out. I dodged, but my cursed skirts tangled about my legs. He pressed me against the table, the wood digging into my back. A shout came from across the room, but neither the man nor I paid it any heed. I unsheathed my dagger and slashed it across his cheek.

His nostrils flared like a bull's, and his eyes narrowed to slits, but he backed away. I tightened my grip on my dagger.

"You'll pay for that, spawn of Loki," he said in a snarl. "I'll tear your gown from your body and have you here on the floor."

As though I'd been stabbed with a burning blade, intense rage shot through me. He charged, and I held my dagger loosely, as Leif's brief training had taught me. I would geld him like a horse; he would never threaten a woman again.

Before the Northman could reach me, Leif stepped in front of the rampaging Northman, his legs spread bracingly. "Ulric," Leif said, his voice deadly, "stop now, or by Thor, I will kill you where you stand."

Ulric halted, but his small eyes flashed with a burning hate.

"Curse you, Leif. If you will deny me my rights, then I will cut you down."

Leif's countenance darkened murderously. "You have no rights to claim. She is an ally, which you well know." He took a step forward. "And I do not take threats lightly."

The scene was like that of a wolf challenging its alpha. A dark cloud of impending violence seemed to descend upon the hall. Those still conscious watched the interplay between the two men with growing anticipation, and I tensed, prepared for battle.

Ulric answered Leif by pulling an axe free from its fastenings on his back.

"So be it," Leif said, and shot forward before Ulric could even lift the heavy axe.

He struck Ulric beneath his chin so hard his neck snapped back. Ulric swung his axe, but Leif struck him again and again in the face until blood sprayed from his nose. Leif's blows were as fast as viper strikes and utterly merciless. Again, Ulric swung his axe. Leif dodged, and the axe split one of the long wooden tables in two.

Many of the men roared their approval, but I could only watch in grim silence.

Ulric charged again, axe raised, but Leif had grabbed a knife. He met Ulric's charge with a powerful upward thrust of the blade. It lodged in Ulric's heart, and the Northman fell to his knees. The axe clattered to the floor. After drawing one last struggling breath, the rest of Ulric's body followed.

My heartbeat thudded in my ears as I stared in disbelief at the dead Northman at our feet. I had expected this to end with Ulric felled into unconsciousness, not death.

"Get this failed usurper from my sight," Leif said, a look of disgust twisting his features. "Burn the body."

Two men immediately moved forward to do as he asked. Grunting with effort, they lifted the broken body of Ulric into the air and carried him from the room.

The drumming sound of tankards hitting the table began soon after. "Olafsson! Olafsson!" the men chanted.

I stood in a sort of shock over the callous disregard for the dead—even if the man had been a disgusting cretin. I turned to Leif. "I hope you haven't killed one of your own on my account."

He glanced pointedly at the dagger I still clutched in my right hand. "And I am to believe you had no plans to use that?"

"Not to kill. Only geld, which would've been a just punishment for one so foul."

Leif laughed humorlessly. "Deprive him of his manhood? Princess, he would have begged you for death. No, my punishment was much more humane."

"Humane?" I said with an incredulous stare. "He is dead!"

"You don't understand our ways, and yet you pass judgment. These men follow me of their own free will. They can leave at any time, but while they are under my leadership, they are not to challenge me." His eyes darkened. "I warned you to stay in your room, and you paid me no heed. He would have taken great pleasure in raping you before all. What were you even doing down here?"

My cheeks flushed, and I bristled. "He never would've had the chance. I don't need a man to defend me; I can protect myself."

"You can—you've proven that before—but that doesn't mean you need to go looking for dangerous situations to put yourself in."

My anger ignited. "And I suppose it's my fault he attacked me, then? I shouldn't have been there—being all female and tempting?"

"Of course it's not your fault—"

"I came here to find your seer, not look for danger," I interrupted, more than a little disgusted at the implied blame. And, if I was being honest, still a little shaken up from the sudden outbreak of violence. "Obviously she isn't among you lot of barbarians, so I'll look elsewhere." I turned on my heel to go.

"I haven't been afraid many times in my life," Leif said suddenly, "but I was afraid when Ulric threatened you." He reached out and touched my cheek, and I was so shocked by the sudden touch that I froze. "I've never felt such rage."

Horribly, I thought of my dream earlier that night, of Leif nearly kissing me. My eyes dropped to his mouth, and horror washed over me as I realized I was actually contemplating what it would be like to feel his lips on mine. He took a step closer to me, and my gaze jumped to his. My heart pounded when I saw the flare of heat trapped within the icy blue of his eyes.

You want him, a part of me whispered, and I stamped down on that part of me with a hiss. He was a *Northman*.

I pulled back, remembering why I'd come down to the hall in the first place—to find the seer. Before I could say anything else, the doors to the great hall opened. Leif's attention shifted—reluctantly, it seemed—to the hall entrance. I turned to see two men enter. They weren't the same men who had left with Ulric's body, but they appeared much the same as the others. Tall, blond, bearish.

Leif caught the eye of Gunnarr and made a sharp gesture with his chin. Gunnarr moved toward us, pulling his axe free.

"Who are they?" I asked.

"I don't know," Leif said.

The men strode toward one of the tables nearest to us, and I took an unintentional step back when I saw them. Their faces looked like melted wax, as though they'd been badly burned early in life. Their brows drooped heavily, almost into their eyes. One's nose was as prominent as a horse's, the other's was barely there, like a snake's. Ordinarily, such a sight would move me to pity. Gazing upon these men, however, the fine hairs on the back of my neck stood up. I shivered as though a cold wind suddenly howled through the hall.

If they noticed the rising tension in the room, the drawn weapons, they gave no sign of it. They tore into dark loaves of bread voraciously, seemingly unaware of their environment. And yet they had an aura about them of malevolence, as if a sudden movement might provoke them to violence.

The one with the snake nose leaned toward the other and spoke rapidly in a language I didn't recognize. It was harsh and guttural, and all at once, I froze. I had heard such a language before. In the crow's vision.

"We should see who they are," Leif said, and took a step toward them, a determined set to his jaw. My hand shot out and grasped his arm. He glanced down at me in surprise.

"This hall has seen enough blood for the night," I said in a low tone.

Leif's brow furrowed, but he did not attempt to remove my hand.

Were these the jötnar we hunted? Though they were easily the tallest men in the room, they weren't giants. And yet . . . I remembered the sound of their language. *Your enemies are closer than you think*, the Morrigan had said, and the stag in the wood had said giants were stirring up the creatures of Éirinn. Still, engaging them here, without knowing for sure who they were and what they were capable of, was folly. I glanced at Leif and Gunnarr. Leif had just slayed one of his own. What might he do with an enemy? I wouldn't risk it.

A female servant entered the room then, her bearing much less timid than that of the handmaiden who had waited upon me. Her wide hips swished as she made her way to the jötnar's table fearlessly. I tensed, suddenly afraid for her. "My lords," she said, "your rooms have been prepared, and I am sorry for your wait." Her eyes surveyed the room, a look of disgust on her face. "The hall is in poor condition at the moment. Would you

163

mind taking your meals in your rooms?"

They shook their disfigured heads and stood, towering over the woman. "You may show us the way," the one with the prominent nose said, his Gaelic as guttural as his own language.

The servant nodded slowly, as though she had trouble understanding. "Follow me," she said after a moment.

From what Leif had told me, I thought the jötnar would be so hungry for human flesh that they'd attack the woman right there in the hall. Though nothing happened, I couldn't deny the skitter of warning across my skin.

Leif watched them with an alert wariness until they finally left the hall. As though a great storm had passed, the tension disappeared from the room. Gunnarr lowered his axe, and I let out a slow breath.

"Should we follow?" Gunnarr asked. "I didn't like the look of them. We can cleave their ugly troll heads from their bodies before they have the chance to attack."

"You can't attack someone just because you don't like the way they look," I said, though I had to admit I understood the feeling. "You don't even know who they are."

"I know they raised the hair on the back of my neck," Gunnarr said with a look of disgust. "That's enough for me."

"Perhaps the seer has the answer?" I said with a glance at Leif. I was happy to have an excuse to talk to the seer. Leif still hadn't said anything, and his face was a mask of stone. "Perhaps she can divine whether they are friend or foe."

Leif shook his head. "She can only see what the gods allow;

her answers and power are limited."

"Then we shouldn't waste time asking her," Gunnarr said, almost eagerly. "We should interrogate them ourselves."

Were all Northmen so eager to die, then? "Still," I said, "it's better to find out all we can."

"Gunnarr, Ciara is right. It's foolish rushing into a situation we have no knowledge of."

Gunnarr's face fell. "Ask the seer, then, but come get me before you do what needs to be done. It's been ages since I made use of my axe."

I hid a smile at Gunnarr's words. He sounded so much like Conall, but my amusement disappeared when I realized who I was comparing my clansman to.

"Where can I find her?" Leif asked.

"Sleeping in one of the rooms above us," Gunnarr said with a jerk of his chin toward the ceiling. "Where else would she be? She's as old as Odin."

"Which room?" I asked.

"First door on your right—just follow the smell of the herbs she always brings along," he said with a Conall-like lip curl.

Leif walked past us and wrenched open one of the heavy doors. "Let's see if she will answer."

"Do you bring old women with you on all your raids?" I asked as I hurried through the doorway—I'd never been so eager to leave a place. With Ulric's attack and the strange men appearing, the king's great hall seemed as forbidding as a crypt.

"On quests as important as this one I do."

We both scanned the dark entryway as the doors slammed shut behind us. The flames of the wall torches flickered and danced, casting ominous shadows, but if there was anyone hiding in the dark, they were utterly silent.

I moved toward the stairs first, and Leif followed, our footsteps muffled by the rugs upon the stone floor.

Trepidation filled me; my every step felt heavy. If those men were truly jötnar—or in league with them—the whole city could be in danger. The fact that they were here, in King Sigtrygg's castle, seemed to suggest he wasn't the ally Leif thought him to be.

If our enemy had already made it to Dubhlinn, where else in Éirinn might they be? Were my sisters even still safe at home?

I feared the answers.

The smell of sage was so strong outside the seer's door that I wondered how I hadn't noticed it earlier.

Leif knocked once, but the door was ajar just enough that Leif's fist opened it farther. The smoke from the sage streamed out of the room and wrapped around us, almost choking in its intensity.

"Sigrid?" he called with a cough and a wave of his hand at the smoke.

"Come," a gravelly voice answered.

Leif crossed the threshold, and I followed him into the darkness. It took a moment for my eyes to adjust, for the room was lit by only a single candle, and the seer sat far away from its light. I could make out a woman bent forward with age, clutching a gnarled wooden stick. Gray robes hung from her body, and they rustled as though made from stiff muslin when she gestured for us to sit.

There was only one other armchair and a small bed, so I took the chair while Leif stood beside me. The seer lit another candle at the rickety table beside her. In the flickering light, she appeared even more ancient, her face as weathered as a rock worn by a thousand years of wind and water. Her hair was as gray as her robes, wild and half braided.

"What is it you wish to know?" she asked.

"There are strange men here," Leif said, his voice low. "Are they in league with the jötnar?"

The seer watched the flame of the candle for several long moments. "The jötnar have nearly as much magic as the gods. They can assume many forms."

"You didn't answer my question," Leif said, frustration evident in the set of his shoulders.

"Then you didn't listen."

"What do you see of the kingdom of Mide?" I asked, my hands gripping the skirt of my gown. "Is my family safe?"

She turned to me, her eyes almost milky with age. "This kingdom you speak of is shrouded by a dark mist that even my eyes cannot penetrate."

"What do you mean?" I asked, a sick anxiety growing with me. "Tell me, are my sisters safe?"

"I tell you again, child. There is something that prevents me from seeing the fate of your kingdom."

The Morrigan? I thought. My anxiety for my family grew until I feared I'd be sick. The strong smell of the sage and the lingering pounding of my head injury didn't help. Suddenly, Leif's warm hand touched my shoulder, and I glanced up to find him watching me with sympathy.

"You have other concerns," the seer continued. "A new power that frightens you."

Leaving my own body. I still failed to see how it was a power, but it certainly frightened me. "I need to learn to control it. I need to know what it *is*."

"You are too weak now, and you lack the discipline and true desire to master it."

I leaned closer. "I was told you could help me." Though that wasn't strictly true. The Morrigan had never promised the seer could help . . . only told me I should find her.

The seer drew farther into her robes. "You are surrounded by darkness. Your life hangs by a single thread, and I cannot see what the outcome will be."

I glanced up at Leif again, and he must have seen the desperation in my eyes, for he said to the seer, "What does that mean? She may die, so you refuse to help her?"

Unperturbed by his angry tone, the seer shook her head. "She must undergo the test before the power can be mastered." She drew a raspy breath as though talking had become taxing on her withered body. "You must remember that your power connects you to the spirit realm. It could save your life"—she looked at Leif—"and his."

"Why is it the nature of seers to speak in riddles?" Leif demanded.

"I can only see what the gods choose to show me. We are all helpless to their whims."

"You can do no more, then?" Leif asked. "Isn't there anything you can do to divine the fate of Ciara's family?"

"This land is not ours. There are ancient beings here, creatures like our gods in the north, and they also have control over what I can see." She watched me for a moment until unease joined the sick feeling in my stomach. "They don't want me to see the fate of your family."

With those forbidding words, she blew out the candle, plunging her corner into darkness again.

Leif made a noise of disgust and made to leave. I came to my feet. "Thank you for speaking with us," I murmured.

"Your power," the seer said quietly, and I paused, "is a door as real as the one in this room. Do not be afraid to go through it."

More riddles. But I could see she was trying to help me, so I nodded once. "I will remember."

I followed Leif into the dim hallway and closed the seer's door behind me.

I wanted to run to the stables, leap astride Sleipnir, and gallop back to Mide. But I couldn't. Of course I couldn't—I was exiled for attacking my own father, and the jötnar might already be here in this castle. But my sisters . . .

Fear gripped me like a hawk's talons tear into a mouse.

"Ciara," Leif said, concern etched into his face, and it nearly broke me. "Your family . . . just because Sigrid couldn't see them doesn't mean anything happened to them."

I stepped closer to him—I couldn't help it. I wanted someone to tell me they were okay, that nothing had happened to them, that this feeling I had meant nothing. "We lost eleven days in the Faerie Tunnel, Leif. There are men here who could be in league with the jötnar, and they could have easily been to Mide and back."

"They could have," Leif agreed, "and I understand your fear, but you can't let it cripple you. Much as I hate to sit idle, I think it may be best to watch and wait—at least until morning." He crossed his arms over his chest. "Unless you know more than you're telling me."

I thought about lying, but Leif seemed more restrained now than he had in the great hall. "I have seen men like them before in a vision. Their strange language is what gave them away as jötnar, yet they are clearly not giants. For this reason, I held my tongue." His body tensed like a bow, and I reached out to touch his arm. "You said we should watch and wait," I reminded him gently. I could feel the need for violence thrumming just beneath his skin, and I understood it. Had they been responsible for one of my beloved sisters' deaths . . . there was very little that would stop me from slaughtering them like sheep.

"If given the chance," I continued, "I can get inside their heads, perhaps find out more."

Leif let out his breath. "You're right." Some of the tension seemed to leave him, and he turned to go. "It's late. I should find Arinbjorn." Before he left, he gestured toward my head. "Your injury—is it better?"

I smiled. "Much." I'd almost forgotten about it. The pain had reduced to a dull ache that I could easily ignore.

"Good. Will you stay in your room now that you've seen I had reason to warn you?"

My eyes narrowed. "Yes, and I don't need another warning. I can take care of myself."

He grinned like he had expected me to answer in exactly that way. "Good night, then."

"Good night," I muttered, and hurried into my room.

I closed my door and leaned against it, suddenly exhausted. With all that had happened, I realized with a blooming unease that we had yet to see the king.

There might be more enemies under this roof than just the two strange Northmen.

12

The sound of a low horn in the morning announced the return of the king and his party. The castle's servants flew into an organized frenzy, preparing the hall and rooms for its master. I watched with tensed muscles, as though I was preparing for battle.

I had a wealth of nervous energy even though I'd spent much of the night afraid that if I fell asleep, the Morrigan would reveal something else to me—like the fate of my family. I tried not to worry about my sisters, but just thinking about them made me long for my lost home. Today, though, I swore I would banish everything but this quest from my mind. There was much more to concern myself over. The king was problem enough, but I was also wary of encountering the strange men from last night.

As I entered the hall, I was relieved to find it set back to rights after the Northman celebration last night. Servants jostled past me, carrying ornate candlestick holders, golden bowls of fruit, and baskets of bread. I could smell boar being roasted on its spit. Red-and-gold embroidered cloth covered the tables, a high-backed throne had been given the place of honor, and already, dancers, jesters, and minstrels were arriving. These were the makings of a feast, but instead of engendering a feeling of joy, I felt only a cold apprehension.

"A feast, a great feast for a successful raid," a loud baritone of a voice called behind me.

I glanced up to see a man unremarkable in appearance save for his height, dressed in a tunic of red and gold, as though he wished to match the tablecloths. He did not wear a crown upon his head, but it was clear from the way his eyes surveyed the room possessively, and the richness of his clothes, that he was the king.

He took notice of me, the only lady in the room in a sea of servants, and hastened to my side. "I thought I knew of every guest in this castle, but I confess, I am at a loss as to who you might be." There was no accusation in his tone, only curiosity, his light brown eyes watching me with interest.

"Forgive me, your grace," I said. "I arrived in the company of Leif Olafsson."

Loud footfalls behind me announced another's presence, and the king and I both turned. Leif stepped forward, his brother just a step or two behind him, and the king greeted them both with a wide smile. "Olafsson! I am honored to have you at my court."

Leif gave a stiff bow. "My thanks for sheltering my men until I could return."

"You mean until you could make your escape." King Sigtrygg laughed. "Ah, well, it was no hardship on my part. Though they have run my servants ragged." His eyes shifted to me. "But I was surprised to find a great lady such as this in your company. I am still waiting for an introduction."

"This is Ciara Leannán, Princess of Mide."

I reluctantly lowered into a curtsy. When I rose again, there was a light in the king's eyes, a sort of greedy hunger. "A warrior princess accompanying you. What a perfect alliance. I should have known who you were the moment I saw you. The dark-haired warrior daughter of the king of Mide. I had wondered why you weren't at your father's side."

I stiffened. "You've seen my father?"

He smiled, but there was nothing friendly in the gesture. "I have only just come from Mide. The king was more than hospitable." His smile widened. "Indeed, I feel richer just having dined at his table."

It was hard to imagine my father allowing this king to dine in our halls, but I was more concerned with news of my mother and sisters. "Then my family is well? My mother and sisters?"

"The queen and the princesses were in excellent health when I left only a few days ago," he said, and I let out a breath in relief. "Your mother was equally hospitable after the king and I came to an agreement."

An agreement? The king of Dubhlinn was responsible for the raid on the monastery. It had seemed like my father was more inclined toward battle with Sigtrygg than peace. But that was a fortnight ago. What had happened to change Áthair's mind? "I hope it was an arrangement of peace."

"We came to a very peaceful arrangement in the end," the king agreed, but there was still something about his tone that was off. I couldn't trust him.

The king's eyes fell on Arinbjorn, who was shifting from one foot to the other as though he'd rather be running than standing by idly. "This boy looks just like you," he said to Leif, "but he is much too old to be your son. He is your kinsman?"

"My brother," Leif said.

"Brother to a great warrior. Are you as skilled?"

Arinbjorn crossed his arms over his chest. His expression mimicked the arrogance of his brother's. "As skilled in what?"

Had this been one of my sisters, I would have been mortified at the audacity of such a question, but Leif only grinned.

"In battles, son," the king said, a slight edge to his voice. "In raids, in warfare."

"No one is as skilled as my brother," Arinbjorn said with a proud glance at Leif.

"They say the princess comes close," the king said, "and there are two Northmen here who claim to have abilities no one has seen before. It makes me long for a coliseum. How I would love to pit your skills against one another."

His wistful look shot a fiery disdain through my heart. "Such barbarism is long dead, your grace," I said.

"A pity. I shall have to satisfy my bloodlust with raids like any other Northman."

A curse sprang to the tip of my tongue, but I managed to suppress it. "If you'll excuse me, I must be sure my horse is being properly cared for," I said with a shallow curtsy.

Leif pushed Arinbjorn toward me. "Go with her," he said.

His brother looked as though he would protest, but then he nodded.

Sleipnir was no doubt well cared for, but I was sure that if I stayed a moment longer, I would forget myself and say something that would bring the wrath of the king down upon my house and clan.

The stables were quiet. It seemed everyone was preparing for the feast in the castle, and there wasn't a single groom to be found. The soft sounds of the horses and the smell of fresh hay soothed some of my anger at the king. He might have been polite, but I couldn't help but dislike him. Not after everything he had done—raiding and pillaging our kingdom and many others like a Northman. He had a falseness to him that I didn't trust.

Arinbjorn leaned against the wall, a sulky expression on his young face. His eyes followed my every movement as I checked Sleipnir for soundness and fed him a handful of grain.

"You needn't be so sullen," I said. "Would you rather listen to the blustering of a foolish king?"

A smile peeked out at the corner of his mouth before he could hide it. "I am not sullen. I only wish my brother hadn't sent me from the room like a page boy."

"He did you a great favor. Be thankful."

He walked closer until he was peering into the stall. "I remember this horse."

I patted Sleipnir's neck fondly. "He's difficult to forget."

"You weren't riding him when you tried to kill me."

"I wasn't trying to kill you, as I'm sure you well know."

His gaze met mine accusingly. "I wasn't a worthy opponent?"

"It wasn't your skills that stopped me; it was my sister. The two of you must have been born the same year, and I saw only her face whenever I looked at you. I did my best to merely subdue you instead of taking your life."

Much of the bluster seemed to leave his stance. "We had a sister once, though I don't remember her as well as Leif does. But I remember well enough, and I know what happened to her." His hands clenched into fists. "That was why I stowed away against Leif's wishes. I am her brother, too, and I should have a right to avenge her."

I touched Arin's arm. "It's a terrible thing to lose a sibling."

"She was murdered by the jötnar," he said in a snarl, as though I had said nothing at all. "Her body was the only one that wasn't just a splatter of blood and gore. They wanted us to know they'd slaughtered her."

A jolt of apprehension raced through me. "Why would you

think that—that the jötnar wanted your sister to be found?"

"Because it was obvious. She was the only one left. Why do that if they didn't want us to find her?"

"Yes, but why your family? Why single you out?"

Arin stood a little straighter. "Because my father, and now Leif, are the greatest raiders in the north."

I could understand how they'd think the jötnar would challenge them in such a way, but there was something that made me think it was more ominous than that . . . a feeling that skittered up my spine.

"I'm young still," Arin continued, "but that doesn't mean I don't want my chance to defend my own family."

"It's a worthy quest."

Arinbjorn looked almost eager. "Then you'll convince Leif I should be part of it? That I, as Finna's brother, also have the right to hunt them down?"

I smiled and shook my head. "You overestimate my influence on your brother, I'm afraid."

"I don't think I do. I have never seen Leif treat a girl as he does you. It's almost like—"

A terrible scream, agonizing in its intensity, rent the stillness of the stable. Arinbjorn and I froze, and the hair on the back of my neck stood on end.

It came again, a keen ending in a strangled breath.

I ran toward the source of the sound. Just outside the stable, a trail of blood darkened the hard, packed earth. I glanced back at Arinbjorn, who met my look with a grim expression of his own. The blood had splattered the side of the barn, and drops of it pointed the way to a dark corner.

With a cold dread gripping me, I followed the trail, careful to mute my footfalls.

There, in a dark corner, was one of the strange men from last night—the one with the nose like a snake. He loomed over the prostrate body of a young girl, his back to us. I stepped closer, Arinbjorn just behind me. The girl's hair had broken free of its pins, and it spilled around her. Her soft brown eyes were glassy and unseeing, and with a start, I realized it was Aideen.

A crunching noise brought my attention back to the man. He turned, and in his hands was an arm, torn from Aideen. The hand was curled into a fist; she had fought before it was torn from her shoulder. Chunks of flesh were missing, and I reeled with horror when I realized why. Blood dripped from the snake-nosed man's mouth, staining his teeth red.

Leif and I hadn't been sure these men were inhuman, but now it was clear this was no mortal man. Though large by any human standard, he still wasn't the size of a giant. His monstrous appetite, however, seemed to prove he was, no matter his size. I reached out with my mind but grasped at nothing; his gaze went everywhere but my eyes, and I needed that connection. I spied a nearby pitchfork and grabbed hold. Brandishing it before me like a spear, I said, "Leave the girl, or I will run you through."

The Northman fixed me with a grim smile. "Why? I think we both know you can do little to stop me. Besides, she is already dead, and her flesh is sweet."

Behind me, Arinbjorn retched, and my own stomach roiled. This was truly the work of the devil. "I cannot allow you to desecrate her body."

He dropped the arm with a sickening thud and spread his own arms wide. "Then let us pit our strengths and see who is the stronger."

Before I could move, the Northman launched himself at me, faster than should have been possible for a man of such size. He knocked me to the ground. I barely had time to raise my make-shift weapon before he was on me again. He landed three blows across my ribs, and I felt the bones bruise but not break. I forced myself to my feet again. Still he avoided making eye contact with me, as though he sensed my intentions.

The Northman circled me like a shark, and Arinbjorn caught my eye, stalking toward him out of the darkness. Abruptly, the man turned, fixing the boy with his gaze. He charged like a bull, slamming into Arinbjorn's middle. The breath was knocked from Arin in a rush, and he lay on the ground, stunned. I ran toward them, the tines of my pitchfork aimed toward the Northman's gut. Before it could make contact, he dodged as agilely as a dancer. He used my own momentum against me, grabbing my arms as I ran by and flipping me onto my back.

Arinbjorn shook off his daze and tried to push himself up.

"Run," I shouted at Arinbjorn. "Find Leif."

I pushed myself upright again, furious at the thought that I'd been knocked down not once but twice. I gave the stubborn boy a shove toward the castle before meeting another head-on assault from the Northman.

I felt his flesh give way to my sharp pitchfork, and I stumbled back. He glanced down at the protruding wood from his side and pulled it free as though it were merely a thorn. After snapping it in half, he threw it on the ground at my feet with a taunting grin. His eyes locked onto mine, finally giving me the opportunity I needed to reach out with my mind.

It was like being plunged into pitch-black darkness, like finding myself lost in a strange wood during a moonless night. A flood of vile emotions crashed over me: loathing, hunger for flesh, bloodlust. He wanted to tear me apart and eat the flesh from my bones.

I struggled to maintain control of his mind, but it was as slippery as an eel. And strong. There was no way a mind this strong was that of a mere mortal.

His hands shot out and wrapped around my slim throat. He lifted me until we were eye level, my legs kicking uselessly. I clawed at his hands. I pried at his fingers. My lungs burned, desperate for air.

I will not die, I shouted in my mind. *I will not be eaten.*

I clung to the weak hold I had on his mind until the pain in my head was like repeated blows from a hammer. Black spots appeared on the edges of my vision. I would lose consciousness soon, and then it would all be over.

My eyes closed against my will.

Then a great door appeared in my mind, bright light shining

behind it. It was a dying girl's hallucination, but I was still drawn to it. All at once, I remembered the seer's words to me: that my power was a door. I still didn't understand, but a part of me reached forward, the darkness all but taking over my vision, my body dying for lack of air. I wrenched the door open.

I drowned in a sea of light.

But then I could see in startling clarity. Again, I was above it all, looking down upon the carnage like a bird. I watched the Northman choke the life from me. I watched my legs continue to kick to no avail.

My body was lit up like the sun, but the Northman was darkness itself. His body was smoke, black and fathomless. But in the very center was a pulsing red spot. I was drawn to it as I was drawn to the door. The arms of my body had no strength left, but this form, this floating ghostly form, had limitless power. I reached into the very core of his chest and grasped the red energy. It beat against my hand like a frightened bird, and I squeezed, crushing it in my fist.

In a rush, I returned to my true body. The Northman's hands fell away from my neck, and I hit the ground, gasping for breath.

With a groan, I rolled to my knees, only to collapse again with a coughing fit. After a moment, I forced myself up again and stumbled toward the Northman.

He was prostrate on his back. His eyes stared at the sky, cloudy and unseeing. I watched for several heartbeats, and his chest rose and fell shallowly. It was clear that he was dying.

A jagged piece of the pitchfork handle remained. Without a moment's hesitation, I staked the Northman through the heart. He made not a single sound as the life left his body. I thought of Aideen, and of Leif's innocent sister, both slaughtered like animals. A chill of unease spread over me at this new power, but when I looked at Aideen's abused body, I could only feel relief that her murderer was dead.

Now the deed was done, the energy seemed to leave me all at once, and I swayed on my feet. My body ached as though I'd been trampled by wild horses, but I forced myself back toward the castle. I had to be sure Arin was safe, and Leif would need to be told; the other Northman would have to be dealt with—hang the consequences.

The sounds of minstrels and the smells of roasting boar and freshly baked bread signaled the feast was well under way in the great hall by the time I made my way there. I cracked the door, aware that my gown was torn, dirt and blood had formed a paste on my arms and face, and my hair would be more fitting for a banshee. Every breath was searing pain through my injured throat, but this was no time to rest and recover. At first glance, I couldn't find Leif in the room full of merrymakers and the bustling Dubhlinn court.

By the grace of God, Arinbjorn walked into my line of sight, and I waved to catch his attention. He hurried to my side. "I've been searching for my brother but have only just discovered he is in private conference with the king," he said in a rush. "Are you unhurt? You look . . ." He winced. "You look relatively whole."

"I'm sure I look terrible, but at least I'm not dead," I said, my voice rough with the damage done to my throat. "I won't be able to enter the great hall looking like this, but we must find the other man who was that monster's companion. Have you seen him?"

Arinbjorn shook his head. "No. I searched the entire hall for Leif, and I would have noticed that man."

My stomach dropped at the news. Whose flesh was he feasting on if not the boar's? "Do you know where Leif and the king are speaking?"

"One of the servants told me. It's not far." He strode away, and I followed as best I could, my lungs protesting every breath.

Arin halted in front of a thick wooden door. When he lifted his hand to knock, I stopped him and put my finger to my mouth in a sign of silence. Voices drifted out from the room, both of which were familiar to me.

"I have told you everything I know of the men calling themselves the Bane of Odin," the king said.

"They aren't men," Leif said in a voice full of disgust. "They're monsters."

"They are strong fighters whatever they are, though I've heard rumors of rather . . . dark appetites. But enough of that. What of the princess you bring to my court?" His tone turned almost gleeful, and I grimaced at the door. "She is a price worth more than gold."

"She is not for sale."

The king lowered his voice, so that I was forced to press my ear against the door like an eavesdropping servant. "She's worth a small army. Men you're in need of for your cause." My hands tightened to fists when Leif did not immediately respond. "Hear me out, warrior. The princess is the heir to the throne of Mide, and a legendary warrior in her own right. Once they discover I have her, there's nothing her clansmen wouldn't give to get her back. I'm not so proud as to think I can keep her here against her will—I know I lack the power to imprison someone with her abilities—but with your aid, I could hold her for ransom. My own son cost over a thousand head of cattle as ransom, and the princess and heir is worth so much more."

The king's words made no sense. Had he not told me earlier that he'd made peace with my father? Why risk his wrath and vengeance by holding me for ransom? Worse, Leif didn't seem to be arguing with him.

Finally, Leif said, "What do you propose?"

I turned on my heel and stalked away.

"Princess Ciara, wait," Arinbjorn whispered urgently.

He caught up to me despite my angry strides. "Leave me," I said.

"You didn't hear my brother agree, he wouldn't—"

"I heard more than enough."

Silenced by a sharp look from me, he still followed me doggedly to my room. He watched as I gathered my few belongings: my sword and the clothes I had arrived with, thoughtfully

185

mended—no doubt by Aideen, who now lay in pieces outside the stables.

"You cannot leave," he said, his eyes pleading. "What about those men who may be jötnar? You must explain what you found to Leif. I don't know how you defeated that monster, but I know my brother will need your help."

"Why should I stay? You were witness as well as I, and I won't stay here as a captive." I was so enraged that I shook all over.

"What of the quest? You would abandon it?"

I stopped, one hand on the door handle. In truth, I hadn't thought further than my own escape from this castle, and his words stirred an unwelcome twinge of guilt. "What would you have me do? Wait in my room until your brother comes to put me in chains? He has betrayed me." An aching pain swiftly followed that statement; I was a fool to have ever trusted him. To have ever thought he could be anything but my enemy was the worst kind of mistake.

"You don't know that for sure," he said weakly.

"I know enough not to take the risk."

I opened the door and stepped into a wall of Northman chest. With an angry hiss, I jumped back.

I faced Leif with my weight balanced on both legs, my hand loose at my side, prepared to unsheathe my sword at the slightest provocation.

His eyes swept over my body, seemingly seeing me for the first time. "What has happened, Ciara? Are you injured?" His

186

face darkened. "Did one of my men—"

He reached toward me, but I jerked away.

The sudden concern reflected in his voice and countenance set my teeth on edge. "You dare ask after my well-being after you've made such an agreement with the king?"

Leif's eyes shifted to his brother behind me. "Arin, leave us."

Arinbjorn's jaw tightened for a moment, but he nodded stiffly and strode out of the room.

Leif watched him go before turning back to me. "There is no arrangement I've made with the king save where I'll sleep this night. Enough of this. Address me directly. What injury have I done you?"

His obvious confusion had my anger fading, and I grasped for it like a drowning man reached toward the surface of the water. "Do you deny conspiring with the king to hold me for ransom?"

"I absolutely deny it. Why would I agree to an act that would guarantee the loss of alliance between you and me?"

"For more men. For the army you need," I said, feeling my argument slipping away with every breath. "You can't deny the conversation even took place; both your brother and I over-heard."

He let out a sharp laugh. "He did agree to lend me more men and ships, but it's something he is bound by oath to give me. You know this."

"I know what I heard," I said, my hands in fists at my side. "You never denounced his plan."

"Then you didn't stay long enough. Have I not shown you I can be trusted? I killed one of my own men in defense of your honor."

I shook my head. "He could have been someone you wanted to kill anyway for insubordination, and I was only the excuse. How am I to know? I barely know you!"

He took a step toward me. "You know me enough to almost kiss me."

His words snatched away my breath. "Perhaps, but I didn't."

"You want to," he said, and that fire I'd seen before in his eyes lit again. "You want to do more than that."

Heat scorched my cheeks. "What right do you have to say such things to me?"

"I have no right, and I can't make you trust me either. You can always come up with a counterargument, but in the end, you will have to choose: Will you be my ally and trust me, or not? Besides," he said with a grin, "did you believe I could ever hold you captive against your will?"

The last of my anger escaped me in a sigh. "I don't know what to believe of you, that much is clear."

"We're allies, and I would never betray my ally. I am a man of my word. Honor is the only code we uphold, and I would die for it."

His words rang true, and I had to admire that about him. It almost made me feel bad that I'd doubted him. "Then how did you leave things with the king? Was he not angry when you refused to hold me captive?"

"Furious, actually. But not enough to dare test his might against mine. You have nothing to fear from him."

"There are worse things in this castle than a pompous little king," I said.

Leif stilled. "What do you mean?"

"I came upon one of those hideous men from last night . . . cannibalizing my maidservant. He may not have been the size of a giant, but his strength was far beyond a mortal man's. Can you make any sense of it?" I was reminded, suddenly, of the old gods appearing to us as crows and ravens and stags. "Do they have the power to transform themselves?"

His brows furrowed. "Many of the jötnar have power over the elements, even over nature itself, but I haven't heard of the ability to transform."

I thought of the awesome beauty of nature, and nightmarish images of the snake-nosed Northman tearing into Aideen's arm filled my mind. "But surely their behavior goes against nature. . . ."

"Not all the jötnar are evil. Even Lord Odin's mother is jötnar."

I shook my head at him. "And you didn't think this was information I should know?"

"It never came up. The jötnar we must destroy are the ones who call themselves the Bane of Odin."

I remembered the king saying that during his conversation with Leif, and I frowned. "Are those . . . creatures we saw last night in league with Sigtrygg?"

Leif considered for a moment. "Sigtrygg is constantly seeking strong allies, and I'm sure they took advantage of that. I wouldn't put it past the king to join forces with them. I think Sigtrygg may be even more interested in raids than my own people. He isn't satisfied with merely being king of Dyflin; he wants to be king of all of Éirinn."

My stomach dropped at the news. "I knew he had designs on Mide, but I didn't realize he was that power-hungry."

"Enough so that he would form an alliance with abominations," Leif said, disgust clear in his voice. "We shouldn't remain in this city for much longer. The creature that attacked you—where is he now?"

"I killed him." I touched my neck and took a shuddering breath. I could almost feel his hands around my throat once again.

"Alone? If he was truly jötnar, then how could such a thing be possible? Did the Morrigan lend you aid?"

I shook my head, for once unoffended by his skepticism. The snake-nosed Northman was a superior foe; by all rights, I should have been dead. "I can't explain it. He nearly choked the life from me, but I was able to grab hold of his mind and fight back. When I did, something strange happened. . . ." I trailed off as I tried to think of the right way to explain what had happened when I could barely understand it myself. "I separated my spirit from my body and was able to crush the giant's heart."

He nodded slowly, and I could tell he was as perplexed as I was. "I thank the gods you were able to—it scares me when

I think of what could have happened . . ." He glanced at my throat and swallowed.

I lifted one shoulder and let it drop as though the mere memory of the battle with the giant—and what I'd found it doing to that poor girl—didn't absolutely fill me with terror.

"Had you ever done that before—separated your spirit from your body?"

I hesitated. "Just once. After the battle in the Faerie Tunnel. I had no idea it was a new manifestation of power." That thought reminded me of Leif's kindness in caring for me, and I felt a blush creep over my bruised throat.

He reached out and ran a finger gently along my jaw. "Are you in pain? I cannot stand the thought of you being nearly killed."

I stifled the delicious shiver that trailed along my spine at his touch. Why did he have this effect on me?

His eyes swept over my body, to the bed behind me. My pulse quickened. Unbidden, wanton thoughts of tearing the clothes from his body, my nails digging into the flesh of his back as I pressed myself against him came upon me. My body filled with heat. At the same time, disgust churned within me. What maid had thoughts such as these? About a murderous *Northman*, no less.

And now, a boy who had no intention of marriage—did the Northmen even marry?—who surely only wanted a night of pleasure, watched me with desire. He was my ally now, yes, but how could I forget that he had been my enemy? My lips parted to bid him good night, but the words would not come.

He took a step toward me, his gaze intent on mine. He was close enough to touch. Close enough to kiss. My breath hitched in my throat. I wanted him. For a moment, the temptation was so intense, I nearly succumbed to it.

He is a Northman, I reminded myself harshly.

I ducked my head and pushed back against his wide chest. "I cannot."

Desire still burned in his eyes, but he took a step back. "You would deny you want this as much as I?" I could hear the disappointment hidden behind his words.

"I don't deny it," I said softly, "but it comes at too high a price."

He took a step back. "I won't push you. It's enough that you continue to trust me."

I flashed him a smile. "I never said that."

A hesitant knock sounded from my door and we both turned. "Brother?" Arinbjorn called. "I must speak with you."

Leif pulled open the door, and Arinbjorn hurried through, his features tense. "The other man has fled. I discovered it just now from a servant."

Leif tensed. "Did the servant see where he went?"

"Only that he took his warhorse and headed toward the north end of the city."

"Then we must follow. Arin, ready the horses. I will bring whoever is sober enough to come."

"I'm sober," Arin said.

Leif put his arm around his brother. "You must stay here. You have the makings of a great warrior, but that time hasn't come yet. Ciara and I will track the other and, after defeating it, return here."

Arin frowned. "I would rather go with you, brother."

Leif's expression brooked no argument. "You're fortunate that I haven't sent you home with an armed guard. You may remain with our men, but you will not go directly into danger."

He nodded stiffly, and I shot him a look of sympathy. I knew it was hard at that age to be told you couldn't fight, and yet I understood why Leif wouldn't want his brother to face such danger. When I was only a little older than Arin, and my powers had barely manifested, I was riding on the beach when I spotted the sails of a Northman raider. I'd begged Fergus and Conall to let me stay, but they'd dragged me from the shore like a wolf will prevent a young cub from joining the hunt. Luckily, that particular battle had gone no farther than our shores.

Arin might have already learned the basics of fighting, but he wasn't skilled enough to face these monsters—none of us were. I glanced down at my torn gown, suddenly desperate to change into my own clothing, my familiar armor. I looked up to find Leif watching me.

"I am sorry you cannot have a moment to rest," he said gently. His eyes fell on my neck, and a muscle in his jaw twitched. "Your throat will likely cause you the most pain."

It was one of many bruises and injuries, but I had long set aside the pain. It would torture me later, when I was at rest, but while I was still active and focused on other things, it was more than bearable. "I'll be fine." I took a step back, away from him and away from the concern in his eyes. "I'll join you in the stables, but first I must change. This gown restricts my movement far too much."

Arin snickered. "Not in pieces like it is."

I shooed him away with an answering grin. "Go. Leave me. I'll join you both soon."

13

After an affectionate good-bye to Arin, who surprised me by throwing his arms around me for an embrace, Leif and I mounted our warhorses. Leif had somehow acquired a massive chestnut horse, its broad back and powerful shoulders strong enough to carry two men comfortably. I suspected he'd merely helped himself to any in the king's stable, and if so, it would be only what the king deserved.

Four of Leif's men had managed to rouse themselves, and after donning chain mail and leather armor, mounted their own borrowed chargers.

Leif brought his horse beside mine, the evening breeze ruffling the silver wolf's pelt he wore over his shoulders. "Remind Princess Ciara of your names again," he said to his men. "It's only right that she should know the names of the men she will fight beside."

"You already know me," Gunnarr said with a grin. He was the one who reminded me so much of Conall that I couldn't help but smile back.

"I am Ulf," another said in a rumbly voice. He was so large I wondered if his horse would be able to keep up with the rest of us.

Another moved his horse forward. "And I am Olafur. You'll remember me because I'll be the one to bring him down— jötnar or not." He grinned menacingly, and the others laughed. I smiled because I would remember him more for the dragon tattoo on his neck.

Leif motioned for the young warrior to the right of me to speak. "Eadric," he said. Both his hair and beard were in elaborate braids. His manner was aloof, as though he was ready to be off and had no time for our introductions. I thought he would prove to be a merciless fighter.

I gave them as graceful a bow as I could from atop Sleipnir. No meaningless platitudes were necessary with this lot; their attention had long since shifted back to Leif.

"We head for the north gate," Leif said, already urging his horse into a canter.

We followed him through the filthy Dubhlinn streets, an unpleasant tugging sensation growing in my abdomen the closer we got to the gates. With the sun setting, the city was loud, filled with people hurrying to finish the day's work. Aside from the sound of the horses, our party was grimly silent.

Leif pulled his charger to a stop once we passed through the north gate. "North?" he asked me.

I scanned the ground for signs of passage, but there were no tracks in the hard, rocky earth to follow. Sleipnir snorted impatiently. A wind teased the ends of my hair as I faced north, and the air turned unnaturally cold.

"North," I agreed.

We urged our horses into a breakneck pace. The farther north of Dubhlinn we went, the colder the wind grew, until it seemed as though nature itself shuddered at the passage of such an abomination.

After hours of galloping until the wind had whipped our faces raw, alternating with intervals of allowing the horses to slow so they would not be blown, we stopped at a stream to let the horses drink.

Leif surveyed the banks warily. "There won't be any other Gaelic monstrosities to slow us, will there?"

Olafur patted his horse, whose sides were already heaving. "Is this land as dangerous as ours, then?"

"I pray not," I said. "I have traveled far across Éirinn and never encountered so much as a wisp, but as soon as I joined Leif on his quest, I have encountered creatures I'd only heard tales of. But then, the hunter in the Faerie Tunnel told us the giants have been disturbing them."

"It cannot be much farther," Olafur said. His small eyes scanned our surroundings. "He didn't have much of a head start."

"We'll catch up," Leif said. His gaze shifted to me and gentled. "Are you ready to ride? You are not light-headed or nauseous from the injury to your head?"

I scoffed. "If you think me so debilitated, then you've made a terrible mistake in choosing me as your partner in this upcoming battle. Even with the odds of six against one, we will be fortunate to escape with our lives."

Amusement shone clearly on his face, and spread throughout the other men, but Leif said nothing as he mounted his horse. A wave of nausea and dizziness assaulted me as I pulled myself onto Sleipnir, reminding me that I hadn't fully recovered. I kept a firm grip on Sleipnir's mane, furious at my body for proving Leif right.

The horses charged forward, ready to resume their steady pace. I let Sleipnir have his head, and he and the stallion Leif rode matched each other stride for stride. The pain of my throat and throbbing of my head threatened to engulf me like a wave, a burning torture with every breath, but I wrestled it back down until all I could feel was the thunder of the horses' hooves.

God knew I would need my strength.

We caught up to the horse-faced jötunn in the dead of night, the moon high above us as though lighting the way. He'd made camp in the middle of a meadow. The cattle in the field kept their distance and stayed huddled together as if they sensed a wolf among them.

He'd lit a great fire, the smoke billowing upward brazenly.

He reclined before it, his back against a tall oak tree. Like the snake-nosed jötunn I'd managed to kill, this one could pass as a regular man from afar. And from his relaxed position, it was clear he didn't fear discovery.

Leif drew his sword, and the others readied their axes and shields. They urged their horses forward, and I followed at a distance. The thunderous pounding of their hooves alerted the jötunn, and he jumped to his feet, his face hideously twisted in the firelight.

He laughed and held out his arms. "You are too late now. We will tear you apart, piece by piece."

At the word *we*, I pulled Sleipnir to a sliding halt, a warning cry to the others dying on my lips. Two other jötnar appeared from the cover of smoke. I'd taken them for trees, but now to my horror, I realized my mistake. We faced three now instead of one, and with a terrible sinking feeling, I knew we'd meet our deaths here in the darkness.

Leif's charge couldn't be halted in time. The first jötunn struck as fast as a bolt of lightning. He ducked out of the way of Leif's sword and cut his horse's legs out from under him with a battle-axe. His horse crashed to the ground, but Leif leaped off his back at the last moment. A clash of metal upon metal sounded in the night as Leif's sword met the jötunn's axe.

Gunnarr and Ulf hurried forward to assist Leif. One of the giants cut Ulf from his horse, his axe sending a spray of blood from Ulf's throat. Ulf fell from his horse with a painful thud.

As the chaos of battle washed over me, I realized that we'd

never discussed strategy. These were seasoned men who'd fought many battles together, and I was used to my own clansmen who knew to cover me while I sought control of the enemy's mind.

The pounding of heavy-booted feet interrupted me before I could decide on the best course of action.

A giant with hair as dark as the night sky thundered toward me, his lips peeled back in a feral grimace. He brought a great axe down, and I dug my heel into Sleipnir's side to dodge the attack. I feared I wouldn't have the strength to meet his blow head-on, so I galloped around behind the giant and swung my sword into his back. He whirled with an angry yell and parried my attacks. With each blow met, he pushed back against my sword until my arm was screaming with the effort. Though I was astride Sleipnir, I didn't have the advantage of height. The black-haired giant loomed above us, so tall that the tips of Sleipnir's ears only reached the monster's knees.

I wouldn't last long in a physical battle, but I needed a moment when I wasn't in danger of having my head cut off to reach out and take control. Ordinarily, I had to make eye contact in order to take over someone else's mind—it was the strongest connection and ensured I had complete control—but the giant wasn't cooperating. However, there was another way. I'd trained only a handful of times at increasing the distance from which I could control another, and my success rate hadn't been high. Still, I would make the attempt here and now.

I wheeled Sleipnir around and galloped a short distance

away—enough to give me a breath of time. Concentrating on the dark-haired giant, I reached out for his mind. Slippery darkness waited for me, as difficult to grab hold of as water. The giant froze. Sweat beaded my brow as I struggled to maintain control. His mind was as powerful as the giant's I'd fought in Dubhlinn—only my sense of his emotions differed greatly. The hatred was there in abundance, toward the Northmen and especially toward their strange gods, but there was more . . . a flash of a woman being carried away by a brawny man with flowing hair and a braided beard.

A part of me wanted to grasp hold of the memory and analyze it—was there more to these savage giants than mindless killing?—but I didn't have that luxury. The giant fought me for control, managing to break free just enough to begin a slow march toward me. I didn't have to be in his mind to know that once he reached me, he'd tear me apart.

Possible solutions raced through my mind. Could I take his life force as I'd done in Dubhlinn? But *how*? Both times, I'd been nearly unconscious. I tried to search within myself for the strange door of light, but all it resulted in was relaxing my hold on the giant.

The earth around me shuddered as his speed toward me increased, and I scrambled to wrestle control again. My head pounded with the effort, but I managed to slow his advance.

I could see only one way out of this: I'd have to hope my hold on him was enough to give real power to an offensive attack. With the barest touch of my heels to Sleipnir's sides, we shot toward the dark-haired giant. I struck out with my sword, my eyes on the area of his chest above his heart, but at the last moment, the giant raised his axe.

My sword bit into his arm, cutting down to the bone. He dropped his axe with a howl of pain. I attacked again, shoving the tip of my blade up into his chest. A flash of surprise drifted across our mental connection, followed swiftly by thoughts of the woman again and intense feelings of love and regret.

His mind went dark as he crashed to the ground, leaving me standing rather dumbfounded.

All around me, the sounds of axes striking each other was nearly deafening. Gunnarr aided Leif while Olafur and Eadric battled the giant who'd killed Ulf. Most of the others had been divested of their horses. The poor beasts' bodies lay in mangled heaps upon the ground, and a sharp, sudden fear stabbed through me as I thought of Sleipnir. Never before had I feared for my great warhorse, but these weren't normal men.

To my right, the jötunn that Olafur and Eadric battled shook the earth with his every movement. The warriors were forced to dodge the giant's feet like mice. A terrible, strangled yell momentarily drew my eye. Olafur had misstepped, and the jötunn had crushed him. Eadric hacked at the jötunn's giant ankles as the monstrosity chopped Olafur's head from his body. Without Olafur's aid, Eadric would soon fall.

My eyes closed in concentration, I reached for the giant's mind. I connected with nothing but empty air—the distance was too great—but Sleipnir shot toward the enemy with barely any urging. Eadric's shield gave way under the giant's powerful blow, and I grabbed for the giant's mind, finally connecting in time to keep him from crushing Eadric under another hit from his axe.

But all too soon, my fragile hold slipped away. My many wounds had reopened and were bleeding freely. My muscles shook with fatigue.

Out of the corner of my eye, I saw Leif battling with the horse-faced jötunn. To my surprise, the monster was now as tall as the other giants.

Despite the horse-faced giant's size, Leif seemed able to deflect his attacks, the muscles of his arm bulging as though they would soon burst free. With a loud shout, Leif executed a series of attacks so rapidly, I could barely track them with my eyes. The giant, too, could only defend himself against but a few of them. A great torrent of blood gushed out from the giant from multiple wounds, but before any of us could relish our victory, the giant slammed into Leif and knocked him to the ground. He immediately seized Gunnarr and crushed him.

Three were now dead.

Again the fear raced through me, that we would never leave this battle alive.

Leif's eyes met mine, and I watched his mouth begin to form the word *retreat*.

Before he could, the remaining two giants towered over us, and I felt the first dark tendril of despair wrap around my heart. Sleipnir wheeled around, taking me to safety against my will. The horse-faced giant took hold of Eadric by the arms and swung his body out toward the other giant. The other giant grabbed hold of Eadric's legs, and both giants pulled.

They tore Eadric in half amid agonized screams and the sounds of torn flesh and tendons, his body pulling apart at the joints as easily as a roasted duck.

Outmatched, weakened, and easily defeated, we had no chance—but I still had my horse. Beneath me, Sleipnir's muscles quivered, waiting for my command. My heels barely touched his sides, and he shot forward.

My breaths came in pants as my heart pounded almost painfully against my chest. My hand shook so badly from fear and fatigue that I could barely hold my sword. Still, I reached for the horse-faced giant's mind. I couldn't use him as a bodyguard, but I could stop him. It felt like my mind would tear apart, the pain almost blinding. But I couldn't give in to it.

The horse-faced giant froze in place. His face twisted with the effort of fighting against me, and dark spots danced before my eyes as I felt my fragile hold on him give way.

The giant raised his axe to deliver what would certainly be a death blow, and Sleipnir jumped out of the way so suddenly I lost my seat.

I landed hard, my breath leaving my lungs in an instant. With my gaze skyward, I saw a black bird making slow circles above us.

In one stride, the horse-faced giant was upon me again. It was my own mental powers that kept me breathing—I forced my protesting lungs to draw air. I rolled to the side to avoid his axe. He brought it down again, but this time, it met with a clang of metal. Leif stood between us, meeting the giant blow for blow.

I stumbled back to my feet. The earth trembled, and I jerked my head up to see the other giant bearing down on us. As fast as he was, he was slowed by obvious injuries to the tendons in his legs. I watched Leif repeat the move on the horse-faced giant before us. He slid beneath the axe's downward swing and sliced the giant just above the ankle.

With a roar, the horse-faced giant stumbled back. Leif stood in front of me, blocking my body with his as the other giant reached us.

Up close, their height was dizzying. One's head was so massive and deformed, it looked like a craggy mountain face. Leif charged, but the giant grabbed him like a child would a toy. He held Leif aloft, his fingers tightening around the entire middle of Leif's body. In moments he would be crushed like an insect.

My mind lashed out, snatching the giant's like a bird of prey. Something warm and wet began to drip out of my nose. I forced him to drop Leif and touched the tip of my finger to my upper lip. It came back red with blood.

The next instant, I was airborne.

The horse-faced giant roared in my face. His fingers were longer and thicker than my legs, and he wrapped them ever tighter around my middle. I struggled wildly, trying to gain even an inch of breathing room. His grip only tightened. I bit down on the finger nearest me, but there was no reaction.

Leif shouted as the giant who held me in his hand kicked him viciously in the ribs.

Releasing the other giant, I called again, and the power within me struggled to respond. The horse-faced giant's fingers continued to close around me until with a scream, I felt every rib give way. With a burst of energy born of desperation, I blocked out the pain and switched my hold to his mind. His fingers lost their grip on me, and I fell in a broken heap next to Leif. If Leif had the power to heal himself of such trauma, it would certainly not be in time.

Through my haze of agony, I felt a warmth touch my fingers. Leif had reached out to me, his hand just brushing mine. I longed to grab hold, but I could no more wiggle my fingers than I could stand. My sweet sisters' faces flashed before my mind; a pain far deeper than that of my broken bones twisted inside me. I had failed them.

A dark desperation gripped me as the horse-faced giant laughed above us. I wouldn't lie here limply and accept my fate. I would not.

Something snapped within me, even as the blood streamed from my nose and my many wounds. My eyelids fell closed, darkness swallowing me whole. The door of light appeared once again, though this time, I could sense movement beyond the threshold.

Pull yourself through, a voice called.

Not without him, I thought.

With the last of my waning strength, I took hold of Leif's hand. I could sense the giants looming above us. Inwardly, I dragged myself and Leif toward the door.

Agony shattered my body in a million pieces. The black nothingness of death threatened to take hold, but I fought it, my gaze fixed on the lit doorway.

I fell through, my fingers entwined with Leif's.

In a free fall, our bodies descended through blinding white light.

And then there was nothing.

14

I blinked slowly into awareness. Bright sunlight beat down on my body, deliciously warm. The grass cradled me like the plushest down. A soft breeze teased my hair and stirred the leaves in the tree above me. But in a rush, I remembered.

I jolted upward as if I'd been branded, coming to my feet in a surge. I braced myself for an onslaught of pain, but there was nothing. When I gingerly touched the sites of my old wounds, I found nothing but healed skin.

A copse of trees surrounded me. They were like wardens of the woods, their leaves gently waving in the breeze. The trunks were so wide and gnarled there could be no doubt they were ancient, and for a moment, every muscle in my body tensed. Surely we had not stumbled into the Faerie Tunnel again.

"Leif?" I called, softly at first, then with increasing anxiety when I heard no response. I spun in a circle, my heart pounding rapidly. "Leif!"

The breeze picked up, drawing my eye to the softly rustling golden hair on Leif's head.

He lay in the shade of one of the enormous trees, his limbs jutted out at strange angles to his body, as though he had been flung to the ground in a state of unconsciousness.

I sprinted to his side. Painful talons of fear held me in their grip as I watched his chest for the telltale rise of a breath. His clothing was shredded, but the skin underneath was smooth, as though already healed. After an agonizing moment, he took a breath. It was shallow, but there. Relief made my shoulders sag.

"Leif?" I said again softly. His eyes fluttered, but he did not stir.

My gaze traveled from his chest to his legs; even his leather leggings had been torn apart, yet there was no blood, no bruising, no sign we had nearly left this world. How long had we been here?

Tentatively, I moved the leather and chain mail covering his torso aside, but as soon as my fingers touched the warm skin beneath, Leif's eyes flew open.

I jumped back as though scalded, and his lips twisted into an ironic grin. "By all means, princess, continue your intense scrutiny," he said in a voice much gruffer than usual. "I can only hope you have found everything to your liking."

Warring desires to embrace him and choke the life from him

vied within me. I settled for glaring.

"Surely I do not deserve such a look after once again narrowly missing the chance to walk down the halls of Valhalla."

Mollified, I softened my expression. "I was examining you for injury. Have you healed so quickly, then?"

With a groan, he rolled to his side before pushing himself laboriously to his feet. He swayed for a moment as if he'd lose his balance, and I darted out my hand to steady him. "Not even I can recover so quickly from such a battle." His gaze swept over me. "Though it appears you have."

"You speak the truth, but I don't how it happened. I don't even know where we are."

"I'm sure it's somewhere with an abundance of Celtic monstrosities," Leif said, taking in his surroundings with a wary expression. "What's clear is that you transported us somewhere the jötnar couldn't follow."

Now that Leif was on his feet and, if not fully healed, surely on the way to being so, a new anxiety gripped me. "Yes, but how will we return if I don't even know how we got here?"

"We'll worry about that later. First, we must find water."

He strode away as though he knew where he was going, and it was then that I heard it, too—the quiet murmuring of a brook.

We followed the sound to its source, only a short distance from where we had lain. The brook cut a path through the trees, the water so beautifully clear it sparkled like gemstones as the sunlight struck it. Leif cupped his hands and drank without hesitation, gulping greedily. Watching him drink, I became suddenly aware of my own thirst, my throat as dry as sand. Eagerly I knelt down, cupped my hands, and drank. The water was as cold as a mountain stream, and so sweetly delicious, I drank numerous cupfuls before my thirst was finally quenched.

Wiping the excess water with the edge of my cloak, I sank back on my heels.

Leif sat down heavily beside me, and for a moment, we stared at the stream and breathed. "I think it's time we figured out where we are," he said.

"What do you remember?" I asked, thinking of the shining doorway.

Leif's jaw tightened. "All of my men dying. The jötnar nearly killing us both. And . . ." His eyes shifted from the water to my face. ". . . your hand upon mine."

His intense gaze captured my attention for a moment, and I bit the inside of my cheek just to prevent my traitorous body from closing the distance between us. I glanced down at his hand beside me, the visible tendons and veins proof of its strength. And yet we had failed.

I imagined the jötnar continuing their path of destruction all the way to Mide, and my breaths came faster. "A doorway appeared in my mind, and a voice told me to pull myself through." I met his gaze. "But I couldn't leave you."

He touched my cheek with the hand I had only just been admiring, warmth spreading down my body. "I'm grateful you saved me. I'm only sorry you had to. It's clear we were spared so the quest will continue. We'll find a way back."

But what then? With all our strength, we barely survived. I couldn't say the thoughts aloud, as though giving voice to them would grant them power over me.

A whispering came from the trees above us. Subtle at first, like a soft breeze rustling the leaves. It soon grew to a level where it was apparent words were being exchanged, though the language was beyond either of our understanding. It sounded as organic as water flowing over rock, or the wind howling through branches.

I glanced back at Leif, and he nodded—an unspoken acknowledgment that we were not alone.

The water joined in, murmuring in the same language as the trees, adding to the cacophony. Amid this chaos, a door appeared within the tree nearest us, and a brightly lit beast stepped through.

It was a graceful, long-legged dog, its fur tawny as a lion's. It watched us with intelligent gold eyes. In those eyes, I could almost make out another form, a willowy figure of a woman. Another goddess?

"I see you have found the healing waters," a softly melodic voice said, whispering through the trees and into our minds. It seemed these were not the dog's words, but rather another being speaking through the dog. The dog's intelligence was clear, but I believed the true owner of the voice used the dog to allow her to see without being physically present.

The dog's expression was open and friendly, but even so, I remembered my last encounter with an animal imbued with immortal powers. I'd have to choose my words carefully. "We beg forgiveness if we've trespassed. We were in a battle for our lives, and whatever I did to bring us here was an act of desperation."

"You can't trespass if you are invited. And I know all about your battle; your wounds were tended to."

"Then I hope you'll pass along our thanks to whoever was kind enough to tend us," I said. "May I ask, then, where are we?"

"You are in the realm of the Tuatha Dé Danann," the voice said. "I am Brigid."

A little jolt of recognition ran through me. "You are the goddess of healing," I said, mostly for Leif's benefit. "It must be you to whom we owe our thanks."

The dog made a soft sound of acknowledgment.

"What I don't understand, though," I said, "is how we got here." I thought back to the terrible moment when Leif and I had nearly died, when the door of white light had opened in my mind. What was different about *this* time?

"Someone opened the door on this side—the door that connects our realm to yours," the voice said, as though any of that made sense.

Leif and I shared a confused look. "And how long have we been here?" Leif asked.

"This realm is one without time," the voice said, "but in your land, several weeks have passed."

I felt the color drain from my face; my head pounded a

213

warning. Not again. Nightmare images of my sisters and clansmen at the mercy of those monstrosities flashed before my mind. Plenty of time to continue to Mide. Plenty of time, even, to sail north to Leif's homeland for reinforcements. As far as they knew, the only two warriors with the power to stop them had disappeared.

"Weeks?" Leif demanded, his expression as grim as mine. "We must go back."

The dog's head tilted to the side. "If you were to return now, how long do you think you could survive against the Norse abominations?"

Leif's jaw tightened. "We lost this battle, but we learned from it. We won't fail again."

"You have both been given great gifts; Ciara, you were born with otherworldly power." The golden eyes of the dog met mine before shifting to Leif. "And you, Leif, made a pact to achieve it."

I stepped closer. "Who am I? How was I born with such power?" Something like awareness teased the back of my mind, as if I stood on the threshold of answering a great mystery.

"You will know—in time. The knowledge now would only hinder you, and it is not my truth to tell. Though by now you must realize you are not mortal." Her words hovered in the air. I'd always known I was something more than human, but it was still as shocking as a blast of ice-cold wind to have it confirmed by an ancient being.

The desperation to know the truth about my power didn't

lessen with her warning, but I knew arguing with her decision not to tell me was most likely futile. I tried a different tack. "Then am I immortal?"

Her eyes met mine, wisdom swirling in their depths. Again, I saw the figure of a woman hidden within. "You mean, can you not be killed? The answer is that you will live much longer than your fellow man, and yet, a well-aimed arrow could still take your life. It is this touch of immortal blood that has brought you here."

"If I am immortal," I said slowly, still wrapping my mind around the revelation, "then are we powerful enough to defeat the jötnar?"

"You say you have learned from your battle, but it is not I who can determine that. You must go and speak with one who is the most experienced in war. She will give you the advice you both need if you are to defeat the giants."

I was almost positive she spoke of the Morrigan, especially since this was the realm of the Tuatha Dé Danann. "Forgive me," I said, "but why can't the people of this realm aid us by fighting the giants? Surely you're more experienced and powerful, and if you were to lend us your aid—"

But the dog shook its golden head. "Once, we could have done so. Once, we could have walked upon the land and made physical changes to it. Now it is the Christian God who rules Éirinn, and we are only shadows of what we once were. We have physical forms only in this realm. Even healing you had to be done in this realm instead of the mortal world—there, we can only act through visions or appear as animals."

I glanced at Leif and thought of the Valkyrie. "And what of the gods of his land?"

The dog's gaze landed on Leif. "They have a greater hold there, but even their influence is slipping. They sought out the greatest warrior in their land to help aid in the fight against the giants, and they asked that we send our most powerful warrior. When we realized Éirinn itself was in danger, we agreed."

It was hard to believe I would be considered by anyone to be the most powerful warrior, and especially by ancient immortal beings, but I also knew there was much of my power that was as yet untapped.

"You are eager to return to your realm," she continued, "but before you go . . ." She indicated with her head a leather bag beside her, unnoticed until now. "Gifts for you."

Tentatively, I took a step forward and retrieved the bag. From within the deceptively small container, I pulled out the most beautiful armor I had ever seen. Black-and-silver leather leggings and chest piece reinforced with chain mail for me, and black-leather-and-chain-mail armor for Leif. Sturdy leather boots for us both. Leif smiled when I pulled free his silver wolf-pelt mantle; whether it was new or merely repaired, I could not tell.

"These are beautiful gifts," I said, stroking the supple leather.

"Beautiful and useful," the voice said. "You will find them to be stronger and more agile than other armor. The chain mail will deflect any blade."

"Armor even Freyja and Odin would be proud to wear," Leif said. "You have my thanks."

"And mine as well," I said.

The dog nodded before taking a few steps away. She paused and looked back, the invitation to follow clear.

A breeze swirled around me then, the whisper of a kiss atop my head. "There is greatness in you, Ciara of Mide, beyond even what you have accomplished so far. It matters little where your power comes from, only that you have been given it to protect your people as the Tuatha Dé Danann once did."

An answering hope bloomed in my chest.

The tawny dog wove agilely through the ancient forest, dappled sunlight making the leaves shimmer above us. Gone was the melodic voice, and though the dog seemed to have an intelligence far beyond that of a normal beast, the sensation that a powerful being had taken possession of it had disappeared.

The farther it led us, the darker the woods became, until even the tree trunks were black. A mist snaked through the trees, cool against our legs, and almost as high as the dog was tall. Here, the once-dappled sunlight struggled to penetrate the dark leaves, casting everything in shadow. The dog trotted along at a steady pace, but even it seemed more alert, its ears twitching this way and that. There was a pregnant silence, like the way the air seems to shiver in anticipation for a coming storm.

Leif, who had been following closely at the dog's heels, fell back until he was beside me. "After encountering hellhounds the last time we were in the woods together, we should stay close."

I nodded once, moving toward him until our arms brushed with each step. Much as I hated to admit it, I took comfort from his closeness, from the feel of the warmth radiating off his body.

A rustling drew my attention to the branches above. Countless shiny, dark eyes stared down at us. I touched Leif's arm, indicated with my chin the murder of crows watching us.

One opened its beak. *Caw-caw-caw.*

Soon another joined in, and another, until the trees were full of the cawing of crows.

Even the dog flinched. She came to a stop in front of us, and Leif and I tensed into fighting stances. The birds began flapping their wings until the forest echoed with the sounds of them.

Then, just as suddenly, the crows fell silent. Black smoke poured from the roots of the trees, slithering along the ground. It stopped mere feet away and solidified into a figure.

She was dressed as though prepared for battle, attired completely in supple black leather nearly identical to the set I'd been given. It clung to her like a second skin. Her head was still that of a crow, and beside me, I could feel Leif shudder.

The Morrigan's eyes bore into mine, her expression unreadable. When she finally spoke, her voice so harshly distorted by the crow's beak, I flinched as though anticipating a blow. "I see Brigid has healed you both, though you scarcely deserved it after losing that battle so spectacularly."

At that, the dog made a chuffing sound as if in farewell. She shook herself off once before bounding away like a deer, disappearing into the mist.

While our attention had been on the dog, the Morrigan had moved closer. Now she stood only a foot away. She leaned still closer, and Leif tensed beside me. "Hear me, Northman. You will both fail. An army of men could never defeat the jötnar—even with your power. This last battle proved that. You failed because you still fight separately. You"—her crow eyes found Leif's—"have the strength and fighting ability of a god. And you"—those eerie eyes slid back to mine—"have the mental prowess to command an army of men. Yet you do nothing to combine those powers. You are both arrogant and foolish beyond measure."

Her words prickled against my skin. I thought of Leif and me battling two different giants—why hadn't I immediately gone to his aid? It seemed obvious now that I should have taken control of the first giant's mind long enough for Leif to bring him down. And yet I was so used to relying mostly on my own abilities. Was it hubris, then? Did I believe I was strong enough—physically and mentally—to defeat a giant on my own? "If we learn to work together, then will we be able to overcome them?" I asked.

The Morrigan tilted her head. "Perhaps. But then again, there is another way." She took another step forward until I could feel the cold emanating off her as surely as I could feel Leif's warmth beside me. "In addition to her many other abilities, Ciara has the ability to call upon an army of great power."

A jolt of surprise ran through me. "But how? I—"

"It requires a great sacrifice." Her eyes darkened, turning to two drops of blood for a fleeting moment. "A blood sacrifice."

I took a step back. "Then, no . . . I could not—"

"How many?" Leif asked, his face a mask of stone.

A slow, awful smile curved the Morrigan's lips. "The Northmen do not shy away from blood sacrifices, do they? The blood of two hundred men must be offered as payment."

The breath rushed from my lungs as though I had been knocked onto my back. "It cannot be done—it will not be done."

"Tell me more of this army," Leif said.

I grabbed his arm. "Stop this. The price is too high."

"The price is high," the Morrigan agreed, "but the price will be higher still for Éirinn if you do not pay it. I have foreseen it: without this army, you will fail. Even now, the jötnar have returned to Skien in the north, and Fenris will bring this battle to our shores." Her attention shifted to me. "I have shown you the consequences, Ciara, and you still tell me the price is too dear?"

Panic bubbled up within me, as I faced this choice I could never make.

"Tell us of the army," Leif repeated.

"It is composed of warriors who cannot die, of men who are accomplished in battle." The Morrigan leveled her gaze at Leif. The feathers upon her head quivered for a moment. "They are warriors who have already died."

15

The crows above us flapped their wings at the Morrigan's pronouncement, and icy cold water swam through my veins. "How can the dead fight battles?" I asked.

"They are the army of the undead," the Morrigan answered cryptically. Her gaze shifted to Leif. "This one knows of fallen warriors who live to fight again. He hopes to be welcomed into the halls of Valhalla himself one day."

A look of surprise and almost hope flashed across Leif's face. "Do you mean that Ciara will be able to call upon the *einherjar*?"

Frustration grew within me. "Who are the *einherjar*?"

"I believe he's referring to the warrior souls who are taken by the Valkyrie to Valhalla," the Morrigan said, a glitter of amusement in her eyes. She turned her attention back to Leif.

"But Ciara is a daughter of Éirinn. She cannot call forth the *einherjar.*"

Leif's disappointment was clear in the drop of his shoulders.

"If not them, then who?" I asked.

"Your own people," the Morrigan said. "Brigid gave you gifts of armor, but I have swords that will pierce even the tough flesh of the jötnar." She pulled two swords from the mist at her feet, swords nearly as tall as Leif. "For you, Northman," she said, handing him a sword with an ornately tooled grip. A Celtic knot made up the pommel. "This is Vengeance, so named because it feeds on the need for revenge." She turned to me and presented me with a sword as beautifully crafted, only the pommel was a miniature skull. "And for you, Ciara of Mide, I give the Sword of the Fallen."

I took it reluctantly. As soon as my hand wrapped around the grip, the sword thrummed, coming to life as though it had been asleep.

"This sword is the key to summoning the army of the undead." Her tone turned sly. "Wouldn't you like to give the dead a noble purpose?"

"Not at the cost of damning their souls," I snapped.

The Morrigan's eyes flashed menacingly in the shadowed light. "Then you have sentenced the people of Éirinn—and your remaining sisters—to death."

Anger rose so fast within me I nearly choked on it. "You wanted me to fight for this quest and so I have, but if this was your intention all along, then I will not be manipulated. Leif and I will fight together, and we'll defeat the jötnar, backed by an army of men with flesh and blood and beating hearts." I shook all over, the sudden fury causing my vision to redden on the edges. "Tell me how to return."

The Morrigan stared at me for several moments, her expression dangerous. It was only my boiling anger that kept me from fearing that she would tear out my heart as easily as she had the hellhounds'. "You need only open the door."

As soon as she said it, I became aware of the other part of me, the ethereal part that could open doors of light and steal a jötunn's life force. I indicated for Leif to follow me before striding away, eager to be free of the Morrigan's tainted presence.

I'd nearly made it out of the crows' wood before I realized Leif wasn't behind me. I swung around, only to find the Morrigan and him finishing a conversation. Leif nodded once and turned away. Anger writhed within me at the thought of his taking the Morrigan's side. "What were you discussing?" I asked as soon as he caught up to me.

His eyebrows were drawn down low over his eyes, as though he was lost in thought. He glanced up, and a wry smile appeared on his face. "I was begging her not to kill you, princess. Ancient war goddesses don't savor being scolded like children."

My eyes narrowed. "I doubt that. You're no silver-tongued peacemaker."

"It doesn't matter. I'll stand by you, Ciara. Summoning the army is your choice to make. We'll fight the jötnar together." His smile turned teasing. "I'm not sure what use an army of dead Celts would be anyway."

I returned his smile in spite of myself, my anger draining away as quickly as it had come. "Then we must return."

I closed my eyes and sank down within my mind as easily as submerging myself in a bath. The sound of the wind in the trees, the rustle of animals, everything but the sound of my heartbeat disappeared. I could see the doorway, light shining just beyond. With my eyes still shut, I reached for Leif's hand, felt its calloused warmth strong against my own.

In my mind, the door became as big as a castle's, the yellow light as bright as sunlight.

I stood upon the threshold with Leif's hand firmly in my own. The light engulfed me, and I let myself fall.

The sickly sweet scent of rotting flesh was the first sensation to greet me as I stumbled, disoriented and nauseated in a field. A cow's low came to me on the breeze, and I blinked my bleary eyes. Slowly, Leif came into focus. He was crouched next to me, head down, as though he was as disoriented as I was. Somehow we were clothed in our gifted armor, though I had no memory of putting it on. I leaned on the hilt of my sword.

And then I saw them—what was left of the men we had fought with.

Skeletal fingers lay near me, the meat picked from the bones. A torso just beyond them, ribs exposed, the remaining flesh putrid and covered in flies. I covered my nose as the wind changed direction, blowing the smell of the fallen Northmen toward us. Bones were scattered about as though animals had feasted upon them, though I had my doubts the remains had been set upon by animals at all, having seen what the jötnar were capable of.

The breeze caused something long and black to flutter upon the rocky ground, and I froze.

Leif came to his feet, and I gripped his arm, my fingers digging into the muscle. I blinked rapidly, tears already obscuring my vision.

"Ciara?" Leif said, but then he saw it, too.

I took one step, and then another, until I fell to my knees beside what remained of my beautiful warhorse. They'd torn him to pieces, the dull gleam of bone so garish against the red of his flesh. His mane had been what caught my attention, attached to his severed head. The eyes were rolled back until only whites showed.

Tears streamed down my face until I could no longer stifle the sobs. I'd had this horse since he was a colt; I'd trained him myself. Losing him was like being exiled all over again, like losing the last piece of my connection to home . . . to Mide. Worse still was the *way* he was killed. He must have been terrified.

"Forgive me, Sleipnir, forgive me," I said over and over. Tears burned over my cheeks, falling like rain. I was choking on my words, choking on the sobs in my throat.

Leif placed a firm hand on my shoulder. I trembled as anguish and grief crashed over me. He hauled me to my feet and into his arms, and I held on to him as though he was the only thing keeping me standing. "We'll gather what's left of them and build a great pyre," he said into my hair. "They will have the funeral they deserve."

He held me until I no longer felt like the grief would pull me under like the tide. Slowly, he disentangled himself from me and walked over to a tree with a trunk only a little bigger than his leg. With a powerful swing, so fast his mystical blade blurred, Leif sliced the sword through the trunk as though it was nothing more than straw.

The tree plummeted to the ground, and we set to work cutting branches from it and gathering enough dried sticks to build the pyre. It was difficult work, and Leif had to guide me in the building of it, as I had never done anything like it before. My body relished the work, and my mind was thankful to have a goal.

Night had fallen by the time we finished.

When only Sleipnir remained to be added to the pyre, Leif stopped me as I bent to retrieve Sleipnir's head, the tears blurring my vision. "Allow me to do this for you."

I shook my head. "No, you've already gathered the men who you had known and fought beside. I won't have you bear my grief as well."

"It's no burden," he said, but he stood aside when he saw the determined look in my eyes.

I picked up what was left of Sleipnir and carefully placed it on top of the pyre. Stroking his cheek one more time, I bowed my head. "Forgive me, Sleipnir. You deserved far better than this."

Leif handed me one of the torches he had lit. His expression grim, he touched the flame to the bottom of the pyre. "Fenris and all the men and jötnar who have joined with him will be destroyed."

I added my own flame to the pyre. Soon, the jötnar would burn, too, and I would be the one to light the fire.

"We must continue on to Mide before we return to Dubhlinn," I said to Leif as we huddled before the light of our campfire. In the distance, the funeral pyre still burned. Exiled or not, I couldn't continue without knowing my family was safe. So much time had been lost between when I'd left and now. "I must be sure my sisters are safe. And . . . we will need more horses."

"And after we reach Dubhlinn?" Leif asked. He turned to look at me, the reflection of the flames in his eyes. "You told me once before that you would only fight this battle in your own land, but now that you know the jötnar have amassed in the north? What then, Princess?"

Leif and his men would sail on to Skien, leaving the shores of Éirinn far behind. I hated the sea. I'd never even been on a boat, much less a Northman longship . . . but I also knew I couldn't stay here and do nothing.

I met Leif's gaze, and something squeezed my heart when I saw the worry he wasn't bothering to hide. He was afraid I'd say I wouldn't go.

"I will go with you," I said. "I will see this quest to the end."

He reached out and pulled me to his chest. His arms wrapped around me like iron bands. "I'm glad you agreed on your own. I would have carried you away by force if you had not."

I laughed to hide the fact that my heart was now racing erratically in my chest. "You haven't the strength."

His heated gaze met mine, and the laughter died in my throat. My traitorous eyes drifted to his full lips. His mouth descended upon mine before I could protest. With both hands, he cradled my face, his tongue teasing my lips until I opened them.

Our tongues met, and the reaction within me was like the sudden flash of lightning. I wanted to tear his chain mail from his body, to run my fingers over the smooth skin beneath. The pull of lustful desire was so strong, I shook with it. As heat built inside me, my mind sought to remind me this was a man who had no right to touch me so familiarly, who was a Northman, but I was deaf to it all. His fingers trailed down my neck, leaving burning heat in their wake.

More, I thought, deepening the kiss.

I had never been kissed before—no man would dare.

I do not ask, he had said, *I take*.

I shouldn't have enjoyed it. But I did.

"Finally," Leif said as he trailed kisses down my neck. "I've wanted to do this for a long time."

I tilted my head to give him better access, a small sound escaping me as his lips touched the sensitive skin. But just at that moment, the flames from the funeral pyre caught my attention, and I stiffened. The acrid stench of burning flesh wafted toward me. Gently, I pushed against him and leaned back. "This is wrong. We shouldn't do this while the men who fought beside us burn close enough for me to feel the flames."

Leif appraised me with heavy eyelids. "Was it so terrible kissing me, then?"

I felt heat rise from my core all the way to my cheeks in a flush. "No."

"Shall I try again?" he asked, his gaze raising my temperature still more.

Yes. "No."

He nodded as if he'd known that would be my response. I pulled my knees to my chest and rested my chin on them as a cold wind stirred my hair. "I have a proposal for you," Leif said, his voice a mere murmur at my side. "If we spend this night in each other's arms, then I give you my word that I will do nothing but sleep beside you. The night is cold, and we both have lost so much."

There was no manipulation in his voice. Absent, too, was his usual gruff overconfidence. In the darkness, it was merely one soul asking the other for warmth and comfort.

"Just for tonight," I whispered back.

We lay down upon his silver wolf mantle, my back to his chest. He wrapped his arms around me, and as the welcome warmth flooded me, I closed my eyes against the tears that threatened. In Leif's arms, I realized the turmoil and mental anguish I'd felt toward him was unfounded. Leif was a Northman, an outsider, but he accepted me more than any of my own clan ever had.

For I couldn't help but think that no one had ever held me like that, nor had I needed them to.

But on this dark night, I didn't dare pull away.

As the sun rose the next morning, the ground was cool with mist and dew, but the last wisps of smoke of the funeral pyre were still drifting to the sky. I clenched my jaw to keep the tears from flowing anew and bent to touch the pile of ash, picturing Sleipnir as he once was.

Bowing my head, I sent up a prayer for Sleipnir and even the Northmen who had fought beside me. *Give me the strength to exact revenge.*

We kept up a grueling pace on foot all the way to Mide. We were silent and focused, and I missed Sleipnir with every step. In spite of my pushing Leif away, like I had so many times before, things seemed to have changed between us—as though we had both bared part of our souls. For the first time, I felt a breath of hope. With our combined strength, there was little that could stop us.

Buoyed as I was by these thoughts of our near invincibility, the feeling dimmed when I thought of actually going home again. What reception would I receive when I entered the bailey? Would my father bar my entrance to the castle? More important, what would I do if he tried? I knew the answer to that; I knew that I would shout the truth about the jötnar threat from the middle of the castle grounds if I had to. My clansmen might not believe me, but they had a right to know what would soon threaten them—if it wasn't already an immediate threat. Again, a jolt of fear for my sisters shot up my spine. I had to see them again, exile or no exile.

I glanced at Leif running beside me, the sun turning his hair to gold, and I knew that whatever I was about to be greeted with, we would deal with it—together. He caught me admiring him and flashed a smile that I returned easily. A friendship and alliance forged by bloodshed and shared loss.

A gull cried nearby, and I slowed my pace. When I took a deep breath, the salty tang of the ocean breeze filled my nostrils, bringing forth a torrent of memories. The familiar scents of home.

Only . . . another smell presented itself—stronger than the others. The acrid smell of something burnt.

On the crest of the next hill, we stopped. My father's castle loomed before us on the next rise, and the longing for my home struck me in the chest like an arrow.

The smell of burning in the air became stronger, and the

first pinpricks of fear pierced my abdomen. "Wait for me here," I said hurriedly to Leif. "My father would have your head on a spike."

His jaw tightened. "I will not."

"Leif, please—"

He crossed his arms. "Where you go, I go," he said.

I glanced from his determined face to the outline of my father's castle in the distance. I hadn't the time to debate. "Fine. We go together."

We sprinted down the hill and climbed the treacherous cliff-side of my father's castle. Only two guards waited for us at the gates, their faces gray and gaunt.

"Princess Ciara!" said the man I belatedly recognized as Faelan, Fergus's brother. His presence was an ominous sign, as he was a farmer, not a warrior. "What are you doing here? We thought you'd been exiled."

"I was," I said, bracing myself for whatever instructions my father had given him in the event I came home.

"Brádan," he said to the gaunt man next to him, "hurry and notify the queen her daughter has returned."

Confused now that he should send for my mother instead of my father, I take a step toward him. "Faelan, where is my father?" I asked.

Faelan stilled, and the panic that had engulfed me since I smelled fire began to smother me. "Princess, it is not for me to say . . ."

His gaze skittered away from mine, back toward the keep,

the wall of which prevented much of my view, but I was suddenly desperate to see inside.

I grabbed his arm. "My sisters—where are Branna and Deidre?"

"Safe, milady. With your mother in the keep—"

I strode past him, Leif following close behind. I had to see them, had to see my father, who would shed light on what had transpired.

Once we had passed through the gates, the bailey was strangely absent of life. No animals bleated, no voices carried on the wind, no people hurried about their day. As I reached the bailey's center, it became clear where the taste of ash was coming from.

The chapel was a blackened ruin. My first thought was a Northman raid, but there were no other signs. No bloodstains or other remnants of a battle. No other buildings had been damaged, only the church.

I ran to the broken door, my heart pounding. Chains lay in a pile on the steps, links severed as though cut. I hadn't stepped through this doorway for so many years that, for a moment, I couldn't move. My hand shook as I pulled open what was left of the door.

Leif kept me from falling as I let out a strangled cry.

So many bodies, all men, dressed for battle. Weapons littered the floor, or lay clutched in blackened, skeletal hands. The smell of charred flesh, wood smoke, and ash was so strong I leaned over and gagged. Most of the men had died near the door of the church, as though they had attempted to fight their way out.

Shaking, and with tears pricking my eyes from the remnants of smoke, I scanned the bodies for signs of Fergus or Conall.

I stumbled forward, tripping over blackened legs and grasping fingers. Furiously I searched through the ash until my hands were black as pitch. Tears mingled with the ash until fat black droplets tracked down my cheeks. Leif stood guard at the door, his expression grim.

I found what I had been seeking on the steps of the altar. With trembling fingers I retrieved it: my father's golden circlet.

Nearby was a corpse who had fallen still grasping his sword, and I immediately recognized the jeweled hilt. Like the other bodies, the skin had burned away from his bones, but still I knew. Unlike the others, this body had been beheaded. I touched the skull as pieces of me broke away inside. My breaths were coming faster, mingling with my trapped sobs. I clutched the circlet so hard I felt the weakened metal begin to give way.

The anger was building within me, a fire feeding on my uncontained grief. I wanted to find whoever had done this, to tear them limb from limb. I wanted to burn their village to the ground.

A soft noise came from the entrance of the church, and I turned to find my mother standing next to Leif, her face pale and drawn.

"Máthair," I said in a rush, hurrying to her side. "What has happened here? Áthair . . ."

"He is dead," my mother said, her voice raspy and devoid

of emotion, as though she had spent weeks in the throes of grief and hadn't quite emerged as the same person. "He is dead along with some two hundred of your clansmen." Her eyes met mine, and I sucked in a breath in pain when I saw the loathing reflected there. "And you weren't here to protect them thanks to your faithless attack on your own father."

Burned alive. Two hundred men, including my father. The ground seemed to open up and swallow me whole. "Who set fire to the church?"

"King Sigtrygg's men," she said, and Leif's head jerked up. "It happened only days after you were exiled. Sigtrygg was angry that his raid on the monastery had failed because of your father, so they retaliated. He came on a Sunday like the pagan Northman he is," she said with a look of revulsion toward Leif, "and his men surrounded the church. They took the women and men who couldn't fight as slaves, and the others—your father and his men—they slaughtered and locked them in the church to burn."

A horrified silence descended upon me as I thought of what my clansmen and my father must have gone through—and the evidence was still at my feet. As I looked at the remains of what had once been living, breathing men, the number two hundred kept repeating itself in my mind. It couldn't be a coincidence. The Morrigan had made it seem like the sacrifice of two hundred men would be something yet to come—something I would have to choose for myself—but I saw the truth now. The truth was that it had already happened.

Worse, Sigtrygg had come on the Lord's day—just as the Northmen raiders had seven years ago. No doubt the only reason my mother and sisters had survived was because ever since that day, they had attended Mass at a different time from everyone else. In case the church was attacked again. I felt the anger continue to build. How could I have believed that duplicitous king when he told me he and Áthair had come to a peaceful arrangement? My father never would have made a treaty with him.

"And Fergus and Conall?" I asked. "What of them?"

"They were among the two hundred," she said. My stomach rolled. Sleipnir. Áthair. Fergus and Conall. Was there no end to the horror? "As was Séamus."

Her words bit into me, and I couldn't help the flood of images of all the men I'd once loved. I thought of them fighting for their lives before finally being consumed by flames, and tears stung my eyes.

"I don't understand," I said with a desperate edge to my voice that even I could hear. "King Sigtrygg told me he and Áthair had made peace—he said he'd dined with him in the hall."

"He dined in our hall," Máthair said, with such disgust she was practically spitting, "but it was after he'd burned the church to the ground. He forced our servants to wait on him, and he sat across from me as though he hadn't just brutally murdered my husband. He sat there and told me it was his *mercy* that allowed myself and the princesses to live, but I know he's only keeping them alive as a bartering tool—he thinks we answer to him now."

I quaked with revulsion when I realized: my father and the others had already been killed by Sigtrygg while I stayed and dined in his castle. When Sigtrygg threw that great feast, it was because he had been successful in assassinating my father and murdering my clansmen.

"I fail to see how any of this is Ciara's fault," Leif said, his voice steadying me.

She narrowed her eyes. "If she hadn't attacked her father with her loathsome ability, then she would have been here to stop him."

"That seems like poor logic," Leif said, and Máthair's expression grew even colder.

"Máthair," I said, reaching out to her only to have my hand sneered at. I let it drop to my side. "Máthair," I tried again, "I am desperately sorry for what I did to Áthair, and even more sorry and ashamed I wasn't here to defend them against such treachery, but I cannot shoulder the blame for this—this was Sigtrygg's doing. He's the one who should pay."

"Oh, you're sorry, are you?" she said, jabbing her finger toward me. "Sorry won't bring him back! For once your demonic abilities could have been useful!"

She was yelling now, and I was momentarily stunned. I'd never seen her raise her voice like that—it was almost as if Áthair's death had caused her to become unhinged.

"I'm not invincible," I said quietly. "Not even I could have escaped a burning building."

Leif had been listening to our exchange with a concerned look upon his face. Now he gestured toward the remains around us. "Why have they not been laid to rest?"

"This is their tomb now," she said, her voice shaking. She wrapped her arms around herself as though cold and turned her attention back to me. "I should have never agreed to raise you! You've brought destruction upon this family just as I promised your father you would."

I jerked back as though she'd struck me. Her words rang out in my mind, and though I tried to push away the meaning behind them, the horrible sinking feeling was enough to confirm the truth. "Then . . . you are not my mother?" I asked in a small voice that didn't even sound like my own.

"Of course I am not," she said. "You are a monster, born of your father's pathetic moment of weakness. He begged me to raise you as my own baby after I lost my own infant in childbirth. Only your nanny knew the truth, and she died while you were still a child—no doubt because of your malevolent powers."

I felt sick. *No,* I wanted to scream at her. *No, you're lying. No, there has to be another reason why everyone in my family is fair-haired and light-eyed . . . everyone but me.*

With the truth out, Máthair's facade of being a caring mother completely fell away. True loathing was apparent in the flash of her eyes, in the piercing cold of her expression. If my father had strayed from his marriage vows, and I—with all my frightening abilities—was the result, then I almost could not blame my mother for her hatred.

My pulse was pounding in my ears, my vision turning blood-tinged. "Just who am I, then?"

"You are the daughter of the king," she said, disgust clear in her tone, "but it was the Morrigan who bore you." An image of the Morrigan as a crow tearing out the hellhounds' hearts appeared in my mind, and I wanted to claw at my own face. *She's just like her,* my mother had once thought about me. *Too powerful. Too dangerous.* Now I knew who she was talking about.

"She seduced your father on a battlefield, appearing naked before him, and he was so overcome by lust he had her right there among the dead. She would not raise you herself, and we were too frightened of her to refuse. You are cursed, part demon—you taint this chapel by your very presence."

I thought of the memory I'd seen in my father's mind all those weeks ago when I'd taken control of him—of the Morrigan appearing to him on the battlefield—and I felt a piece of my heart shrivel. I thought of the way he'd paled when I'd told him of the Morrigan's vision—the mere mention of the Morrigan's name had frightened him. There had been so many signs, and I'd been foolishly blind to them all.

"Your father banned you from this church, praying it would spare us from God's justice. He turned back to God, tried to atone for his sin on the battlefield, but it was all for naught." My mother's words were like sharp nails piercing my heart. "He died in the end, leaving me alone to deal with . . . everything. Sigtrygg, this kingdom, *you.* I agreed to take you on as my own child, but that was before you attacked your own father. You're dangerous, you've always been dangerous, and now that he's gone, I see no reason to continue the charade." She looked at me in disgust, and something died inside me. "You shouldn't have come back here. There's nothing for you here."

She turned on her heel and started to walk away. I wrapped my arms around myself protectively, hearing the echo of every time I'd been called monstrous and evil, of every fearful look and whispered aside.

I bent forward as though punched in the gut, and Leif reached down and hauled me upright. "She has gone mad with grief. Don't let the poisonous words she spews render you incapacitated," he said into my ear.

I almost let her walk away. I almost let that be the last thing she said to me, but then I thought of my sisters, and this kingdom, and the fact that I was the true heir of Mide.

I felt the warmth of Leif's hand on my arm, strong and comforting, and stood tall. I might have been the daughter of the Phantom Queen, but it was that blood that would allow me to defend my kingdom and my world from the real monsters who threatened it.

"No, you're wrong," I said, and she turned slowly. "This is my kingdom. Those are my sisters—no matter that I only share half their blood. My father was the king, and for better or worse, I was raised as a princess of Mide."

Her eyes narrowed. "It's true. Your father named you his heir, but what good is it now? This kingdom has been claimed by Sigtrygg."

I thought of not just Sigtrygg, but the greater jötnar threat. "Then leave with my sisters while you can. Take Branna and Deirdre and flee to another kingdom; we have other allies—"

"I cannot leave your father," she said in a growl. "Of course I will not abandon him and this clan."

I glanced at the charred remains of the men surrounding us and swallowed hard. She wasn't in her right mind, but I still had to try to make her see reason. With Sigtrygg harboring jötnar under his own roof, Mide could be in very real danger. "Please, Máthair, there are worse things than Sigtrygg that threaten this kingdom. I was given a vision of Éirinn—"

"Stop!" Máthair snapped. "I won't listen to such pagan nonsense. You taint this sacred ground by even uttering such a thing."

"You'd do well to listen," Leif warned. "Your daughters' lives could depend on it."

"And who are you to say?" Máthair demanded. "By the look of you, you are a Northman. What is the true reason, then, for your alliance with Ciara? Did she seduce you as her mother once did the king?"

I flinched at the implication as Leif drew himself up to his full height. "We owe you no explanation."

She turned her attention back to me. "You are not welcome here. With Sigtrygg alive, this kingdom is no longer yours."

It was clear she wouldn't listen to anything we said. And with Sigtrygg in league with the jötnar we'd encountered in Dubhlinn, we didn't have time to make her see reason. I wanted to grab her by the shoulders and shake sense into her, but there was nothing more important right now than the quest.

"We will need horses," I said, choking on the last word. There wasn't a horse in the stables equal to the one I'd lost.

"Take them, then." She wrapped her cloak tighter around her and walked away without a backward glance.

Leif grabbed my arm. "Sigtrygg is responsible for this, and he will be dealt with."

Sigtrygg. I thought of what the pagan king had done to my clansmen, to my father—to my kingdom. The rage grew until all I could see was red. I wanted to find the men who had burned the church and slaughter them like pigs. "I want him dead." Just then my body was filled with an impossible amount of energy, as though I could take on the whole of Sigtrygg's army. It built and built until my muscles thrummed. I tasted blood on my tongue and wanted more.

Leif took my face in his hands and met my eyes. I hated to think what reflected back at him. "Then we will make it so."

"Two hundred men, Leif. They died, and for what?"

Leif was quiet, his eyes searching mine. Finally, he said, "Their deaths needn't be in vain."

The Sword of the Fallen blazed to life on my back. I felt something inside me rise up to answer. "No. This is what the Morrigan wants, what she wanted all along."

"The Morrigan wants our quest to succeed." He took a step back from me. "She told me how to raise the army."

My hands shook with the need to hurt something. "I knew you weren't begging her for my life; I should have never trusted you."

"I told you before that it was your decision. She held me back and told me the ritual in case you had a change of heart."

"A change of—and what, suddenly decide that yes, I wanted to use the blood of two hundred innocent men? She is no benevolent goddess. What if the ritual damns their souls?" My words lashed him like a whip, but he stood unflinchingly before me.

"Regardless of why I was told, these men are dead. They were slaughtered like animals in a place your people consider sacred. You have the power to make their deaths worthy; they will have given their lives to bring forth an army strong enough to destroy the jötnar." His hands curled into fists. "An army strong enough to bring Sigtrygg and his jötnar allies to their knees."

Revenge, the darkness born inside me the moment I walked into the chapel seemed to whisper, or perhaps it was my own mind cracking beneath the pressure of so many unbearable losses. Thoughts of storming Dubhlinn with an unstoppable army rose unbidden to the forefront of my mind.

I knew Leif was right. Sigtrygg could be on his way at this very moment—the hideous jötnar beside him—to finish what he'd started in my kingdom, and I needed an army.

The only things standing between the vile king and my kingdom was us.

I pulled free the Sword of the Fallen. It glinted in the light, and a faint hum came from within the blade. I met Leif's gaze.

"What must I do?"

17

Leif crouched and touched his fingers to the ash and soot upon the floor. "Blood and ash is required for the ritual—your blood."

I glanced down at the gleaming blade. It was as if it whispered what must be done, a quiet voice in my mind. "The sword must be anointed with blood and ash. What then?"

"Then you must say: 'So the Phantom Queen's blood flows in my veins, so shall I summon the army of the undead.'"

I stared at him. "You knew about the Morrigan." I was in complete shock that he hadn't said anything, and I flinched when I remembered what we'd both witnessed of the Morrigan—what must he have thought of me?

"I knew only that you shared blood, not that she was your mother."

"You knew I was kin to such a gruesome being, and yet you . . . kissed me? And now that you know she is my mother . . . ?"

"My desire for you has not changed. What do I care who your mother is? I kissed you when I thought you were all Celt, after all." He smiled teasingly, even amid the carnage at our feet, as only a Northman could. I couldn't yet return it, but I appreciated the gesture nonetheless.

Relief that he hadn't judged me for the Morrigan's horrific actions bloomed in my chest. "I can't express to you how much your words mean to me."

"You could always show me," he said, and his gaze dropped to my mouth. It brought a reluctant smile to my face, even as desire stirred within me. My breath stilled as he reached out and touched a lock of my hair. "Later, then," he said.

I forced my mind back on the task at hand. "After I have performed the ritual, what will happen?"

"She didn't say, but we'll soon find out for ourselves."

A trace of unease spread down my spine even as the Sword of the Fallen thrummed eagerly for my blood. I held out my hand, and with the other, made a shallow cut along the palm. Blood immediately flowed, and Leif took hold of my injured hand gently. He sprinkled the ash he had collected over the wound, the black soot mixing with the dark red.

All at once, my vision darkened at the edges, and all sound seemed to disappear. As though I had performed this ritual a thousand times before, I took hold of the blade of my sword and smeared the mingled blood and ash along it. It disappeared on the blade like water in the sun.

The church was still. I could hear my own heartbeat, the thrumming of the sword in my hand, and a louder pulsing—the heartbeat of another realm. I slammed the point of my blade into the floor and said the words that would summon an army powerful enough to save us all.

An earsplitting *boom* and a wave of power rippled outward. The bodies at our feet crumbled into dust, and the dust was sucked away by the wave of power, leaving nothing but the men's weapons behind. The silence that descended after was deafening.

I took a shaky breath and pulled the sword free. A tremor began, the ground beneath our feet quaking with increasing intensity until the glass of the few remaining windows shattered. A cold fog descended, obscuring our vision. Leif grasped my arm and pulled me close to his side.

The quaking continued, and we braced ourselves for something terrible to come. And then, as suddenly as it had begun, it stopped. The fog ebbed, revealing a ghostly sight.

My father stood before me, two hundred men at his back. My heart sounded like the fluttering of birds' wings in my ears. Gray-faced they stood before us. There was no scent of decay. They were devoid of any smell at all. They were completely outfitted in the same black armor as Leif and I, claymores strapped to their backs. The black of the leather was a strong contrast with the faded color of their skin. It was as though I viewed them from underwater. No details of their bodies aside from the armor they wore could be seen sharply. They were hazy, one foot in this realm, another in the next.

"Áthair?" I asked, unsure if it was truly my father or merely something that resembled him.

"Princess Ciara, daughter of the Phantom Queen, we have heard your summons." He made a fist with his hand and crossed it over his chest in a strange gesture of respect. The others immediately did the same. This, then, couldn't be my father. But just as I doubted it, he said, "Though I never would have agreed to such a blasphemous ritual in life, after being shown the destruction that awaits Éirinn without this army, you have my blessing."

I bowed my head. "Áthair, I'm glad for your blessing, because knowing I couldn't defend you when your life was taken has nearly destroyed me."

"It is not you from whom I crave vengeance."

Before I could respond, a sound drew my attention to the back of the church. It was the sound of a hoof hitting the steps of an altar. A horse as black as pitch trumpeted an impatient whinny. "Sleipnir?" I said in a rush. "How?"

The warriors parted as my massive warhorse approached. His coat was as glossy as a raven's feathers, with no hint of the trauma that had befallen him. But as he drew closer, I saw the difference: his eyes were no longer a horse's warm brown, but rather the deep red of a wraith.

When he was close enough, he dipped his head, snuffling my hands. I threw my arms around his neck, tears slipping down my cheeks. He might have had eyes like the devil now, but he was still Sleipnir. I was not afraid of him.

"The king and your horse have retained their identities," Leif said in the midst of my reunion, "but it would seem the rest of the warriors have not."

I glanced up to find Leif was right. The warriors lined up in perfect rows, their arms still held over their chests, their faces emotionless.

My eyes scanned the warriors, searching for Fergus and Conall. I found them standing at attention, the same as the others. When I approached them, no flicker of recognition appeared on their faces; they remained eerily still. Not far from them was Séamus, and the bleak nothingness I saw reflected in his eyes was almost more painful than seeing his loathing.

"You're right," I said to Leif, deep regret weaving its way into my heart. It had been foolish to believe I could have everything. "They don't know me."

"They know you only as the one who ultimately commands them," Áthair said.

"But you remember who you are?" I asked him.

My father shook his head, and I could see he was only a shadow of himself. "The Morrigan came to me just as my soul left my body. She said as king, I would be given the chance to avenge not only my own death, but the deaths of all my clansmen. I remember only what I need to know to bring vengeance upon King Sigtrygg."

I looked at my horse and wondered if he felt the same toward the jötnar. Had he died swearing he wouldn't rest until he had his revenge?

"You'll have your revenge." Leif turned to me: "I'll find myself a horse, and then we should march on Dyflin. So much time has already passed that I have no doubt that Sigtrygg has begun the march here. If not, we can draw him out of Dyflin. With an undead army, I imagine you won't have to rely on ambushes to defeat him—you can fight in open battle."

He strode out of the church, and I was struck by how much having him here was a help to me. It allowed me to focus on what needed to be done. I turned to address the men, their commander now in death as I had never been in life. "Clansmen, to the gate."

I took one last look at the devastation that'd once been the church, my jaw clenched tightly. With a hand upon Sleipnir's neck, I walked down the steps. My macabre army followed silently behind, even their footsteps muffled.

Once outside, I grabbed a handful of Sleipnir's mane and pulled myself astride. The men continued, marching five abreast in perfect unison. My father had fallen in with the rest of them, and with no crown or robe to differentiate himself from the others, he was difficult to recognize. I was glad; already the explosive sound of the summoning and the sight of the silent warriors had drawn a crowd.

"Princess Ciara," the people whispered.

Faelan, noticing our return, hurried to my side. "Milady, who are these men?" He glanced back at the gates—the only entrance into the bailey—and back. "Where did they come from?"

"You needn't know. All you need know is that we will exact revenge on King Sigtrygg and ensure the safety of this clan."

Sleipnir pawed the dirt with his hoof as though eager to be on our way. I couldn't help but agree. I wanted to be gone before anyone recognized these men. I couldn't imagine my fellow clansmen's reactions when they saw their fallen loved ones resurrected, or worse still, their king. With their gray skin and expressionless faces, the identities of the undead would be camouflaged—but not for long.

Sleipnir's ears pricked forward as Leif exited the stable astride a beautiful dapple-gray stallion—my father's warhorse. The horse was temperamental and difficult to ride with everyone but my father, but Leif handled him easily, the horse as calm as a kitten.

"You've chosen well," I told him as our horses greeted each other nose to nose. "That is Abrax, my father's charger."

Leif gave him a pat on the neck. "I chose him because he was the only one in the stable who seemed eager to leave."

I smiled. "He is almost as bad a warmonger as Sleipnir."

"They'll have their fill of it soon," Leif said. "We should leave now. Are you ready?"

I glanced back at the keep longingly. "My sisters . . ."

Leif reached across the horses and touched my leg. "They're safe, and you'll ensure they'll stay that way."

I knew he was right; knew that every moment we remained brought Sigtrygg ever closer. "Warriors," I shouted, "we march to Dubhlinn."

Leif spurred Abrax on, and the undead men immediately began their silent march. Sleipnir danced in place, eager to move, but I couldn't stop myself from turning back to stare at my father's castle one last time.

"Ciara, wait!" a voice cried then from the right side of the bailey. Branna and Deirdre ran toward me, and I immediately threw myself from Sleipnir's back.

I caught Deirdre in a firm embrace, the hairs of her fur-trimmed gown tickling my cheek. Branna wrapped her arms around my middle as tears pooled in her eyes. "Máthair said you'd been exiled! She said you attacked Áthair and ran off with the Northmen, but we knew it couldn't be true."

"It is true, Bran," I said, feeling as though I would be sick. "I can't explain right now . . . but all of Éirinn is in danger."

"Áthair . . . ," Deirdre said, biting her lip as though holding back her own tears.

I touched her cheek. "I know, Deirdre. I'm so sorry. And I'm sorry I was leaving without seeing you—"

"Máthair has lost herself," Branna said, almost fearfully. "She won't let any of the men bury Áthair. She won't even let us leave the keep, but we saw you from our window."

"I'm so sorry, Bran. I would stay here with you if I could," I said, tears stinging my eyes at the fear in hers.

"Please don't go," Deirdre said, her voice so quiet compared to Branna's.

"I must. With Áthair gone, and no heir to the throne, King Sigtrygg will have no opposition. He will come for Mide, and I won't leave your fates in his hands." I hugged them again, each in turn, wishing I didn't have to let go. I touched Deirdre's pale blond braids, remembering not long ago when her hair was only a few soft wisps. "I love you both so much."

"I love you, Ciara," Deirdre said, her voice thick with sorrow.

"Avenge our father," Branna said, her hands curled into fists.

I hauled myself astride Sleipnir once more. "I will," I promised. "I love you both. Stay safe." After one last glance at my beautiful sisters, I touched my heels to Sleipnir's sides, and he surged forward.

I will return, I promised myself, *and I will never let Mide be threatened again.*

The army marched tirelessly, and though the sun's rays burned overhead, Sleipnir and the men never perspired nor seemed to fatigue. When Leif and I stopped for water, none of the undead partook in it, nor did Sleipnir. My father was as silent as the rest of the men, though perhaps his dark eyes blazed a little more fiercely.

It tortured me to think that Branna and Deirdre were being left behind—possibly in danger—but I knew the best way to protect them was to first stop Sigtrygg, and to continue our quest. It was time the raider king of Dubhlinn was called to task for his crimes.

It was when the sun had already reached its peak and was moving closer to the horizon that everything changed. Sleipnir

nearly unseated me by rearing, and the men who'd been marching silently forward suddenly drew their weapons. Though I
strained my ears, I heard nothing but the wind.

A rocky field lay before us, and beyond that, craggy hills.
"Do you think they sense Sigtrygg's men?" I asked Leif, whose
own eyes were scanning the horizon warily.

Abrax snorted and shook his head, but it seemed he was only
responding to Sleipnir, who danced in place with eagerness. I
freed my sword and Leif did the same.

We continued forward, straining for any sign of an oncom-
ing army. It wasn't until we had trotted for several miles that we
heard them in the distance: horses.

"We have the advantage," Leif said. "Get to the next hilltop
and we will ambush them there."

"Onward," I told my undead warriors, barely able to restrain
Sleipnir from charging forward.

When we reached the top of the hill, Leif and I took the
forward-most positions. My army fanned out and stood silently
at attention, their swords drawn.

"Will Sigtrygg be with them?" I asked Leif.

"He loves nothing more than to raid, and he'll want to be
present to take your father's throne."

Your throne, the Morrigan's voice whispered inside me. "I
want him dead," I said, my hand tightening on the grip of my
sword, "but we should capture him first. We need to know
about his alliance with the jötnar."

"Take over his mind to loosen his tongue," Leif said, with

a curl to his lip, "and then he should be executed. He doesn't deserve to die in battle."

"I make no promises," I said through my clenched jaw. "Once I have what I need from him, I may not be able to help myself."

Just then, riders on horseback crested the next rise, saw us waiting, and charged. The shouts of Sigtrygg's men contrasted heavily with the eerie silence of my own army. "Hold," I said, as much to Sleipnir as to the warriors. "We'll pick them off as they climb the hill."

The first two made the climb; Leif lopped off the first man's head, and my sword bit into the other's chest. Still more and more men came, but not nearly as many as our army. Sigtrygg had brought perhaps thirty men in all, as though he had not expected much resistance. And why should he? He'd killed or enslaved most of my clansmen.

But then I saw the true reason he'd brought so few men: the horse-faced jötunn from Dubhlinn—the one who'd nearly killed us—was with Sigtrygg's army. Though Leif had sliced through his ankle, he appeared without injury. With an ally like that, they wouldn't need many men to defeat us.

The horse-faced jötunn was growing before my eyes, and I knew it wouldn't be long before he was the size of an oak tree.

"Leif!" I shouted, and he glanced back at me. I jerked my chin toward the jötunn. I had a moment where fear threatened to disable me in its icy grip, but I shook it off. No, the outcome of our battle this time would be much different. We would not be defeated by this giant.

Some of Sigtrygg's men broke past us, and I watched my army make quick work of them. They moved with the same unnatural speed Leif had; they tried to block the blows, but the undead men's swords pierced them before they could even fully raise their arms. They fell with hoarse shouts, while my warriors remained ever tight-lipped.

I wheeled Sleipnir toward the closest group of my army. I needed them to focus their efforts on the jötunn. With hand on sword, I pointed with the blade toward the horse-faced jötunn. "Bring him down," I said to my army.

Eleven of them responded immediately, surging down the hillside like a shadowy fog.

But before I could follow them, two of Sigtrygg's men rushed me. While I brought my sword down upon one, Sleipnir attacked the other with such ferocity, my breath caught in my throat. With his ears pinned down and teeth bared, he seemed more wolf than horse. Even the shape of his teeth had changed: no longer broad and flat for clipping blades of grass, but with long, pointed canines. He sank his teeth into the other man's arm, tearing the flesh down to the bone. The man's screams were terrible, and I swung my sword in an arc, slicing his throat just to end his suffering.

When I searched for the jötunn again, I was awestruck to find him on the ground. The giant rolled and writhed in an effort to dislodge my undead clansmen who crawled all over him, stabbing him repeatedly with their swords.

I thought of how the monster had once held both Leif and me in his hands, how I'd truly thought in that moment that we would die, and then I glanced down at my phantom horse. What had he endured after we'd left? They'd killed him and ripped apart his corpse. As if reading my thoughts, Sleipnir charged toward the fallen giant.

But before I could vault down and end the monster, Leif appeared.

His face twisted in fury, he plunged his sword straight through the jötunn's heart. The giant writhed one last time and then was still. With arm muscles bulging, Leif yanked his sword free again. He met my gaze from across the field, chest heaving. But that look said so much: his men who were slaughtered had been avenged.

My undead clansmen immediately moved on to the remaining human soldiers, and I followed.

"Sigtrygg!" Leif shouted, and I followed his line of sight to Sigtrygg astride a dark gray charger. In contrast to his plainly armored soldiers, the king wore robes trimmed in fox fur, a small circlet of gold upon his head. Rage boiled up in me at the sight of him, and Sleipnir threw back his head and trumpeted a warning.

Before Leif could charge after him, more of Sigtrygg's men attacked, dividing Leif's attention. I was on my own.

I didn't even need to touch my heels to Sleipnir's sides— he galloped toward the king without prompting, his ears flat against his head. Sigtrygg was pale—he knew what I was capable of—but he raised his sword to meet mine.

Our blades rang out across the field. Sleipnir took a chunk of flesh from the gray charger's neck, and its screams added to the brutal cacophony.

Despite my training with Leif, the king was still the superior fighter, and he would have knocked me from Sleipnir's back had he not met my gaze with his. I reached out with my mind and latched on to his, forcing him back.

"How are you alive?" he demanded through gritted teeth, even as his mind struggled against mine. "They found no trace of you. Mide should be mine!"

But he thought of much more than Mide. I saw designs on the rest of Éirinn, on the Northman lands beyond, and farther. All of this, because of an alliance with the jötnar.

Shock and disgust warred within me as memories flitted through the king's head: the jötnar coming to him, offering him the chance to take over the known world with them. Offering him the chance to be the king of so much more than Dubhlinn.

"You brought one jötunn with you, but what of the others? What of the ones that have been free to roam Éirinn?"

He refused to answer, so I ripped into his mind until he was screaming for mercy.

"Where are they?" I demanded again.

This time, he didn't dare refuse me. "Their leader called them north. He is preparing to move his army as one."

"You have betrayed us all by joining forces with creatures

who will burn Éirinn to ashes. You will never be king of Mide."

He struggled pitifully against my hold, and I smiled grimly.

"I will defeat you in battle, and then I will take your crown for myself, pagan. It's time a Celt ruled Dubhlinn again."

The king surprised me by laughing. "We are alike, you and I. You should admit the truth: you want my kingdom for yourself."

Vengeance had been my primary motivation, but there was something that stirred within me at the mention of his kingdom, a burning ambition I'd never known I had.

"You called me pagan, but you are no better—what is this spell you have cast over me if not dark magic?"

His point seemed to reverberate through my mind. With my undead army around me, and as the daughter of the Morrigan, how could I sneer at those considered pagan when I was no better? With an angry shove, I released his mind.

He landed on his back, his sword thrown a few feet away. I dismounted in a rush and stalked toward him. Sigtrygg struggled to stand, no doubt dazed from his hard fall.

I kicked his sword toward him. "Pick it up," I said in a growl. This was a duel, and I wouldn't cheat by using my mind control on him. He would die fairly—by my blade alone.

As soon as he picked up his sword, I attacked. He would have been skilled had he not been greatly weakened already by my mental attack, and my thirst for vengeance made my sword swing true. He parried two of my swings, even kicked me back with a boot to my abdomen. But on the third, my sword sliced open his chest. Even with blood spilling out of the wound, he continued to come at me.

He swung again, but I knocked his sword aside and kicked powerfully. He fell down again with a mighty crash and did not try to rise. I stood over him with my sword raised. "I will show you no mercy, just as your men gave none to my father."

I pierced his heart, and his eyes bulged as the blood spilled upon the ground.

Leif strode over to his side and spat upon the ground. "May you never enter Valhalla."

We watched as he shuddered once and then was still.

I turned to see the fate of his other men, and a chill went through me. My undead warriors had defeated them all— messily. They stood above the carnage as remorseless as stone.

A noisy crunching came from behind me, and I turned to find Sleipnir devouring one of the fallen soldiers, his teeth easily tearing into the flesh. Blood covered his nose and mouth, frighteningly unnatural. A low groan of horror escaped me.

The battle had drawn carrion birds, and they flew round and round above us, waiting their turn for whatever was left. Leif stood at my side, his face a stony mask. Abrax pressed close to him, as though seeking comfort from the horror before us.

"What have I done?" I whispered.

After Sleipnir had his fill, he walked toward us, blood dripping from his mouth and splattering his legs and chest. Abrax danced away from him nervously. Even I had to steady myself. I felt like crying; what had I done to my beautiful horse? But then again, he was a savage beast now, fit for the daughter of one of the most vicious ancient beings Éirinn had ever known.

If he was aware of our fear, he showed no sign of it. He shook himself like a dog and twitched his tail, and if it hadn't been for the blood and gore upon him, he would have been just as he always had been. I held out my hand to him, but Leif pushed it down with a shake of his head.

"He won't hurt me," I said, both to myself and to Leif.

Sleipnir lowered his head to be scratched, and I let out my

breath. After rubbing the soft hair under his forelock, I hauled myself astride. The undead warriors stood once more at attention.

Leif strode over to Sigtrygg's body and retrieved his sword and crown. He presented them both to me, and I raised an eyebrow questioningly. "You've killed Dubhlinn's king. The city is yours."

Yes, affirmed the voice inside me, as the burning ambition took hold again. There was much good I could do taking it from the hands of a half Northman many despised for his constant raids on neighboring kingdoms. "Bring it with us for proof, then, but I will not wear such filth upon my head," I said.

He nodded approvingly and hid the circlet away in his mantle. Once astride Abrax, he said, "We should travel until nightfall, though I suspect it's only the two of us who will require any rest."

My eyes shifted from the carrion birds, which now fought over the remains of Sigtrygg's army, to my own motionless warriors. After such a frightening display, I almost wished I could send them back from whence they'd come. If it hadn't been for the thirty men and terrifying jötunn they'd slaughtered as easily as sheep, not to speak of the countless battles ahead of us, I would have.

"Onward, then," I said.

The undead marched behind us at a swift, ground-eating pace, and the mere thought of them behind me tensed all the muscles of my body.

We might have won this battle, but as I glanced back at the undead men following me, I knew the greater war was to come.

I hoped the terrible price I'd paid for my army would be worth it.

The wind howled, scattering embers from our campfire. By nightfall, we'd made camp north of Dubhlinn, perhaps a day's march away from the city. Though my belly was comfortably full from the brace of rabbits we'd feasted on, the eerie sight of the undead army standing in the darkness like silent sentinels chilled me bone-deep. Leif sat beside me before the fire. He was close enough that I could feel the warmth coming off him in waves, and yet much too close for comfort. For some reason, I couldn't stop thinking of a conversation I'd once overheard between my father and mother, one to decide my fate as a woman. I was already sixteen and had not been brought up as the future lady of a house, nor had I any womanly skills, save sewing. My mother had asked my father what would become of me; should they not begin a search for a suitable husband?

"Ciara is too powerful for any man to take her as a wife— too unpredictable," my father had said. "He will either attempt to break her spirit and die trying, or hate and resent her for being stronger. She is a warrior, not a maiden. Better to concentrate your efforts upon Branna and Deirdre, raise them to be great ladies of our clan."

I'd never heard my mother's response, for I'd clutched my chest and raced to my room before the sob could escape my throat. It was a terrible thing to have my fate decided without my consent, without even a single word of input, but even that wasn't as painful as my parents' consensus: that I was too repulsive for marriage.

But not long after, I came to realize my father had given me a gift. Girls of my standing had two paths in life: marriage or the nunnery. My father had opened a third path to me, one where I could live my life with all the freedom of a man. The only cost was that it came with the soul-sucking burden of loneliness.

And now, my father was mere feet away as I sat willingly next to a former enemy. Although after everything I'd done, it seemed to be the least of my crimes.

In calling them back from the dead I'd no doubt damned my clansmen and father, but there was a part of me that took great satisfaction in the revenge they'd given me. And if they were necessary to destroy the jötnar, then there was an even greater part of me that didn't regret dragging them back from the dead. I shivered at my thoughts. Where was this growing sense of ambition coming from? Had it always been there, lurking in my subconscious?

Gently, Leif turned my face toward his. "What troubles you?"

Many things, I thought, but didn't say. I didn't want to air my memories of my parents' belief I was unsuitable as a wife—not to Leif. Besides, there were more pressing issues. My gaze shifted to my army of undead clansmen.

"No war was won without sacrifice," Leif said. "This army has gifted you with revenge upon Sigtrygg—who not only murdered your father and clansmen, but was in league with the jötnar—and the kingdom of Dubhlinn. Your army is a weapon; we will use them to crush the jötnar. When our lands are safe, you'll release them, and perhaps they will sleep in the peace you Christians always talk of."

A hint of a smile touched my lips. The Northmen's concept of an afterlife was anything but peaceful. "And what if our roles were reversed? What if you were the one to call forth your father and friends? For every trace of who they were to be gone, and for only walking corpses to be left? To watch them tear apart their enemies in mere minutes?"

"My father would accept such a fate with great zeal. Any of us would be proud to be *einherjar*, to be called upon to fight after death."

I sighed, exasperated with the forever blood-hungry Northmen. "But if my father still retained his sense of self, he'd be filled with nothing but shame."

Leif gestured toward the silent men in the dark. "He stands as motionlessly as all the others. Your father as you knew him is gone. What is left will save us all."

I touched his hand for a moment, but then the echoes of my parents' conversation reverberated through my mind. *A warrior, not a maiden.* I withdrew my hand. "You give me sound advice and more than a little comfort."

He held my eyes. "I'm not your enemy, Ciara. I may have been . . . once. But that changed the moment I met you on the battlefield."

I tried to laugh him off. "Because I defeated you so soundly?"

"Because you spared my brother. Because something about you made it impossible for me to look away."

He was melting my resolve, yet still I fought it. We had allied ourselves together, and I had overcome the sense that he was my enemy, but I couldn't shake the long-held belief I had that I wasn't fit to be loved as other maidens were. I barely knew myself; how could I in good faith give myself to another? But Leif's face blocked it all out. There were only the two of us in the darkness—alone.

"Your sister," he said suddenly, and I froze. "Was it one of my own who killed her?"

Pain for me showed on his face—and regret. "It was a Northman, yes," I answered, "but certainly none of the men who accompany you." Very quietly I added, "She was only a child when I watched her be killed."

"She was murdered . . . in front of you?"

"I've watched my sister being murdered in my dreams so often I know every detail," I said, almost to myself, "down to the stray eyelash that had fallen on her cheek."

He looked ill for a moment, and then angry, his jaw flexing. "I see my sister, too, in my dreams, and I can't imagine how I would be now if I'd seen it all happen." His eyes flicked to mine. "If I could take your memories from you and spare you that pain, I would."

Almost against my will, I leaned toward him. "The proposal you made last night," I said quietly, "will you hold to it again tonight?" My craving for closeness was a siren call I couldn't resist; and indeed he was the only one who could understand me now.

He laughed under his breath. "You'll kill me yet," he said. But in answer, he pulled me down beside him and wrapped us in his fur mantle.

This man who had once been my enemy—with his strong arms around me—made me feel safer than I had in weeks, but still I did not succumb to sleep. "I still fear for Mide . . . and for my sisters," I whispered into the darkness. Leif was silent, but I could tell from the slight shift of his body toward mine that he was listening. "We've killed King Sigtrygg, but soon others will come. They will see my father's death as an open invitation to seize the throne—through marriage or by force."

"Then you must take the throne for yourself," Leif said. His words resonated through me like the vibrating strings of a lute.

Yes, whispered the voice inside me, and for once, I wasn't sure if it was my own or the Morrigan's. By law, I was my father's heir, but I wasn't sure if Máthair would contest it. Would she reveal the truth of my birth—that I was a bastard not even entirely human—or was my exile binding? Mide was a valuable kingdom, rich in resources. Without a powerful force to rule it, it would always be susceptible to other strong and ambitious kings.

"I'll need help if I am to take Mide from my mother," I said.

"I am your ally, princess," he said. "One day you'll see that."

As I drifted off to sleep, I thought, *Maybe I already have.*

❖❖❖

The dream stole upon me with such vivid imagery I knew it was more than just a dream.

I stood in the hall of the ruins of a great castle. Stars shone clearly overhead through a massive hole in the ceiling; roots pushed their way up through the stones of the floor, leaving cracks in their wake; hundreds of vines wrapped around the stone staircase before me.

Dark mist poured in, flowing around me like silk. If I stared long enough, I could just make out the form of a woman. Suddenly, the destroyed room was filled with crows. Their black feathers fell to the floor, solidifying into the figure of a woman who remained hidden in the shadows of the great hall. "You know the truth of your birth now," the Morrigan said.

"Yes," I said, my hands curling into fists at my side. "Though I'm still not sure why you went to such an effort."

"We are not without our own seers, and we knew of the giants' plans long before they stirred from their realm. I refused to stand aside and watch them destroy the land that was once mine. I may be too weak to battle with these monsters, but I could create someone who could. Your father's bloodline gave me the perfect warrior. You."

Confusion slowed my reaction. "His bloodline?"

The dark mist swirled until a vision of a woman in gauzy white robes stretched her arms out to the sun as it rose, the pale yellow rays bathing her in its light. The moment it touched her, the gorge behind her was illuminated, and other priestesses in white robes moved toward the light.

"Your ancestors the druids once lived and worshipped

alongside the Tuatha Dé Danann, harnessing the power of nature to give them abilities beyond that of mere mortals: the gift of healing, the gift of sight, and the ability to travel between realms." Her eerie gaze, dark and fathomless, fell upon me. "The druids have died out just as the Tuatha have been driven out of the mortal realm, but traces of their bloodlines, though rare, remain. Your father carried one of their oldest bloodlines, and it gave him the potential for great power. Power that was lying dormant, waiting for immortal blood to awaken it. Together, we made a powerful weapon."

One born for it, the Morrigan had said when she'd first appeared to me.

"Why? Why would you create me? You knew the monster you'd send to the world."

She smiled, but the gesture was one of cunning rather than benevolence. "I needed a warrior with the power of the ancients. I cared nothing for the price."

My head ached with the dissonance of the faith I had always believed in, and the truth that I could no longer deny.

"The new god's influence is spreading, but the old gods live on," she said. "I would do anything to protect this land. Seduce a pitiful king, bear a child and allow her to be raised by foolish mortals who know nothing of the old ways, even join forces with gods from the north."

I thought of the way the Morrigan had appeared alongside the ravens in the Faerie Tunnel—the ravens who had turned out to be the Valkyrie. My eyes widened. "Do you mean the Valkyrie? You joined—"

"The Valkyrie are but messengers for the more powerful gods of the north. They chose their own warrior to right the mistakes made by their gods, and it was I who led him to your doorstep."

She looked completely unrepentant that in leading Leif to me, many of my clansmen had died in the ensuing battle with Leif's men. It made me feel sick, like I was partly to blame, even if I hadn't been consciously aware of my part in bringing them to our shores.

But it also brought me Leif. The thought whispered through my mind, and I couldn't deny how thankful I was for it.

"So you came to me in a dream to gloat about how you manipulated my father and bent others to your will?"

"I came to warn you," she said, bringing forth a vision of Leif battling jötnar with all his strength. "Unlike your power, which you were born with, the Northman's was bestowed upon him as a gift from the gods, but it doesn't make him invincible. You will soon sail north, and once you arrive on the North-men's shores, you will lose all access to the realm of the Tuatha Dé Danann. There are other ancient beings who guard those shores, and I cannot cross them. You may find yourself without allies in the end. You have to be strong enough.

"Your only hope will be to master your abilities before you arrive. Become the warrior queen you were meant to be." The mist transformed into rippling ink-black feathers. "Do not fail." With a *caw*, she completed her transformation into a crow and took flight.

269

The march to Dubhlinn wasn't long, but it was long enough to torture me with thoughts of the Morrigan's words. It seemed especially ominous that she'd said Leif wasn't invincible. I kept sending him worried glances, but he was lost in his own thoughts, no doubt anxious to return to Arin and his men. The apprehension seemed to spread through Leif and me, until we became almost desperate to arrive. I was queen now, yet there was no time to formally take the city, nor to decide what would be done with Sigtrygg's wife and family. His wife was a Celt, I knew, so she might have fled to her father, the High King. I thought of my own mother, refusing to leave, refusing to even bury the remains of her husband. I doubted Sigtrygg's wife would be as devoted—not many in arranged marriages were. Still, with the High King behind her, Sigtrygg's wife could pose a problem I wasn't prepared to handle.

I didn't anticipate anyone in the city protesting my claim to the throne, not with my nightmarish army at my back, the king's crown in my hand, and my own intimidating reputation, but I knew if I had any hope at all of retaining the kingdom of Dubhlinn for myself, then I'd have to leave behind someone to hold the city.

I stole a glance at Leif, noting again the lines of tension there. He feared for Arinbjorn, I knew. We'd been delayed for so long now, anything could have happened while we were away. His men had been told to prepare the ships, but that was weeks ago. Did they even believe us to be alive?

If they had waited for us, and if the ships had been made ready, then we would set sail tomorrow. I shuddered as I thought of the dragon-headed prows, the square sails. How I had always loathed that sight. Now, all too soon, I would be on board them as we sailed north, at the mercy of the sea and sky.

I felt completely unprepared, and though Leif had eased my concerns over sailing in general, I still questioned how comfortable the journey would be.

"What do you do if it rains?" I'd asked Leif the night before, when my anxiety over sailing had reached the point that I could silently think on it no longer.

He had grinned and said, "We get wet."

I'd imagined just how miserable this journey could be and decided not to ask any further questions.

But I couldn't keep all my concerns at bay as we marched toward the city. I glanced at my undead warriors. They followed in our wake, showing no sign of fatigue though they hadn't slept. It wasn't until we reached the bridge into Dubhlinn that I realized we'd be leading them into the city. The boys with no shoes I'd seen the first time we rode through came to mind. Was I bringing monsters I knew very little about to the doors of innocent people?

"I think the army should wait here—at the gates," I said to Leif.

"Why? We must travel to the city to get to the ships, and it'd be foolish to leave them here only to return for them later. I'd rather you have the extra protection; we can't know what awaits us in the city. Sigtrygg's men might challenge you for the throne."

I glanced back at my morbid army, their faces gray and their march tireless. Leif did have a point. We might need them. "I'd rather not turn them against my own subjects, but I suppose I will if I have to if the people of Dubhlinn challenge us."

Leif nodded his approval.

"And what of Sleipnir?" I asked. "Can I trust him in a stable with other horses?"

"You fear he'll devour the other poor beasts in the stable? He's been beside Abrax this entire time and hasn't so much as licked him."

"He knows Abrax, though. The others . . ." I trailed off when Sleipnir's ears suddenly pricked forward. Sensing the other horse's alertness, Abrax did the same.

A band of men on horseback was riding toward us. Leif and I warily drew our swords and waited on the bridge.

As soon as they were close enough to identify, Leif sheathed his sword. I smiled when I saw who was in the lead. "Arin," Leif said with relief clear in the smile on his face, "it's good of you to come to meet us. Saves me the trouble of tearing the city apart to find you."

"Find me?" his brother said, shaking his head. "You're the ones who've been missing for ages." He smiled as he met my gaze, but then as he noticed the undead at our back, the expression rapidly turned to apprehension. "Who are those men?"

"My army," I said, unable and unwilling to explain further.

"The army we used to destroy King Sigtrygg after he killed Ciara's father and burned two hundred of her clansmen," Leif said grimly.

"That's terrible, Ciara," Arin said, his whole face drawn in sympathy.

"The whole damn city turned on us while you were gone," one of the men riding with Arin said. "Sigtrygg's men tried to round us up and hold us prisoner, so we were forced to kill them all and burn the castle."

"Sigtrygg never did know how to pick the winning side," Leif said. He turned to me with an ironic smile. "It would seem your castle has been burned, my queen."

Arin and the Northman shared a look of confusion. "Queen?" Arin asked.

"I'll explain everything later," Leif said. "What I need to know now is: Have the ships been made ready?"

Arin's face lit up. "They have, brother. Not only our ship, but four others."

Leif nodded with approval. "Enough for two hundred men." He glanced at the army at my back. "Living men, anyway."

"Men and horses," the other Northman said. "The ships are filled with weapons and food stores—enough to replace those we lost. We raided the city after we beat Sigtrygg's men back."

"Did you leave any alive?" Leif asked.

"Some yielded," Arin said, and I could see from the brightness in his eyes that he had relished his first battle. "Though not many remain alive. Sigtrygg thought his army of fifty men would be enough to take us, but they were wrong."

I was surprised by how few men Sigtrygg had left behind to defend his city. We'd defeated the small battalion Sigtrygg brought with him, but surely his army consisted of more than eighty men. "Where are the rest of Sigtrygg's men?"

"Raiding," Arin said matter-of-factly.

"The ones remaining will be given a choice, then," Leif said. "Join us in battle as was originally promised by King Sigtrygg, or be executed by their new queen."

I thought of my clansmen who'd been burned alive by Sigtrygg's men. The men who now stood behind me, fueled by the blood of the fallen. "What use do I have for traitorous men?" My hands tightened on the reins, and Sleipnir tossed his head. "What use are men who steal into my church on the Lord's day and burn it and my clansmen to ashes?"

"More bodies to block the blows of the jötnar," Leif said. His tone was calm, but the fire inside me burned still brighter. "Not all of the men were guilty of attacking your clansmen, Ciara."

"Those who had nothing to do with it may come to battle. Those who did . . . will die."

We entered Dubhlinn with much more fanfare than I would have liked. Leif and I rode side by side, followed by my army of fallen warriors. Leif's men rode ahead and called out to the people as we rode by, "People of Dyflin, King Sigtrygg is dead. Behold your new queen, Queen Ciara!"

A loud clamor of surprise went through the crowd, which drew even more people from their houses. They lined both sides of the road and stared at me as I rode past. With most of Sigtrygg's men defeated or captured by Leif's, there was no one to contest my claim, and the people of Dubhlinn didn't seem to mourn the loss of Sigtrygg. The peasants who were originally from the north disliked him for being half Celt, and the Celts who lived in Dubhlinn disliked him for his raids on Éirinn.

I overheard murmurs in the crowd. "Her horse's eyes are red," a man said, and his observation rippled through the crowd.

"Who are the men who follow her?" another asked, clutching her son to her side.

I glanced back at my army, but they didn't break formation. Leif and the others rode along as though they were used to such scrutiny from a loud crowd, but I found the attention unsettling. It wasn't until I noticed one of the small, dirty boys I had seen the first time we rode through the city that I was able to smile.

He waved vigorously as I drew nearer, his cheeks spattered with mud. "Queen Ciara!" he called, and I responded to his wave with one of my own.

This was what we stood to lose if we couldn't defeat the jötnar: this boy and all the others like him. My sisters—more innocents who would lose their lives to the giants if I didn't stop them. I would think of them when I boarded a ship I'd always despised, when I journeyed far from Éirinn. They gave a face to the nameless destruction that awaited this land and its people if we failed.

In the distance, smoke from the still-smoldering castle rose to the sky. In this, at least, I had my revenge. Sigtrygg's men had burned my church, but Leif's men had burned his castle. It was just an unfortunate thing that the castle happened to be mine now.

"It was a mistake to burn the castle," Leif said, as though voicing my own thoughts. "Now we'll have to bed down in the stables for the night."

As Leif spoke, one of his men slowed his mount until he was keeping pace with us. "We slept in the ships last night. Not all of the castle was burned. We only set fire to his throne room."

"And what of the servants and Sigtrygg's family?" I asked, spurring Sleipnir through the crowd. "You left them unharmed?"

"His son was one of the men who attacked us, so we killed him, but the servants are still alive. His wife pleaded for mercy, and we allowed her to take her belongings and leave the city."

"His wife is the daughter of the High King," I said to Leif, turning over the implications in my mind.

"Will it be a problem?" Leif asked.

"Each kingdom in Éirinn has autonomous rule, and we merely pay tribute to the High King. Sigtrygg and the king may have had an alliance, but a battle was fought fairly, and I was the victor," I said. "By rights, his land is mine." Even if the High King's potential revenge was an issue, it was one for a later time. We had bigger problems to deal with now—like the jötnar potentially taking over the world.

By then our party had reached the castle courtyard, but unlike the last time Leif and I had been there, now there were no guardsmen at the gates. No servants rushed out to attend to us. The smoke, coming from the middle of the castle, wafted lazily toward the sky. The air was ripe with the smell of burned wood, and a much more pungent smell, one I was all too famil-iar with: charred flesh. My army spread out behind us once we came to a halt, and my gaze fell upon my father. As though he felt my stare, he turned his head, and our eyes met. An awareness burned in his once again, and I thought of his need for revenge.

"Where are the men who yielded during your battle?" I asked Arin.

"We threw them in the dungeon," Arin said, pride over his accomplishments evident in the swell of his chest.

"I want all of them brought before me," I said with a glance at my father. I couldn't rest until I had dealt with them.

Leif nodded toward his men. "Erik, Oleif, bring one man before the queen at a time. It's time they answered for their crimes."

"I'll go," Arin said, but Leif held up his hand.

"You will stay," Leif said, and Arin glared at his elder brother.

Erik and Oleif dismounted and strode toward the castle. It wasn't long before they returned, each dragging a man in chains behind them.

Erik approached first with his captive, yanking him forward viciously, until the man stumbled and fell before Sleipnir. My horse's ears immediately shot back. When he bared his sharp teeth threateningly, I placed a single hand on his neck.

Pale-faced and filthy, the man scurried backward out of the reach of Sleipnir, only to be forcefully stopped by Erik's foot.

"Enough," I said to both Erik and Sleipnir, who each seemed to wish harm upon the prisoner. I turned to the captive in the dirt. "Erik has brought you before me to give you a choice:

swear fealty to me and join my army, or be executed for your attack against my allies."

Shakily, the man stood and bowed his head. "I will gladly serve you, my queen."

"I accept your fealty," I said, "but as your queen, I must know, what part did you play in Sigtrygg's attack on Mide?"

At the dark look in my eyes, the man began to shake anew. "I was only supposed to help the others take down Leif's men here in the city," he said, his eyes casting about as though unsure what the correct answer was. "We tried to ambush them, but they still defeated us."

"And you never left Dubhlinn?"

"No, my queen," he said, glancing back and forth fearfully between Leif and me.

"Remove his chains," I said to Erik. "He will sail north with us."

The man dropped forward with relief, and I waved the next captive forward. Unlike the first, this man did not shake or show fear of any kind. He was as tall as Leif and even bigger around. He met my gaze with defiance. I despised him on sight.

"Tell me of your involvement in Sigtrygg's attack on Mide," I said, my tone sharp.

"I killed people," he said with a grin that was more the bearing of teeth.

Oleif strode forward and shoved the man in the back of the head so hard I could practically hear his neck snap. "Answer your queen properly."

The captive narrowed his eyes. "I killed *your* people. Burned their church to the ground because they were too stupid to get out."

As the sudden rage within me nearly took my breath away, there was a strange stirring behind me. The undead warriors had shifted as one, their focus now on the captive. My father moved toward him, his expression fierce.

"What was Sigtrygg's plan?" Leif asked before I could respond.

His eye still warily on my father, the captive answered, "King Sigtrygg pretended to want a treaty with the king of Mide, and it was your father who invited us to his kingdom. But then, he didn't expect us to arrive on the Lord's day," he said with a nasty sneer. "They were as easy to slaughter as lambs. Your father included," he added, boldly meeting my gaze.

"Brave words for a man who is about to die," I said, relaxing my hold on Sleipnir. He stalked forward menacingly. I drew my sword. "You have confessed to killing my clansmen, and for this, I will have justice."

He stood unblinkingly before me, his eyes cold and unafraid. Had he worn the same unfeeling expression as he killed my family? Movement caught my attention, and I halted Sleipnir. My father had drawn level with me. He glanced up at me and freed his sword, determination evident in the set of his shoulders.

I would execute the man quickly by beheading, but I doubted any punishment my father had in mind would be as swift. As I looked at the condemned man, I could hear the screams of the two hundred dying men, burned alive.

"He is yours to do with as you will," I said to my father.

There was no hesitation. He sped forward so quickly his movement was blurred, and I could only see the result: the captive's entrails pooled at his feet. Beside me, Arin leaned over and was sick, and even my own stomach churned.

Even more disturbing was the silence that this gruesome display was carried out in. My father had uttered not a single sound, and he returned to his place among the other warriors just as quietly.

Based on my father's reaction, it was clear the man had been the one to behead him, and some of my disgust was tempered by righteous anger. He deserved to die, and I would seek out every single one of the men who were instrumental in killing my clansmen.

As the blood continued to spill around the executed captive, I said grimly, "Bring forth the others."

Four more men were executed, and twenty-two were added to our army. It seemed Sigtrygg had taken a small band of men to Mide, but it was only the first man who produced such a reaction in my father. I killed the rest myself, ending them swiftly. I couldn't prevent Sleipnir from devouring their corpses, his unnatural behavior too disturbing even for Leif's battle-hardened men. None had become sick at the sight like poor Arin, but they had left in a hurry, with the excuse that they needed to make final preparations on the ships. By the end, I wished I could escape the gruesome scene.

After our macabre tasks were done, I'd ordered the people who had been taken as slaves from my kingdom be found. Some were, but many had already been sold and taken far away. Each loss made me want to kill Sigtrygg all over again.

With so much to be done, darkness came much too soon and not soon enough. I was exhausted and longed for my bed at home in Mide with its warm furs and downy pillows. Here I would receive no such luxury. I spent my first night as queen bedded down in the stables. Though it was only the throne room and surrounding halls that had burned, the smell of smoke lingered, strong enough to cause our eyes to water ceaselessly. In contrast, the stall was warm, and the hay smelled sweet. In the past, I would've slept in the same stall as Sleipnir. But now not even I was willing to lose myself in vulnerable sleep beside a creature whose eyes glowed red in the darkness.

I tossed and turned, unable to find a position comfortable enough to rest. I missed Leif's strong arms around me, the smell and feel of his soft fur mantle, the clear night sky above us. Without the excuse of acute grief and the lonely, cold nights on the run to push us into each other's arms, we'd gone back to sleeping separately. But now I wondered why I thought it was necessary to maintain modesty—who was watching? Who would even care? Angry with myself now, I squeezed my eyelids shut . . . only to open them again at the sound of a boot rustling the straw of the stall.

Leif stood over me, his expression hopeful and sheepish both. He held his leather chest piece over his shoulder. My eyes swept over his muscular form, clearly revealed by his light linen tunic and leather leggings. "I couldn't sleep," he said, and lay down beside me as if he belonged there.

Pleasure bloomed within me at the thought that he had felt the same as I. I rolled to my side and met his heated stare. "I couldn't either," I admitted. "I'm nervous about this trip north." He was quiet, so I kept talking. "I've never been anywhere but Éirinn, and I've never been on a ship—not even a fishing boat." I rubbed my arm, feeling strangely vulnerable revealing such comparatively inconsequential fears. We'd faced far greater dangers. It felt silly to admit I was afraid of a wooden boat on the water.

He shifted so he was facing me. "I don't want you to worry. The journey north is an easy one this time of year, and I've sailed it many times. But at the same time, I understand that sadness and fear of leaving your own land. I know how difficult this is for you, but I'm so happy you're coming with me—that I can share the beauty of sailing in open water with you."

His words made the tension in my muscles melt away. I trusted him, and if he said it would be okay, then it would be. "I'd like to share that with you, too."

He touched my cheek, his thumb just barely brushing my lips. "I don't know if I can hold to our agreement tonight, Princess. I want to kiss you. I want to do much more than that, but I wouldn't want to tempt fate."

Desire rose so quickly within me it became an aching need. Before I'd even formed a rational thought in my head, I leaned over him and pressed my lips to his. He pulled me closer until our chests were flush against each other. Our lips parted hungrily, his tongue meeting mine, setting my whole body aflame. My hands slipped beneath his tunic, and it wasn't long before he sat up and pulled it over his head. His armor had hidden several tattoos. A skeletal dragon curled around his shoulder blade; both biceps were covered with beautifully intricate knotwork patterns; and across his back was a massive war hammer, encircled by chains and runes.

I drank in the sight of them, tracing each one with my fingertip. "These are so beautiful," I said.

"I will tattoo every inch of my body if you'll keep touching them like that."

I smiled. "No scars to mar them. You've been victorious in battle—at least, until you met me."

A growled laugh escaped him, and he pulled me down beneath him.

Our tongues met again as his hands swept over my body, leaving trails of fire everywhere he touched. He kissed me until we both panted for breath, until I could think of nothing but the steely hardness of his muscles, the fullness of his lips. My nails raked his back as he kissed the side of my neck. My feverish desire seemed to spread to Leif, until there was a desperation to our touches.

Suddenly, he pulled back, a pained look on his face. "What

is it?" I asked, and the distance between us and cool night air seemed to bring me back to my senses.

"There's something you should know," Leif said, his mouth drawn in a grim line. "You asked me once what it was I traded to the Valkyrie for my power."

My stomach twisted inside me. How could I have forgotten? Whatever it was, it wasn't good, and I wanted to reach out with my hand and silence him before he could continue.

"I traded my life."

I froze. I needed to know what he meant, but at the same time, I dreaded his answer. "What do you mean?"

I watched Leif swallow hard. He didn't want to tell me. "The Valkyrie gave me the many abilities I would need to defeat Fenris and the other jötnar, but after I succeed, they will sacrifice me and take my soul to Valhalla."

The roar of blood in my ears sounded like a river. "Why would you do such a thing?" I whispered finally, my mouth bone dry.

"I had to, and I would do it again. I care for you, Ciara—it's why I told you the truth about this before we went any further—but there is nothing I wouldn't do for revenge on the jötnar who took my sister from me."

It was then that I realized two things: I cared for him, too—far too much. And I couldn't watch him die.

A sob caught in my throat. Why bargain with his life? But even as I thought it, I knew I'd do the same.

"You should have told me before," I said. *Before you kissed me like that. Before I realized how much I—*

I stood, suddenly desperate for escape. I couldn't allow myself to think about this—not now. It had sneaked over me slowly, this caring . . . this depth of feeling for Leif. It was bad enough carrying such a burden when we were merely former enemies. It was something else entirely to know I felt this way about him and that he would be sacrificed at the end of our quest.

"Where are you going?" Leif asked as he watched me move toward the stall door.

Sensing my presence, Sleipnir's head appeared atop his own stall door. He nickered to me softly in greeting. "For a ride," I said.

After freeing Sleipnir from his stall, I pulled myself astride. I needed time away from Leif. Time to prepare myself for a voyage far from anything I'd ever known.

Time to lock my emotions away in a box where they belonged, lest they drag me under.

Sleipnir and I wandered throughout the city in shadow and darkness, our way lit only by moonlight. My mind tortured me with images of Leif dead in many different ways: torn apart by giants, felled by a sword, beheaded by the Valkyries. I felt sick and alone, and I hated myself for running away like that, but I couldn't stay. My body still burned for him. I couldn't just lie back down beside him as though nothing had happened, as if I hadn't just learned we might succeed in our quest only to lose him.

For a while, I considered seeking out Sigrid to see if she would divine the same terrible fate for Leif. In the end, I decided to let her have her rest. I'd be on a ship with her soon, after all. I would train with her and grow stronger, and maybe that would be power enough to save him.

You don't know that he can be saved, my mind reminded me painfully, and I squeezed my eyes shut.

That didn't mean I planned to stand by and watch it happen.

After a time, the smells and sounds of the nearby sea called to me, and I guided Sleipnir toward the quay. The sound of waves lapping at five Northman ships greeted us, Sleipnir's hooves falling on the wooden planks adding their own music. The dragonhead prows, illuminated in the soft light of the moon, gave the appearance of great slumbering sea monsters risen from the deep.

I pushed my thoughts of Leif aside and focused on the journey ahead.

With so many ships out of port, Dubhlinn would be left vulnerable. We would need the lion's share of men to come with us north, but some trusted men would need to stay behind to guard the city. Unfortunately, the only men I trusted aside from Leif were dead.

As I approached the ships, I expected feasting and raucous drinking from Leif's men, but instead, all was quiet. I watched the wind toy with the ropes securing the currently deflated square sails. In the morning I would be aboard, nothing between me and the weather but the clothes on my back. I'd be on the largest ship, Leif's own, with his brother and men. It would be uncomfortable, crowded, cold, and have a total lack of privacy. Even so, there was no turning back now.

A figure came toward us from Leif's ship, interrupting my thoughts and pricking Sleipnir's ears forward. As he drew closer, I recognized Arin.

"You couldn't sleep either?" he asked, his face pale and his eyes excited.

"No," I said. Looking at Arin's earnest face, I realized he would know the men as well as Leif. "Arin, are there any men among you whom you trust?"

He looked momentarily taken aback, but pleased I had asked him such an important question. "Some of the best went with you and Leif to battle the jötnar," he said, "but there are still many others who are trustworthy."

"I'm in need of men who'll remain here and hold Dubhlinn until I return."

"Leif always said Erik and Oleif have the minds of chieftains," Arin said. "They acted quickly in the attack against us while you were gone, and they commanded us well."

I nodded thoughtfully. Erik and Oleif had also been quick to carry out Leif's orders. They were both capable men, and I'd liked how Oleif had enforced respect of me from the captives. But they couldn't hold the city on their own. Ideally, we would leave behind a small battalion, but I wasn't sure how many Leif could spare. It would be best if one of Sigtrygg's captured men remained behind to give the Northmen guidance. Mentally, I sorted through the men I'd interrogated.

"Have you had contact with the remainder of Sigtrygg's men?" I asked Arin.

"Some. They wanted to sleep in their own beds this night, but we didn't trust them enough." He pointed to one of the longships in the middle. "Most are there."

"So there are none you trust? What of the first captive we interrogated? He seemed honest enough."

Arin swallowed visibly. "He hasn't been a problem. I wouldn't trust him with my life yet, but he seems battle-hardened."

"I would speak with him, then," I said, dismounting from Sleipnir smoothly.

Arin watched Sleipnir with a wary look. "I can get him for you," he said.

"Not necessary," I said, already walking toward the ship. My boots thudded dully on the wooden quay and were soon joined by Arin's.

Arin shot me a sheepish smile, as though he didn't want to be left alone. "I'll come with you."

Together we approached the longship, and even in the dark I could see it was beautifully built, sleek and streamlined. It creaked gently as the waves rocked it. Inside, I could make out the dark forms of slumbering men, but there was one who leaned against the mast, already alert to our approach.

I recognized his tall, wiry form as the man I was looking for. "I'm glad you're awake," I called out to him softly.

He straightened and made his way toward us, stepping over

legs and torsos. "My queen?" he asked as soon as he had stepped off the ship.

Now that he was closer, I could see sweat beading along his thinning hairline, and a nervous cast to his eyes.

"I only wish to speak with you," I said, as I took in our surroundings for myself. Was there something I had missed? Something to put this man on alert? I glanced at Arin, but he didn't seem alerted to any unseen danger. "But first, I want to know your name."

"Donal," he said.

His gaze skittered away from mine, and I felt a twinge of pity. "Donal, when the sun rises, we'll sail north. Dubhlinn will be left vulnerable."

He glanced over his shoulder. "This is true, my queen."

Again, I searched the quay for any sign of danger. "What are you afraid of, Donal?" My question seemed to take him by surprise, and he jerked. When he couldn't meet my eyes, I realized the awful truth. "You're afraid of me," I said quietly.

Using fear to command men is for the weak. My father's words whispered through my mind. Long had I fought under my father's command, but I'd never seen him use such tactics to gain respect or obedience. I thought, too, of the Morrigan, how even the sight of her caused my skin to erupt in goose bumps. Was that what strangers saw when they looked at me? A monster hidden behind a woman's form?

"Have . . . have you come alone?" Donal asked. "Not with your army of bones?"

I stilled, and beside me, Arin shifted uncomfortably. "Why would you call them that?"

If possible, Donal grew even paler. "When I look at them . . . I see only skeletons and red flames where their hearts should be."

I thought of the way I saw my undead army. They were shrouded in mist, and it seemed to take a great effort to make out any details on their faces, but they didn't look like skeletons to me. "They look like any other warrior," I said.

"Not to me."

"You have the sight," Arin said, awe in his tone. "Were you Sigtrygg's seer?"

Donal took a step back. "Seer? I—no. No, of course not."

Arin looked at me with confusion plain on his face. I remembered how Sigrid was respected by the Northmen, or at the very least, tolerated. "The sight is considered heretical in our culture," I explained. "Something only pagans use."

Arin snorted. "No wonder you Celts were so easy to raid."

I gave him a warning glare and returned my attention to Donal. "And what do you see when you look at me?"

"My queen, I . . ."

"No harm will come to you, Donal. I am only curious."

He took a steadying breath. "Crows' feathers in your hair, death at your side."

I nodded slowly. I didn't need a seer to tell me what such symbols meant. At least he hadn't said I looked like a skeleton. "And when you think of our quest in the north? What do you see then?"

"I see you riding a horse made of fire instead of flesh, the ground quaking beneath you. Nothing else—nothing helpful. This sight never shows me anything but symbols and riddles."

He sounded frustrated, and I could empathize. "Thank you for being so forthcoming with me, and I hope . . . I hope to earn your respect instead of your fear."

He bowed his head as though ashamed. "What did you wish to speak with me about, my queen?"

"When we leave for the north, I would like for you to stay and advise those who remain behind. Will you do this for me?"

"It would be an honor," he said, a tentative but relieved smile on his face.

I touched his shoulder and was happy when he didn't flinch away. "Thank you, Donal. Rest in your own home this night, and in the morning, report to the castle courtyard."

After thanking me, he hurried away into the night, and I turned to Arin. "What about you? Are you ready to sleep?"

Arin shook his head. "I'd rather sleep on the ship as we sail. Helps to pass the time."

"Then help me find Oleif and Erik. With Donal's touch of the sight, I think ten men should be able to hold the city, but I want their opinions on who should stay behind."

I started toward another longship, but Arin's words stopped me. "I'm not afraid of you, you know."

I turned back with a smile. "I'm relieved to hear it."

"That army you have is pretty terrifying, but you aren't."

I smiled and rubbed the top of Arin's head. "Nothing should

be terrifying to you after seeing what that monster did."

He smiled, his teeth bright white even in the dim light. "I could help you fight one next time."

His arrogance was so like his brother's it was like a vise upon my heart. "You could not, and you will not. Any more talk like that, and I'll be sure to leave you behind."

"You're as bad as Leif."

I leaned in close. "I'm worse." I straightened and moved away. "Now, come. We must find Erik and Oleif."

He followed reluctantly, and I vowed to myself and to God I would not allow any harm to come to him—no matter how badly he might wish it upon himself.

The sun rose much too soon, and by the time I'd finished deciding who'd stay behind with Oleif, Erik, and Donal, I could only rest my head on Sleipnir's neck and greet the sunrise with an irritable squint. Arin sat on the quay not far from me, his back against a post.

The men who'd slept on the ships now made the final preparations. I watched as two men wrestled with a massive wooden cage full of ravens, and my eyebrows drew together.

"Surely we won't be eating those," I called out to one of the men. The birds quieted at the sound of my voice, their eyes trained on me as one. It was eerie, but not in a threatening way.

The man glanced down at the cage before looking back at me. "We bring them to be sure we're staying close to land."

His words made a quiver of anxiety run through me. Soon we would be at the mercy of the open waters. The man carried the cage to the largest ship, and it was in the light of day that I realized there were distinct differences. The largest, which I recognized as Leif's, had a prow that was so ornately carved it was almost beautiful. From a distance, all I'd seen was the gaping maw of the dragon, but up close, I could see the knotwork so lovingly carved. The sail had not yet been raised, but I knew it to be white with a bloodred skeletal dragon insignia. I only hoped it would strike fear in the hearts of the jötnar who saw it bearing down on them, as it had in mine when I saw it appear along the coast of Éirinn.

Beside Leif's ship was another that was shorter by at least twenty feet, but much wider and sturdier. Onto this ship the men led various livestock, including many warhorses taken from the former king's stables. Tarpaulins were secured in the middle, providing a semblance of shelter for the animals.

"I hadn't realized you Northmen had different types of ships."

Arin gave me that same look of surprise he always did when I showed my ignorance of his people. "You thought we only had the longships? But how would merchants transport goods or livestock?"

He had a point, of course. "Then that ship there"—I pointed to the one animals were being loaded onto—"is a merchant ship?"

He nodded. "We call it a *knarr*. The rest are longships, but

Leif's is the largest, with room enough for thirty-two to row."

Just then hooves thudding dully on the quay alerted me to the approach of someone, and as I turned, I saw Leif with my army following. My army marched slowly but steadily until they reached the quay. I watched as one by one, they stood at attention, awaiting my command.

Leif guided Abrax until he was level with Sleipnir. Arin took one look at his brother and suddenly developed a fascination with untying a knotted rope far across the quay from us. I stood my ground as emotions warred within me: anger and frustration over his stupidity in trading his own life, but also that burst of joy I had whenever I saw him now. I tried not to drink in the sight of him, but I shamed myself by staring at him like someone dying of thirst stares at fresh water. How could I lose him? He dismounted, and I did the same. "You never returned," he said, his expression guarded.

I tried to hold on to my anger, and I wove it around me like a shield against the hurt in his eyes. "I had to gather men who would stay behind. Dubhlinn cannot be left undefended."

He moved closer to me, until I could feel the heat radiating from his body. "You ran away."

"You told me you'd be dead at the end of this," I said, unable to keep the anger from my voice. "All this time, we've been together, and you fail to tell me we might defeat the giants only for you to lose your life. You didn't think it was something I should know?"

A muscle in Leif's jaw twitched, and I couldn't tell whether he was as angry as I was, or hurt. "It's always been my burden to bear. I've thought of telling you many times, but always I decided not to. What difference would it have made? But last night, that all changed when . . ." He trailed off for a moment. "When I thought we'd do more than sleep. When I thought we meant more to each other. And when I did tell you, you left in the middle of the night without another word."

I flushed. "I was angry, Leif. I'm still angry—both that you would do such a thing and that you let me grow to care for you as much as I do." I swallowed hard as emotions threatened to boil up again; I hadn't cried when I was exiled, and I refused to cry now. I looked into his eyes and saw the hurt I felt mirrored back at me, and suddenly, I realized being angry at Leif was pointless. He'd made his decision long before me, and there was more at stake now than just our relationship and feelings for each other. I didn't have the luxury of wallowing in self-pity. "But I shouldn't have left. I couldn't bear to face it. I still can't."

He reached out and took my hand, his own warm and strong. "You care for me too?" he asked, a grin playing at the corners of his lips. I shoved his chest with one hand but didn't let go with the other.

"I thought it was obvious. And now that we both know that, how can we go on when your life is forfeit at the end of all of this?"

His expression reflected the sorrow I felt. "We will go on as we always have—together. Either one of us can die at any point during this quest we've taken on; pushing each other away won't make that any easier to bear, and the result would still be the same." He tilted my chin up to look at him. "We're stronger together, Ciara."

"Then don't die," I said, my voice a whisper of pain. "There must be a way to change your fate."

"I made a choice before I ever even met you, but if it helps, I do feel sorry for it now. I would do it again to avenge my sister, you must understand, but I'm sorry for it."

I shook my head. "Then if you won't find a way to undo it, I will."

He laughed. "If anyone could change the fate of the gods, it's you."

I frowned—I knew he was trying to put me off. "Are you afraid changing your fate would mean you'd lose the strength you've been given?"

"I'm saying I didn't enter into such a pact lightly, and I know the Valkyrie won't suddenly change their minds or decide to be merciful."

It felt as if he'd reached inside my chest and grabbed hold of my heart. "So you're going to die. There's nothing to be done about it. You're just a lamb led to slaughter."

He snorted. "We're all going to die. I could've died at any point in this quest so far—there are no guarantees."

"But if you survived until the end, if you finally succeeded in killing Fenris, then you'd still let yourself be killed by the Valkyrie." I knew I was pushing him; I knew he wanted me to drop it, but I just couldn't. I wanted to hear all the terrible details, even as it felt like nails hammered in my chest with each word.

His eyes met mine, and for just a brief moment, I saw it: the fear. It hurt me worse than imagining my own helplessness in his coming execution. But then he grinned. "I never said I wouldn't put up a fight." I let out a rush of breath, and he gave my hand a squeeze. "Enough of this. Come with me. I have something I want to show you."

His smile was infectious, and I tried to push aside my worry, at least for now. He led me to the ship that was his, where it sat, graceful, long and narrow in the water. He helped me on board, and as the ship gently swayed beneath my feet, he led me to the stern. Two tarpaulins had been rigged so that a small piece of the ship was afforded some privacy; one cut off the stern from the rest of the ship while the other blocked the sun overhead.

I gave him a questioning look, and he answered by pulling aside the tarp. Spread out over the ship's planks were soft furs, a trunk, and even a chamber pot. Tears of surprise and relief stung my eyes.

"For you, my queen," he said with only the barest hint of a teasing smile. "It's my hope that you'll be at least a little more comfortable than the rest of us—protected from the sun, and most of the wind and rain."

I felt my heart soften at his gesture. "This is the kindest thing anyone has ever done for me." I meant it.

His answering smile was wide. "I wanted to make this journey bearable for you. There's nothing like being on a ship in the open water," he said, pride lighting his face as he looked out at his ship. "Nothing like that rush of feeling when the waves threaten to topple you, but the ship glides atop them—nothing save a battle."

"I still don't understand how you Northmen navigate these seas. What if we lose our way?"

Leif snorted. "I have never lost my way. I use the sun and stars to guide me." His face tipped up to the sky, and he closed his eyes for a moment. When he opened them again, he nodded as if confirming something for himself. "The winds are favorable today, which means we'll make good time."

"How long until we reach Skien?" I asked, dreading the answer.

"We won't be sailing straight into Skien," Leif said, and I glanced up at him sharply. "We'll be sailing to Bymbil, my homeland."

"And what of Skien?"

He grinned. "You *have* become bloodthirsty." He gestured toward the *knarr*, which had already begun to sink lower in the water with the weight of all on board. "You didn't think I would deliver such prizes to Fenris, did you? These are treasures to profit my own village. Now that I have the army I set out for, my father will call upon every freeman who owes him a favor, and we'll sail for Skien with an army far greater in number than Fenris has ever seen."

His plan was a sound one, but a faint shadow seemed to pass over me, warning that no battle goes as planned. "We may win this yet," I said, arguing with the shadowy feeling that had sneaked over me. I refused to fail this quest. "So how long will it take to sail to Bymbil?"

"Only a fortnight if the winds favor us."

So long! Nausea churned within my belly as though I was already being tossed around by the waves. Could this narrow ship even survive rough water?

"Have you ever sailed through a thunderstorm?" I asked suddenly.

"The North Sea is rife with storms, but this ship has always weathered them. I'll deliver you safely to the north, Ciara. You have nothing to fear."

I nodded, my attention shifting to the men who were hanging brightly painted shields on the sides of the ship for storage. An impressive cache of weapons had already been stored under loose planks, but Leif and I continued to carry our own swords.

"Which ship will carry my army?" I asked. They stood as still as statues upon the quay, neither fidgeting nor shifting their weight.

"As one of our greatest assets, we should distribute them evenly on each ship."

I knew this was in case the ship holding them sank, and I was once again struck by my fear of open water. "That is a sound plan, but what of Sleipnir?"

"The *knarr* is the only ship big enough for him, and I'll be sure there is plenty of livestock—should his . . . appetite return."

I frowned deeply. "Let's hope it doesn't."

As Leif and their men made their final arrangements, I took one final look at Dubhlinn and prayed it wouldn't be my last.

Despite my trepidation, when it came time to set sail, the excitement and pride of Leif's men flowed through me, as energizing as a lightning storm. On each ship, thirty men rowed us out of port, while forty undead men clustered together at the stern. They would need no shelter nor food, and even the space they occupied was minimal, as they never moved. The seer was also on board with us and had chosen a place to sit far from everyone else—by the cage of ravens. Leif had made sure she was on the same ship as I was. I hoped I could make use of my time by practicing my abilities—I had a fortnight to master them.

Leif and I stood at the bow of the ship, and when the great square sail bearing his insignia was lowered at last, a feeling like joy took flight within me. The ship glided forward on the relatively calm waters of the port, Leif's ship the point of the V formation they'd all assumed. Still, I couldn't help but glance back at the coast of Éirinn, fading faster as the wind grabbed hold of the sail.

Arin held on to the mast and crowed with unchecked delight. Leif's face split into a grin, and even the most battle-hardened men jostled and spoke with each other as cheerfully as if it were their first voyage as well. Leif pulled me down next to him to sit and reached out to catch the water's spray. With blue skies above, and the waters relatively calm, it was easy to relax.

"Will you tell me of your land?" I asked, watching the

sunlight dance across the water.

"What do you wish to know?"

"Anything. I want to know what to expect."

"There are mountains and lakes, rivers and fjords, but it isn't as cold as you might think," he said, and I could hear the faint smile he wore as he spoke of his homeland. "The water is bluer than the sky, and every child is born knowing how to sail a ship. Water is our life source, but we farm, too."

"Are you a farmer as well as a sailor?" I asked, a teasing note in my voice.

"My father owns land, yes, which will one day be mine, but I wouldn't say I'm a farmer."

"Then you're a sell-sword who owns land?"

He let out a short laugh. "I'm not a sell-sword either. I owe no one fealty but my father, who is jarl."

"Jarl?"

"Your people call them earls. He is jarl of a village half the size of Skien. It's how I came to have so many ships and men to sail them."

I stared at him in surprise. "How have I not heard talk of this?"

"Titles are not as important in the north. We judge a man more by his prowess on the battlefield. The men and women of the north are freemen, and freemen can make their own way in life. If you earn enough on raids, you can become a landowner with riches enough to be jarl."

His words seemed to strike me in the chest. Monasteries

burned and desecrated, holy men slaughtered, piles of stolen treasure. "The earnings from raids," I said slowly, "you mean . . . all the treasure you have stolen and killed for?"

His face darkened like a sudden storm. "We do not steal. There are few things worse than a thief."

"Forgive me. I fail to see the difference."

"The victors of a battle deserve the spoils. You took Sigtrygg's sword and crown; would you call yourself a thief?"

Anger flared within me at the accusation, white-hot, but just as quickly, it faded. Was I not equally violent? Had I not killed and destroyed? There were five graves behind us to remind me of my true nature, and countless others that were unmarked from years in battle. There was a darkness within me, and how could there not be? My mother was the Morrigan.

"I suppose you have a point," I conceded grudgingly.

He grinned. "I can only imagine how much of a struggle it was for you to admit that."

I nudged my shoulder into his but couldn't hide my own answering smile. It was little wonder we were so drawn to each other. We weren't so different.

Leif put his arm around me, and again I was struck by how relaxed he looked. I turned my attention to the sea, surprised by the beauty of the sky and the water. I'd seen it from the shore all my life, but there was something about the sparkling splendor of the sun on the waves that intensified the natural beauty.

The throaty croaking of ravens pulled me from my reverie of the water, and I looked up to find the seer watching me.

"Should I go now to speak with Sigrid?" I asked Leif.

One of the men seated across from us, Thorin, overheard. "It seems we're risking the wrath of Njord by having two women on board who practice *seidr*."

Leif gave him a hard look. "We're lucky to have such powerful abilities on board. No more talk of them as though they're cursed—not on my ship."

Thorin returned his attention to the sea, and I turned to Leif. "What does *seidr* mean?" I asked.

"It's difficult to explain," he said, and fell into a thoughtful silence. Then he added, "There are many aspects of *seidr* . . . but I've seen you demonstrate most of them."

A jolt of surprise ran through me. "There are others who can do the things I've done? There is a *name* for it?"

He shifted again as if uncomfortable. "Rarely. It's a . . . dark art. Most are wary of someone who practices it because it's a magic that affects the mind by illusion, magic, or control."

"And my mind control?"

"Odin is the only one who is capable of something so powerful . . . and you."

"Do you know much about it, then?" I asked, desperate to know more. My powers were growing and transforming—from being able to mentally control another, to separating my spirit from my body, and finally to calling upon a shadow army. It was frightening and thrilling at the same time.

"Not any more than most in my village—the only *seidr* we've experienced is the ability seers have to divine the fate of the gods, but beyond that, you'd have to ask Sigrid." He turned to me. "You are the most powerful *seidr* user I've ever known, and it's these abilities that will make the difference in this quest—I have no doubt about that."

"If I can master them in time," I said, worrying my lower lip with my teeth. "I should go speak with Sigrid."

I started to stand, but Leif put his hand on my arm. "Tonight would be a better time," he said. "This may be hard to believe, but watching you and Sigrid performing *seidr* would make the others nervous, and they're especially superstitious on the water."

With a snort of disbelief, I shifted so I was pressed against the hard muscles of his side. "Who knew you Northmen were so delicate?"

"We're as fragile as petals."

"I can see that," I said as I watched the men around me doing various disgusting things: everything from nose-picking to urinating over the side of the ship.

I just kept my eyes on the waves, the sun beginning its descent, casting its golden-orange rays over the water. It wasn't long before my sleepless night caught up to me, and my eyelids drooped. I stood unsteadily, not yet used to the water beneath my feet. "I believe I'll test out that nest of furs you arranged for me," I said to Leif.

He tried to pull me back on the bench. "Rest here with me."

"Tempting, but I've never been able to sleep in the presence of others," I said, with a nod toward the other men on board. Not only was I often plagued by nightmares, but I never felt comfortable relaxing my guard to the point necessary for sleep.

"That could become a problem for you," he said with a grin, "but go. Enjoy your privacy."

I smiled back at him as I picked my way carefully to the stern. Forty of my undead men parted for me, and as I passed through them, my shoulders dropped. I couldn't find my father, but Fergus was among them, his once animated face expressionless.

I stopped to touch his cheek, sorrow biting into me so strongly my breath hitched. "How I wish I could still talk to you," I murmured.

He didn't respond, and I didn't expect him to. I passed beyond the tarpaulin, and the undead men wordlessly moved into place before it, a wall of flesh between me and the rest of the men on board.

I lay down upon the soft furs and covered my eyes with my arm, letting sorrow and regret slam down upon me like waves.

When I woke next, it was so dark I had to blink several times to assure myself my eyes were open. Beside me came Leif's soft breathing; sometime in the night he had joined me, and I could only sigh at his audacity . . . even as I was secretly glad for his company.

Something had woken me, though, and I lay for a moment,

listening to see what it was. The sound came again: my name followed by the pungent smell of sage.

The seer was calling me.

I stood carefully but was pleased to see my body had already adjusted to the movement of the waves. I drew aside the tarp and froze in wonder.

The moon illuminated the ship, falling upon the resting men and joined by countless stars. The light was so beautiful, so pure, and it shimmered silver on the dark waters. I stepped forward, and the men of my army parted again for me.

The Northmen slept in long bags made of leather and trimmed in fur. Not all were sleeping—Arin and another Northman, one who was not much older than I, sat playing a game near the mast. I found Sigrid beside the cage of ravens, and the birds seemed agitated in the light of the moon. Their feathers were so ruffled they resembled blades, jagged against the night sky.

"You wish to know more of *seidr*," she said, her voice just loud enough to be heard above the waves.

"I do, but more than that, I want to know how to control it."

"There is darkness in you," she said, and I could feel her eyes on me, "enough to destroy everything you care about. You will be a great and terrible queen."

For a moment, her words cast a spell upon me, showing me what could be. With my own abilities and my army of men, I could rule all of Éirinn. Mentally, I pulled myself free from the net of ambition. I would not fall prey to power-hungry visions. "My will is far greater than the darkness within."

"Tell me," the seer said from within the shadows of her robes, "is your mind control strong enough to take over the jötunn's mind?"

I stiffened. "How did you—"

"You have great powers, but you only use them when you're impatient and desperate during battle. You have practiced them, but you were forced to do so and reluctant. The number of *seidr* abilities you have is on the same level as a god's—mind control, sending your spirit from your body, summoning the dead—and yet you have mastered none of them."

Then what am I supposed to do? I thought but did not say. My tongue lay limp in my mouth—dumbfounded by the seer's words.

You must put your full efforts into mastering them as you never have before, she answered in my mind, and I jerked in surprise. "You wanted to ask me how I know these things about you. I know them because I have mastered the only *seidr* I have: visions and fate."

Then how can you hear my thoughts?

Because we are connected by the seidr *we both practice,* she answered in my mind, reminding me eerily of the Morrigan. "You have much to learn," she added out loud.

"I don't have long to train," I said, my thoughts slow and confused. "How am I to master so many skills?"

She shook her head as though frustrated with me. "You've had the key to doing so all along. Tell me, how is it that you control another's mind?"

"Because the Morrigan is my mother," I said, unsure what answer she wanted.

"Your immortal blood is what gifted you the ability in the first place, yes, but *how* do you control another's mind?"

I glanced up at the clear night sky as though it held the answer. "It's hard to put into words. I sink into myself and reach out with my mind. . . ."

"You are doing it wrong," the seer said, her tone becoming increasingly emphatic. The ravens beat their wings against the cage in response. "Your power lies not in the recesses of your mind, but in your *spirit*. Your mind is but a pale echo of what your spirit can do."

Her words resonated so strongly within me that I could feel the hum of their truth, along with a twinge of horror. I'd been wielding my powers wrong since they first manifested—could I have saved the Northmen who fell to the jötnar?

"Yes," the seer said, and my gaze jumped to hers and narrowed.

"Get out of my mind," I said in a growl.

"Detach your spirit from your body. It's the only way you'll be able to control a being as powerful as the jötnar."

"And how am I to do that during battle?" I demanded. "My body will be limp, unconscious—unprotected."

The seer's pale white hand shot out and pointed toward my undead clansmen behind me. "Do you not have powerful warriors who can stand guard? If you want to win the battle against the jötnar, your only hope is to stay safely apart and detach yourself from your body—only then will you gain control."

"I cannot abandon the others! How am I to remain safely apart while they battle for their lives?"

"Do not be a fool," the seer said, her tone sharp now. "Are you so great a warrior, then? You believe yourself to be more skilled at swordplay than the jarl's son?"

"No," I said.

"Then it's time you learned. Come with me." She walked to the side of the ship, and I followed, close enough that the spray created a fine mist on my face. "Look into the water."

I gripped the ship's side and leaned over, momentarily mesmerized by the moon sparkling over the water's surface. The next thing I knew, a dagger was held to my throat.

I didn't dare move. "What are you doing?" I asked carefully.

"Call your warriors—you have an army of undead at your command," she said.

"Or what? You'll kill me?" I didn't think she would kill me—Leif would kill her in retribution, for one thing—but I also didn't know her well enough to say for sure. Tentatively, I reached out with my mind toward hers.

"Perhaps," she whispered just behind me. "You don't know because you haven't the strength to breach my mind."

Before I could respond, she pushed away my attempt to enter her thoughts as easily as a grown man bats away a curious bee. It was clear her mental prowess was far greater than mine. My heart felt like it would break my ribs it was pounding so hard.

How do I call them? I wanted to shout at her, but I didn't want to waste my breath. I had a feeling she wouldn't answer me.

I tried to ignore the cold feel of metal against the sensitive skin of my throat and let my eyes fall closed. I reached out with my mind, but this wasn't like trying to take control of someone else—I wasn't making eye contact with anyone, for one thing, so I didn't have a specific target—but I could feel them. I could *see* them, though my eyes were closed. Shadowy forms wreathed in smoke. I could just make out their skeletal forms beneath.

Help me, I thought, and when nothing happened, I thought more desperately, *Help me!*

I could sense them appear just behind Sigrid, but with surprising speed, she spun us around so that I faced my warriors. Fergus—I'd recognize him anywhere—and Séamus. The two I'd had the most connection to in life? Whatever the reason, they were here now, ghostly and strange and magical.

Sigrid dropped the dagger from my throat. "Call them off now," she said.

"You took a great risk just doing that," I said, rubbing my throat. "What's to stop me from having them rip you to pieces?"

"You've learned to summon your warriors to guard over your body when you're vulnerable," she said, "but there is still much to learn. You need me."

I did need her, and I let out a hiss of frustration. "Did you really have to threaten me with bodily harm? Would it not have been easier simply to explain how to summon them?"

"I could have, but it would have taken you twice as long to

master. As I said before, you only use your power when you're in a desperate situation. This was the only way to contrive a situation where you felt threatened so that you might finally recognize how to access your power."

I shook my head, inwardly cursing the Northmen. Only they would think putting someone's life in danger was the best teaching method. I hated to think how they taught their children.

"We will continue tomorrow night," the seer said, already moving away toward her seat at the bow of the ship.

"I hope I survive," I grumbled.

"I do as well," she replied, "for I sense a storm is coming that will test us all."

21

We practiced only at night for the next five days. Hours and hours spent searching for that door in my mind—the one that had saved me from the jötnar twice. Two of my undead clansmen would stand watch over me while I forcefully pushed my spirit from my body. I couldn't do it fast, and I couldn't even do it reliably—one night I failed to do it at all, and I think if it hadn't been for my undead army, Sigrid would have bashed me over the head with her gnarled stick. It wasn't until the sixth night, though, that I realized what I'd been doing wrong: I'd been thinking about it too hard. The harder I concentrated, the more my conscious mind told me it was impossible, and then I couldn't do it at all. I had to free my mind and think of the result instead, of my spirit floating high above my body. Only then was I able to release my spirit from my body the moment I closed my eyes.

Then I entered the furthest recesses of my mind, threw open the door of light, and plunged through it. I knew this time was different from all the other moments I'd attempted to leave my body. Everything was clearer, less hazy, and I felt stronger than I had before.

Seeing my unconscious form below me was as disconcerting as it ever was. My body lay slumped on the rough wooden bench of the ship, the bright spot of my heart glowing strongly. My undead clansmen were even more astonishing to behold: their bodies were nothing but skeletons surrounded by swirling black smoke. The two bright red hearts that animated them had ethereal silver chains that connected to my own heart. I touched my chest with my ghostly hand but felt nothing but mist. No matter how many times I'd seen it, it was still difficult to believe.

With my body safely guarded, I was free to soar high above the ship like a bird. Or a ghost. Untethered, I watched the sleeping forms of the Northmen, the water black and fathomless, the ships gliding along. I saw the bright red hearts of everyone on board, including Sigrid's.

Then I had only to think of the beat of her heart, and I was there. Standing before her, I reached out and grasped her heart, feeling it beat steadily in my hand as she gasped and clutched her chest. Before the rhythm could be interrupted, I let go.

In the next instant, I returned to my body.

I walked over to her, expecting to hear her censure. Instead, she grinned at me.

"Now you are ready."

The next day, under a sky so blue it hurt my eyes to stare too long, the men sat around the mast corrupting Arin with stories of gods that were excessively violent or bawdy or both. My grasp of their language had always been elementary, but these past few days in such close quarters had changed my knowledge to close to fluent—at least in what I understood.

My mind was wandering, but I couldn't help but hear some of it, especially when I heard them mention the word *jötnar*.

"And then the giantess Skadi came to avenge her father," Agnarr said, his dark beard nearly the color of the bear's pelt he wore over his shoulders, though both were crusted with salt from the water that sprayed us all near constantly. His matching dark eyebrows rose in a suggestive leer. "She wore form-fitting armor, but her big breasts were bare, and every god who lay eyes on her wanted her beneath him, no matter if she was jötnar or not."

"So, this giantess's father was murdered by the gods," I interrupted, my arms crossed over my own chest protectively, "and when she came to avenge him, all the gods did was look at her with lust?"

Agnarr shook his head. "They made reparations to her, of course. She was able to choose any husband from among the gods she liked, but she had to make her choice based only on the sight of the gods' legs and feet." Agnarr stood and flexed his hairy calf muscles while the rest of the men roared with laughter.

Drawn by the riotous sound, Leif appeared at my side as I stared at the men with confusion. "But why would she choose them based on such a ridiculous reason?" I asked.

"It's just part of the legend," Agnarr said, with a glance that said it was what *I* said that was ridiculous.

"So who did she choose?" Arin asked. His eyes lit up like my sisters' did during story time.

"She picked the fairest legs she could, hoping they belonged to Baldur," Agnarr continued, "but as it turned out, she'd picked the legs of Njord." Again, the men laughed.

"Baldur is said to be the most handsome of the gods," Leif said to me.

"As beautiful as you, Leif," one of the other men called.

"Better to be beautiful than so ugly even maggots can't stand the sight of you," Leif called back to answering laughter.

"And who is Njord?" I asked.

"The sea god," Leif answered.

"And was he so terrible a choice, then?"

"He was a terrible choice for an ice giant who lived on the highest mountain peaks where the snow never melts," Agnarr said. "For nine days, Njord endured her cold, dark Thunder Home, before finally demanding they return to the sea. He hated the constant howling of the wolves and the cold that froze his piss the moment he relieved himself. But when they stayed for nine days in Noatun, Skadi found the cries of the seagulls so abrasive her ears bled by the end of her time spent there. Unable to agree on a place to live together, they parted ways."

"So her father was murdered, and all she got was a failed marriage instead of vengeance?" I asked, finding myself bizarrely sympathetic to this giantess who hated the sounds of the sea.

"Just whose side are you on?" Leif asked, draping his arm around my shoulders companionably, but still I couldn't shake the thoughts of the giant whose mind I'd controlled. More and more, it seemed the jötnar weren't the mindless evil I'd believed them to be, and I hated the sympathetic turn my own thoughts were taking. Did enduring a serious offense and wrongdoing justify an evil act in turn? I didn't want to think of them as anything but completely evil; I didn't want to recognize the parallels between their stories and those of humans. It was a wholly pointless endeavor, however, since they had to be stopped—no matter what their original quarrel.

"Either way, she became the goddess of winter," Agnarr said, "for which she should be grateful."

"Then . . . some of the jötnar are also your gods?" I asked, truly confused now. Were we to fight the gods themselves?

"Some are," Leif answered, "and some are not." He said this as though it should immediately illuminate everything in my mind, but before I could puzzle it out further, a voice drew our attention.

"Dark clouds spotted," one of Leif's men said grimly.

Indeed, the wind picked up, rippling the sail and slapping the rope against the mast. I stood, my eyes on the horizon. Something about this particular storm made the blood in my veins turn cold.

I sense a storm is coming that will test us all, the seer had said.

Leif turned to Arin and the rest of his men. "Make ready for the storm."

After lowering the sail, the men around us, including many from my undead army, took their places at the oars and prepared to row. Once the storm's strong winds caught the sail, we could be knocked completely off course.

Lightning lit the sky, a powerful crack of thunder followed, and I heard the horses on the other ship scream.

The black waters churned, as dark as the angry sky above us.

"We have angered Thor," Agnarr said. The braids of his beard were almost the color of the sky. "He beats upon his anvil, showering the sky with sparks."

"No god is angry with us," Sigrid said. "We have been steered into the storm by the sea itself."

"Njord?" Agnarr asked.

"No, this has the feel of something much more malevolent." Her milky eyes stared at the dark sky before turning back to me. "You didn't do your job well enough, Queen of Dubhlinn. You left behind someone loyal to Sigtrygg and the jötnar."

"What do you mean?" I demanded, already impatient with her cryptic answers. "What does that have to do with the storm?"

For once, she took pity on me and clarified. "A spy. Someone sent word to Fenris that the two of you set sail for Skien."

Instantly I thought of the Celtic seer. Had his fear of me been an act? He was the only one who stood out in my mind, though it could have been anyone. "The jötnar have such power?"

"They control as much magic as the gods when it comes to the elements, and the sea is no exception." Her milky gaze shifted to Leif. "They will be steering you toward something worse than a storm. Be on your guard."

An interrupted shout from the bow of the ship was our only warning as the prow slammed into a massive wave. Leif grabbed hold of me with one arm, the other clutching the mast. The rest of the Northmen braced themselves, holding on to the sides of the ship. Water collected rapidly in the hull, soaking our boots.

When next I looked at the remaining ships, they had all fallen back, with ours in the lead. Undead men upon each deck joined the rowers, adding their superior endurance. Following Leif's lead, the oars split into black water, forcing the ships forward despite the strong winds. Still the waves crashed over us, soaking our clothes and hair as the falling rain did the same. The assault upon my senses was truly like nothing I had ever endured, and I longed for shelter.

I scanned the water as we made agonizingly slow progress forward, afraid of what I would see. The black sky seemed much too close, the waves mountainous. Lightning arced across the sky, and the biggest wave yet swelled before us. The ships rode it to the top, but as soon as we had crested, we plummeted back to the unforgiving water below.

In the next instant, I was airborne. I heard Leif scream my name as the wind and rain blinded me. I plunged into the freezing-cold waters, a wave burying me before I even had a chance to get my bearings. I struggled to the surface, gasping for breath only to have my mouth filled with rain and seawater.

Sputtering and barely treading water, I watched as the ships continued on . . . and disappeared behind the massive waves.

The horror that I was now very much alone in a dark and stormy sea descended upon me, nearly sinking me with its weight. Again and again the waves hit me, and I had to kick furiously just to keep my head above water. I forced myself forward in the direction the ships had gone, my way only occasionally lit by bolts of lightning.

I cannot die here, I thought, though it seemed all of nature had turned against me.

That was when I felt something large brush against my leg.

I wanted to scream but could not; the rain and seawater would fill my mouth as soon as I opened it. Again, the unknown creature bumped against me, and this time, my boot scraped along it, giving me an indication of its size. This was no shark. The thing was bigger than the ship, and I knew at once this was a sea serpent.

Lightning lit the sky again, and I glanced behind me. From out of the water rose the end of a scaled tail, and it was only a moment before I realized the creature was headed in the direction of the ships. As it rushed by me, I grabbed on. Its scales bit into my hands, but if the creature realized I now clung to it, it gave no indication.

The sea serpent seemed to pick up speed. Waves slammed over my head, and I gritted my teeth. Lightning flashed again, and there, not far from us now, were the ships. The relief I felt was so powerful I nearly relaxed my hold on the serpent's tail, but then I realized this same creature that was so generously giving me a ride was also dangerously close to the ships.

It continued on, so close now I could see the oars striking the water. Closer and closer I came until I could make out a form in the water. Leif was swimming toward me, a tether of rope swimming behind him. He must have jumped in after me, only he'd been smart enough to anchor himself to the ship first. I was so relieved that he'd come after me—that he hadn't left me for dead.

"Leif!" I tried to shout, but received a mouthful of water for my efforts.

The serpent dragged me forward until I crashed into Leif and let go of the creature's tail. Leif's strong arm wrapped around me, the other still holding on to the rope.

"Ciara, thank the gods," he shouted, waves and rain interrupting his words.

"Sea serpent!" I shouted back, pointing toward the ships, praying he could understand me.

His head jerked back toward the ships. "Hold on," he said. I wrapped my arms around his waist, and he pulled us along the length of the rope, hand over hand.

Water gushed over the side of the ship, and I glanced up. The sea serpent rose from the sea behind the ships, as massive as a mountain. Its head was like that of a dragon, its body of a snake. Its jaws opened wide, great swords instead of teeth, and I heard the shouts of men. The rowing stopped as everyone on board the ships grabbed their weapons.

Helplessly, I watched as the creature's head descended toward the men on board.

22

Its teeth were met by the swords of the undead. They'd all moved as one to parry before the mortal men could even rise. Around us, the storm still raged. Rippling through the water came the sea serpent's tail, and it coiled around the ships like an enormous chain.

We were almost to the ship. Leif grabbed hold of the rudder, and I reached out with my mind—through the wind and rain, past the grim and frightened minds of the men on board, until I could feel the creature's noticeably different thoughts. There were no words in its mind, only images and emotions. The anticipated thrill of destroying the ships, the sweet taste of human flesh—something it so rarely chanced upon—and fury and confusion at being deflected in its goals by my undead army, tainted creatures it had never encountered.

I waded in and snatched control, wrapping its consciousness with hundreds of invisible chains. The tail around us froze.

The sea serpent sent a flood of threatening images through our connection: it would find me, and then it would bite my head from my neck. Nauseous and cold, I felt fear churn within me as I was forced to watch myself being killed and eaten repeatedly, but still I held fast.

Leif grabbed hold of the ship's rudder and boosted me up to waiting hands. He followed behind me, collapsing beside me on the deck as we both gasped for breath. He recovered faster than I did and hauled us both to our feet.

"I would hold you just to assure myself you were safe if I could," he said, "but for now, it will have to be a promise."

My heart beat unsteadily in my chest.

The sea serpent's consciousness fought mine, until I struggled to hold on. It was too strong; I was losing control. Below us, its tail wrapped around the ships.

I squeezed Leif's waist to draw his attention. "The tail will crush the ships. Hold on to me!" I yelled, and Leif wrapped an arm like a band of iron around me.

I didn't have time to explain my plan to Leif. All those nights of practice allowed me to instantly access the door in my mind: I separated myself from my body and fell limp against him.

I could see Leif shouting fearfully at me, scooping me off my feet and clutching me to his chest, but I couldn't worry about that right now. I knew he would keep me safe.

Closer now, I could see just how large the serpent was. Its

head was wider than the ship, its teeth as long as swords. It was green and blue, its scales iridescent in the flashes of lightning, wicked spikes running the length of its body.

If I didn't crush it from the inside, it would easily destroy the ship and everyone on it.

Finding the glowing red pulse of its heart wasn't as easy as finding it on a human. Its massive size, and the fact that most of its body was still in the water, made it difficult. I floated above, unsure, as my undead warriors kept it at bay. I thought of what the seer would tell me to do, and suddenly, I realized: my form was all spirit—I could go underwater without needing to draw breath.

I dived into the black, churning water. I couldn't see anything but darkness and a vague form of the monster, but I didn't need to. Its heart was enormous—one-third the size of the ship—and glowed brightly enough to light up the water around it. I plunged my hand into the serpent's chest and grabbed hold as best I could.

It quickly became obvious I wouldn't be able to crush this heart—it was far too large. Someone would have to kill it with an actual blade. I was holding it enough to throw off its rhythm, giving someone else time to finish it.

When several moments passed and nothing happened, I realized I'd have to convey what needed to be done. I thought of the way the seer had taught me to summon my warriors, and I reached out to them—I could see them, their skeletal forms awaiting my command.

I'm holding it captive; now you must finish it, I said through our link.

I could see what my undead clansmen could: the serpent frozen as though the lightning had struck it. A gleam of metal, and then I saw it: a sword protruding from between its eyes. One of my clansman had pierced the soft underside of the serpent's head.

Its head and neck came crashing down, narrowly missing the mast. Even still, it landed on the deck so hard the ship nearly capsized, and some almost found themselves lost at sea. We held our breaths and watched as the serpent was quickly swallowed by the churning waves. At last, it was no longer a threat. I closed my eyes at the relief of having survived such an attack.

When I came to myself again, I touched my hand to Leif's chest. He still held me, so close I could hardly breathe.

"Ciara," he said in a breathless rush. He put me down but didn't let go—in fact, he pulled me toward him again until I was pressed against his chest. "By the gods, I didn't know what had happened to you." He leaned back just long enough to put both hands on either side of my face, and then he kissed me, and we were both heedless to the rain pouring over us, the thunder booming overhead.

"I had to stop the serpent long enough for my warriors to kill it—I'm sorry, I didn't think there was time to explain," I said when he pulled back again.

"You frightened me more than the monster," he said. "You

aren't the one who's supposed to die."

"Neither of us will die—look at the creature they sent after us, and we defeated it." I touched his wet cheek. "We don't have to accept your fate."

He leaned into my touch for a moment before turning back to his men. "The sky is lighter ahead. Keep rowing!"

The men took up their places once again, though the serpent had damaged several thwarts from where it had landed, costing us several rowers.

I watched the *knarr* anxiously, but it continued on, though it rode much lower in the water than the rest of the ships. Frantically, the men on board shoveled bucketful after bucketful of water. Sheets of driving rain continued to fall even as the waves brought more water over the sides of the ships.

The undead showed no sign of being bothered by the storm, and indeed, did not even appear wet. They rowed tirelessly as the last of my strength gave way and I sank to my knees.

And then Leif was there, lending his strength to me. Together we surveyed the ships, anxiety sinking vicious claws into me every time we crested a wave. I had nothing left to give should things go terribly wrong, and worse still was the knowledge that there would be nothing I *could* do should any of the ships start to sink.

Then the rain, as suddenly as it had come, slackened. The clouds went from black to gray, and the mountainous waves transitioned into hills.

When the sky lightened so much so that we could see clearly

again, and the rain became only a light mist, the living men upon every ship let out a roar.

"Thor has spared us," Agnarr said.

I shook my head as I gazed slowly at the smoothly sailing ships on either side of us. "No. We saved ourselves."

Sigrid stepped forward, somehow barely wet. "The storm was designed to drive your ships into the sea serpent." She looked at Leif. "Fenris knows you're coming."

Leif's arm tightened around me. "Then he'd better prepare."

That night, I lay beside Leif and stared up at the blessedly clear night sky. I couldn't enjoy the breathtaking beauty of the glittering stars, though, because I was shivering so violently my teeth audibly clacked together. Everything was soaked from the rain and seawater—our clothing, the furs, our cloaks. Leif had fallen into an uneasy sleep, but my tremors became so powerful that I jerked against him.

"Ciara, what's wrong?" Leif asked, his voice gruff from sleep. He sat up. "Your skin is like ice."

He pulled me toward him, but my limbs were stiff and uncooperative. When he started stripping my clothes from my body, I managed to unlock my jaw long enough to protest. "What are you doing?" I demanded.

He dragged over one of the leather bags the men used for sleeping—the fur around the top was wet, but the inner fur was dry, and *warm.* "Forgive me," he said. "You should have told me how cold you were—all I could think about was collapsing on these furs and sleeping."

"It's all right," I said, my words broken because of my chattering teeth.

"Getting in this will warm you, but not in your wet clothes," he said with a pointed look at my soaked tunic, boots, and leather leggings. "You'll have to trust I won't take advantage of your nakedness."

"Of course I trust you," I managed to force out.

He efficiently and quickly stripped me of clothing and light armor, and I was too cold to blush, too numb to even appreciate the feel of his hands upon me. And then the fur surrounded me, and after a few quiet minutes of shivering, it finally calmed.

"Better?" he asked, a strange tone to his voice. I met his gaze, and heat rushed through me as I realized his efforts hadn't been so efficiently detached after all, for even in the darkness, I could see that his eyes burned with desire.

It ignited something within me. All that we had been through together, all the times he had helped me and challenged me—the feel of his lips on mine, the comfort he gave me just lying chastely beside me each night. All of these things rushed through my mind, and I realized, I wanted more. I wanted him.

But as much as I felt the stirrings of desire within my own body, I wouldn't give in to them—not here. Not covered in sweat and salt, surrounded by men and separated by a mere piece of cloth.

"Leif," I said quietly, "thank you for jumping into the water to save me."

"There's no need to thank me," he said, his gaze intent on mine. "I think I've made it clear I would do anything for you."

His words made my stomach flutter more than the most romantic poem ever could. I didn't think there was anyone who would say that about me—that they'd do anything for me. Not even my parents. It made me realize how much Leif meant to me, how terrifying it was to think I might one day lose him.

I couldn't bear to think about it.

"You have no idea how much that means to me," I said, and I felt my throat tighten.

"It makes it difficult not to come over there when you look at me like that," Leif said, heat flaring in his eyes.

"I want more of you—all of you," I said, the words tumbling out of my mouth before I could stop myself. "But not on this ship, not . . . without a bath."

He laughed, and he leaned down to kiss my lips gently. "Then we will wait, for I have wanted you all this time, and I will wait as long as it takes." His gaze swept over my form hidden beneath the leather and fur. "Even if it brings me physical pain to know you're naked right now."

I smiled as a blush again warmed my body. As he lay back down to sleep, I made a promise to myself and to him: we would find a way to save him.

I couldn't lose him.

23

The days at sea that followed the storm were uneventful. The sun shone in abundance as we sailed closer to Leif's home-land, and after a fortnight had passed, I was desperate for rain, if only to wash the salt from my body. My hair no longer flowed freely, but instead was a tangled mess of waves. Every inch of my skin and armor had a coating of gritty salt, both from the sea and my own sweat. Despite such deterrents, Leif and I shared the same bed of furs each night, though we did nothing but sleep. I appreciated his respectful restraint, but it was torturous all the same.

And just when I thought I couldn't take another day at sea, Leif called for a raven to be released.

"If I'm right," he told me as I watched the bird soar away

hopefully, "we aren't far from land."

"How will the raven tell us?" I asked.

"If it returns, then it couldn't find land."

I watched the sky that day like I had once watched it for storm clouds, but the bird never returned. I paced even more rapidly in the little space I had. The thought of land made the ship now seem desperately small. A light breeze teased at my hair, sending stray pieces into my eyes, and I pushed them away irritably.

"Land ahead," Leif said, and as though he had conjured it with his words alone, mountains rose in the distance.

The V of ships headed for a small spot in between the mountains like geese flying toward a pond. But as we drew closer, I realized the spot was a fjord.

The men rowed, and a hush fell over us all as the ships sailed into the narrow inlet. A mist rose from the clear, cold water as verdant mountains rose on either side. Sunlight filtered in from the clouds, dancing upon the glittering water.

I felt eyes upon me and turned to find Leif watching me intently. "What is it?" I asked.

He smiled. "I am only enjoying the sight of you seeing my fjord for the first time."

"It's far more beautiful than I could have imagined," I said. "The mountains are so green here."

"You expected snow and ice?"

What *had* I expected? Whenever I thought of the land where the Northmen came from, it was always bleak and dark in my mind. A cold, barren wasteland. Certainly not the awe-inspiring beauty of the soaring cliffs and glassy waters. "Yes, but this . . . this is almost as beautiful as Éirinn. Why, then, do Northmen plague our lands?"

"The fjords are impressive to look at, but we lack the fertile farmlands of the south."

"So you take ours," I said with a nod of understanding.

Leif grinned, his mood much too buoyant at the sight of land to be brought down by even my provocative questions. "We take them after defeating their owners; they are the spoils of war."

"Yes, I'm sure it's a hard battle against farmers."

His gaze shifted to the fjord. "Most of *us* are farmers. You'll see."

Warrior farmers, I thought, but didn't say. Up ahead, a quay jutted out into the water, its planks covered by at least one hundred people. They must've caught sight of the red skeletal dragon when we entered the fjord. Cheers of excitement carried back to us on the wind. So different from the screams of terror they would be greeted with in Éirinn.

Behind them stood rows of wooden, thatched houses—not unlike the ones in Dubhlinn, only larger. The crowd was mostly made up of women and children, though there were also a few older men, and men who must have stayed behind to watch over the village.

I glanced up at Leif, this man I was so drawn to and yet knew so little about. An answering excitement bubbled up within me at the thought that maybe I would have the chance to learn more about him.

The men rowed our longship to one side of the quay, the *knarr* on the other. The three remaining longships were rowed all the way to the shore, where their shallow hulls breached. As soon as the ships were secured, men streamed off, eager to see the loved ones they'd left behind. The bloodthirsty warriors I'd come to know transformed into loving husbands and fathers; even the most fearsome of them were surrounded by laughing children. Here they were not dragons, only ordinary family men.

Sigtrygg's men were nearly indistinguishable from the Northmen. All were equally filthy, for one thing. The sea had not been kind. But I also heard many speaking in the Northmen's own language, conversing as easily as warriors who have fought battles together would do. The close confines of the ship had done much for bringing us all together.

Arin greeted a young girl about his age, both shyly smiling at each other, but clearly thrilled to be reunited. Leif slipped an arm around me, a relaxed smile on his face. He didn't seem to be looking for anyone in the crowd, only relieved to be home. Again I wondered at his life before we met. Had it been a lonely one?

Then a slim woman approached us, and I stiffened in surprise. Perhaps I had been wrong to assume he had left no one behind.

"Leif," she said, "I thank the gods you have returned. Shall I prepare a feast in celebration?"

Something in me relaxed as I translated the Norse words. A servant, then.

"Thank you, Zinna," he said. "Tomorrow night we will feast, and we've returned with food to replenish the larders. We must give our allies time to arrive. But why has my father not come to greet us?"

A shadow passed over her face, and she bowed her head. "He has been unwell these past few weeks and mostly stays confined to his room. He's been looking forward to your return, though, and reserving his strength for the feast."

A muscle in Leif's jaw flexed. "I'll go to him as soon as we are settled."

Zinna's almond-shaped eyes shifted to my face, but she did not voice her silent question. Leif caught her questioning look. "This is Ciara, Queen of Dyflin and Princess of Mide. Let everyone know her commands are to be followed as if I had given them myself."

Zinna nodded. "Of course. Welcome, Queen Ciara."

Some of the gaiety of the crowd dimmed when they caught sight of my undead army, remaining on board the ships. They glanced at one another and murmured, clearly unnerved by what they saw. "These are men of Hel," they said to one another.

One of the men unloaded Abrax and Sleipnir, and the sight of the black stallion with red eyes nearly silenced the crowd. Some of the women cried out, and I heard the same name repeated over and over: Helhest.

I turned to Leif, my brows knitted in concern and question.

"Helhest is the steed of Hel, and is said to be a plague-bringer," he said. "Hel is a daughter of Loki, and she maintains the realm of the dead." To his people, he raised his hands. "There is nothing to fear from these warriors and this horse. They are our allies, sworn to defend us against the jötnar."

His words had a calming effect, but still, many shot distrustful glances toward the ships and my horse.

Leif smiled, his mood lighter than I'd ever seen it. "Come, it's time to show you my home."

"I will follow you anywhere as long as there is a bath at the end of it."

He laughed. "Did the rainstorm not count?"

I shook my head as I smiled back at him. "Even if it did, that was a week ago."

"I'm sure we can find something for you to bathe in." His gaze held mine for a moment—a promise of things to come—and my stomach fluttered.

Though the majority of the villagers were down by the ships, I could tell the village was as busy as any city. We passed a blacksmith forge, horseshoes and weapons upon the walls in place of a sign; stray chickens and pens of sheep and goats; a stable for the horses; various shops with pottery and baskets; and everywhere, wooden shields and iron axes.

We stopped at the base of stairs leading up to a longhouse. Shields bearing Leif's insignia hung from the wooden planks. "This is the great hall," he said, and continued through the door.

Once inside, I paused as I took in the massive room. The ceiling soared above us, while the room itself seemed big enough for one hundred men. Upon every wall was some symbol of death: antlers, skulls, weapons, shields, Leif's dragon insignia. Even so, the objects were arranged in such a way that there was a wild beauty to them. The smell of smoke wafted over to me from a large fire pit in the middle of the floor. The hall was as dim as a tavern.

On one side of the room sat a dais covered in skins and furs instead of rugs. Two large chairs, their backs and arms made of antlers, waited. Leif stared at them, his lips slightly parted as though surprised.

"Your father had the other made for you," Zinna said, coming up behind us.

He paused as though taken aback, darting a look toward Zinna that was fraught with confusion and concern. "Has he been so unwell that he hasn't been able to hear the needs of the village?"

She averted her eyes. "He has made do, but I know he has looked forward to your arrival."

"I'll go to him soon." Leif turned to me. "Shall I show you to your room?" he asked. "You've waited for a bath long enough."

I smiled and followed as he led me into one of the side hallways.

"Is everything all right?" I asked quietly.

"My father was injured long ago, and he's never really recovered," Leif said. "He has trouble walking, and at times, the pain is so bad he cannot get out of bed. But he's always been able to do his duties as jarl." He let out a pained sigh. "The fact that he has brought in another chair for me can only mean he has become too ill to continue."

I reached up and touched his cheek. "I'm sorry, Leif," I said, hating the pain in his eyes.

He took my hand and kissed the palm. "I must go. Do you need anything? Zinna will help you with a bath, and I will return as soon as I can."

"Of course, go—don't worry about me."

This time he kissed my lips gently before leaning in and whispering in my ear, "I look forward to tonight."

Heat spread outward from the core of me and traveled up my neck. My eyelids fell closed as he pressed another kiss on my neck. I knew I was in danger staying here with Leif. The more I learned of him, the more I felt my convictions toward him disappear.

He had never seemed more human.

After bathing, my skin and hair scented with lavender instead of sweat and seawater, I felt more relaxed than I had in weeks. I waited as long as I could for Leif, but after weeks spent on board a ship with little sleep, I slept like the dead.

The next morning, I opened my eyes to an empty room and immediately squeezed them closed again with a groan. How could I have fallen asleep? I had so badly wanted to be with Leif, especially after having a bath that made me feel attractive again. As I sat up in bed, another thought entered my mind: Had Leif even returned? I wasn't usually such a deep sleeper, but I must have been more exhausted than I'd thought.

When I finally left my soft bed, I found that Zinna had kindly laid out both a tunic and a gown for me, but in this land I was a stranger to, I preferred to stay in my leather armor. I tugged on the tunic to wear beneath my armor, which, to my surprise, had easily come clean with merely a wet cloth, the leather as soft and supple as it had been when first gifted to me.

A firm knock came at my door, and I opened it to find Leif, dressed in a long belted tunic, leather leggings, silver wolf's fur mantle, and tall leather boots. A single chain hung around his neck, a dragon biting its tail as the pendant. His hair was freshly washed and braided, his teeth white as he smiled down on me.

Our gazes caught and held, and soon his mouth was descending as I rose to meet him. He tasted of honeyed mead, and as his wide hands took hold of my hips and brought me closer, I nearly pulled him into my room.

"You are so beautiful," Leif said, "and if I wasn't sure someone would come and drag us out of this room before we had a chance to enjoy each other, I would gladly forgo greeting our allies."

I shook my head, but a pleased smile touched my lips. "That's what you said last night, but you never showed."

He laughed. "I did, but you were sleeping so peacefully I couldn't bear to wake you."

"I didn't even hear you come in." I tilted my head. "What kept you?"

A shadow passed over his face. "My father. He is much worse than I'd anticipated."

I reached out and touched his arm. "I am sorry. Is there anything I can do?"

He grinned. "I can think of a few things you can do to comfort me, but I'm afraid I don't have time at the moment to dedicate to it."

"Will a kiss suffice?" I asked, letting out a little laugh as he pulled me toward him.

He kissed me again with a growl of frustration. "Come with me before I change my mind. We'll walk to the docks, and you'll see how domestically we live here."

I followed him back into the quieter hall, where a fire still blazed and many servants hurried about their different tasks. "Do you have cattle and sheep? I won't consider it truly domestic unless you do."

"Of course." He stopped and called over one of the servants, who quickly answered his summons. "Would you bring us some *skyr*?"

She nodded and hurried away. When she returned again, she brought with her small wooden bowls full of a creamy white food.

"Try it," Leif said, handing me one of the wooden spoons.

I dipped the spoon in, surprised by how thick it was. When I tasted it, there was a tartness on my tongue but also quite a bit of sweet. "Delicious," I said. "How do you make it?"

"It's made from cow's milk strained through cloth. We usually make it when we make our cheese."

This was much more domestic than I'd ever imagined the Northmen being, but I refused to admit I'd only ever thought of them eating raw meat and drinking ale and mead. We continued out of the longhouse and made our way through the village. Everyone we passed was busily working—the blacksmith hammering horseshoes, a fisherman gutting his fish, women weaving baskets, and children laughing and playing. There was no great show of notice when Leif passed by. He was one of them, not someone to be worshipped as many of our kings were.

The smell of the sea blew in on the breeze, triggering a painful homesickness. I thought of my sisters and Máthair. I could almost feel the softness of Deirdre's hair, or the fierceness of Branna's hugs. *Soon*, I promised them.

A low horn sounded from the shore behind us, and I turned toward the sound, my eyes scanning the distant waters.

Leif did the same. "One of my father's allies has answered my summons," he said as the ships' banners came into view. "We will need all the help we can get for the battle against Fenris."

Though there was no danger, my heart continued to race along in my chest. A low horn sounding and dragon-prow ships in the water had a different meaning for me, though even in this, my heart was changing.

Many of the villagers were already down at the quay to await the Northmen who had come. Two new ships now stood next to Leif's, and the occupants were watching my army still on board them with as much distrust as the villagers had shown.

As the newcomers disembarked, I searched for their leader, curious to see who would be fighting alongside us. A slow smile took my face by surprise when I saw who it was.

A woman.

There was no doubt she was the leader, with her beautiful mantle of sable fur atop leather armor and longsword strapped to her hip. Her hair was worn in intricate blond braids upon her head, and her face was as fierce and angular as an eagle's. The men followed in her wake as she approached us.

"Rúna," Leif said. They clasped hands in greeting before she pulled Leif in for a firm embrace.

"I have brought you forty men," she said. Her green eyes shifted to mine. "You are the Celtic queen?"

"I am Ciara," I said, surprised she had already heard of me. Word spread fast through these northern lands.

"Rúna is my aunt," Leif said with a fond smile, "my father's only sister and a jarl in her own right."

"And where is my brother?" Rúna asked with a smile. "Or does my arrival not warrant a greeting from the jarl?"

Leif touched her shoulder. "I was told upon my own arrival that his condition has worsened to the point that he can rarely leave his bed, Aunt, but he may join us in our feast tonight."

Her smile faded. "It pains me to hear that. I will go to him, then. But first: What is the plan? How many others will respond to the summons?"

Leif gestured for us to follow him back toward the longhouse. "I can count on Jarl Thorsten and Inghard to bring more men, but neither will be able to bring as many as you. They should arrive by tomorrow, and then we will sail to Skien."

When we entered the longhouse, the three of us sat around the fire pit in the main hall, and a servant brought us mead to drink from horns capped with gold.

"You plan to attack from the fjord?" Rúna asked Leif.

"Yes."

"Hm," she said. "Do you have a map?"

He paused, considering. "You think it would be better to attack from behind the city?"

"So they won't see us coming," I said, understanding dawning. The Viking longships were fast, but the fjords were narrow. They would be seen before they could make landfall, and giving the jötnar the chance to transform was a death sentence. "They will be anticipating an attack—the sea serpent showed us that."

Leif nodded. "They'll be expecting us."

"Sea serpent?" Rúna asked, confusion knitting her brows together.

"There was a jötnar spy in Dubhlinn who sent word to Fenris of our movements," he clarified for her. "Fenris in turn sent an *ormr* to deal with us, but"—he glanced at me with a smile—"Ciara dealt with it easily."

I laughed. "I don't know about 'easily' . . ."

"Either way," Leif said, "it's dead and we're alive." He stood and squeezed my shoulder gently. "I'll go get a map of Skien."

I turned my attention back to Rúna, who was watching me over the flames of the fire.

"You *are* beautiful," Rúna said appraisingly as I took a sip of the mead. "I can see why he keeps you by his side."

"And you are as bluntly outspoken as Leif," I said. "It's no wonder you're related."

She smiled. "It must be in the blood. It's been too long since I've seen him." She took a sip of her own mead thoughtfully. "The last time was when his sister, Finna, was still alive. Two winters have passed since then. And now my brother has taken ill. Have you seen him? Is his condition truly that bad?"

I shook my head. "He has been too ill to leave his bed, but I hope to make his acquaintance tonight at the feast."

"Worse than I thought," she said quietly. A shadow of sadness crossed over her fierce face. "It's mostly because of my niece that I'm here. She was a kind and lighthearted girl, one who would have made the best of mothers. What happened to her was a fate that should never befall anyone, let alone someone like her."

I thought of my own sister, and my hands tightened into fists. "We'll stop them," I swore.

Her sharp gaze met mine. "Tell me of your army. They say they never sleep nor move around the ships, only stand there as though you had brought statues to life."

"How have you heard of them?"

"News of them traveled with the summons."

Silence descended upon us as I contemplated how much to tell her. How to describe the men I had once loved who were now shells of the men they'd once been? "They have only seen one battle, but none fell," I said. "They strike as fast as vipers and never tire."

Rúna leaned forward. "But how did you come to have such an army?"

I thought of the two hundred men who had died, including my father, and the walls within me rose. "I paid a very high price."

Leif returned then, a rolled-up piece of leather tucked under his arm. He dragged a table over by the fire and unrolled the map. As we crowded around it, I examined the whole of his homeland for the first time: a jagged piece of land mostly made up of rivers, fjords, and mountains.

"Most of your land looks uninhabitable," I said, my finger tracing all the lines that represented water. "It's impressive you manage to have any farms at all."

"Was that a compliment?" Leif asked, humor shining in his eyes.

I made a rude sound in the back of my throat. "Don't make me regret giving it. Let's plan our strategy."

Leif grinned but turned back to the task at hand readily enough. His finger traced the lines of rivers leading from his village to Skien. "We could sail the ships up the rivers that end up to the north of Skien. From there, we can approach on foot."

"That is a much better ambush strategy," Rúna said. "I doubt they'll have any sentinels—they believe themselves to be invincible." She peered closely at the map. "If I'm not mistaken, though, there is a glacier nearby that will only slow our progress."

"We'll avoid it. But you're wrong, they will have watchmen." He glanced at me. "Now that Fenris knows we're amassing an army."

Rúna nodded grimly. "Then we will have to move swiftly."

As they continued to debate the best rivers to take, a subtle fluttering sound drew my attention to the window.

A great black bird stared back at me from outside the glass. My first thought was that it was the Morrigan, come to offer her own advice, but then I remembered she had told me she could not come to this land. The bird let out a low croak, and I realized it wasn't a crow, which the Morrigan always appeared as, but a raven instead. Unlike a crow, it had a tuft of feathers just above its beak. I followed the line of its sight and realized it wasn't looking at me at all.

It was watching Leif.

24

The rest of the day had progressed quickly: deciding strategy, gathering weapons, and welcoming another ally. The raven that had so intensely watched Leif through the window had flown away, though the sensation we were being watched lingered. Fear crept over me as I thought about Leif's agreement with the Valkyrie. Were they watching to make sure he kept his end of the bargain?

That prickly wariness still had not left me by the evening feast. As we entered the main hall, the din of a room full of voices greeted me. It seemed that the entire village had come to celebrate the return of Leif and his men. The smells of roasting meats, fresh-baked bread, and freely flowing ale and mead scented the air, and many eyes were upon me as I walked beside Leif.

He reached for my hand, and I took it. I had to resist the urge to clutch his hand to ease my worry that I would lose him at the end of this. I pushed such thoughts away before they could drag me under. I refused to live in fear.

Leif led me to one of the two chairs on the dais and clasped my hand again once we were seated. When I glanced at him, I could see that his face was pale.

"Are you all right?" I whispered.

His answering smile was a nervous one, and I shifted uncomfortably in my seat. My eyes scanned the people in the hall, searching for Leif's father in the crowd, but I could not find him. But all who met my gaze greeted me with a welcoming smile. I thought of the reactions of my own clansmen should I place an outsider in such a place of honor and sank down in my chair. I had seen so little of this land so far, and nothing was as I had expected.

Leif stood—reluctantly, it seemed to me—and the hall quieted. "Freemen and women, I've brought back a powerful ally as promised." He turned and held out his hand to me, and I got to my feet beside him. "This is Ciara, Princess of Mide, Queen of Dyflin. She single-handedly brought down a jötunn and defeated King Sigtrygg. Her prowess is well-known in Éirinn, and her abilities rival my own."

Loud murmurs of approval followed Leif's impressive introduction of me, and I was surprised by how much I wanted to live up to such words.

"She brings with her a powerful army—men who do not

easily fall. And we have sent call to our allies. Some of you have already lost men and women to the jötnar, and though you still mourn for your dead, there is only one thing that can ease your suffering: revenge." Many nods and shouts rang out from all those listening. "Tomorrow, we will sail to Skien and defeat Fenris in his own city."

Another roar of approval soared up at this, and Leif flashed his teeth. "Who here will join in the battle ahead?"

Men from the ship were the first to step forward, to offer themselves as warriors. Their wives nodded their approval, their chins held high with pride. As if caught up in the ritual of it all, Sigtrygg's men volunteered as well. It surprised me that though Leif's father was jarl, he still invited the men to volunteer, rather than forcing them into service. Others from the village stepped forward, all pledging their aid.

But when Arinbjorn stepped forward, Leif shook his head. "No, Arin," he said. "Not this time."

Arin's face darkened in an impressive imitation of his brother's. "Did I not prove myself battle-ready in Éirinn?"

"You did, but I had no choice there. You will stay here and watch over the village; you haven't yet come of age for battle."

Arin's face fell, but he bowed his head tersely. It was clear Leif would not be dissuaded.

After the last man had offered himself to the cause, the servants brought forth enormous iron cauldrons. It took two strong men to carry each steaming cauldron in, and when they had placed them before the table, one of the men turned to Leif.

"For the *blóta*," he said, and handed him a bowl full of a dark liquid.

Leif brought forth a long-handled brush from the bowl. "By this blood, we ask the gods for strength and good health in the battle to come."

Everyone in the room repeated the prayer, and then Leif flicked the brush until droplets of blood sprayed through the air. One drop landed on my forehead, and I touched it tentatively as it tracked down my face. The Northmen around me bowed their heads and murmured thanks to Odin or Freyja, but I could only stand in an awed sort of silence. There had been a time when I would have sneered at their ritual, been disgusted by the pagan sacrifice, but now that I was one of them . . . I could only see the good intentions behind it.

After making a full circuit around the room, Leif brought the bowl of blood to the foot of a crudely carved statue. He sprinkled more blood on it before returning to the front of the room.

"Let us feast," he said.

Two of the servants immediately pulled out the steaming meat from the cauldrons, while others piled food high on tables so long they ran the length of the room. Roast lamb and pork, dried fruits and nuts, salted fish, fresh fish, and bread so dark it was nearly black. Our table was set with wooden bowls and plates, sharp knives, and horns of mead. I sat beside Leif at the head and watched with an amused smile as everyone, but especially the Northmen we had sailed with, fell upon the food as though they were starving.

"I'm relieved that's over with," Leif said in a low voice to me.

I shot him an incredulous look. "So you *were* nervous."

"It's the first time I've addressed the freemen without my father and led the *blóta*." He frowned. "I'm not sure what's keeping my father—I don't relish speaking in front of so many."

I set my knife down to better stare at him. "This is what frightens you? Speaking in front of a crowded room?" He nodded sheepishly. "Well, if I hadn't noticed you were pale beforehand, I would not have even thought you were uncomfortable. You did a good job."

"I imagined I was speaking to them in the midst of a battle."

My laughter took us both by surprise, and soon, he was joining in.

The children finished first as children do, and their high-pitched laughs and screams punctuated the din as they began chasing one another about the hall. The now familiar sound of the Norse language flowed around me, and I leaned back, savoring my dessert of honeyed fruits and nuts.

I was happy for the feast, happy Leif and all of his allies could take part in it, for it might be the last feast we enjoyed for some time.

The feasting and dancing lasted long into the night, and after Leif had his fill of the bountiful food, he sat upon his throne wrought from wood and antlers with a horn of mead and watched. Many came to him, talking of the upcoming battle, or of more mundane matters, but always his eyes were upon me.

I enjoyed his gaze. Forgetting myself, I'd drunk far too much mead and danced until my legs were shaky and my cheeks were flushed. When he was finally alone, he caught my eye and gestured to the chair next to him, thoughtfully padded with furs. I fell down upon it in a heap.

"You are enjoying yourself here, among all these pagan barbarians," he said, with that teasing smile so familiar to me now.

I leaned my head back and smiled. "They may have horrid table manners, but never have I met a more welcoming people."

His gaze dropped to my mouth, and I felt a wave of desire lick up my stomach. But before he could say anything else, Agnarr's deep voice resonated from his place around the fire pit.

"Arin has just asked me to tell the tale of the jötnar," Agnarr said, pausing to take a sip from his horn of mead. "Do you know it?" he asked one of the small boys nearest him.

"No, Agnarr," the boy said, his eyes wide.

Agnarr smiled and glanced at me. "Neither, I'm sure, does the Celt." He gestured for me to join them around the fire. "Come, it would be good for you to hear the story of the enemy we will face tomorrow."

When I stood, Leif followed, and the others made room for us on the wooden bench.

"Long ago," Agnarr began, and everyone gave him their rapt attention, held captive by his rich voice, "in the void that existed before time began, two opposing forces reigned. In the north, it was ice and wind and rain, such that nothing could survive. And in the south, it was a blistering heat. It was from this meeting of ice and heat that the first being was formed: Ymir. He was a giant bigger than any of the mountains on earth. A jötunn son and a jötunn daughter sprang forth from his armpits as he slept—the first of the jötnar, the Frost Giants.

"When Father Odin later slayed Ymir, the giant's blood formed such a deluge that all but two jötnar drowned. From Ymir's flesh the earth was formed, and the rocks were formed from his bones. His skull became the sky above us, and his blood, the sea. The two remaining jötnar repopulated their race: some who would later help the gods . . . and others who would turn against them."

"What do they look like?" asked the boy seated at Agnarr's feet.

"Tall as trees, faces craggy and deformed, and claws on their hands," Agnarr said, and I thought of the few we had already encountered with a shudder. "But some are so beautiful not even the gods can resist them."

Good and evil, ugly and beautiful. The jötnar didn't sound so different from mortals, though I'd yet to encounter a human enemy who feasted upon the slain. The boy asked for more stories of the gods, and Agnarr gladly launched into another bawdy tale.

Soon, Rúna joined us, making everyone roar with approval with her tales of successful raids. I found even I was laughing at these Northman stories, but I could tell Leif was distracted. Half the time he watched me with such hunger in his eyes my stomach twisted with desire and I could hardly breathe. The other half of the time, though, he watched the entry to the hall for his father.

"Perhaps you should go to him," I said after his eyes had drifted to the doorway yet again.

"It would only insult his pride. He would see it as an unspoken proclamation that I believe him to be too weak to join us."

My brow furrowed. "Isn't he too weak? He's been bedridden this whole time, after all."

"Yes, but he said he'd be here," Leif said distractedly. "Going to him would mean that I no longer trust his word."

I shook my head. The Northmen's prickly pride made little sense.

"Aunt Rúna," Arin shouted above all the other voices, "tell us of the wolf you kept like a dog."

Rúna grinned. "There's a good lesson in that for you, nephew."

As the others roared again with laughter, a small commotion drew our attention to the entrance of the hall. A grizzled man dressed richly in dark velvet and fur leaned heavily upon his cane. Zinna and a woman I assumed was another servant hovered at either side of him, watching as though they feared he'd fall at any moment.

Leif jumped from the bench and strode forward to offer his arm, and the man took it after a moment's hesitation. The hall went silent, and some Northmen even bowed their heads. So this was Leif's father. He walked with a painfully pronounced limp, one of his legs so badly scarred and shriveled it was now deformed.

"Father," I could hear Leif say, his voice low, "are you sure you're well enough?"

The man brushed away his concern, but his voice sounded weak when he answered. "I wouldn't miss a feast."

Leif led him into the light of the fire, and as my gaze settled on the older man's face, I froze, every muscle in my body going stiff. The blood pounded in my ears.

The man's gaze shifted to mine, and so many feelings hit me at one time that I felt as though I would burst. They clamored within me, screaming to be heard.

A Northman looming above Alana and me, cutting off our escape—

—the axe in his hand stained red—

—a deep cut from his eyebrow down to his cheek dripping blood—

The scar splitting Leif's father's face from his eyebrow to his cheek was unmistakable.

"Father, this is Ciara, Queen of Dyflin and Princess of Mide," Leif said, holding his hand out to me with a proud smile. Confusion flitted across his face when I did nothing but stare at them both.

Leif's father bowed his head to me. "I am Jarl Olafsson, but you may call me Frey."

I clenched my hands into fists to hide how badly I was shaking. That voice. My sister's murderer's name was Frey Olafsson.

Blood for blood, he had said. And then he'd taken the dagger to Alana's throat.

Leif grabbed hold of my arm, steadying me. "What's wrong? Are you ill? Do you need to sit down?"

I could feel that I had no color in my face. My knees threatened to no longer hold me. So many times I'd thought of this moment—of what I would do if I was able to confront this man again—how I would tear his mind apart and force him to slit his own throat as he once slit my younger sister's. But the vicious man who had been my sister's attacker was no longer there. In his stead was a broken-down old man, one who could barely make it out of bed, who could barely stand on his own two feet.

And he was Leif's father.

"You murdered my sister," I said, the words torn out of me before I could stop and think.

I couldn't look at Leif, but I felt him stiffen in shock beside me. His father's ice-blue eyes—*Leif's* ice-blue eyes—stared at me with a slowly dawning realization.

"You murdered her before my eyes, and I have long hoped my father's injury to you was fatal. I see that it wasn't, but I hope your suffering has been unbearable."

He flinched before my words, but it wasn't enough.

"May you live another ten years in agony," I said, my voice thick with unshed tears.

I fled before he could respond, leaving the room full of horrified silence.

25

I barred my door. But it wasn't long before Leif came. He called softly through the door at first. When he got nothing but silence, his cajoling tone turned demanding.

"Ciara, let me in," he said. "We have to talk about this. Don't make me apologize through the door."

"Go away, Leif," I snapped, my shoulders hunched almost to my ears. I didn't know how I'd face him. Never had I felt so far from home as I did at this moment. I'd risked everything to join him on this quest, even more so when I traveled to the land of my clan's enemy. And now, despite knowing who his father was, I still wanted Leif.

It made me sick with confusion and rage.

"Don't make me break down this door," he threatened, and

it so incensed me that I strode over to the door and wrenched it open.

"How dare you—"

He plunged both hands into my hair and kissed me, his full lips soft against mine. I felt my eyes flutter closed before I finally pushed him away. "No. Why would you think you could kiss me right now?"

He let out a shuddering sigh. "I'm sorry, Ciara. I don't know what to do—I can't stand the thought of us going back to the way we were when we first met . . . not after all we've been through."

He reached toward me, and I jerked away.

His nearness was torture. I wanted to throw myself into his arms and bury my face against his chest, but then I would look up at his eyes—Jarl Frey's eyes—and see Alana dying again.

"Don't pull away from me," he said. "Not now. Not again. I am not my father."

"Did you know?" I countered. "Did you know your father murdered my sister? I told you the story—how could you not have known?" I suddenly felt sick. "Were you *there*?"

I backed up in horror, but he grabbed hold of my hand. "By all the gods, I swear to you, I didn't know until the moment you recognized him. I stayed here when he went on raids to Éirinn to keep watch over Arin and Finna."

I believed him, but it didn't make it any better. "I can't bear to look at you right now, Leif."

He looked like he wanted to argue, but he relented and

moved toward the door. Just before he left, he turned to me and said, "Just because it's my father doesn't mean I don't understand how you feel. I made it my life's mission to track down the jötnar and have my revenge for what they did to my sister. She was murdered, too, and if I came face-to-face with her murderer . . ." He trailed off, but his eyes were so full of sorrow and sympathy for me that I had to look away.

I was left alone for a time, while I paced my room like a caged animal. What would my father say if he knew I'd come face-to-face with Alana's killer and done nothing? And Máthair?

No, there was only one option: I would have my revenge.

It wasn't difficult to find the jarl's room. The door with heavily carved knotwork gave it away. To my horror it was only one door down from my own bedroom. I'd been separated from my sister's murderer by only a few walls this whole time.

I waited in the shadowy hallway until one of his servants left his room, and then I opened his door and strode in as if I belonged there. I gripped the hilt of my sword as my eyes adjusted to the darkness.

The feast had ended long ago, and I knew with the jarl's injuries he would retire early. He writhed on his bed, his breathing ragged and pained, and I could tell it was his leg that tortured him. I hated this broken man. Hated him for taking away my right to confront him for killing my sister, to demand justice. How could I demand justice from an infirm, elderly man? A man whose injuries had clearly been punishment enough all these years. Did he even remember killing my sister? Or was she just one of many faceless victims?

I stalked over to him, my blade catching the light of the fire as I passed by. As I stood over him, I contemplated all the ways I could kill him: the point of the blade thrust into his heart, a slash to his throat as he'd done to my own sister, a stab to his gut to make him die slowly and miserably.

He moaned in his sleep, and my hand turned white on the hilt of my sword. This man was nothing like the one from my memory—the heavily muscled monster. Now he was only a shriveled old man. I sighed heavily and took a step back.

"Jarl Frey," I said, just loud enough to wake him. His eyelids fluttered for a moment, and then those ice-blue eyes stared up at me.

"Have you come to put me out of my misery, then?" he asked, his gaze flicking to my sword.

I shook my head in disgust. "I told you before—you don't deserve such mercy."

"Then why have you come?"

"I want to know why you took my sister's life, but I know you won't be able to tell me. I'm sure she was only one of hundreds you've killed in your miserable life."

His eyes clouded over with pain. "You're wrong. I do remember."

I had the briefest sense of reaching toward his mind, and then I found myself completely immersed, as real as if I suddenly dived below the surface of the sea. There was no resistance from him. Not even the smallest protest that I had grabbed hold of his mind.

Show me the attack on my father's castle, I commanded, and the memories were wrenched toward me so fast I flinched before them.

There was Jarl Frey's longship landing on our shores, his men pouring over the sides with eager shouts. But Jarl Frey hung back, his hand upon an adolescent boy's shoulder.

"This is your first battle, so stay close to me," he said. "Your mother will skin me alive if one of the Celts kills you."

The boy grinned and flexed his lean muscles. "I'm stronger than I look, Uncle."

The memory shifted, moving rapidly through the battle that took so many of my clansmen's lives. And then the boy appeared again—seen through Jarl Frey's eyes. The boy stayed close at first, but they were soon separated by the chaos of battle. When Jarl Frey caught sight of him again, he was on the far side of the courtyard. The boy managed to take down one or two of my clansmen before another struck a blow to his side, placing him in the path of another man. With a jolt of recognition, I watched as my own father strode toward the boy, sword drawn. The boy tried to deflect my father's attack, but he was knocked back easily. With a twinge of horror, I watched my father run him through with his sword. The boy fell, his eyes wide and unseeing before he even hit the ground.

Jarl Frey let out a feral cry as a new flood of memories crashed over us: his nephew as a tiny infant cradled in a woman's arms, the boy learning swordplay from Frey, the same woman again who could only be the boy's mother, her eyes a unique mixture of worry, sadness, and pride as the ship set sail.

It was about this time in his memories that my own mother and sisters appeared. From Jarl Frey's viewpoint, there could be no doubt that we were the family of the king of Mide as we rushed toward the safety of the castle, dressed in our fine velvets and furs.

He contemplated killing my mother at first, but then when he saw my sister and me, his mind changed. *Blood for blood*, he had thought. *The king's daughter for the death of my sister's child.*

I watched him kill my sister again, felt her heart beat as fast as a bird's beneath his hand that restrained her. I watched and reminded myself why I hated him. Why I wanted him to suffer. But even with these convictions in my mind, I still saw the boy as a helpless infant in his mother's arms. I felt Jarl Frey's immeasurable pain at losing his nephew.

The memories skipped ahead—I supposed I was subconsciously calling them forth. Jarl Frey threw his crutches to the floor, fell to his knees at a beautiful woman's feet—his sister, the mother of the boy—and bowed his head. Her hair was so pale blond it was almost white, and tears streamed down her face. Icy shock trickled through me as I realized it was Rúna. But no harsh words came from her—only terrible sobs as she wrapped her arms around her brother.

His pain was a living thing that grew and grew no matter what poultices were used or how much he rested. Still he maintained his conviction that his actions were justified—that the innocent girl had deserved to die. But as the years passed, and his leg only worsened, he saw the truth: that he had angered the gods. He regretted what he had done, but in the darkness of his room at night, he admitted the truth to himself. He regretted it the most because it had crippled him, and he was now no longer able to be the warrior he always had been.

I pushed Jarl Frey's mind away from me as though it was tainted and came back to myself. I stared down at him, curled so pathetically on the bed. He had suffered far more than a quick death would have given him. The hatred in me for this man was an old, old hurt, one that had been allowed to flourish and take root deep inside me. It wouldn't easily be removed, but it was no longer strong enough to wish him further torture.

"My regret tortures me," he said when I relinquished his mind, "but I know it does nothing to take away your own pain. The gods saw fit to take my own daughter from me, and now I know your sorrow."

"I still cannot forgive you," I said, my jaw clenched around my words. "Not even for Leif."

Another tremor racked his body, and I left him there, suffering in his bed.

But I could no longer revel in it.

2ᛟ

I spent the night on board Leif's ship, surrounded by my undead army. After I left the jarl's room, I escaped outside, simply unable to face Leif. I wanted to go to Sleipnir's stall, but I knew it would be the first place Leif would look for me, and I couldn't talk to him—not yet. We would have to work together in battle, but I couldn't bear to be near him under his father's roof. The night was long and sleepless. My mind tortured me with endless images: my sister's death, meeting Leif's father, and worst of all, every touch and kiss and gentle word I'd received from Leif. It all felt like I was betraying my clansmen, my sisters, all over again. But even as I struggled with the weight of betrayal, I knew I could never abandon the quest. I'd seen for myself what my undead army could do against a jötunn foe, and it gave me hope that we would defeat Fenris and his army in the end. I owed it to my sisters and remaining clansmen to fight . . . and win.

By morning, I was a jittery, sleepless shadow of myself. Sequestered away from Leif and the others, I'd missed out on the battle preparation, and for once, I felt unprepared. But as I watched men and women march onto the quay, ready to defend themselves and their world from the jötnar threat, I felt my weariness disappear. They lined the sides of the longships with shields of many different colors: red, orange, white, green, blue. All with runes I'd never seen before. They climbed on board weighted down by armor and swords, until the ships hung low in the water. It was a terrifying and glorious sight.

As though sensing the battle ahead, the eyes of the undead warriors had come alive, a fierce sort of hunger alight in them. I prayed that their sacrifice would be worth it; that we would be the victors against the jötnar.

We'd gained two more longships in addition to Rúna's, and so it was with a fleet of eight that we set sail for the rivers west of Skien. After a roar of well-wishes sent from the people who stayed behind in the village, quiet settled over the ship; the only sound the waters lapping at the sides.

Leif was the last to board, and the sight of him brought me shamefully close to sobbing. He wore the armor gifted to him in the Morrigan's realm, his silver wolf mantle blowing softly in the wind. He looked tall and dangerously beautiful. I stiffened as he approached me, and hurt flashed across his face.

"I went to your father last night," I said quietly.

He nodded slowly. "I know you left him alive, and I thank you for that. I'm sure it couldn't have been easy."

"I went to him planning to kill him, but it was harder knowing that he regrets what he did," I said, unable to look at Leif. "It would have been easier to execute an unrepentant murderer."

He reached out and lifted my chin so I was looking him in the eyes. "You had mercy on my father, but you cannot extend the same mercy to me?"

I took a step back until he was no longer touching me. "I'm trying, Leif," I said, and I felt as though my heart was being torn from my body. "I'm trying not to see you as my enemy."

He reached out and grabbed hold of my shoulders. "Ciara, you cannot continue to push me away. We're about to go into battle together." He gave my shoulders a little shake. "We may never see each other again alive after this. What can I do to make you see how much you mean to me?" Suddenly he straightened. "Sigrid said that now you're strong enough to penetrate the jötnar's minds. You should try it on someone whose mind you couldn't breach before."

He had my full attention now. "You want me to try to take over your mind?"

"I trust you."

His words were like shards of ice to my heart. "Still, I don't think you realize just how . . . intimate it is. I could see your every thought and memory if I wanted to."

"I'll accept the risk."

"I'll be gentle," I said. He smiled a sad smile.

I reached out with my mind and stepped through into his easily, as though I'd never been barred from Leif's mind before. His thoughts swirled around me like leaves on the wind, and I snatched one free from his stream of consciousness.

It was me from the day we met on the battlefield, only it was an image of me I'd never seen in my own reflection. I brandished a sword against him, but instead of looking inexperienced and childlike as he'd once accused me of being, my whole body was taut with power. My black hair streamed behind me, my dark eyes flashing at him fiercely. I lifted my chin and met his gaze, and I could feel his reaction: it was as if he were ensnared in a spell.

Image after image appeared before me: me looking surprisingly beautiful in the cave in which I kept him prisoner—and Leif's knowledge that he could escape, but chose not to, just to stay with me a little longer—hundreds of little moments remembered from traveling together on Sleipnir, the first moment we kissed, the many battles we'd fought together, seeing his own land through my eyes.

In every image, in every moment, I was beautiful and strong and passionate.

You love me, I thought, awestruck.

The revelation hurt me more at this moment than it would have to suddenly discover he didn't care for me. He loved me, but I couldn't move past the knowledge of who his father was.

I love you more than I've loved anything—even the thrill of battle. His words resounded through me, all the more intense because I could feel without a shadow of a doubt that he meant them.

The shock pulled me free of his mind, and once I returned to my body, he pulled me to my feet. His hand was warm on mine, and my heart pounded furiously in my chest.

"Now you know the truth," Leif said.

I felt something inside me break.

The sun was setting when the longships beached on the shore of the river. Faster than I would have thought possible had I not seen it so many times before, the men disembarked. Sleipnir and Abrax were brought ashore, and my undead army followed. Leif mounted Abrax, and I pulled myself astride Sleipnir.

"We will attack after nightfall," Leif said as we gathered around him. "We must kill as many as we can before they have the chance to grow into their giant height, but even in their smaller forms, they are faster and more skilled than you. Stay together." His eyes met mine over the heads of all the others, and I nodded my assent. "Let's go."

The total number of men had swelled to over three hundred, and yet I still feared it wouldn't be enough to stop the jötnar.

Sleipnir and Abrax trotted side by side as we followed the river east toward Skien, leading the army to what would be death for the vast majority of them, at least the ones who were still living. Rúna rode a little behind us; there was no fear on her face, only determination. She and the other Northmen were glad to have the chance to die in battle, and though I didn't share this particular sentiment, I was willing to do anything to stop the jötnar.

The night sky was clear, the moon full, as though the heavens above had decided to lend us their aid. Our path was lit so well we did not need to light torches, and we marched onward, the landscape a blur of trees and hills and rocky ground.

We continued in silence, the horses' hooves and the light clanking of weapons against chain mail the only distinguishable sounds. In the distance, light from fires in the city loomed. Unlike Leif's village, this city was much larger—nearly the size of Dubhlinn—and was surrounded by a high wooden wall. Beyond it was the fjord, and I could only just make out the sails of numerous longships—perhaps thirty at the least. At the top of the next hill, Leif raised his arm, and the army came to a halt.

He waved one of his men forward—a tall and lanky man with a tattoo of a knotwork snake that slithered up from his neck to his ear. "Scout for us, Arn. I want to know the location of every guard."

Arn sprinted down the hill, and the blood pounded in my ears. Anticipation was the hardest part of a battle. It always felt as though my body would burn up, the blood boiling inside me, every muscle taut. Once engaged in battle, though, all of those sensations would fall away. But more than anything, my body thrummed with the thrill of truly unleashing my power for the first time.

Leif did not give a stirring speech to raise morale for the

battle ahead. These were hardened warriors, raiders who needed very little encouragement to pick up an axe or sword. I could see eagerness in the tightness of their grips on their weapons, the subtle shifts of their bodies, waiting for the word to be given to charge.

So it was for my ears alone when Leif leaned over and said, "Remember, we work together. We'll take them down one by one, and we'll use each other's strengths to destroy them."

I wanted to tell him I loved him, that I was glad I had come north with him, but I swallowed the words. To speak them aloud was a promise I wasn't ready to make. I wanted to blame it on the horrible truth I'd discovered about his father, but I knew it wasn't his father's sins that stayed my tongue, or the fact that he was my enemy. The truth was: I was afraid. Fear clutched at my heart when I thought of what Leif had traded for his power. How could I tell him I loved him only to have him forfeit his life at the end of this? Worse, it would seem like a good-bye, and I refused to believe we wouldn't survive this or that his life would be taken so soon—not after we had survived so much.

"Together," I agreed.

He reached across and touched my thigh, and I squeezed his hand.

Arn returned, only lightly out of breath from his sprint to the city. "Only two guards posted at this gate, but they aren't alert. They don't expect an attack. There are five scouting near the quay, and two more at the back gate."

"Then I will take over one guard and have him kill the other," I said. When Leif made as if to protest, I continued before he could argue. "This is a job for stealth, not raw power. If you want to preserve the element of surprise, then you must let me do this."

Leif nodded.

I touched my heels lightly to Sleipnir's sides and trotted down the hill. Twenty of my undead clansmen flowed behind me and before me. I'd called them without even realizing it.

Sleipnir's powerful legs ate up the distance, and it wasn't long before I saw the guards Arn had scouted. They stood on either side of the barred gateway into the village beyond. They were true giants, as enormous as the ones we'd fought what felt like a lifetime ago. But as one drew into the light of a torch, I let out a faint breath. He might have had colossal height, but his face appeared human—handsome, even.

There was a terrible moment where this made me hesitate, as though only those who *looked* the part of a monster deserved to die, but then I came to my senses and dismounted.

The ground was cold and rocky, but I sat anyway. My clansmen surrounded me without so much as a whispered command. I closed my eyes and pushed my spirit out as easily as exhaling.

Once free of my body, I could see the swirling darkness that made up the giants. A glowing red brightness in the center of the one closest to me drew my attention, but it wasn't his heart I was interested in. As if sensing a shift in the air around him, the giant turned toward me.

In that instant, I streamed into his mind. Relief hit me powerfully when I found it as malleable as any mortal's. The giant knew I had infiltrated him, but it was as if I'd imprisoned him within his own mind. He tried to threaten me, tried to intimidate me with thoughts of promised violence, but I immediately suppressed them. He watched helplessly as I took control.

I forced the giant to draw the broadsword sheathed at his side. Before the other giant could even realize he was under attack, the giant I controlled ran him through with his sword.

Your speed and strength will be useful to me, I told my captive, but he could only rage at me from behind the walls of his cage.

I used him to push open the two massive doors that barred access to the village beyond, and I heard the pounding of hooves and booted feet behind me. Leif and the others were coming.

As the giant's long legs strode through the gate, he came to an unsteady halt while I took in the horrifying sight of the village.

Blood and gore, thick as mud, were smeared across the walls of houses and drying on the hard-packed earth. The massacre that the jötnar had wrought on this village was plain to see in the firelight. The smell of rotting flesh was so strong I would have gagged had I been in my own body. The salty smell of the nearby sea wasn't even enough to mask the scent. Pieces of people littered the ground—an arm here, a head, a torso. The villagers hadn't stood a chance against them when the jötnar came and claimed it as their own.

As the whole of our army made their way through the gates,

the occupants slowly became alerted to the attack. Fires were lit around the village. I could feel the vibrations in the earth as giants raced toward us, but more disturbing were the mortal men who joined them. They boiled out of thatched huts like ants from a destroyed mound.

I hesitated even as they clashed with Leif's army, swords and axes clattering together in the terrible din of war. Leif had said that long ago there were Northmen who had joined Fenris's cause, but the idea was so foreign to me I hadn't truly believed it until this moment.

Why would they join forces with monsters? I thought, and I directed my thought to the giant I kept imprisoned. He refused to answer me, his silence sullen.

I forced him to respond, commanding his thoughts as I commanded his body.

They tire of the failed promises of the gods, he said. *They tire of sacrificing their animals, their friends and neighbors, even their own lives only to have those sacrifices and prayers go unanswered.*

Despite my qualms, Leif's army and my undead clansmen— the ones who were not guarding my body—had no such hesitations. Their swords and axes flashed in the torchlight, taking down mortal and giant alike.

I threw the giant into the fight, swinging his sword with powerful blows. At some point, I grabbed a discarded shield and was able to use it both defensively and offensively. I kept Leif within my sight as I fought on, taking down as many of the jötnar as I could while I still had one to control. Leif's every move was smoothly executed, the flash of his blade a mere blur of light. He wielded his shield as an offensive weapon as well as a defensive one, bashing the heads or noses of any mortal who battled him. My undead clansmen lent him aid as he fought one of the jötnar, and with a little jolt of recognition, I realized it was Fergus who partnered with Leif to bring them down.

Together they killed three, while still others of my clansmen took down more, and hope bloomed in my chest.

But then the giant I controlled was met with another giant whose powerful blows my giant couldn't block. This one brandished an axe with a blade half as long as Sleipnir. The one I controlled would have one chance to block with his shield, and then it would be reduced to splinters. I had to make it count.

The other giant took a swing, but my giant rolled out of the way, coming gracefully to his feet again. The blade of the other's axe flashed again, this time much faster, and I raised my giant's shield at the last moment. The shield shattered under his enemy's powerful blow, but that gave my giant an extra second to dodge. I brought my sword down across the other's back, feeling his spine give way beneath the blade.

He collided with the ground, and as my giant spun away in search of another enemy, I felt a sword bite into his flesh.

The other jötunn's aim had been true, the blade slipping between his ribs to pierce his heart. But as my jötunn bled to death, his mind became like a yawning chasm, a dark nothingness that threatened to swallow me. I struggled against its hold, panicking as I tried to free my spirit from the dying body. It held on tenaciously, talons of darkness lodged in me. I'd never felt this sensation before. Desperately, I sought the door of light.

I moved as though underwater, the darkness pulling me back with every step. I fell through it, and mercifully came back to my true body in the next breath.

I leaned over and was sick. Tears ran down my cheeks. I shook violently as though with fever, and as I struggled to my feet, I swayed as weakly as a newborn kitten.

Never before had I reacted in such a way to my mental link being broken. Was it because I had connected to an immortal creature rather than a human?

I shuddered again as I worked to gain back my strength. My undead clansmen didn't react, but Sleipnir took a step toward me until I was able to lean against him. I rested my forehead on his neck in gratitude for one shaky breath before I forced myself onto his back. I'd never before considered what might happen if my spirit was caught when the giant I controlled was killed, but I couldn't let it stop me from taking control of another. We had yet to see Fenris, and if I could find him and kill him, all of this would end. He had united this terrible army, and without his leadership and power, they would fall.

Urgency nipped at my heels. I hurried Sleipnir on, but as we drew closer to the gates, Leif's army was pushed back—out of the city and onto the rocky field beyond. At least forty-five of the jötnar still stood, and they loomed above Leif's men and my undead clansmen. Most of the Northmen allied with the jötnar had fallen, easily felled by my undead army, but the losses on our side were significant as well.

The jötnar continued to thunder toward us, the ground shaking beneath them. Where they clashed with my undead clansmen, they were taken down, but even then it was taking many more men to stop them.

Rúna was still mounted, but she faced her own enemy—a giant continually hammered her with his axe. Her shield wouldn't hold much longer. I had to do something or she'd be defeated. So, surrounded by my small band of undead clansmen, I threw myself from Sleipnir's back, sat on the ground, and pushed my spirit free. As I watched, untethered, Rúna's shield finally gave way, sending a shower of splinters to the ground.

I wrenched control of the giant she fought. I forced him away from the battle with Rúna and made him bring his axe down on a nearby giant instead. The giant's suddenly strange behavior must have been enough of an indication to Rúna that it was I who controlled him now, for she quickly moved on to another battle.

I took down five of the jötnar with my controlled giant before his fellow giants realized he was now an enemy and turned on him. When two collided with my giant so powerfully the giant's legs gave way, I prepared myself to leave his body the moment before he died. In the next instant, my giant's thrust with his sword was deflected, and as I saw the other giant's sword arcing down on him, I bailed myself out of his mind.

When I returned to my body, it was to a searing pain in my head and weakness so intense I could do nothing but lie where I'd collapsed.

The ground trembled around me, and I knew there must be more jötnar coming for me. I forced myself up, panting, blinking sweat from my eyes. The undead who guarded me swarmed over the threatening giants, and I tried desperately to push myself to stand. Above the ringing in my ears came the heavy thud of boots, and then Leif pulled me to my feet.

"Ciara, are you hurt?" he asked, his voice barely detectable amid the terrible buzzing in my ear. I could only lean heavily against him and shake my head.

The sounds of battle all around were deafening. Most of the men had already been killed, torn apart by the jötnar as though they were little more than children's playthings. Perhaps fewer than fifty remained. Rúna still lived, and she used both the remains of her shield and axe to slice her way through.

Even my own army had suffered a loss; the jötnar had discovered that removing the undead's head from his body would stop him, and perhaps fifty had fallen.

Then from the distance sounded a howl that tore through the night sky, the sound more frightening than even the sound of the hellhounds in the Faerie Tunnel. Everything seemed to freeze.

From the city strode a true giant, bigger even than the ones we fought now; the earth shuddered with each step he took. Unlike the others, whose leather armor seemed to stretch and grow as they did, this giant wore massive chain mail and two bears' pelts as a mantle. By his side was a wolf, as big as Sleipnir and just as dark. The jötnar fell back at the sight of the giant, as though waiting for his command.

"Fenris," Leif said in a snarl, though by then I had already figured it out for myself.

The giant beat his axe against his shield once, and then charged. With great, leaping bounds his wolf tore through the ranks of men, biting them in half. Our men scattered, screaming, but Fenris grabbed them and tore them apart. One he caught by the neck and squeezed so hard with his massive hands that the man's head popped free of his body.

My body was very nearly at its limit, but I couldn't stop now. I freed the Sword of the Fallen from its sheath and summoned every one of my undead clansmen to me.

Take him down, I commanded.

They sprinted forward in that way that appeared as though they weren't even touching the ground. Half split toward Fenris, the other toward the wolf. The beast snarled when it met my army; it rolled and dodged like a snake, but my undead clansmen continued their assault. The wolf's massive teeth could parry a sword, but I knew it would not be able to fend them all off.

I returned my attention to Fenris only to see his gigantic hand sweep toward my men and brush them aside as though they were nothing more than mice. They tried to swarm up his great tree trunks of legs, but he kept dislodging them before they could make purchase. This wasn't working. I needed to do something more.

"Leif, will you guard my body?"

His arm tightened around me. "You don't even have to ask."

"You must get me closer to Fenris."

He nodded tersely, reluctantly, but he didn't argue. He knew what was at stake. After mounting Sleipnir, he pulled me astride, wrapping his strong arms around me.

From my vantage I could see the rest of the terrible battlefield. Emboldened by my army's attack on Fenris, what was left of Leif's allies gave their aid to bring down the terrible wolf. Blood continued to spray through the air as the beast found mortal flesh to be more giving than undead.

"Together we bring Fenris down," I said with a glance at Leif. This was the moment we would change our fate. I would make it so.

"Together," Leif agreed.

Sleipnir needed no encouragement. He raced as fast as wildfire toward the fallen giant, and with a terrible wrenching, I forced my spirit free from my flesh. Unconstrained, it flew above the carnage like a bird. I could see the darkness the giant was made of, so oily black I couldn't make out the glow of red that was his life source.

My eyes searched desperately for the telltale sign of red. Still the churning darkness within him hid the pulse of his life source. And then I saw my father climb the giant's chest. My father's eyes met mine—he could see me even in my spirit form.

The point of his blade pressed against one spot in the giant's chain mail, and then I saw it: the red, beating heart.

Focused on the giant's one weak spot, we didn't see Fenris raise his other hand until it was too late. He grabbed my father and squeezed so hard and fast that his body was crushed flat, an explosion of bones and dust falling to the ground. Silently, I screamed for the second death of him. I plunged both hands into the giant's chest and pulled free his enormous, pulsing heart.

The giant froze, his mouth twisted in a terrible grimace as I clutched his heart. In this final moment, though, my strength was failing, and cold fear trickled through me at the thought that I might not be able to complete the mission. I thought of Leif, how I had need of him, and suddenly he was there, his expression grim and determined. I glanced back at Sleipnir and my body, and I saw it was safely on the ground, Sleipnir standing protectively over it. Leif drew the shining sword gifted to him by the Morrigan, held it by the hilt with both hands, and slammed the tip of the blade into the heart. Fenris shuddered once and was still. I nearly cried with relief. I returned to my body, and pain seared through me, the agony almost blinding— like forcing a joint out of its socket. Weak beyond measure, I fell to my knees.

But even though their leader had fallen, the other jötnar seemed to be in the grip of a blood frenzy and did not stop. Leif killed two himself with the aid of two of my undead clansmen, while Rúna and my army felled the rest. Finally, the gruesome battle came to an end, and the ground was littered with the giants' massive, destroyed bodies.

Through my exhaustion, I smiled as I watched Sleipnir have his fill of the jötnar blood, glorying in the justice of consuming them just as they had consumed innocents. The relief I felt at their deaths was so sweet I felt joy burst through me. I closed my eyes. My sisters were finally safe; for the first time, I allowed myself to picture them: Deirdre's shy smile, and Branna's loud laugh. I'd been afraid before to think of them too much, afraid we'd fail and I'd lose them. But now I drank up the sight of them, if only in my mind. Though the cost had been great, we had brought an end to the threat against our lands. Still, there was a part of me that struggled to accept that it was really over; that we had won. My family and clansmen were safe; Éirinn was no longer fated to be reduced to ashes.

Leif strode toward me, and a relieved smile split my face. But there was that unease in my stomach, that fear that we hadn't won yet. And then, just as the sun rose on the horizon, I heard the ominous flapping of great wings.

I froze even as my gaze darted to Leif.

27

"Leif!" I shouted. The great black birds were threatening. I could feel it in the heaviness in the air, the thrum of it like the tingle just before lightning strikes.

There were six of them, inky black against the pale dawn sky. Their wings were spread impossibly wide, creating great buffets of wind. I had seen these birds before.

The Valkyrie.

As they descended, their wings created such a powerful wind that everyone in the radius around Leif was knocked flat. Torn from Sleipnir's back, I fell through the air. One of my undead clansmen caught me, preventing me from breaking my body against the hard earth. His cold arms released me almost immediately, and when I looked into his face, I saw it was Fergus.

Sleipnir landed beside us with an impact that would have broken the bones of a mortal beast.

Beyond us, the birds transformed.

I squinted through dust and the cacophony around me to see they had become six bronzed women, wearing the same shining golden metal armor Leif had described. Their black wings spread wide, each wing touching the tip of the next Valkyrie's wing. And Leif was trapped in the middle of their terrible ring, effectively separated from his allies. And though they were the ones who had bestowed his power upon him, and both of us knew what would be his fate, I still drew my sword.

"Leif Olafsson," they said, all speaking at once, "you have fulfilled your quest."

He bowed his head once, but I saw that his hand never relaxed on his sword.

"Fenris led the revolt against the gods," they continued, "and we granted you the power to stop him. In doing so, we made you the most powerful warrior on earth. Odin allowed this under one condition: you could only remain this way to complete your quest." They moved to form a wide circle around Leif. "It is your abilities that will make the *einherjar* unstoppable." In one fluid motion, six swords were drawn. "You have done well, Northman, but now it's time to come with us to Valhalla."

No. A violent, uncontrollable anger seethed within me, and I drew my sword and summoned the rest of my undead clansmen to me. My body might have weakened, but I would wield my army against these pagan goddesses; I would have them tear the wings from their backs and rend their flesh to pieces.

Rúna was shouting something, but I was deaf to everything but my need to help Leif.

Protect Leif; defend him against the Valkyries, I thought to my clansmen, and they surged forward.

The Valkyries attacked Leif then. He blocked with his shield and parried with his sword, but they hemmed him in. Panic rose within me, choking in its intensity. He would hold his own, but not forever. Not even Leif could fight endlessly against six goddesses with swords.

My undead clansmen reached the Valkyries as I struggled to pull myself astride Sleipnir. I'd succeeded in controlling the jötnar's minds, but these were war goddesses. My whole body shook violently, my heart shuddering in my chest. Even so, I had to try.

Two of the Valkyries turned to face us. Swords clashed violently as my undead clansmen attacked, easily running through their defenses.

With my hands thrust in Sleipnir's mane, I wrapped the strong hairs around my palms and gripped them tightly. I hoped it would keep me mounted.

I closed my eyes and sought the power that would allow me to battle the Valkyries on more equal footing—I hoped. But it wasn't as easy as it had been before; the power seemed to dance away from my grasp, until with a scream of frustration I finally accessed it. There was a tearing sound so terrible I wondered if I'd finally freed my spirit one too many times, but when I glanced once at my body, I knew I was still alive. My spirit surged toward the closest Valkyrie, and my desperation was a living, breathing thing.

I plunged into impenetrable darkness. The strength of her mind was the same as the stag's had been in the Faerie Tunnel. It was like being lost at sea on a cloudy night: nothing but black nothingness no matter where I searched. Again and again, I threw myself against it. When that failed, I moved on to the next Valkyrie. And the next. All had minds of steel.

Their taunting laughter filled my mind. *You are not strong enough, little Celt. Leif will die, and you will be next.*

Three Valkyries surrounded Leif, but all were engaged with my undead warriors. These were Norse goddesses with abilities far beyond my own. I streamed back to my body, but the moment I became conscious, my heart shuddered. I pressed my fist against my aching chest, and after a breath, it resumed beating reluctantly. I didn't need to be a healer to know I didn't have much time—my body had reached its limit. But I had the blood of ancients, the blood of the druids and the blood of the Tuatha Dé Danann, and I knew what I must do.

For only death itself would stop me from saving Leif.

I sank deeply into my mind and found the door of light— it was my connection to the realm of the Tuatha—and fell through it. I called for the Morrigan, imagining her as I'd seen her last: with a headdress of crows' feathers. Black fog poured in, ominous as storm clouds. And she appeared before me. For the first time, I gazed upon the Morrigan in mortal form. Her skin was as pale as marble, her hair as dark as pitch. But her eyes were still a terrible blood red. She was dressed for battle. Her armor was as black as night, a mantle of greasy black feathers upon her shoulders. I knew she couldn't appear in Leif's land to fight for me, but there was one way she could help me.

I need the power to stop them. Will you lend it? I asked.

The Morrigan's answering grin was more frightening than her glower. *I thought you'd never ask.*

The black fog that seemed to travel with her swirled around me, and then I felt it: a swelling of power, a renewal of energy, the healing of my broken body.

I thanked the Morrigan and returned through the glowing door to my body in a rush, my heart beating strong now, my strength returned tenfold.

I had an army of undead at my command, powerful goddess-given *seidr*, and a flesh-eating charger. I could stop them—I had to.

I called upon five of my clansmen, summoning them to me instantly. Together, we streamed toward one of the Valkyries. They engaged her in combat, separating her from her sisters while the other Valkyries battled Leif and the remainder of my clansmen.

Their black swords clashed with her golden one, and she kept them at bay, fighting them all at once, as easily as a seasoned fighter could battle a child. Still, it was enough to distract her. I forced myself free of my body and targeted the glowing golden spot in her chest that was her heart. I plunged my hand in, my triumph reverberating through my body as I grasped her life force.

Now! I told one of my clansmen, and he thrust his sword into her immobile heart.

Her face was frozen in shock as she crashed to the ground.

I had felled one, but there were five more. As I turned my attention to the next, a horrible sight greeted me.

The Valkyrie who stood over Leif raised her sword.

No! I shouted inwardly, snatching out with my mind to take control of her—to stop her before she could do the unthinkable. I was plunged into impenetrable darkness once again, but I felt her hesitate.

You cannot hold me long, she taunted. *He has always been destined to add to the ranks of* einherjar, *and we have made sure from the very beginning that he would be the best warrior the world—and Valhalla—has ever seen.*

Suddenly I remembered what Arinbjorn had said all that time ago in the stables. When he said their sister was killed on purpose so Leif would find her. I remembered learning from the Northmen that the jötnar weren't that different from the gods, and that some were even intermarried or related by blood.

You arranged for Finna to be slaughtered, I thought to the Valkyrie, horror washing over me.

The Valkyrie laughed, the sound eerie and humorless. *We did. Leif Olafsson was already the best raider the north had seen—he would have sailed the world, bringing knowledge of our gods to many people—but we needed his power as an* einherjar. *His power would be better used in Valhalla to fight for the gods, and what better way than to have him train here in Midgard?*

You manipulated him. You murdered his sister! And now you'll take his life?

She answered by shoving me mentally so hard, my physical body crashed to the ground. An agonizing pain assaulted my head, so terrible in its intensity that I could only cradle my head and scream silently as I lost control of her mind, of everything, as I was myself lost to the agony.

Two of her sisters escaped my undead clansmen. They grasped hold of Leif. The Valkyrie who held Leif immobilized raised her sword.

I pushed away my pain to find Leif. Time seemed to slow as our gazes caught and held. "I love you," Leif mouthed.

A sense of urgency exploded within my chest, and I streamed toward him. But the distance was far, too far.

The sword flashed and fell.

I watched as Leif jerked once and then was still.

Something inside me shattered. A scream tore from deep within me, so intense and powerful it was like a wave of destruction. Everyone froze.

Before I knew it, I had wrenched my soul from my body and appeared next to the Valkyrie who had killed Leif. Black anger and a terrible, soul-destroying grief rent through me, and I exploded through the Valkyrie's mental defenses, ignoring her as she fought me like a wild animal. Her arm shook as it rose against her will, and she screamed in anguish as I forced her to plunge her sword into her own chest.

I returned to myself before I could become trapped in her death spiral.

Four remained.

I stalked toward one, darkness rolling off me like a black fog. My spirit burst free of my body and slammed into her mind, and I forced her to kill herself amid her mentally screamed threats of death and damnation.

I killed them all, one by one, tearing their golden hearts free of their bodies.

Breathing hard, I returned to my body once more, and fell to my knees by Leif's side. Far above me, the sky darkened with storm clouds as though my emotions were being mirrored by the elements.

I had torn the Valkyries' hearts free, but it was mine that was dying.

I leaned forward until my head rested upon his still-warm body and I wrapped my arms around him. Losing Sleipnir and my father could in no way compare to this pain . . . this emptiness inside me.

"Please don't leave me," I whispered. "I was a fool to think I could live without you, and I will do *anything* if you'll only come back to me."

Lightning flashed, its sudden luminance only emphasizing how dark it had become. A boom of thunder followed.

A figure appeared before us. He wore a gray, hooded cloak

and gripped a gnarled staff. Bushy eyebrows hid only one startling ice-blue eye. The other was missing, as though plucked from its socket. Only skin remained. His long white beard was streaked with gray, but instead of looking old and helpless, he only appeared more powerful. A raven sat on each shoulder, watching us with eyes that seemed to contain the entire world.

"Odin," I said, recognizing the father of all the Norse gods from my time spent with the Northmen. I tightened my grip on my sword.

He said nothing, only took in the scene with his eye. After a moment, he walked over to the closest dead Valkyrie and touched her shoulder with his staff. She shook her head and came unsteadily to her feet. It took everything within me not to kill her all over again. Her eyes flashed as if she wanted to do the same to me, but Odin merely caught her eye and shook his head.

He walked around to each fallen Valkyrie and brought each to life just as he had the first. I silently seethed. Soon all six stood next to him, resurrected as though nothing had happened, while Leif lay unmoving on the ground.

"Father," one of the Valkyries began, but he held up his hand.

"Muninn," Odin said to the raven on his right shoulder, "show us your memory of what happened here."

The bird let out a croak and took off with a flurry of wings. He flew over us in a great circle, and once he had done so, the air shimmered. In the sky above us, the events that had transpired replayed. We saw our battle with the jötnar, the defeat of Fenris, and the coming of the Valkyries. Odin watched without expression as the Valkyries turned on Leif and battled against my fallen clansmen. I was held in the grip of agony as I watched Leif die for the second time. After all six Valkyries had fallen, the images blurred before finally dissipating into the stormy sky like smoke.

"So it was for vengeance that my Valkyries were killed," Odin said, his voice deep and thoughtful. "But it was revenge for the death of one of my people, not a Celt."

"He means more to me than even my own people," I said to Odin. "I would kill your Valkyries a hundred times if it meant I could bring him back." Apathy freed my tongue. What had I to fear of Norse gods? I had lost Leif.

"How were you able to do this?" he asked me. He paused as the raven on his left shoulder whispered in his ear. His eyes shifted to mine. "You have the blood of a Celtic goddess. The immortal daughter of the Phantom Queen."

"Father," one of the Valkyries said again, "we were only doing as you asked of us."

Odin nodded thoughtfully. "It is true. I asked you to bring the warrior back to Valhalla after he completed his quest. But I didn't ask you to threaten the Celtic queen; doing so violated the alliance you had made."

The Valkyrie seethed visibly. "Her intentions were to stop us."

"It seems justice was had here—you took the life of her ally, and the Celtic queen exacted revenge. A truce will be called."

I stood next to Leif's body with my hand on the hilt of my sword. "You speak of justice. The man I love is dead, while the beings responsible still live. Worse, it was they who manipulated him into trading his life in the first place. They drew the jötnar to the village where his sister was; they made sure Leif would find her slaughtered."

Again, the raven on Odin's left shoulder whispered into his ear. Odin turned to me. "It's true. We wanted Leif Olafsson's soul early—it won't be long before the jötnar launch an assault on the realm of the gods. We rule over the mortals of Midgard; it is our right to manipulate mortals as we see fit. But I am not without compassion, and I like a wager. Leif Olafsson's soul is already in Valhalla. Do you think he will choose you over its golden halls?"

"I don't know what he will choose." My eyes narrowed at the six Valkyries. "I only want him to be given the chance."

Odin smiled. "I like you, Ciara of the Phantom Queen. You are a true warrior, one who isn't afraid to fight for what she wants." He fell silent for a moment as though lost in thought—or listening to one of his ravens. "I will take you to Valhalla. If you can persuade your Leif to return to Midgard with you, then I will send his soul back into his body."

The relief and swelling hope hit me so hard my knees nearly crumpled beneath my weight.

"Thank you, Odin, I—"

"If you fail," he interrupted, "you will neither return to

Midgard nor stay in Valhalla. I will send you to Freyja's death fields, and you will be forever separated from the one you love."

I understood the risks: my very soul was in danger, and I could be beyond saving. But I also knew Leif would accept such a price without a moment's hesitation, if it were my life on the line.

"I won't fail," I said.

Odin stepped forward and put his hands on the upper part of my arms. He smelled like smoke and earth. "Let's go, then," he said.

At once, the Valkyries exploded into their raven forms and took to the skies, feathers falling in their wake. Odin's two ravens joined them, and then we were spinning wildly, as though caught in the midst of a storm. I could see nothing; I could hear nothing but the scream of wind in my ears. Faster and faster we ascended, spinning all the while, until I felt like a leaf caught in a hurricane.

Just when I was sure I would die from the onslaught, it stopped.

Odin released me, and I fell to the ground. Every bone and muscle in my body shrieked in pain, but not because of the fall. The world had changed; I felt as weak as a kitten once again, and the pressure on my body was so intense I couldn't even cry out, only grit my teeth together. Everything around me blurred and shifted, as though I was peering through smoke, and I lay in the fetal position, unable to move myself forward. There was no way to take note of my surroundings, no way to do anything but cling to the ground beneath me.

"You should be proud of yourself for still being alive," Odin said from somewhere above me. "If it weren't for the part of you that is immortal, this realm would tear you apart."

At his words, the pressure built to a tugging sensation that intensified until a sweat broke out all over my body.

"It's your mortality that's holding you back now," he said, and I could sense him walking in a slow circle around my fetal form. "You really should hurry. Your body won't be able to tolerate much more of this."

His words triggered me to release my mortal self, and I threw open the door within my mind, bathing myself in its golden light. My spirit separated from my body, and I stepped free. The pain vanished as quickly as dousing a candle's flame with water. But as I gazed down at my body, still wretched and prostrate on the ground, I knew Odin spoke the truth: I didn't have much time.

"Clever girl," Odin said, his eye now on my ethereal spirit form.

"Where is Valhalla?"

Odin smiled as his gaze shifted to somewhere behind me. I turned, and a massive eagle let out its shriek into the sky. It flew above a colossal longhouse, the roof made of thousands of shields. There were more windows and doors than I could count, and the whole structure was made of bright, shining gold. Above us were two suns and a moon, and the sky was gray, as though a storm would soon be upon us.

"Mind the wolf Fenrir at the western door," Odin said. "He will know you are no *einherjar*."

Before I could ask him anything else, he disappeared, leaving me with nothing but an unsettling urgency. One of his ravens, though, kept track of me from the air. I sprinted forward, faster in this realm than I would have been on earth, and the raven followed, casting its shadow above me. It took me mere seconds to reach the doors—heavy with gold and with snakes for handles—but when I wrenched them open, all hope that this would be an easy task fell away.

The hall was bigger than any castle I had ever seen, bigger even than the city of Dubhlinn. The rafters were made of spears, and there were tables so long I couldn't see the ends of them. They were filled with food and drink—fruit and cheese and meat, honeyed mead and cold ale. And there were more men and women than all the armies I had seen put together. They crammed the hall and filled the tables, their voices and laughter carrying to the spear-tipped rafters. Finding Leif among so many was going to be as hard as finding a single grain of sand in the sea.

I would have to do this as I did everything else: one step at a time. I walked and searched, for how long, I couldn't say. All the while, my body called to me, and the tugging sensation became nearly unbearable. Still, I pressed on.

I quickened my pace but began to feel the tautness of the link to my body stretched nearly to capacity. I had searched only half the hall, and I knew I was rapidly running out of time.

But with my spirit form came quickness of thought. I was the Morrigan's daughter; I had a communion with the dead. If I couldn't continue my search, then maybe I could summon the dead to me. I thought of Leif; I thought of the way he smelled, the deepness of his voice, the iron-like strength of his muscles. But mostly, I thought of the way he made me feel: like I had finally found where I belonged.

Just then a bellow of pain rang out somewhere in the middle of the hall, the sound echoing off the walls. Voices near me fell silent as a tall, golden Northman came sprinting toward me. Leif had found me.

He stood before me, his chest heaving for breath though I was sure he no longer needed to draw it. His arms reached out and drew me to him. "Ciara, no. No, you cannot be dead. Please tell me this is only a hallucination brought on by Valhalla mead."

He pulled me into his ethereal chest, solid to me in my own spirit form, but strangely absent of everything that made him his familiar self: no warmth, no smell, no . . . heartbeat.

"I'm not dead, and you're not hallucinating," I said in a rush to Leif, who had yet to realize the danger we were in.

"Then what are you doing here?"

Again, my body called to me, and I put a hand on Leif's arm. "I'm here to bring you back . . . if you'll go with me."

For a moment, Leif was so quiet I was terrified he would say no, and then the grin that had once enraged me spread across his face. "How could you doubt me?"

Relief bloomed within me, and I returned his smile. "Because all you've talked about since the moment we met was Valhalla."

He touched my face. "That was until I fell in love with you."

I leaned into his touch, imagining how it would feel when we were back in our proper bodies. "We don't have much time," I murmured.

He tilted my chin up to look at him. "Before I leave the golden splendor of Valhalla, I need to know if you love me."

"Yes." The word came from deep within, and once I had spoken it aloud, I realized just how true it was. I felt a blush steal over me even as something within me clicked irrevocably into place. Leif had *died*, and with him, my inability to see him as he really was. He was kind and merciless, frustrating and encouraging, beautiful and dangerous. But most of all, he was *not* his father.

My gaze dropped to our feet. I felt shamed by how I'd responded toward him when I'd learned of what his father had done—not in love and understanding as he had, but in coldness and distrust.

And it only took his death to make me realize it.

I shook my head. "I'm so sorry, Leif—"

His finger traced down my cheek, his eyes intent on my lips. "Don't apologize," he said, "I understand. My reaction would have been worse had our circumstances been reversed. You can apologize and make it up to me all you want when we return to Midgard." He took hold of my hand and gave a little tug. "What did you trade in order to bring me back?" he asked as we strode down the golden hallway.

"Odin seemed to think you would never want to leave Valhalla, so only your agreement was required," I said, and related everything I had seen after Leif's death.

His ghostly eyebrows shot up when I described the vengeance I took on the Valkyries on his behalf.

"I was a fool to think only my mortal life would be payment enough for the gifts the Valkyrie gave me. They had plans for my soul as well." He glanced around him at the tables filled with other warriors. "There was a time when I would have gladly accepted such a fate, but"—he pinned me with his gaze—"everything has changed now."

I squeezed his hand in response and prayed that Odin would hold to his part of the bargain.

Leif must have read my mind, for he said, "I doubt my agreement to leave is the only thing needed before we'll be allowed to return to the mortal realm."

As we pushed open the same massive doors I had opened before, a sinister growl greeted us.

I froze, cold fear eating its way through me. An angry mob behind us, and a wolf guarding the door. "Is this not the way I came in—the eastern door?" I said in a hushed whisper to Leif.

"It is."

"Then tell me that wasn't the growl of a wolf."

The growl came again, louder and closer than before. Leif gave me a shove. "Go. I am *einherjar* now. It won't attack me, and I can distract it."

"And then what, Leif?" I demanded in a hiss.

"Just go," he said, and gave me another stubborn push.

A snarl came from just behind us, and I ran. The scenery—a rocky cliff overlooking a fjord—rushed by. I heard Leif jump in front of the wolf, but it easily dodged him and came after me. I risked a glance back. Its enormous paws thudded as loudly as a horse's hooves, and it was massive—bigger than a bear. Bigger than any animal I had ever seen on earth. Its yellow eyes were trained on me, hungry. Its teeth were like daggers in its mouth. It no longer growled, only raced after me silently with single-minded intent.

I wasn't sure what would happen if it caught my spirit form, but neither did I want to find out. Even my unnatural speed was only fast enough to keep me just ahead of the wolf.

My body called to me from somewhere just ahead, and in a moment of horror, I realized I couldn't lead this bloodthirsty wolf straight to my undefended body. I veered suddenly left, and jaws snapped just inches away. My mind raced and I desperately sought a solution.

"Leif!" I shouted, and then he was there, beside me as though he had always been.

"What's your plan?" he asked.

"I need you to grab hold of it," I said, glancing back again to confirm that it was still right on our heels. "Do you think you can?"

"Not for long, but yes."

"I won't need long," I said.

Leif slid to a stop and flew back at the wolf, grabbing it by its massive jaws. It flung its head from side to side viciously, but Leif held on. I scanned the wolf's body for the telltale red glow—the heart that was its life source. His black fur gave way to swirling golden smoke, and within the smoke was a glowing red heart. I plunged my hand into its chest and tore it out.

The effect was instantaneous. Its eyes rolled back in its head as it slammed to the rocky ground. In my hand, the red heart pulsed. I had only to return to my body and squeeze, and the ruthless creature would be no more.

"Stop!" Odin's voice rang out, thunderous and mighty. It echoed over the cliffs. He appeared before us, his eyebrows drawn low over his eyes threateningly. "You cannot defeat Fenrir here. He is meant to be defeated during Ragnarök. To kill him now will destroy time as we know it and render all prophecies useless."

I held the life source aloft. "Grant us free passage back to the mortal realm, and I will return the wolf's heart."

Odin held out his hand and summoned my body. "Granted."

With my body so close, the magnetic pull to return to it was nearly unbearable. I felt stretched as tight as a drawn bow, but I wasn't eager to return to the agony my body suffered. "When I return to my body, then you will send us back."

Odin met my steady gaze. "You have my word."

I nodded as I moved closer to my body. With a deep breath, I closed my eyes and let my body pull my spirit back into it.

I gasped in shock. The agony crashed over me, contracting all the muscles in my body until only a wretched sob escaped. In my hand was still clutched the red heart. Odin reached down and took it from me after I found that I couldn't even command my fingers to let go.

"Is this truly what you wish, Leif Olafsson?" Odin asked from somewhere above me.

"I cannot be without her, Father," he said simply. I would have smiled if I could.

"Then go," Odin said.

He held up his hand, and the world exploded in light.

I plummeted back down to earth, the wind screaming in my ears just as it had during my ascent. My stomach had slithered into my throat as the tunnel of wind I was encased in shot toward the ground. Blind and deaf to everything but the wind around me, I'd lost track of Leif.

Just before I would have smashed into earth and shattered all my bones, I slowed and landed gently on my feet. The wind dissipated at once, but this time, I wasn't left disoriented. It took only a moment to register my surroundings: the slain giants littering the ground were indication enough. I had been returned to just outside of Skien.

My army waited in a silent formation nearby, while Sleipnir nickered a soft greeting. With a hurried touch of my hand to Sleipnir's nose, I strode toward Leif's body.

The sight of him lying so still upon the ground, the blood staining the grass beneath him, sent panic clawing to free itself within me, but I stamped it down. "Come on, Leif," I said quietly, intently.

I was rewarded with his eyes rolling behind his eyelids, and the pulse at his neck throbbing. He drew a single gasping breath and then another, and then his eyes flew open. I could bear it no longer. I threw my arms around him as great, forceful sobs took over my body.

Leif's eyes widened. "I didn't know you could cry like that."

I laughed and cried harder. "I can summon the dead, but I'm not dead inside." Softer I said, "I really thought I would lose you."

"Never," Leif said, his eyes bright with restored life. Slowly, he stood, and I kept my arm around him to steady him. He smiled down at me. "See? I am whole. Thanks to you."

And then his arms were around me, and our bodies were pressed so tightly together it seemed what we desperately wanted was to be one. He kissed me, and I tasted salt from my tears.

Eventually we pulled away. We still stood upon a battlefield littered with fallen giants. Nearby, my undead army watched expressionlessly. Memory returned, and with it came a wave of horror as I remembered Leif's aunt had fallen when the Valkyrie had descended. I jumped to my feet, my eyes scanning over the many bodies, but there was no sign of her.

The sound of horses approaching made me turn, and I saw Rúna upon a blood bay charger. I let my breath out in relief.

"Leif!" Rúna shouted as soon as she was close enough to be heard. The only sign she'd been injured was a smear of blood dripping from her scalp. She urged her horse on until she was level with us, and then she dismounted so fast she nearly crashed to the ground. Leif steadied her with a hand upon her shoulder.

Rúna threw her arm around Leif's neck and pulled him close. "Thank the gods," she said, her voice hoarse. "How did you survive?"

Leif lifted his head and looked at me. "Ciara stormed Valhalla." A slow smile crossed his face. "She even swore she'd do *anything* if only I'd come back."

I jerked in surprise. "How did you—"

Leif's gaze met mine. "Did you mean it?"

"Of course—"

"Then let us make a pact here and now that we will forever be allies."

I smiled. "*Just* allies?"

He laughed and pulled me into his arms. "You could never be *just* an ally to me. Someday soon, our alliance will become much more permanent."

His words were characteristically arrogant, but I found I couldn't argue with them. I tilted my head back, and he kissed me again.

"I love you, *meyja*," he said.

He kissed me as only someone who has dodged the scythe of death can kiss. "I love you, Leif," I murmured. "But don't call me *meyja*."

His laughter chased the darkness from my heart.

We spent the rest of the day burning the remains of the dead. It took all our strength to pile the jötnar bodies together in an impressive fire, but it was necessary labor. There was a danger in leaving such creatures behind, even if they were dead. Legend had always held that powerful beings could regenerate if even a finger were to survive. I didn't rest until I tasted ash with every breath I took.

We built great funeral pyres for those we had lost, sending the burning bodies out on longships docked in Skien. I found my father's crown, only inches away from his bones. Sadly, I drew my finger across the tarnished metal, remembering the man he once was. I carefully gathered his bones and added them to the pile, wishing I could give him more than a hasty end-of-battle funeral.

"Does this make you jarl of Skien now?" I asked as we stared at the mountainous remains of Fenris.

He nodded once. "We are slowly taking over the world, you and I."

That same ambitious hunger reared within me, but I turned away from it. "I must return to Mide, Leif."

"Soon," he said, and something almost like contentment warmed my stomach.

As Leif and I stood side by side on the quay, reflections of the burning ships shining on the water, I clasped his hand in mine as my heart sang thanks for one thing.

We had challenged the gods and won.

24

Our return voyage was much less eventful than the last, which was something of a miracle for us. Still, it was long and tiring—full of hot sun and endless salty spray.

When at last we landed upon the shores of Mide, my father's castle looming over us from above, I vaulted down from the longship I had once feared. As I took that first step on the rocky, sandy shore, I could hardly prevent myself from falling to my knees and kissing the ground in thanksgiving. But I had barely enough time to tilt my head to the sun's warm rays before a horn bellowed far above us.

My heart sped up in my chest. Though technically I was the cause for the horn's bellow, it still filled me with fiery dread. Habits died hard. The Northmen meant so much more to me now. I might not have been ready to forgive Leif's father for what he had done to my sister, but it was Leif and Arin and Rúna and all the others who had taught me that not every Northman was a monster, just as the minds and stories of the jötnar had taught me that not every giant was completely corrupted by evil. Darkness came in many forms, and it was wrong to think that any being was beyond redemption. Even the Morrigan had moments of goodness.

"We must hurry," I said to Leif, who joined me at my side. "They will think we've come to raid."

"It's no more than your mother deserves," he said with a smirk.

"Perhaps. But my sisters and remaining clansmen do not."

Arin ran over to us, his expression eager. "Will there be a battle?"

Leif turned to his brother with a stern look. "Stay with the ship."

We had started up the rocky path when I heard it: the unmistakable sound of warhorses. The jangle of chain mail and weapons followed, and I doubled my pace. We had to make it to the top of the cliff, else we'd be funneled just as the Northmen I killed once had.

I glanced back at Leif. "Tear off a piece of your linen tunic—and hurry." He did as I asked, ripping free a piece of cloth that was a dingy white, but white nonetheless. "I will go on alone. I don't want to alarm them."

He looked for a moment like he'd argue, but in the end nodded his assent.

I held the cloth aloft as I came to the top of the steep rise.

Before me stretched a contingent of thirty men, led by the High King of Éirinn, Brian Boru. His banner of crimson and gold flew high above him, and he rode a little apart from the rest on a white charger. The sun glinted off his dark gray armor menacingly. My heart continued to race along in my chest, for I had not forgotten that it was his daughter who was married to King Sigtrygg.

"Peace," I said clearly in Gaelic, easily slipping back into my native tongue. "I am Ciara of Mide, and this is no raid."

The king frowned. "Ciara, Queen of Dubhlinn, who has allied herself with Northmen?"

I raised my chin and met his dark gaze. "The same."

"What brings you here with Northman longships and an army at your back?"

"I have come to assure myself of the safety of my sisters and clansmen," I said.

"They are well enough now that we are here to guide them," the king said.

"Then you must know the king, my father, has died," I said, unable to prevent the torrent of images—the charred remains in the chapel, dying for a second time in an explosion of bones and ash—from racing through my mind.

The king shifted in his saddle. "Yes, another king dead. King Killian of Mide, your own father. You are here to seize his lands, I suppose?"

My eyes narrowed dangerously. "It was King Sigtrygg who killed my father, and no fewer than two hundred of my clansmen, and I was right to seek vengeance against him. As eldest daughter, I am my father's heir. The kingdom of Mide is mine, and I've returned to claim it."

"It was your mother who said you'd been banished," the king said, and I saw his hand tighten on the grip of his sword. "You no longer have a claim here."

I stood before the High King of Éirinn, a man who outranked me, but I would not cower before him. I had faced foes much greater than him, and I would take what was mine.

"The blood of my father, the king of Mide, flows through me, and I will assume my role as protector of this land. Retreat, sire, or I will be forced to slaughter your men."

Angry voices rose at my insolence, but I held my ground.

The king leaned forward and locked eyes with me. "I'd like to see you try."

His men cheered as I retreated back down the path, my jaw set. Leif waited for me near the shore with what was left of my army of undead standing at attention.

I marched to the forefront of them. "There is an army at the top of this cliff. Kill them. Spare the king."

I pulled myself astride Sleipnir as Leif mounted Abrax. The few Northmen who had returned with us waited, unabashedly eager for battle.

"This is my fight, Leif."

He grinned. "I appreciate your efforts to emasculate me so early in our relationship, but you know I cannot resist a battle."

A laugh escaped me in spite of myself. "We aren't married

yet." I tossed another smile over my shoulder at him as I urged Sleipnir up the rocky path.

Leif and the other Northmen followed, but my undead army surged past me, their feet never seeming to touch the ground. Strangled screams greeted them at the top of the cliff, and by the time Sleipnir delivered me to the top, nearly every man was dead.

"Stop! Enough," I said when the High King dropped his sword at my feet.

"I yield," he said, his face ashy pale in the bright sunlight. Seven of his remaining men circled around him bravely, though they, too, were deathly pale.

"Do you recognize me as queen of Dubhlinn and Mide?" I asked, the Sword of the Fallen held ready in my hand.

He dipped his head once. "You are hereby granted both kingdoms to rule and protect."

I smiled slow as death. "It would be my honor, your grace."

The castle bailey was quiet with an almost palpable unease. Leif and I rode our horses right to the doors of the keep, where I knew my mother waited inside.

"Máthair," I called, because I knew her by no other name.

It wasn't long before she came, followed by my sisters, whose golden hair brought tears to my eyes.

Her hands were in fists at her sides, and her face was as welcoming as a hailstorm. Worse still were my sisters' reactions: they kept their eyes firmly on the floor, never meeting mine.

"Where is the High King?" my mother asked.

"Defeated," I said, and she sucked in a breath.

"You killed him, too?"

I flinched. "Defeated but not dead."

She crossed her arms defensively. "Why are you here, Ciara? You aren't welcome."

Leif shifted in his saddle threateningly, but I raised my hand. "I may not be your daughter, but I am the eldest daughter of the king of Mide. I have come to claim my birthright, to keep Mide safe and to rule as its queen. This is my kingdom, these are my sisters, my clansmen. No harm will come to them while I rule. My alliance with Leif Olafsson will usher in a time of peace between our kingdoms and the Northmen."

Máthair stood in stunned silence, and my gaze shifted to Branna and Deirdre behind her. Both were thin and pale, but Branna now looked at me with cautious hope in her eyes. What had happened while I'd been away?

I dismounted and approached them. Máthair shifted so she was standing in front of my sisters, and I glared at her through the hurt. Surely she couldn't believe I'd harm them?

"I came back, Bran," I said, addressing the one more likely to rebel against Máthair. "Just as I promised you."

"It's too late now," Branna said, her tone quiet and sullen.

"What do you mean?"

Branna crossed her arms defensively, and Deirdre shifted uncomfortably. "I'm betrothed now—we both are. It doesn't matter if you're here now, because we'll never live as a family again."

It shouldn't have surprised me, and yet, all I could see before me were two little girls. They'd been raised all their lives knowing that they'd be betrothed when they came of age. Their marriages would have formed necessary alliances, and perhaps if they'd been lucky, Áthair would have taken pity on them and married them off to men no older than thirty years. But though it wasn't unheard of, betrothals at their ages were far too early. I could understand why rebellious Branna chafed beneath this edict and soft-spoken Deirdre was apprehensive and fearful of what was to come. But lucky for them, *I* was queen now, and I would forge my own alliances.

I glanced at my mother, and a slow smile bloomed across my face. "Then we'll break the betrothals."

Máthair stiffened in shock, and I almost pitied her. "What? No. You cannot—"

From a relaxed position on his horse, Leif grinned as though watching a highly entertaining sword fight.

The matching smiles on Branna's and Deirdre's faces were well worth any anger from Máthair.

"I can, actually. I'm the queen." To my sisters, I said, "Consider your betrothals broken."

"Branna was betrothed to the High King's son," Máthair said, her voice desperately sharp. "We cannot just tell him no."

"I'm sure the High King will agree to whatever Ciara tells him," Leif said. "He was soundly defeated just now, but Ciara spared his life."

Branna threw her arms around me, and I rested my head on hers. "Thank you, Ciara," she said. "You don't know how much I've fretted over this."

After a moment, Deirdre joined in the embrace, and I let my breath out in a rush. Home. Family. I would never let any harm come to them now that I was queen. "My sisters should be able to marry whomever they please."

"Such promises," Máthair said with a sneer. "You know nothing of being queen, of making essential alliances. Part of growing up is in sacrificing one's happiness for one's clan."

I shook my head. "I may not be an experienced ruler yet, but I do know I have power enough to keep Mide and this clan safe. What good is my power if my sisters must be bartered off to ensure we will have allies to come to our aid?"

The sound of many boots hitting the earth drew our attention, and I turned to find Arin and the other Northmen entering the bailey. My undead army followed, stony and gray-faced.

I caught Arin's eye and waved him over. "There is someone I'd like you to meet," I told Branna, while Deirdre ducked behind her shyly. Arin joined us, a wary expression on his face. "Arin, these are my sisters, Branna and Deirdre."

Branna curtsied before him, and a wide grin split across Arin's face. Máthair looked as though she had eaten something rather sour.

"I've formed an unbreakable alliance with Arin's brother," I said with a shared smile with Leif, "so you'll be seeing much more of both of them in the future."

Before my sisters could even react, Máthair let out a noise of utter frustration. "I've heard enough of this madness. Branna, Deirdre, come with me. Your father would be devastated by such a betrayal—to ally herself to a pagan barbarian. Ciara will destroy this family." She turned on her heel and stalked off, but I called out to her before she could disappear within the keep. Reluctantly, she turned her head.

"You may have your opinions on my choice of alliances," I said, "but I must know: Will you contest my claim for the throne?"

Her back stiffened. "I don't really have a choice, do I?" At my look, she sighed. "No," she said, the word sounding as though it was wrenched from her forcefully. "Girls?"

Deirdre wrapped her slim arms around me once more, and I kissed the top of her fair head. "Go, now. I'll come find you later."

"I'm glad you're home, Ciara," Deirdre said before hurrying after her mother.

Branna hung back, her eyes still on Arin. "Will I see you at dinner?"

He glanced at Leif once before nodding. "I hope so."

Perhaps it was in our blood to find the Olafsson men irresistible. Smiling, I gave Branna a little nudge. "Better go before Máthair comes looking for you."

Branna threw her arms around me again. "I prayed every night you'd come home, Ciara."

"And I prayed I'd come home to you," I said with a kiss on her head. "Now, go."

When she was out of sight, I shifted my attention to my undead army. "There is something I must do," I said to Leif.

❖❖❖

"This is a mistake," Leif said later, when I had assembled my undead clansmen in the remains of our chapel. They stood emotionlessly, though they stood upon the ashes of their violent deaths.

I shook my head as I pulled the Sword of the Fallen free. "This is what must be done."

"And if your kingdoms are challenged and you need them again?"

I turned to him with a hint of an ironic smile. "I'm surprised, Leif. I would think you of all people should realize that if I cannot hold these lands with my own power, then I don't deserve to have them at all."

He crossed his arms over his chest obstinately. "They are part of your power."

In answer, I sliced the palm of my hand across the blade of my sword. It thrummed loudly as my blood was absorbed. This time, the words came to me without having to be told.

"So the Phantom Queen's blood flows in my veins, so do I release you from your oath to me. No longer will you be forced to walk upon the earth. Instead, I leave you free to rest in peace."

An explosive *boom* rent the air, and the men before us shattered into a cloud of ash. Sadness and regret fell upon me like a veil, but over it all was a feeling of peace—the peace I had granted my clansmen, and the peace I felt for doing what was right. My atonement for the death of so many had only just begun—

The soft step of a leather shoe on ash alerted me to someone's presence, and I turned to find the graying form of Father Briain. As his gaze drifted over the remains of the chapel, I realized just how terribly lost he must feel.

"It will be rebuilt," I said, my voice quiet but strong.

His rheumy eyes met mine, the relief on his face profound. "As queen, you will be welcome in the new chapel."

It would be many years before I would feel welcome in church—if ever—but I said nothing of this to Father Briain, only smiled and touched his shoulder as I passed by.

But as I walked outside, another pile of ashes halted me as suddenly as though I'd been shot with an arrow.

"Sleipnir," I whispered, echoes of the first time I found him broken and bloodied on the battlefield reverberating through me. How could I have forgotten he was as bound to my blood sacrifice as the others?

Though as I touched what was left of my courageous warhorse, there was a part of me that knew this was how it was meant to be. For how long could I have kept an undead skeletal horse with a gruesome appetite for flesh? I mourned him for what he once was. Losing him again ripped open old wounds, old losses: my father, Fergus and Conall, my clansmen, even my mother, who was never really mine to lose.

But as Leif wrapped an arm around me in silent comfort, I swore I would forge a new life, one of peace.

That night after a strained dinner with Máthair that tensed
every muscle in my body, and then a subsequent two hours practicing sword fighting with Leif that finally siphoned my energy,
I stumbled into my room with Leif, weary to the bone—until
his gaze met mine.

"It becomes difficult not to touch you when you look at me
like that," Leif said.

Another two weeks at sea with him had stolen any notion for
propriety I might have had. When the red haze of desire flared,
I fanned the flames. "Who says you can't touch me?"

He let out a cross between a laugh and a groan before reaching for me. The kiss was hurried, desperate, but as we pulled
back for a breath, his touches became gentle. He traced the line

of my jaw, pressing kisses along the side of my neck. I helped him out of his tunic and chain mail, and he reached for the fastenings of my armor.

"You'll have little need for armor now," he said, putting it to the side as he removed each piece.

I lay down on the bed with a sigh. "Oh? And what would you have me wear instead?"

"Nothing." He pressed a kiss to my bare shoulder. "But I don't think you'd agree."

My lips curled into a smile. "You're right."

"Then let me dress you as I would my wife," he said, pressing another kiss to the hollow of my throat, "with gold and furs and silk."

I pushed him back until I was on top, my hands braced against his wide chest. "You are forgetting that I am a queen in my own right. I can clothe myself in gold and furs and silk."

He laughed, the motion shaking through me. "I could never forget that you are a woman who can take care of herself." His smile melted away as he pulled me down to his mouth. "But that won't stop me from wanting to shower you with gifts."

Any response I might have had disappeared as his mouth and tongue rendered me speechless.

Though I didn't recall falling asleep, I woke to the sound of rustling wings. I sat bolt upright in bed, my heart racing in my chest. Beside me, Leif slumbered on, unaware, but I knew the Morrigan had come for me.

From out of the fireplace, tendrils of black smoke flowed. They outlined the form of a woman just before solidifying into the Morrigan. She was dressed in a gown of black, a mantle of crows' feathers on her shoulders. Though I had seen her many times since that first vision, my skin still erupted in goose bumps at the sight of her. There was no ignoring the undercurrent of darkness and violence that lay just beneath her surface.

And I am just as dangerous, I thought.

"So you are a queen now," the Morrigan said with an expression I would almost call pride on anyone else. "Power becomes you." She tilted her head. "Soon all of Éirinn will come to know what you have done for them, and though many will be grateful, there will be others who will want to test their might against yours just to see who will come out the victor." Her gaze shifted to Leif's sleeping form. "And the two of you together will only draw powerful beings to you like flies."

There was a compelling truth to her words, and for a moment, despair descended upon me like the heavy weight of chains. "Then we will draw together for strength and thwart any who would threaten us."

A wide, approving smile curved her lips. "You truly have grown into your power, Ciara of Mide." She turned to go, but I held out my hand to stop her.

"Why didn't you tell me I could call upon your power in battle?" I asked.

Her expression remained unapologetic. "I had intervened as much as I dared. I could not fight your war for you; destroying the jötnar was your quest. You needed to believe you only had yourself and your Northman lover to rely upon, but I have always done everything I could to see that you succeed."

Her eyes met mine, and something inside me seemed to shift. "Have you ever loved me as a mother?" The words were torn from me without conscious thought.

She let out a self-deprecating laugh. "I'm not sure I'm capable of such an emotion," she said, but just as a dagger of pain stabbed through me at the thought that no parent was able to love me, she added, "But if I were, you are the only one for whom I've felt anything remotely close to it."

Before I could respond, she leaned forward and pressed a kiss to my hair. Then in a flurry of feathers, she was gone.

31

I sat upon Mide's throne of white, my gown the glittering silver and black of the night sky. To my right sat Leif Olafsson, the Giant Slayer, my former prisoner and soon-to-be husband and king.

A crow let out a *caw-caw-caw* just outside, and my lips curved in a slow smile.

ACKNOWLEDGMENTS

Deo gratias.

Beyond has always been special to me because I nearly put it aside, but Ciara and Leif just wouldn't let me. Their voices, as it turns out, are pretty hard to ignore. And I'm so glad I didn't, because with the help of many, many people, their story has been brought to life.

Thank you to my husband for everything he does (the list is long and exhaustive), but especially for keeping the kids entertained while I literally locked myself in a room to work on edits. I love you forever and always.

For my mom and dad, who always believed in me, no matter what. And for my mom's willingness to read every version of this story . . . times a million. I'm sorry for the animal peril! I'm also sorry for refusing to change the ending. . . .

For my in-laws, Mike and Carol Leake, who have always been so proud and supportive—and they were always happy to take the kids any time I needed time to write!

For Karina Sumner-Smith, who never doubted Ciara and Leif's story could—and should!—be told. Our Skype conversations on plot ideas (and everything else) were pure genius—it's like we should write books. . . .

For my editor, Alice Jerman, for loving this book just as much as I do and working tirelessly to make sure it was the absolute best version it could be. Your edits were brilliant. I'm sorry I kept you on the phone for insane lengths of time talking about writing and chickens and everything in between. Thank you for falling in love with this book!

For my agent, Brianne Johnson, for her persistence in finding the absolute best home for *Beyond*. I literally couldn't have done this without you, so I hope you realize just how appreciated you are!

For everyone at HarperTeen for all their hard work on this book—most especially for the gorgeous cover that was everything I could have hoped for and more.

I have an enormous family, and every single one of them is supportive and encouraging to an incredible degree. Thank you to all of you—my grandmothers, all my aunts and uncles (including my favorite aunt and uncle), cousins, most especially my cousin Kelsey Cox, who has always been my partner in this writing journey through her inspiring and insightful critiques. You've been my best friend since we were kids, and I'm so glad to share a passion for writing with you! Love you, cousin.

I have an amazing group of friends, so thank you for all the playdates, book club meetings, and thousands of text messages, all of which helped me keep my sanity as I navigated being mom to four extremely small (but so, so adorable) children and writing/editing a book.

For my chickens for being so fun to watch. I'm kidding. I wouldn't actually thank my chickens . . . who would do that?

For my aunt Patty Fahey, who would have loved this.

PRONUNCIATION GUIDE

Celtic names and words

Áthair: ah•her

Ciara: keer•a

Each-uisce: ach (said in the back of the throat; it almost sounds like "ugh") •ish-kay

Éirinn: ay•rin

Flidais: flee•dish

Máthair: ma•her

Sluagh: sloo•ah

Tuatha Dé Danann: too•uh•huh dey dah•nuh•n

Norse names and words

Einherjar: ane•hare•yar

Huginn and Muninn: hoo•gin and moo•nin

Kráka: krah•kah (crow in Old Norse)

Jötunn/Jötnar: yo•ton / yo•nar

Meyja: meh•yah (Girl or maiden in Old Norse)

Seidr: say•der

Sleipnir: sleep•neer

AUTHOR'S NOTE

I first fell in love with Ireland when I was just a little girl, and my mom would excitedly tell me of our family ancestry—her side of the family was nearly 100 percent Irish. The superstitions, folklore, and mythology of the Emerald Isle always captivated me, and I absorbed everything I could about the creatures my ancestors once believed in. Irish history is fascinating, particularly in the early centuries, when it was wild and untamed and full of more kings, queens, and princesses than a fairy tale. I couldn't resist setting a story in a country full of rich legends and folklore. I just had to decide *when* I wanted it to take place. So when my parents returned home one year from a trip to Dublin with pictures of an ancient Viking village that once made up Dublin, I knew. Vikings and Ireland? I couldn't think of a better combination.

I love the history of Ireland, but I also love Celtic and Norse mythology, and I used both of them as inspiration for this historical fantasy. Though I took some creative liberties. The Wild Hunt, for example, wasn't led by Flidais in the old legends but usually by Odin. Fenrir, the wolf that guarded Valhalla in the book, is actually bound by an enchanted fetter and not in Valhalla at all. Despite these deviations, I found both Celtic and

Norse mythology to be remarkably similar and to complement one another well, despite being from two different parts of the world. The Morrigan and the Valkyrie, for example, played the same sort of role on the battlefield. And even though Ireland during the eleventh century was almost entirely Christian, the superstitions, legends, and folklore always remained. They still feared the *sluagh* and the each-uisce; talked of the Fey and the Little People. The Norse and the Danes—the Northmen—came with their own set of beliefs of powerful gods and monstrous jötnar, further contributing to a land steeped in legend.

For the historical element, I tried to stay true to what life was like in Ireland and Norway in the eleventh century. The battles—both the armor (or lack of it in the Celts' case) and the tactics—were representative of how Viking raiders and Celtic warriors fought. Leif's village and longhouse were fairly typical of Viking life, and the same could be said of Ciara's castle. And as I fell into the endless wormholes of researching that history, probably the most exciting thing was when I could make a piece of history work in the story. King Sigtrygg, for example, was real. He was King Sigtrygg Silkbeard, and he was half-Irish and half-Norse. He really did raid other kingdoms of Ireland, just like a Northman. And worst of all, he really did burn two hundred men in a church after a raid of Mide. So he probably *did* deserve what happened to him in my version of the story.

Dubhlinn, though it really irritated Ciara, really was known as Dyflin to the Norse. They took over Dublin in the ninth century, and you can still see remnants of their wooden settlements today in Ireland. Because of this, the Norse and the Irish often intermarried, so there was this bizarre situation where the Norse raiders were feared and hated, but then they were also forming alliances with the Irish by marrying their princesses.

The myths and historical setting of *Beyond a Darkened Shore* combined to form a rich tapestry that lent itself as the perfect backdrop for Ciara and Leif's world. As with the mythological aspects of the book, I took some creative liberties, and I hope my readers—particularly those who specialize in Irish history—will indulge me.

For more information on the specific myths in this book, please read on!

GLOSSARY

Celtic Mythology

Brigid: Brigid was a Celtic goddess of fire—of the forge and the hearth—among many other things. She was generally seen as a motherly healer type of goddess. She was the first daughter of the Dagda, who was the chieftain of the Tuatha Dé Danann, and also the wife of the Irish King Bres, making her a queen among the goddesses.

Each-uisce: This is a water spirit similar to the Scottish kelpie, but far more vicious. As Ciara tells her sisters, it can take the shape of both a horse and a handsome man to lure victims to their deaths.

Flidais: As with so many things in history, there's a debate as to what her actual role was as a goddess, but for my purposes, I chose to focus on the belief that Flidais was the goddess of the woods—much like Artemis in Greek mythology.

Morrigan: Also known as the Phantom Queen. She is as mysterious as she appeared in the book. Sometimes portrayed as a triple goddess—made up of three separate sisters—I chose to focus on her main role: as war goddess and keeper of fate on the battlefield. She is often shown flying over the battle in the form of a crow.

Sluagh: A term for the "restless dead" who hunt for souls in a flock of shadows. They were said to appear when someone was on their deathbed, waiting to steal their soul.

Tuatha Dé Danann: Translates as the "tribe/people of the goddess Danu" (the mother goddess of Ireland) or as the "tribe of the gods." These were an immortal race of people with supernatural power who lived in another realm—the otherworld—in pre-Christian Ireland. The Morrigan, Flidais, and Brigid were all examples of such goddesses.

Wild Hunt: A folklore known all over Europe, where a powerful god would lead a hunt through the woods, riding a horse as black as midnight, with ghostly hounds racing ahead. The old myths never really say *what* they're hunting, but the implication (and fear) is generally that they're hunting living people or souls.

Norse Mythology

Einherjar: Warriors who have died in battle and are brought to Valhalla by the Valkyrie.

Fenrir: The third son of Loki by the female jötunn Angrboda. He was a giant, terrifying wolf that was kept bound (the legends never really specify where) by an enchanted fetter created by the dwarves because he would eventually bring about the end of the world and the gods (see Ragnarök below).

Huginn and Muninn: Translates to "thought" and "memory" from Old Norse; these are the names of Odin's ravens that fly all over the world and bring him information.

Jötunn/Jötnar: A race of giants who were banished from Asgard (the realm of the gods) to live in Jötunheimr, one of the nine worlds of Norse mythology. As Leif mentions, they have a complicated relationship with the Norse gods—sometimes antagonistic, sometimes friendly or neutral. Many of the gods, including Odin, descended from the jötnar, and some of the gods even intermarried with them.

Midgard: One of the nine realms, or worlds, in Norse mythology, where mortals reside.

Odin: I could spend a page on all the many beliefs about Odin in Norse (and Germanic) mythology, but a simplified version is that he was one of the principal gods, a warrior god who was also talented in magic and runes. He is usually portrayed as an old man with a long beard and only one eye because he traded the other for wisdom.

Ragnarök: The Norse version of the apocalypse. When the wolf Fenrir escapes, a great battle takes place and many of the gods are killed.

Seidr: This belief is as complicated as Leif and the seer make it seem, but a very simplified way of defining it is that it was shamanism that could alter fate.

Valhalla: Heaven, Viking-style, where warriors who died in combat can eat and drink and fight for eternity.

Valkyrie: Usually portrayed as winged female figures, these warrior goddesses chose who lived or died on the battlefield.